30 May 1989 was the point in time when Penny J Black first knew depression. This has haunted her on and off ever since. No one even mentioned mental health in those days; they palmed you off with antidepressants, or in extreme circumstances, you were put in an institution and forgotten about.

Her self-treatment was drink, vodka, to be precise. She always held down a job, though, and tried to see herself out of the dark hole she kept slipping back into. Just when she thought she was okay, she'd slip back down.

Her children were supportive, but, in reality, she put them through hell. Her youngest son suffers mental-health issues because of her. In fact, they all suffered, and she is so grateful they are still supporting her.

Mental health is a serious illness, we are now told, and Penny J Black is thankful it is now starting to be recognised. If you've never had it, you don't understand – simple. People tell you to "snap out of it" but that is impossible to do. Writing has helped her a lot; it's good to get those feelings down on paper. Not everyone can write a novel, and it has taken her a long time between starting this and it being on the shelves.

If you think you are suffering, please don't suffer in silence like she had to. #itsoktonotbeok

For my first love, who tragically committed suicide due to mental health.

Jason Charles E Hampshire (Hammy)
16 September 1962 – 30 May 1989
R.I.P.

Penny J Black

NOBODY'S PERFECT

AUSTIN MACAULEY PUBLISHERS™
LONDON • CAMBRIDGE • NEW YORK • SHARJAH

A CIP catalogue record for this title is available from the British Library.

ISBN 9781786933041 (Paperback)
ISBN 9781786933058 (Hardback)
ISBN 9781786933065 (E-Book)

www.austinmacauley.com

First Published (2008)
Second Edition (2019)
Austin Macauley Publishers Ltd
25 Canada Square
Canary Wharf
London
E14 5LQ

I want to thank my kids most of all: Damon, James and Danielle, because as I was writing the book, they hardly saw me. I came home from work and straight upstairs until late. Then I was made redundant, and we went to Corfu for four weeks, where the last few chapters were written. It was then left to collect dust!

It was very painful to write, as although the book is fictional, a lot of it is based on truth. It was upsetting at times to write, re-read and then edit. It delves deeply into my life and the pain I have suffered over the years with love, heartache and tragedy, especially the death of Jason. Even though it was nearly thirty years ago, he still has a special place in my heart.

I recently married a wonderful man, my best friend and my soulmate. It is something I never thought would happen after Jason, especially the continuing heartaches I've had, but that's in the next novel!

Thanks to everyone else who has helped me, and I really hope you enjoy reading it. I would love your comments, whether good or bad.

Twitter - @PennyJaneBlack
Facebook - Penny J Black – Author
Email me - pennyblack_12345@hotmail.com
          hello@pennyjblack.co.uk
Website - pennyjblack.co.uk

Chapter One

Mrs Bannister was watching Nancy as she waltzed up the path, swinging her rag doll as she skipped along. She had been visiting every day since the family moved in across the road a couple of years ago. Mrs Bannister had been walking past the ice cream van when she saw three-year-old Nancy crying, she'd dropped her pennies down the grate, and Mrs Bannister had very kindly bought her an ice cream.

It was a quiet area, with younger couples and families steadily moving into the houses left empty by the ever-decreasing older generation. Mrs Bannister was a sprightly eighty-two-year-old widow who regularly took her West Highland terrier, Scottie, for a walk around the quiet streets and onto the fields behind, and always made an effort to talk to the neighbours, especially the newcomers. She had an aura about her that made everyone feel welcome and relaxed.

Scottie barked and jumped up at the door to welcome Nancy in. She was a beautiful girl, with long, dark wavy hair and big brown eyes. She looked absolutely adorable in her new navy and white school uniform.

'Have you had a nice day at school?' asked Mrs Bannister.

'Lovely, we painted some pictures and the teacher read us a story. What have you done today, Mrs Bannister?' replied Nancy.

'I've been into town and done some shopping. What do you think I have bought?'

'Cakes and sweets!' shouted Nancy excitedly and followed Mrs Bannister and Scottie into the kitchen.

The next few years passed quickly, and Mrs Bannister thoroughly enjoyed watching Nancy growing up. She had no grandchildren, as her only son had tragically died in a motorbike accident when he was only seventeen. She thought her own life had ended that day when the police came knocking on her door but Bill, her late husband, had been a great help to her and time had been a great healer. Bill died shortly before Nancy and her family moved in, and even though she didn't know it, Nancy had been her life since. She had been invited to their house for Christmas every year and this year was no exception.

As Mrs Bannister was getting ready in the early hours of Christmas morning, so she could arrive before Nancy woke up, she heard a strange noise outside. As she looked out of the window, the pavement covered with the glow of fresh, crisp white snow, she saw a small brown pony tethered to Nancy's fence. '*How wonderful,*' she thought to herself, '*Nancy hasn't got a clue about this one.*' She waited until she saw lights come on across the road, grabbed her coat and walked over. She tapped on the door and Nancy's mum, Maggie, answered with a big smile and a finger to her lips. Obviously, Nancy wasn't awake yet. It was only 7:30 a.m. and Maggie had the gorgeous smell of turkey spreading through the house, a great welcome for Christmas morning. As Mrs Bannister and Maggie drank their tea, they heard footsteps creeping down the stairs.

'Good morning, Nancy,' shouted Maggie and Mrs Bannister in unison.

Nancy burst into the kitchen with such a sparkle in her beautiful eyes. 'Please can I go and see what Father Christmas has brought me?'

'Of course,' replied Maggie, and she and Mrs Bannister followed her into the lounge. Maggie had laid all the presents out so that Nancy could read the writing on them and hand them out as she came to them. Maggie got a gorgeous diamond and sapphire eternity ring from her husband Eric and a bottle of her favourite perfume from Nancy and Mrs Bannister, along with other bits. Eric received a gold watch from Maggie and a car cleaning kit from Nancy and Mrs Bannister. Nancy and Maggie bought Mrs Bannister a beautiful china West Highland Terrier ornament. The list of Nancy's presents was endless: a Sindy doll and horse, a toy guitar, and a hat and glove set but when she came to open the last of her presents, she sort of looked disappointed.

'I didn't need any new clothes and I don't wear trousers, and what would I want with this horrible jacket?' frowned Nancy.

Maggie went over to her daughter and took her to the window, where she proceeded to open the heavy green velvet curtains.

'Wow, it's snowed!' gasped Nancy with excitement and then let out a scream. 'Mum, is that my pony?' and hugged her mother so tightly, then ran to her father and hugged and kissed him. 'Thank you, thank you, I love you both so much. What's he called? Is it a boy? Can I go and see him? Where does he sleep?' The questions were so continuous, no one had chance to answer. In her nightie and slippers Nancy ran to the front door and out into the bitter cold of winter and hugged the pony so tightly around its neck, they thought she would have strangled it.

'Where are you going to keep it?' asked Mrs Bannister.

'It's all sorted,' replied Eric. 'I spoke to Farmer Pearson, who owns the land surrounding us, and I've bought two acres off him at the back of our house. I couldn't fence it off or build a stable before today or Nancy might have been suspicious, but I've bought all the wood and a friend of mine is building the fence and two stables next week. In the meantime, he'll stay at Farmer Pearson's.'

Nancy had spent practically all day with her pony, brushing him, riding him up and down the lane, and when it was time for him to be taken to Farmer Pearson's, Nancy was almost shedding a tear, not wanting to part with her new friend.

'What will you call him?' asked Mrs Bannister.

'I don't know yet; have you any ideas, Mrs Bannister?'

'Well, I used to have a dog called Fred. I haven't a clue what you would call a pony,' laughed Mrs Bannister.

Nancy was up bright and early next morning to go and see her pony, whom she had decided to call Sammy, although Eric wasn't too pleased at being woken at 5:30 a.m. to take her and it was just a little too far for her to walk alone. Nancy went to play with her new Sindy doll and horse and started imagining how famous she would be in a few years' time, the best horsewoman of all time.

'Nancy, Nancy, wake up,' shouted Eric. 'I'll take you down to Farmer Pearson's; are you ready? It'll be a lot easier when the stables are built at the back, I might even make a start on them this afternoon.'

Nancy's visits to Mrs Bannister became shorter now she had Sammy in her life, so Mrs Bannister went to visit her instead and ended up chatting more with Maggie than with Nancy. It was lovely to see Nancy trotting around the field, she looked so happy.

Nancy was growing up quickly and it wasn't too long before she looked too big on Sammy, although he never seemed to mind. She was growing into a tall, slender teenager, and it wasn't long before boys started coming along the lane and calling for her. There was a local youth club where there was a disco once a month and Nancy and her friends always went along. Nancy would tell Mrs Bannister all the goings on when she came to visit; it made Mrs Bannister feel younger just listening to Nancy, she was so full of energy and bounce, which made everyone feel happy.

A few days went by before Nancy realised Mrs Bannister hadn't been over, so she nipped across to her house. The door was locked and when she peered through the nets, she could see Scottie lying next to a heap of clothing. She knocked on the window, and Scottie started barking and running around the heap. Nancy realised it was Mrs Bannister and ran quickly home to ring an ambulance. They arrived within minutes and had to break the door down. They found Mrs Bannister barely alive and rushed her to hospital.

Nancy and Maggie followed, and the doctors informed them she had had a stroke and had probably been lying there for at least twenty-four hours. If Nancy hadn't found her when she did, she would have certainly been dead by now. It was touch and go for the next few days, but when Mrs Bannister did finally come around, she had nothing but praise and thanks for Nancy and Maggie. They were pleased she was still alive.

They kept her in hospital for a couple of weeks and when she did come home, a nurse had to visit her every day. She was advised to go into a home, as she had no living relatives, but she was a stubborn old lady and refused.

Nancy and Maggie took turns to look after her. She lived four more months before she had another stroke and died instantly. She was ninety-two years old. Maggie arranged the funeral and rang some of Mrs Bannister's friends from her address book, but she had outlived them all. The funeral was a quiet one, attended by a couple of other neighbours, and Maggie put on a small buffet for the guests.

At fifteen years old, Nancy didn't ride Sammy any more, but they were still the best of friends and the younger children on the lane came to fuss over him and beg Nancy to let them ride him. Maggie admired her for trying to teach them to ride, especially as she was studying hard for her O levels, which she was sitting soon.

One morning an official-looking letter arrived, and when Maggie opened and read it, she nearly collapsed with shock. She rang Eric at work, and he promised he would nip home at lunch time. They sat down, and she handed the letter to Eric, his face contorted with amazement.

'My God, I would never have guessed. She certainly didn't seem to be, well, I'm–I don't know what I am.'

Nancy had been left Mrs Bannister's entire estate: the bungalow across the road, a house in neighbouring Langhall called Barnacre Hall, a long-term rental agreement on Barnacre Hall which was four hundred pounds per month, and her savings and insurance policies, totalling one hundred and seventy-five thousand, four hundred and fifty pounds. Barnacre Hall should at that time become vacant and, hopefully, Nancy would move in and would pass it down through her family. If any money was needed prior to that, they could check with the solicitor, who was the trustee.

When they rang the solicitor, it turned out he had dealt with Mrs Bannister and her late husband for most of his working life. They lived in Barnacre Hall, which had been in her family since the turn of the century, when her great-grandfather made a fortune in the cotton industry. The First World War began, and her great-grandfather was called up and killed in action. After the war her grandfather took over running the factory. Shortly before the demise of the cotton industry, he sold out to a competitor and retired. Her mother married a wealthy businessman but after Mrs Bannister was born, her mother died, leaving her father and a housekeeper to bring her up. When Mrs Bannister married, they lived with her father at Barnacre Hall until he died. When her husband also died, she couldn't face living there, so she rented it out to a former colleague of her husband's and bought the bungalow across the road from Eric and Maggie.

'What are we going to tell Nancy?' asked Maggie. 'She's sitting her O levels soon, this will certainly put her off.'

'I don't think we should mention it to her at all. After all, the letter was addressed to us,' replied Eric.

'I can't believe it, our Nancy coming into all that money! It'll go to her head,' said Maggie.

It took a while for the news to sink in and they kept it from Nancy and plodded on as normal. Nancy received her O level results: two As, three Bs and three Cs and went out celebrating with her friends. For the first time ever, Eric and Maggie hadn't specified a time when she had to be in. Well, she was now sixteen and very sensible. Maggie lay awake, restless, until she heard Nancy's key in the lock and some muffled whispers and laughter from Nancy and her friend, who was stopping the night. She could now relax and soon drifted off to sleep.

It became a regular occurrence, Nancy going out on the town at weekends. Eric and Maggie didn't object as she was a sensible girl, but as with all mothers, Maggie could never sleep until she knew Nancy was safely home.

Chapter Two

Nancy was seeing a lad called Alan; it was nothing serious and she never tended to go out with him, just meet wherever they were ending up. One night at the Rugby Club, Nancy and her friends were nattering, and Alan was there with his friend Jason (Hammy) and a few others who, Nancy didn't really know, although most of the night Alan was talking to a dark-haired female at the bar. When Nancy went over to him, ready to leave, he practically ignored her, so she picked his pint up and poured it over his head, which also wet the girl through. Then she walked off laughing. Janet and Chris watched in horror as did most of the people left. Jason walked over to Nancy and asked if she was all right.

'Of course, I am; it's his loss, not mine,' she replied.

'Can I walk you home?' he asked rather shyly. Nancy looked at him and nodded her head.

As they walked, she realised what an interesting person Jason was. He played the guitar in a local band. He was twenty-one, five years older than Nancy and he was actually very good looking. He also travelled a lot; Holland, Switzerland, Germany and Austria, where he had stayed for almost six months.

When they arrived at Nancy's house, Jason asked if he could see her again. She gave him her phone number and a quick thank-you peck on the cheek for walking her home.

Jason phoned the next day. 'Fancy a drink in my local?'

Nancy had never been in the Alexandra before, although she knew a lot of people who had and said it was good. She arranged to meet him outside the pub at 7:30 p.m.

She got dressed in tight jeans and a fairly tight black top, although not too revealing; just enough to show off a bit of her cleavage and her gorgeously slim figure.

Jason was waiting for her when she turned up at twenty to eight, women's prerogative, and they went inside and ordered drinks. It was a cosy pub with a small games room and a fantastic jukebox, with a good variety of music, from pop to rock and everything in between.

Nancy saw Jason a lot over the next couple of months and this particular night when he invited her back to his flat, she agreed for the first time. It was a small flat, a kitchenette and a double bed in the living room and it was adorned with ornaments and artefacts from his travels. He put some music on and started playing his guitar along to the music while Nancy sat on the bed listening, intrigued and fascinated.

When the song finished, Jason came and sat next to Nancy on the bed and put his arm around her shoulders. She turned to face him, and they kissed, gently at first. The strange feeling Nancy had in her stomach made her kiss him harder. Jason slowly took off her top and his gentle hand was caressing her breasts. The churning in her stomach felt weird and she didn't want him to stop. His kisses were gentler as he undid the button on her jeans and slid down her zip. He gazed into her wanting eyes.

He caressed her with such gentleness and when his hand went down to her vagina, he put his fingers inside in a gentle thrusting motion. She was writhing with delight. He slipped his penis into her waiting vagina and when she let out a small scream, he presumed she was a virgin.

'God, Nancy, I'm sorry, I didn't realise,' he said as he suddenly stopped mid-thrust. She wasn't a virgin; it was the shock at the size of his manhood, but if he wanted to think that, who was she to tell him otherwise?

'It's OK, I want you to make love to me and I have done for a while. I was scared you'd leave me if I'd let it happen sooner,' she replied. He kissed her so lovingly and taking extra care, made love slowly and gently to her.

Her nails were digging into his back and he was thrusting harder. Nancy was enjoying every second. He then kept his penis in her, with smaller thrusts, her legs resting on his back. She suddenly had a sensation which moved all through her body. She moaned and panted with pleasure and it made her head go all funny. Her vagina was throbbing against his penis.

They lay in each other's arms and fell asleep.

She saw Jason almost every night over the next few weeks, then he left on his travels again. She was upset, but he left her with a promise that he would be back.

Chapter Three

One Friday night, shortly after her seventeenth birthday, Nancy and her friends Janet and Christina were in their local night club, Oblivion, when Nancy spotted a man with a lovely large smile on his face and sparkling eyes. She smiled back and turned back to talk to Janet and Chris.

'Who's that?' they asked.

'I've no idea, but he's gorgeous. I like this song, let's dance,' Nancy replied shyly, trying to avoid the man's stare. They moved onto the dance floor and were happily dancing when the mystery man sidled up behind Nancy.

'Do you mind if I join you?' he asked.

'Umm, not really,' Nancy replied, blushing from head to toe, and carried on dancing with her head down.

Janet and Chris decided to leave them to it and went to the bar to order some more drinks. Nancy came to the bar shortly after with the man in tow and joined them.

'Could I buy you a drink?' the man asked. 'I'm Thomas, by the way.' He bought Nancy a white wine and they stood talking for the rest of the night. He was a traffic policeman based in Allington, about ten miles away, but lived in Blacklodge, not so far from Nancy.

Time passed quickly, and it was time for the smoochy records. Neither of them said a word, just drifted onto the dance floor and slowly entwined to the music. Janet and Chris had never seen Nancy like this before, and they had never believed in love at first sight before now, but they looked besotted with each other.

Thomas escorted Nancy home, hand in hand, along the dimly lit streets and when they reached Nancy's house, they stood at the gate under a clear sky, the stars sparkling, the moonlight shining down on their faces, and their eyes locked together with the love that was deepening between them. Thomas gently brushed his fingers along her face and brought his face closer until their lips met, so gently, so lovingly. Nancy's whole body quivered as the feelings inside her stomach churned as they had never been before. What was it? Nerves, butterflies? Her head was starting to spin, and she pulled herself away quite abruptly.

'What's wrong?' asked Thomas.

'Nothing–nothing. I must go in now,' she replied.

'Can I ring you tomorrow?' he asked.

She gave him her phone number and wandered into the house in a dreamlike state. She lay awake for hours thinking of the events of the evening before drifting off into a deep sleep.

She woke with a smile on her face and when Maggie asked if she had a good night, all she could do was smile. Every time the phone rang her heart would miss a beat and after what seemed like hours, Thomas phoned. They arranged to meet and went to the cinema and then for a pizza. They talked and began to learn about and get to know each other. Soon they were inseparable. When she went out with Janet and Chris, she arranged to meet Thomas later. Not a day went by without them seeing each other. Maggie was starting to worry about Nancy neglecting her studies, but Nancy reassured her.

One weekend, Maggie and Eric went up to the Lake District for a well-deserved break. Nancy, Chris and Janet went to their local pub, where she had arranged to meet Thomas and a couple of his friends. They ended up all going back to Nancy's house, the music went on and everyone was dancing around the chairs in the lounge. Thomas was standing at the back of the chair, watching Nancy dancing around, when he suddenly blurted out, 'Nancy, I love you!' She stopped dancing and they gazed into each other's eyes. They didn't notice that everyone saw what had happened and decided to make themselves scarce.

They were alone for the first time and fell into each other's arms. The chemistry between them was electric as Thomas gently stroked her face and neck and their lips touched with a passion neither of them had experienced before. Their eyes were fixed on each other as they caressed and kissed. Nancy's dress was slowly and carefully being unbuttoned until it sexily dropped to the floor, and she was standing in her underwear, a white lacy bra with panties to match. He gently touched her breasts, which made Nancy tingle, and she smiled at him with all the love that was churning inside her.

He unfastened her bra and his lips brushed her bare skin. His tongue, warm and wet, played with her now erect nipple, while his gentle fingers caressed her other breast. He glanced at her as though seeking her approval and they kissed. His hand made its way down to her panties and slipped inside, where he stroked a warm and damp vagina. Nancy was groaning with pleasure and with a smile on her face she undid the buttons on his shirt and eased it off each arm. With lips locked, he reached down to gently ease off her panties while she was undoing the belt on his trousers. As she pulled his zip down, she felt his manhood, it was large and hard and throbbing with passion. She suddenly felt scared and seemed to freeze. Thomas noticed this and kissed her gently on the lips whilst stroking her face.

'Do you want me to stop?' he asked softly. Nancy stood there, suddenly thinking about how Jason had left shortly after they made love.

'I love you, I'm not going to hurt you,' he reassured her and started stroking her stomach.

Nancy smiled at him. 'I love you too,' she said, tugging at his trousers, trying to get them off.

His strong arms lowered her to the floor, then his fingers made their way down to her vagina and entered gently into the warm, damp environment. As they kissed, he moved his mouth from her face to her neck and down to her breasts, sucking on her nipples. The churning in her stomach returned, making her vagina feel very wet and warm. His fingers were gently moving in and out, making her wriggle with excitement. He started kissing her stomach and slowly edged his way down until his tongue was energetically playing with her clitoris. She let out a relaxed groan and stroked his hair while his tongue was racing over her clitoris and then into her vagina. Her body was writhing with ecstasy. He moved back up and placed his penis at the entrance to her vagina. He held each buttock and slowly eased it in, trying not to hurt her. She was digging her nails into his back and it was hard for him not to force it in, but he gave in to the pain in his back and his penis thrust into her vagina with a vengeance. She screamed and dug her nails in harder. The thrusting movements in and out were met with loud groans and her pelvis moving in time with his. They kissed passionately on the mouth, neck and ears whilst still thrusting in harmony together. The churning in Nancy's stomach suddenly moved all through her body, and the force of ecstasy engulfed her, making her throw her head back and moan in short pleasurable breaths, shortly followed by a loud, long moan just as Thomas thrust his penis as far as he could and ejaculated, letting her vagina feel every throb of his sperm as they entered her eagerly waiting body.

Nancy's head felt very strange and she had never felt as happy and relaxed as she did at this perfect moment in time. They kissed with passion and held each other in silence, the air filled with the luscious smell of sex and the deepness of the love they had released between each other, until Nancy took Thomas' hand and led him to her bedroom. They made love all through the night with a passion anyone would kill for and finally drifted off to sleep with the contentment of two people bonded as one.

It was difficult for them to be on their own together, so they tended to spend a lot of time in the stable, where they made love in the hay under Sammy's watchful eye. This was the ultimate excitement for them as they had to sneak about, not letting Maggie and Eric see them. Eventually, Nancy asked Maggie if she could bring her boyfriend to meet them. It was arranged for the following Thursday, when Maggie and Eric had planned to go out later in the evening.

Thomas turned up on time, in smart navy trousers and cream shirt. He had short light brown hair, slightly longer on the top, sparkling green eyes and he was tall and very, very handsome. Nancy had a permanent smile on her face and a sparkle in her eyes, and Maggie and Eric hadn't seen her so happy since the Christmas Day she was presented with Sammy the pony. It was very difficult for Nancy and Thomas to control themselves in front of her parents, and between them they couldn't wait for them to go out.

Thomas was being hounded by questions: Where do you live? What do your parents do? Any brothers and sisters? It seemed never-ending, but he answered each one politely whilst turning to Nancy with the gleam in his eye which only she could read.

After what seemed like hours, Maggie and Eric wandered off to their local pub, discussing the pair. They both liked Thomas and could see that he made Nancy very happy. Within minutes of them leaving, Thomas ripped Nancy's clothes off while she was fighting to rip his off. They were strewn all over the room. Thomas lifted Nancy up with his strong hands resting underneath her buttocks, his fingers caressing her wet vagina as he carried her into the kitchen and put her bottom on the edge of the sink. She wrapped her legs around his back, with her hands on the taps supporting herself. She turned on the tap and with cold, wet hands caressed Thomas' hair, face and back, then her own breasts. The coldness of the water and the stainless steel on her buttocks and his tongue twiddling around her nipples made her reach orgasm quite quickly but Thomas hadn't and carried on thrusting his penis as deep as he could. He lifted her buttocks off the sink, supporting them with his strong arms and leant Nancy against the wall. The movement of her back against the wall and the deep penetration soon had her writhing in constant ecstasy and with difficulty she was managing to move in rhythm with his penis. Thomas recognised the short groans when she was due to have an orgasm and let himself be taken over by the pleasure of ejaculation. It was the perfect love when two people could orgasm at the same time, the throbbing of the penis hard and still inside the vagina and the pulsating of the vaginal wall. Pure ecstasy. Her parents were due back around eleven, and they managed to straighten themselves up by quarter to and put a video on near to the end as though they had been sitting on the settee watching it all night.

Chapter Four

Nancy was due to sit her A level exams and had to see less of Thomas but as she sat in her room studying, her thoughts soon drifted from her books as she dreamed of what they would be doing that weekend. The exams soon came along and even in the silence of the hall where thirty-two other girls sat, Nancy's mind was on other things rather than the maths paper in front of her. Soon the tutor shouted out, 'Stop writing now, please.'

'*Oh, no,*' she thought to herself. '*I've hardly done anything.*' Scouring through the paper in front of her, she saw that most of the questions were filled in, yet she couldn't remember doing it. 'They're probably all wrong,' she told her friends afterwards.

'Well, whenever I looked up, you were staring into space,' replied Janet.

'I think I've done all right, it didn't seem too hard, but we'll have to wait and see. We'll get our results soon enough."

It could not have arrived too quickly with the amount of dread Nancy was feeling. Maggie and Eric wanted her to go to university to study law. She wanted to stay around here and be near Thomas, maybe forget about college altogether and find a job.

The postman arrived before Nancy was up. Eric had taken the day off work specially, and Maggie shouted up to Nancy to get up. When she came downstairs, Maggie thrust the envelope in her face excitedly.

'Please, could I get a cup of tea first?' snapped Nancy, thinking about how she could explain her failure while the tea brewed in the pot. She took her time and when she went into the lounge and saw her parents sat on the settee, eagerly awaiting her to open the envelope, all the things she was planning to say went by the wayside.

'I think I've failed,' she blurted out, bursting into tears.

'Don't be silly, they can't have been that bad, and look at all the time you spent in your room studying for them,' said Maggie sympathetically.

'Come on, open the envelope and find out,' said Eric. 'This will be the making of a brilliant barrister,' he continued.

'I don't want to go to law college, whatever my results,' Nancy replied, opening the envelope. 'Yes, yes!' she screamed, not believing her own eyes. 'I've passed all three, not brilliant grades, but I've passed.'

Maggie and Eric smiled and hugged her. 'We're really pleased, but what did you mean, you don't want to go to law college? You had your heart set on it a couple of years ago, what's changed?' they asked.

'I want to stay around here and be near to Thomas, Mum. I love him. I'll see what's on offer at the local college before I make any final decisions, OK?'

Janet and Christina called around later in the day. Christina passed two, failed one and was a bit miffed that Nancy had passed all three. Janet passed all three with two As and a B.

Nancy got ready and they went out just after tea to celebrate their results. They were in a recently opened wine bar called Toggles, when three gents clad in business suits wandered over and started talking to the threesome. They were all fairly decent looking, but nothing fantastic, but they had the girls in stitches with laughter. The wine flowed all evening and when last orders were called, the boys invited the girls back to their flat to carry on the conversation and the laugh they were all having.

The girls were very merry, in fact quite drunk, and they walked for what seemed like hours, to a dimly-lit street on the other side of town, went through a big dark door and up some grotty stairs until they got to the third floor.

'I don't like the look of this,' whispered Nancy to Janet and Christina.

'Let's disappear,' said Christina.

They all agreed and shouted to the boys, 'Sorry, but we have to go home now, see you around.'

'Not so fast,' replied one of them.

'Run,' screamed Janet as they shot down the stairs and out through the big dark door, the boys following behind.

Janet had always been a faster runner than the other two and when she looked around, the boys were nearly catching up to Christina.

'Run faster, Chris,' she shouted as loud as she could, and as she turned a corner, she nearly knocked a bloke over.

'Hey, watch where you're going,' he shouted.

'Sorry, but we're being chased by some blokes,' she gasped.

'You're lucky I'm an off-duty policeman then,' and he got out his badge, went around the corner just as Chris had caught up, with the boys shortly behind her.

'Excuse me, just what do you think you are doing?' the policeman said as he grabbed two of the boys, literally by the scruff of the neck.

'We were just having a bit of fun,' they replied.

The policeman turned to the girls and asked if that was right.

'Well, we were earlier, but we decided to leave,' Janet replied.

'Then they started chasing us,' said Christina, just getting her breath back.

He turned to the boys, 'You're very lucky I'm not in uniform, else I would have arrested you. Now don't let me see you again, go on, off with you. Right, come on girls, I'll escort you home.'

The following day, Nancy went down to her local college to see if there was anything she fancied doing. Instead of staying with the throbbing headache she had, she brought a batch of leaflets and prospectuses home with her. That evening she was sitting in the lounge, glancing through them whilst Maggie and Eric were watching television.

'Anything interesting?' asked Eric.

'Not really,' she replied.

'If you went to Manchester instead of Leeds to study law, you could come home every weekend and see Thomas,' said Maggie. 'It wouldn't really be any different than living here, you only see him at weekends now anyway.'

Nancy thought about it for the rest of the evening and even had a wonderful dream about the friends she would make at university, the laugh they would have and the special trips home to see Thomas. When she woke up, she rang the admissions department at the University of Manchester and asked them to send her all the details and an application form.

Thomas wasn't too pleased when she told him, but said if that's what she wanted, he was happy for her. He loved her too much to disagree. Anyway, while it was holidays, they saw each other most nights and spent more time in the stable making love than talking about the future.

Chapter Five

Thomas turned up one evening with a grave look on his face. 'We need to have a serious talk,' he said. 'Where's your mum and dad?'

'They're in the lounge, come up to my room,' she replied, feeling very worried about what this talk was about. 'Mum, me and Thomas are going to my room to listen to music,' she shouted.

Thomas sat on her bed. Her clothes were strewn all over her bedroom floor, and she gathered them all up and threw them in a corner as if to ease her embarrassment. Nancy was never a tidy person; Maggie had always done everything for her and whenever Maggie had asked her to tidy her room, she always said she would do it later. The decor was nice and bright; one of Eric's friends was a wallpaper designer and Nancy always had first choice of any weird and wonderful designs. In fact, it was very psychedelic and if you stared at it for a while, you ended up in a state of trance.

Nancy cuddled up to him on the bed, music playing softly in the background.

'What is it? You still love me, don't you? You don't want us to finish?' She was always one for asking question after question before any answers were given.

'Nancy, I love you with all my heart, you have to believe that. But a job has come up that I have been wanting for years, and I have been offered it,' he said with a sadness in his eyes and not being able to look Nancy straight in the eye.

'Ho–how does that affect us, I don't understand?' she replied with a quiver in her voice.

'It's the Royal Military Police, based in Germany. Nancy, it's what I've wanted to do since I was a boy. We can keep in touch, and I'll come home on leave.'

Tears slowly welled up in Nancy's eyes. 'When do you go?'

'In two weeks,' he replied in a soft voice while lifting her face up to face him. 'Come on, darling, let's make the most of the time we have left together. You're still on holiday, let's go away somewhere, then we can spend every minute together.'

Nancy was crying softly and put her head on his chest. He could feel his shirt getting wet with her soft tears and held her tightly, with all his love flowing from his strong arms into her body.

They lay together in the dimly lit bedroom, the music in the background swimming gently all around the room, holding each other as though no one would ever part them when they heard Maggie shouting up to them. Goodness, it was 11:30 p.m., they had been holding each other for four hours. They looked into each other's eyes, which were both sparkling with the tears they had both shed, and kissed each other gently on the lips.

They went downstairs, and Thomas popped his head around the lounge door to say goodbye to Maggie and Eric, and he walked out of the door with Nancy watching him walk down the street. She stood on the doorstep in the cool night air, just watching her lover disappear and the words they had spoken going around and around in her mind, tears trickling gently down her cheeks as she tried to imagine life without her love. Maggie came out and saw Nancy was crying, put her arms around her like she did when Nancy was a child and tried to comfort her. No words were spoken between them. Nancy eventually went upstairs and just lay awake, crying.

The next morning, she told Maggie what had happened and also asked if she could go away for a week with Thomas. Maggie said she would ask Eric and see what he thought. When Eric came home from work, Thomas was already there, and Nancy seemed to be in better spirits. Maggie dragged him into the kitchen and asked if Thomas and Nancy could go away for a week together. He wasn't very keen on the idea as Nancy was only seventeen, but when Maggie explained about Thomas leaving, he agreed as she was nearly eighteen. He went and spoke to Nancy and Thomas and made Thomas promise he would look after his daughter.

At lunchtime, they set off in Thomas' dad's car and drove up to the Lake District, there they found a cosy little guest house with en-suite shower room, tea-making facilities and a trouser press. They unpacked their small suitcase and went for a walk along the banks of Lake Windermere, hand in hand, sharing the precious moments that were passing quickly around them. All of a sudden Nancy dropped back to earth when Thomas whisked her up in his arms and threw her in the lake. He stood there laughing for a while, then took off his T-shirt and jeans and dived in near to her. He came to the surface within inches of her and held her tightly. Every time they tried to kiss, they sank underwater, which made them both splutter, and they ended up in fits of laughter, getting strange looks from the passers-by who had seemed to accumulate on the banks near to them.

They swam for a while and when they got out of the water, Thomas got dressed, but of course Nancy had all her clothes on. They looked a right sight walking back to the hotel, Thomas dry and Nancy leaving a trail of dripping water behind her. The looks they got off people made them laugh all the more.

On the way back to the hotel, they spotted a restaurant which looked nice. They showered and changed and returned to the restaurant for their evening meal.

The week passed quickly, and their days were spent walking, drinking and making love. People they met thought they were on their honeymoon, which gave Thomas an idea for their last night. He disappeared that morning while Nancy was nattering to Sharon and Geoff, a couple who actually were on their honeymoon (unbeknown to her they were to keep her talking) and went into a small antique shop he had spotted. They had a few antique rings, and he picked a cornflower blue sapphire with a diamond in a twisted shape. The shop owner said it was made in the 1920s. He was sure Nancy would love it; she had a lot of costume jewellery with diamante and sapphire-coloured stones in, and sapphire was her birthstone. He ran all the way back to the hotel and sat with Nancy, Sharon and Geoff. Nancy was still nattering away to Sharon. Geoff turned to wink at Thomas and Thomas nodded back; mission completed.

That evening they had arranged to go for a meal with Geoff and Sharon and had found a lovely, cosy-looking restaurant which had entertainment. They managed to get a table in the corner and the waiter lit the candles; a trio were playing soft music in the background. They ordered their meal and sat around talking. It turned out Sharon and Geoff lived in Feniscliffe, which was quite near to Blacklodge, and they were insisting on meeting up when they arrived home in another week's time. Nancy's eyes misted over, and she tried so hard to keep the tears away, until Thomas looked into her big brown eyes and took her hand in his. The tears rolled with a vengeance. Thomas made his apologies to Sharon and Geoff and quietly explained why Nancy was crying.

'We're so sorry, we didn't know,' said Sharon.

'It's all right,' said Nancy, wiping her eyes. 'You weren't expected to. This is our last night together, really. Thomas leaves for Germany on Tuesday and I still live with my parents, so we've made the most of this week.'

The waiter approached the table and took their sweet order. Nancy said, 'No, thank you, I'm quite full.'

Thomas looked at Geoff, shocked, but Nancy didn't notice. Geoff shrugged back at Thomas and nudged Sharon.

'Come on, Nancy, you have to have a sweet,' said Sharon. 'If you don't, I'll feel awful and I was so looking forward to the chocolate cake with lashings of cream on it,' she said with a pleading look in her eye.

'Oh, all right then, I'll just have a small ice cream sundae,' she said to the waiter.

Thomas was so relieved and sank into his chair. The sweets were placed on the table whilst they were all talking between themselves. Nancy picked up her spoon and noticed Thomas was staring at her.

'What's wrong, Thomas?' she asked.

'Nothing, darling,' he replied. 'How's your sundae?'

'I haven't tasted it yet, give me a chance,' she said, turning to get a spoonful of cream off the top. She nearly had the spoon in her mouth when she saw something sparkling on her spoon. She picked it out and turned to Thomas, who was beside her on one knee.

'Will you marry me, Nancy? I love you so much and you could come with me to Germany if we were married.'

Sharon and Geoff were holding their breath and watching Nancy's face for her reaction, as were all the other customers in the restaurant.

Nancy was just in a state of shock and her mind was racing. What would her mum and dad say? Could she leave her birth-town and start again in Germany? Would she make any friends? Would marriage be how she imagined it as a child? Her mind was racing faster and faster when all of a sudden, she muttered a shaky, 'Yes, yes, YES!'

Thomas picked her up in his strong arms and swung her around, nearly knocking over the table and the whole restaurant erupted with applause and "Well dones". Nancy went bright red with embarrassment with the whole restaurant cheering at them. The bottle of champagne which Thomas had on standby was brought out on ice and shared between the four of them. Within a few minutes the DJ who had appeared during all the commotion was announcing it over the P.A. system and inviting Thomas and Nancy to start the evening's dancing off with *Something's Gotta Hold of My Heart.* Thomas whisked her onto the dance floor to claps and cheers, wrapped his arms around her waist and smooched along with the music. The passion rose up inside Nancy like a volcano erupting as he touched his lips against hers and caressed her back. Nancy's hands were gently stroking his jaw as they kissed. The room went silent and it felt as if no one else was there. Nancy could have made love to him there and then, but she controlled herself and became aware of the other couple joining them on the dance floor when they accidentally got nudged. She looked at Thomas and smiled gently.

'I love you with all my heart. The pain I have gone through the last few days at the thought of losing you has been unbearable, I couldn't have coped with you leaving.'

'Shush,' said Thomas gently, placing a finger on her lips. 'I know, it's been the same for me too. I haven't and will never love anyone the way I love you.'

They carried on dancing for a few more smoochy records and then the disco started, and they went back to their table. Sharon and Geoff were grinning like two Cheshire cats. The champagne carried on flowing until the early hours. People kept coming over to congratulate them; it was absolute bliss. Nancy had never been happier. Walking back to the hotel, Sharon and Geoff were ahead of them, staggering slightly with the effects of alcohol, Nancy felt like she was floating. The hotel bar was beckoning, and the owners were still up and had a bottle of champagne ready for them.

'You had all this planned, didn't you?' she asked Thomas. 'Did everyone know apart from me?' She glanced down at the diamond and sapphire ring sparkling on her finger, slightly too big, but beautiful.

When they went to their room, Thomas made love to her with all the gentleness and love in the world, soft caresses and loving touches. Two bodies became one in a way they had never done before, love was engulfing them, and the orgasms were the best they'd had. They stayed in each other's arms all night and well into the morning.

Chapter Six

They packed their suitcase and loaded it into the car, said their goodbyes and thank yous to the owners and Sharon and Geoff, promising to keep in touch. They set off from the beautiful surroundings of the Lake District, taking in the breathtaking views. Once they got onto the motorway, Nancy turned to Thomas, who smiled at her.

'Thanks for last night, it was wonderful,' she said.

'No regrets?' asked Thomas.

'I'm just worried now what Mum and Dad will say. They won't be happy about this, you know,' she replied.

'They'll come around and accept it in time,' he said confidently.

'What on earth have you two done?' shouted Eric. 'I knew I shouldn't have agreed to let you go away together,' he carried on, absolutely fuming. 'She's only seventeen. You're far too young, I will not go along with it and that's final!'

Thomas left with a, 'See you tonight,' and Nancy went up to her room in tears. She could hear Maggie and Eric arguing downstairs and thought about the events of the night before. She had accepted he was leaving for Germany and had been hurting so much inside, coming to terms with the fact, and then he sprung a proposal on her. She had felt obliged to say 'Yes', to save him from the embarrassment of turning him down. She loved him dearly but like Dad had said, she was only seventeen, too young to get married. She'd talk to him later when he came around. The soft music in the background made her drift off to sleep.

In her dream she saw Mrs Bannister and herself as a child with Sammy, riding up and down the lane, willing herself to be a famous horse rider and imagining the stardom and all the famous people she would meet and receiving first prize for show jumping. Mel Gibson was presenting the trophies and the rosettes; he gazed at Nancy with his sparkling blue eyes and her knees began to wobble and her stomach fluttered with butterflies.

'As an extra special prize, would you come to dinner with me tonight?' Mel asked.

'Yes, of course,' replied Nancy with her sexiest smile, thinking, '*God, I have nothing to wear.*' She got back to her caravan, put Sammy away in his makeshift stable and began to cry, 'I can't go to dinner with Mel Gibson, I only have horse riding clothes with me.'

There was a bright flash and a little fairy was hovering above her. 'Don't worry, my child, you shall go to dinner,' and she flicked her magic wand over Nancy's head and the most gorgeous sparkling silver dress encased her body.

'You look beautiful,' said the fairy. 'Enjoy your dinner.'

A limousine came to pick her up at 7:30 p.m. and she arrived outside a huge hotel. The red carpet adorned the floor leading to the huge glass doors. The doorman who opened the door for her was dressed in gold and held his arm out to help her from the car. Mel was standing at the door of the hotel, waiting for her. As soon as she stepped out of the car, he approached her and took her arm to escort her inside. Photographers' flashes were going off in all directions, but Mel only had eyes for her. They walked into the hotel and in front of her was a large circular staircase leading to the bedrooms, a beautiful white marble floor, and the walls were lavishly covered in carved oak. The doors of the restaurant were opened, and everyone turned their gaze towards this beautiful woman on the arm of one of the most famous film stars. They were escorted to a corner table for two which enjoyed more privacy. The champagne was chilled to perfection and poured by the most courteous waiter she had ever come across.

All through the meal they talked, and Mel was very interested in everything she had to say. They talked about anything and everything. Mel was in London, filming, and he asked if she would like to star in his next movie as the leading lady. After the wonderful meal, Mel invited her to his room. Champagne had been ordered and put on ice. They danced around the huge suite, champagne glasses still in their hands, laughing and enjoying every moment. He took her hand and led her into the bedroom, took her face in his hands and kissed her.

'I have never in my life met anyone as beautiful and intelligent as you, Nancy,' he said, softly kissing her again. With a gentle passion, he unzipped her silver dress, which fell to the floor. His lips caressed her nipple as he slowly took off her panties. His lips were gently kissing her stomach as he slowly moved back up to her breasts. Nancy struggled with the buttons on his shirt, but he ripped it off and then loosened his belt on his trousers and undid his button, while Nancy pulled down his zip and eased his trousers over his tight buttocks until they slipped down his legs. Nancy was over-awed by his wonderful tanned body with no underwear on. They fell onto the king size four poster bed, all the while their eyes gazing into each other's. Mel eased open her legs and his large penis was going to enter her waiting body and send her to ecstasy. 'Nancy, Nancy, Nancy,' he repeated over and over. Her body shook with ecstasy.

'NANCY! Thomas is here,' shouted Maggie, shaking her to wake her up.

'Oh God, Mum, why did you have to wake me up? I was just with Me–oh never mind,' said Nancy grumpily and went down to see Thomas.

'Let's go for a walk, we need to talk,' said Nancy. They set off towards the village of Sallbury and walked through the beautifully landscaped churchyard and sat on a bench. The church was lit up and looked beautiful.

'We can't get married, Thomas. Like Dad said, I'm too young, and there's so much I want to fulfil before I'll feel ready to settle down,' Nancy said with her head down.

'But we don't have to get married yet, we can wait a few years. I love you, Nancy, and I want to spend the rest of my life with you,' Thomas replied.

Nancy looked into his eyes. 'I love you too, but I'm not ready for this. I'm sorry, but that's how I feel. Let's just enjoy the next couple of days.'

'If that's what you want,'

'Yes, it is. Come on, let's go.' They walked in silence through the woods and back into the field which led them to the stable. Thomas looked at Nancy with a pleading grin.

'Not tonight, love, I want to be on my own,' she said after reading through his senseless grin. He kissed her and disappeared into the night.

Nancy sat in the stable and talked to Sammy well into the early hours of the morning. He nuzzled her when she cried, as if to tell her everything would be all right. Sammy was ten years old now and not as active as he used to be, but he loved being pampered by Nancy and all the children who came to see him every day.

Tuesday arrived, and Nancy went with Thomas to the station. His mum, dad and sister were there, and he looked embarrassed when his mum hugged him when they called out for his train to leave. Thomas gazed at Nancy while he was still wrestling free of his mother. He kissed his mum and walked over to face Nancy. He gently lifted her face to meet his and couldn't stop his tears. When he saw her silent tears meandering down her face, he took her in his arms and hugged her.

'I'm sorry, I've been really trying hard not to cry; I don't like goodbyes,' she said with sorrow in her voice.

'It's not goodbye, it's I love you with all my heart and I'll see you soon,' he said with tears dripping into her hair.

'Come on, Thomas, the train's about to leave,' shouted his dad.

He kissed Nancy passionately on the lips and shook his dad's hand with his little sister clinging to his leg. He patted her on the head and boarded the train. The whistle blew, and the wheels started to slowly move around. Thomas stuck his head out of the window, waving like mad until he was just a dot on the horizon.

'Do you want a lift home, Nancy?' asked his dad.

'No, thanks, I want to be on my own for a while and I'm going to visit a friend later,' she replied.

'Keep in touch then,' shouted his mum.

'I will,' she whispered with some hesitation. 'I will.'

Chapter Seven

Janet was all ears when Nancy turned up at her house, and after she had enough of being a shoulder to cry on, she said, 'Right come on, let's go and get our glad rags on and hit the town.' Nancy wasn't for it at first, but Janet rang Chris, who turned up shortly afterwards, and Nancy couldn't get out of it.

Tuesday night was a quiet night in town, so they went to Priston, about ten miles away, where there was a night club open.

'Good, there's so many people here from Blacklodge, we should be able to get a lift home later.'

Nancy and Chris went to the loos and left Janet talking to a bloke she knew. When they got back to where they were standing, Janet was on the dance floor with John, so Nancy and Chris went to dance as well. A few more drinks later, Janet and John re-joined them as last orders were called, and they all went to the bar.

Walking back to the table with the drinks, a bloke accidentally knocked Nancy and she spilt a bit of her drink.

'Sorry,' he said as he turned around to face her.

'So I should think. Watch where you're going in future,' as she was wiping her dress where she had a small stain.

'Nancy?' asked the bloke.

She looked at him and broke into a smile.

'Jason, how are you?'

'Sorry, obviously,' he said, breaking into laughter.

'That's not what I meant. How long have you been home? Where did you get to this time?' The usual barrage of questions; that was Nancy all over.

'If I can give you a lift home, I will tell you all about everything.'

The smoochy records came on and Jason took Nancy's hand and led her onto the dance floor. He held her as though he was never going to let her go. His hands were gently rubbing her back as she buried her head in his chest, thinking of Thomas and feeling guilty, dancing with the man who had given her her first orgasm. She had loved him so much but that was then, and this was now.

He touched her cheek gently and she gazed into his eyes. So blue, and she melted into his arms.

On the drive home, he told her how he had settled in Salzburg in Austria and how beautiful it was with all the tavernas, the locals and how friendly they were. It seemed like no time at all had passed when they pulled up in front of Nancy's house.

'I'm home visiting Mum, but I'm planning on going away again in a month's time,' he said. 'I'll understand if you say no, but do you want to go out tomorrow night?'

'You hurt me when you went away, I'll think about it. Will you ring me tomorrow?' Nancy replied, 'About tea time?'

''Course I will,' he said with anticipation.

Nancy lay awake long into the night, thinking about Thomas and the ten months she'd spent with him, the feelings she had for him, the pain she was feeling now he'd gone, which was so much more intense than the pain she felt when Jason had left. Why does life have to be so hard? She'd be eighteen in a couple of weeks and she had thought about leaving for Germany to be with Thomas, but she was starting university in Manchester in October, and Jason was home for a month. All the thoughts were going around and around in her mind and she had a very restless night, tossing and turning. Eventually, she settled and drifted off to sleep.

Janet rang Nancy just after lunch for the gossip.

'Well, he certainly took my mind off Thomas for a while and he's asked me out tonight. I don't know whether to go or not,' Nancy told her.

'Be a devil,' Janet replied. 'I was!'

Apparently, she had known John for quite a while and he'd asked her out on numerous occasions, but she'd always turned him down. When they had dropped Chris off, he invited her back to his place and seduced her, soft music, candlelight, and she enjoyed every minute. 'I'm certainly going out with John tonight, he was fantastic! We could all meet up for a drink,' said Janet.

'Yeah, why not? It'll be easier in company, but I won't be able to go around Thomas' end of town, I may be seen,' replied Nancy.

They arranged to meet in the Alex, and Janet was just passing, of course.

Jason rang just after tea and with the tone of his voice at first was not expecting Nancy to meet him. When she said she would come to the Alex he sounded really pleased. 'I'll be there for eight o'clock,' she said.

'I'm looking forward to it,' he replied.

They had a good night, more so when Janet and John turned up. Nancy was keeping her distance, and she told him later on in the evening they should just be friends and she didn't want to get involved again. He agreed with her until they went back to his flat and made love for most of the night. She woke up in the morning and realised she had come on her period. She was so embarrassed, there was blood all over the sheets. She said sorry and she would take them home and wash them, but he told her not to worry about it. These things happen.

When she went around that night, the sheets were soaking in the bath. She felt so awful; he'd had to handwash them when she had a machine at home. They went for a few drinks in the Alex. He asked her how heavily she was bleeding, and she told him she was always heavy for the first couple of days, then it tailed off pretty quickly. His eyes lit up, thinking that tomorrow night he would be able to make love to her. It was weird talking about female things. She could never talk to Thomas about periods; he just kept away when she was "on". They went back to his flat and when they eventually went to bed, he just held her close to him all night.

The month went by too quickly. She had turned eighteen and couldn't even remember what she'd done for her birthday, with her confused mind. Jason was going, Thomas was coming home on leave in two weeks, promising her a belated birthday surprise, probably taking her out for a posh meal somewhere. She was remembering the restaurant in the Lakes with a contented smile on her face. She should get in touch with Sharon and Geoff before Thomas arrived home, she thought to herself.

The night before Jason was due to leave, they had a bit of an argument in the Alex and Nancy ended up storming out. It was over nothing, but Nancy had thought it would be an easier way for him to let go. Her feelings for Thomas had not diminished at all really, but the way she felt about Jason had been getting stronger. He didn't know about Thomas and vice versa.

Jason followed her out of the pub and chased after her. When he caught up the arguing continued, and Nancy slapped him across the face. He raised his hand to hit her back and when he realised what he was doing, he held her tightly in his arms and said he was so sorry.

'Nancy, I love you. Come abroad with me, I can't bear to lose you.'

'How can I? It's impossible, stupid even.'

They talked about it most of the night, in between making love and in the morning, Nancy helped him pack and saw him off at the station. She didn't feel any pain this time, but it took her mind back to when Thomas was leaving, the same station, the same platform and she cried, not for Jason, but for Thomas; or was it?

Chapter Eight

'*I hate railway stations and I hate this platform. Are they doing this to me on purpose, trying to make me feel guilty and admit to Thomas what has been going on while he has been away?*' Nancy was thinking to herself. '*Typical trains, always late giving me time to think. I HATE THIS STATION.*' She was getting angry, looked at the expected arrival time on the board and walked out onto the busy bus station. Women laden with shopping bags, children being dragged along behind them, whingeing, mothers shouting at them, which made them whinge even more.

It was just over half an hour she had to wait around for his train. His parents had agreed that Nancy met him at the station on her own. They had three weeks with him before he went back to Germany and they knew how much Thomas had missed Nancy. She was wandering now and not knowing where she was going; the people around her just made her want to scream. She came across a pub and went inside and ordered a double vodka and lemonade. She sat down in a quiet corner – not that there were many – and drank. Blokes were staring at this beautiful creature they saw sitting alone in the corner. She ignored all their stares and went back to the bar and ordered another, and then another. God, they were going down so easily, she was so thirsty, and the anger she had felt was subsiding. The blokes who were staring at her earlier were now curious as she had drunk six glasses in a very short span of time.

Shit, she thought to herself and jumped up. She had been here for almost an hour. She ran out and across to the station. Had Thomas arrived and gone? What would he say? Would he be mad? She felt herself staggering slightly as she made her way to the platform, when she heard a voice shouting, 'Nancy, over here!' She stopped mid run and turned around.

Thomas was standing near the phone boxes and she had run straight past him. She was rooted to the spot as she took in his dark hair and sparkling green eyes as he made his way towards her. He looked broader, his beautiful body seemed more muscly than she remembered. He picked her up in his strong arms and spun her around. She felt dizzy.

'Thomas, stop, please,' she cried. He put her down and looked into her eyes. They were filling with tears and he kissed her slowly, lovingly with all the emotion he had stirring inside him.

They retrieved his bags from near the telephone and got into a taxi to Thomas' house. Hugs and kisses from his mum, then Shelly, his sister.

'My, haven't you grown in the last couple of months!' Thomas said to proud Shelly. After an hour or so of catching up on the news, Thomas drove Nancy home, called in briefly to say hello to Maggie and Eric, and left with, 'Be ready for 7:30, I'll pick you up.'

Nancy asked Maggie if she knew where Thomas was taking her tonight, but she didn't. 'I would presume it'll be somewhere nice. Why don't you put that new dress on, the one you wore on your eighteenth?' suggested Maggie when Nancy was getting ready to go out for a meal.

She looked at the long silver dress hung in the wardrobe. She'd worn this when she went out with Janet and Chris on her birthday and met Jason later on in Oblivion. He had slowly peeled the figure-hugging dress off her body, leaving her naked; it was too clingy to wear underwear. They had made love passionately that night, orgasm after orgasm, pure ecstasy. Could she wear it for Thomas? She tried it on and looked at herself in the mirror, the clinging, sparkling fabric which showed every curve of her teenage body. Her bust seemed bigger, looked sexier than before. How did she feel? Would she feel guilty? Would she spill the beans, or could she focus her mind back to Thomas?

She had a long soak in the bath after Maggie and Eric had eventually finished in there. What were they celebrating, she thought to herself as she drifted amongst the bubbles. Where was Thomas taking her? She would have to wear THE dress, it was the most expensive, beautiful dress she had.

She blocked all thoughts of Jason out of her mind and thought about what happened this afternoon, why had she felt as she had. OK, she was annoyed at the station, she had said goodbye to the two people she had loved most on the same platform recently, but welcomed one back as well, albeit for a relatively short period of time. But wasn't that what she had with Jason? *'GOD, FORGET HIM!'* she tried to shout in her mind. *'FORGET HIM, even if only for now.'*

She styled her long dark hair and had a hard decision; whether to wear it flowing, slightly wavy over her slender shoulders, or wear it up to accentuate her slim face and high cheekbones. Once she put her dress on, she decided she would leave it down and scrunched it a little more to exaggerate the curls.

Thomas was on the dot, as usual, and while Nancy was rushing around the house trying to find her shoes, he poured them both a small drink each. Maggie and Eric had left earlier, and she couldn't find her shoes, the anger was returning. Where had she flung them off when she last wore them? Maggie would know. Damn it, she thought, calm down, for God's sake. She emptied the bottom of her wardrobe and routed through all the shoes. Typical, right at the bottom. She slipped them on and walked downstairs to where Thomas stood with glasses in both hands and his mouth wide open.

'You look absolutely gorgeous, darling,' he said, almost drooling. 'Do we have to go out?' he pleaded.

'Yes,' she replied, taking her drink out of his hand. 'You don't look so bad yourself,' she grinned with a mischievous sparkle in her eye. He took her in his arms, and they held each other tightly. She could feel the special bond they had getting stronger every second. After what felt like ages, Thomas took her hand and they got in the car and drove.

They pulled onto the car park of Northgate Manor, the poshest, most expensive hotel in the area. Nancy was ecstatic, she had never been before, and she turned to Thomas and kissed him. 'This is perfect,' she smiled at him.

'We haven't even gone inside yet,' he laughed.

He took her arm and led her up the stone steps leading into the marble reception. Looking around inside the hotel, it was something that you could only dream about; the large marble entrance hall, the winding staircase to the bedrooms. Hang on, she had dreamt about it! Weird.

They made their way through to the dining area, where there was a small bar and double doors with doormen standing each side, which led to the restaurant. Thomas ordered the drinks and they sat at a candlelit table, gazing into each other's eyes. Even though the bar was small, there was no one else there. Too expensive, she thought. The maître d' came over to where they were sitting and guided them into the restaurant. The double doors were opened by the doormen to cheers from the people seated inside.

Nancy looked around. She saw Janet, Chris, Maggie, Eric, Sharon and Geoff, all Thomas' family and more of her friends. She turned to Thomas, tears streaming down her face and hugged him.

'Thank you, thank you, but how did you manage this while you were in Germany?' she quizzed.

'Blame your mum,' he replied with a wicked grin, very similar to the one Maggie was sporting as Nancy looked at her mum.

They sat down at the table and the food was dished up. Very nouveau cuisine; small portions, but perfectly delicious. This must have cost a fortune; how could Mum and Dad afford this? Nancy thought to herself when the comedian was introduced on stage. He was funny, everyone was in stitches; a little bit blue every now and again, which made Nancy laugh more whenever she glanced over at Aunty Elsie's face (Eric's older sister).

Then the disco. Nancy and Thomas were invited to dance to the first record, *Something's Gotta Hold of My Heart*, it was the one they had danced to in the Lakes. Sharon and Geoff were the first ones to join them on the dance floor and soon the small dance floor was full of couples smooching.

Throughout the night Nancy mingled and caught up with people she hadn't seen for a while: Barbara and Maggie from school; Maggie had just found out she was pregnant. She was a bit younger than Nancy, not eighteen 'til October. Her boyfriend Jed was going to stand by her, and she had been offered a council house in Blacklodge. After a good catch-up with old friends, Nancy found Thomas sitting with both sets of parents. She sat next to him and snuggled closely to him.

'Are we getting a taxi home?' she asked. 'You can't drive, you've had too much to drink.'

'No, we aren't,' he replied, reaching into his jacket pocket. He pulled out a set of keys and jangled them in front of her.

'We're staying here?' she asked excitedly, her heart pounding so much it felt like it would burst.

When the last records of the evening came on, people started filtering out of the room, and Thomas led Nancy onto the dance floor. A classic was playing; she didn't know the singer, but the record was good: *Gonna Write a Classic, Gonna Write It in the Attic*, then *Three Times a Lady*. They glided around the dance floor. The people left were watching, never realising love between two people could be so strong it could be seen.

The record finished and after the last of the party had left Thomas took Nancy up the winding stairs and opened the door to the suite. It was huge; there was a dining area, a lounge area, all open plan, with a door leading to the bedroom. Nancy was in her element, noseying around as Thomas opened the bottle of champagne that was waiting for them. There were roses on the pillow of the four-poster bed draped in white lace. '*How perfect*,' Nancy thought as she took her glass from Thomas.

'I love you so much and I've missed you every second of every day,' he whispered into her ear.

'I've missed you, too,' she replied.

They took the champagne into the bedroom. Thomas slipped off her silver dress while his tongue was working down her neck, caressing each breast in turn as he picked her up and gently laid her on the bed. He made his way down to her waiting vagina and kissed and licked while she was writhing with pleasure. She wanted his penis inside her so much, but he wouldn't. He turned around, so he was laid on his back while he was still caressing her clitoris with his fingers, and she was stroking his penis. She had never put it in her mouth before but presumed that was what he wanted; how was it done? She licked the end and placed her mouth onto it, moving it up and down. It didn't go in very far in, but he seemed to be enjoying it by his light groaning, so she must be doing it right, she thought, and she was enjoying doing it to him. It pleased him, that was the most important thing, and she would do anything to make him happy. They continued to make love until they were both exhausted and fell asleep in each other's arms. What a perfect end to a perfect night!

Chapter Nine

It seemed strange at breakfast in the large restaurant all alone. Maggie had arranged minibuses to take everybody home and the whole hotel had belonged to them all night. Maggie had packed a bag for Nancy, with more casual clothes in for the next day, which she was glad about; she would have looked odd in her evening dress at breakfast. The thought made her smile and she looked at Thomas.

'Thanks for last night, it was wonderful.'

Thomas smiled. 'I know, I was there, remember,' he laughed. They both ended up in hysterics, tears rolling down their faces and the waiter giving them very odd looks, which made them giggle even more.

After breakfast, they went for a walk in the hotel grounds. The surroundings were beautiful; it was a crisp morning and the squirrels were scuttling around the grass and trees looking for food. Thomas stopped walking and turned to Nancy and held her arms as he looked into her eyes and asked, 'Why were you drinking yesterday afternoon?'

Shit, she thought to herself, moving her head to look down so she wasn't facing him.

'I don't know, I was annoyed, I don't know,' she replied. 'Leave it, please.'

He held her in his arms, stroking her hair as a silent tear fell from Nancy's eye. After a while they carried on walking, hand in hand. The tension had eased slightly between them and they started planning what they would do for the next three weeks.

They collected their things from the hotel and set off home. When they arrived, Maggie looked anxious; they had called the vet out for Sammy and were waiting for him to arrive. When Maggie had gone in earlier to feed him, she had found him lying down and unable to stand up, even though she had tried to encourage him. Nancy ran to the stable and when he looked up and saw her, he tried to stand up but immediately collapsed again. Nancy sat down and rested his head on her lap while she gently stroked him. Thomas stood watching her and could see the sadness in her face. When the vet arrived eventually and examined Sammy, he said he was lame with old age and suggested he was put to sleep. He wasn't in much pain, but he probably wouldn't be able to stand again and would soon deteriorate. Nancy was crying, she didn't want him put to sleep, but she didn't want to see him suffer either. She talked about it to Maggie, Eric and Thomas for hours and they decided to leave it for a few days to see how he was.

That night, after spending a couple of hours with Sammy, Nancy made him as comfortable and warm as possible, before she went into the house. Maggie and Eric were going out, so Thomas had brought a bottle of wine and a video around for them to watch. They cuddled up on the sofa, which made Nancy feel secure and loved, although she wasn't particularly watching the video.

Nancy got up and dressed and rushed out to see Sammy before breakfast. He tried to lift his head to greet her but struggled. He looked tired. Nancy was stroking his head when he died, he must have waited to see her. She stayed with him for about an hour, stroking him, his head wet with her tears, then she went back into the house and told Maggie, who called the vet.

All the children on the street had heard and all asked if they could see him. Nancy had never seen the children so sad and she felt sorry for them. They all stood around as Sammy was carefully carried out of the stable and put in the back of the horsebox and they all cried as it started driving off. The stable seemed bare without him and Nancy couldn't face cleaning it out yet. She would do it later.

Thomas came around after lunch and they went for a drive to the country and a walk through Salewheel Woods. Nancy was struggling to hold back her tears and much of the day was spent with Thomas holding and comforting her, pretty much in silence.

When they arrived back home, Maggie said Sharon had rung to say thanks for the other night. Nancy rang her and after a brief natter, had arranged to meet her and Geoff that evening for a few drinks in the Bull's Head, a busy although cosy pub which wasn't too far away. Sunday was normally a good night in most of the pubs in the area and there was a disco on as well. Nancy got ready and ordered a taxi; she wore her jeans and a tight blue top. Her jeans seemed a little bit tighter than normal, probably all the food she had eaten the other night. She was to pick Thomas up on the way as it was nearer to his house.

Thomas also had his jeans on, the ones that Nancy couldn't resist him in as they showed off his bum beautifully, and a check shirt. They arrived at the Bull's Head just before eight. The disco was just starting, and Sharon and Geoff hadn't arrived. Thomas ordered the drinks and said, 'This must be a first for you, being early.' He smiled sarcastically and gave her a quick kiss.

They found a table and sat down. Sharon and Geoff arrived shortly afterwards and there was a steady stream of people arriving. By nine o'clock the pub was packed, the music blasting out, and they had to shout to hear themselves. It was a good night and there were quite a few people in they knew who they had a natter to. Sharon asked if they had arranged a date for the wedding yet.

'We're leaving it at least until later next year,' Thomas replied.

'Once they get that ring on your finger, you can't get away with anything,' said Geoff, laughing as Sharon kicked him under the table.

They were all pretty drunk by the end of the night and ordered a taxi home. Sharon had confided to Nancy earlier in the night that she and Geoff were going through a bit of a rough patch, and they arranged to meet on Wednesday in town to have a proper talk about it. It would get Nancy's mind off things if she could help someone else.

That night Thomas made love to her with such gentleness, it made her cry, not because she was upset but because of the love she felt for him. Strong, solid, perfect love. They would spend every minute they could together until she would have to face that platform again.

Chapter Ten

Nancy caught the bus into town and met Sharon. They went to a café and ordered two pots of tea. Sharon was training to be a nurse, which Nancy admired her for, although it wasn't anything Nancy would ever be able to do. Sharon told her that Geoff was really possessive, and she was struggling to cope with it. He wouldn't even let her go to the shop on her own and she wanted to leave him, but she knew that wherever she went, he would find her. She was getting more and more frightened of him. He had never hit her, but she felt it was only a matter of time. Nancy hadn't realised any of this, but they didn't know each other that well. They started discussing what options were realistic. Sharon had to try and put her foot down with him and try and nip it in the bud. A lot easier said than done though, but Nancy offered her refuge at her house if she absolutely needed it.

They left the café and looked around the shops. Retail therapy was what they both needed, they laughed; to spend some money! They went in at least ten clothes shops and tried almost everything on just for the laugh of it. Before they knew it, the shops were starting to close, and Sharon got a bit panicky as Geoff would be due home from work soon. They walked to the bus stop, reminiscing on the bit of fun they had, and arranged to do it again soon.

When Nancy arrived home, Thomas was already there. They had their tea; braised steak, vegetables and potatoes, and Nancy went and got showered and changed. They all sat watching telly when Maggie suggested they started thinking about a date for the wedding and what they both wanted. Church or registry office. 'You've got to remember that venues get booked up well in advance nowadays,' Maggie pointed out to them. They talked about it all evening and Nancy started getting excited. Thinking about the big white wedding, looking like a princess and the quaint cottage that all little girls dream of.

Nancy spent the next day cleaning out Sammy's stable. She laid down fresh straw, cleaned the few rosettes that they had won when she was a lot younger and hung the pictures up all around the stable, which Maggie had enlarged and framed, of Nancy and a lot of the other children, all with Sammy. She made it into a bit of a shrine; she even brought a chair from her bedroom, so she had somewhere comfortable to sit when she felt like being on her own. Thomas had only known straw bales when they used to sneak in the stable and make love. It was always funny as it was so uncomfortable, but sometimes that made it more exciting. They hadn't been in here for a while, as Maggie and Eric had accepted they slept together and let them share Nancy's bed. Eric wasn't happy about it though, but Maggie had reassured him they always used the necessary precautions.

That evening after Nancy and Thomas came back from the pub, Nancy took his hand and led him to the stable. They made love on the uncomfortable scratchy straw as they had done in the past. It must have been the scratching of the straw on her back which made Nancy orgasm more quickly than usual, but Thomas carried on gently thrusting until she was ready again, and when he knew she was going to have her second orgasm he relaxed, and they came together, the pulsating, throbbing, wonderful sensation only that moment can bring.

The following days passed too quickly, and Thomas' last weekend arrived before he set off back to Germany the following Friday. Thomas rang Nancy at teatime on Friday and told her to pack her bags for the weekend, he'd be there in an hour. She rushed around, not knowing where they were going. The nights were getting colder, so she packed a warm jumper, her silver dress, two pairs of jeans, socks, knickers and her walking boots, just in case.

Thomas arrived, and they set off northbound on the M6. The Lakes, Nancy thought to herself. When they arrived at the hotel where they had stayed last time, unfortunately they were booked up, but they did recommend a hotel further down the road and even rang up for them to see if they had any rooms available. They did, and they went and checked in. It was a bit more expensive than the other, but it did have a swimming pool. They went to their room, got changed and went out for dinner, the same restaurant where Thomas had proposed. He could be so romantic at times.

The next morning, they went and bought swimwear and made full use of the facilities. The swimming pool wasn't very big, but it was quiet and the Jacuzzi was the best part, the warm bubbles massaging their bodies as they sat there, arms around each other. It was making Nancy feel horny and she leant her hand over to slyly rub his penis, making sure no one could see her. It was soon hard, but he stopped her as he wouldn't have been able to go anywhere until it had calmed down. When he was able to move, they got dried and went to their room. Thomas threw Nancy on the bed and ripped her swimsuit off with a passion; he thrust his penis into her so hard that she cried out. He held her hands above her head as he thrust harder and harder. It hurt but it was ecstatic, when Thomas was going to come, he stopped thrusting and kept his penis in her vagina, just moving it in and out a little so his body was rubbing hard on her clitoris, and he lifted her bottom up so she could get the full pleasure of her orgasm.

They got dressed and went for a walk in the hills to work up an appetite for food before lunch.

Chapter Eleven

Friday morning came around too quickly for anyone's liking. Nancy felt like she couldn't cope with the tears again and at first refused to go with Thomas to the station. His pleading eyes soon weakened her and before long they were standing on platform two. The train was due in fifteen minutes to take Thomas to Manchester, from where he flew to near his base in Germany. Tears were shed by Thomas' mum. He would be away for six weeks before being on leave at Christmas for four weeks. When his mum let him go, Thomas turned to Nancy, stroked her cheek in his special way that made her tingle, and kissed her with a gentle passion. They stood in each other's arms until the train chugged into the station. Other people clambered on board; Thomas was rooted to the spot, absorbing the love that Nancy gave him. There were no tears in her big brown sparkling eyes.

'I love you so much,' Thomas said, kissing her again.

'I love you, too. See you at Christmas,' she replied.

He picked his suitcase up and strolled towards the train, turning back only once to blow a kiss to Shelly and a sexy wink at Nancy.

He boarded the train and as the whistle blew and the train slowly moved out of the station, he leant out of the window and waved. Shelly was waving and shouting like mad, his mum was crying and Nancy, trying to be strong, just shed a few tears.

She spent most of the afternoon in the stable, reading the letters that Thomas had sent last time he was away. She was getting one every few days, but that soon dwindled to one a week. They were passionate letters that meant a lot to her; it was always difficult to express what and how you felt in a letter, so she could tell how much thought had gone into each one. She would treasure these letters all her life. In the quietness of the stable she broke down and had the familiar pain of being left yet again. She lay on the straw bales, sobbing, and eventually cried herself to sleep.

When she woke up, she went into the house and got a strange look from Maggie. 'Have you seen the state of your hair?' she exclaimed. Nancy looked in the mirror and laughed to herself. She must have been tossing and turning in the straw, her hair was covered in it so much she looked like Wurzel Gummidge! She got as much out as she could and then went for a long soak in the bath.

She rang Janet to see if she was going out. It was Friday night after all, she couldn't stop in and as she hadn't seen her for a while; it would be good to catch up on her news and Janet could always cheer her up.

They went around town. It was packed and there were a lot of familiar faces. Janet was still seeing John, he was getting quite serious, but Janet wasn't. She could have him eating out of her hand and she tended to mess him about a bit. She was always flirting, and fellas flocked around her. Tonight was no exception, it just meant that Nancy had to talk to their friends, and she was in no mood to put up with idiots. She spotted Barbara, her old school friend, and left Janet talking to the three blokes.

The next morning Nancy woke up and went to the bathroom where she threw up. She felt lousy. She went downstairs and promptly stated to Maggie that she was never drinking again. Maggie laughed to herself; she was used to her saying that after a good night out. Nancy spent most of the day recovering, she hadn't felt that drunk, and she hadn't been sick for a long time, especially not in the morning. It was tea time before she could face any food and the smell of Eric cooking. He always cooked on Saturdays, normally some kind of steak with either chips or potatoes. Tonight, it was fillet steak, Nancy's favourite, cooked so there was a bit of redness inside; medium rare when you order in a restaurant.

Nancy went along to the pub with Maggie and Eric later and had a nice chat with some of their friends and a few glasses of wine. A nice quiet cosy evening amongst the oldies, she thought; she was the only one under forty in the Dog Inn, the closest pub to their house. No wonder she didn't come here that often.

She was definitely not drunk last night, so why did she have her head down the toilet again?

'You couldn't be pregnant by any remote chance, could you?' asked Maggie, showing concern.

'No chance,' replied Nancy. She was due to start uni a week on Monday. She was trying to cast her mind back; when was her last period? She really couldn't remember but the turbulence and the upset of the last few months would be why she hadn't had one.

The following Friday night, Maggie and Eric had booked a table at a restaurant to treat Nancy as she was setting off to university on Sunday afternoon, ready to start on Monday. They had talked about getting Nancy a car, a belated eighteenth birthday present; it would probably save them money if they did, she wouldn't use them as taxis as often. They had a word with the mechanic they used, Stuart, and asked him to keep his eyes open for a cheap, reliable run-around. Stuart had rung them earlier in the week; he had found a lovely little

Ford Escort, an R reg that was in good condition and cheap at a hundred pounds. They went to see it. It was rather a bright green, but they thought Nancy would like it; she would certainly stand out from the crowd in that! Stuart had delivered it while Nancy was out shopping, and they put it in the garage where Nancy rarely went. The washing machine and dryer were in there and she only went in when she wanted to put clothes in the dryer.

Eric drove to the restaurant, Chicco's, a little Italian place just outside Great Yarwood, about eight miles from where they lived. It was olde worlde; large wooden beams, low ceilings, very compact, and it was extremely busy. They had a bit of a wait, but the food was glorious. Being in an Italian restaurant, Nancy ordered the fillet steak with pepper sauce. The Italians always cook it better, so she said. Maggie had beef stroganoff and Eric also had a fillet steak but without sauce; he said it ruined the succulent taste, with garlic bread and mushrooms for starters. Eric just had one glass of wine, but Nancy and Maggie polished off a couple of bottles between them. It was a lovely family meal. When Nancy went to the toilet, Maggie, being a little bit tipsy, suggested they leave, telling Nancy about the car till the morning. Eric agreed.

Nancy slept in while almost lunchtime and arose rather groggy. Maggie made her a cup of tea. Eric was due home from work soon, he had arranged to finish early, and she should be able to keep Nancy occupied on the settee until he got home. Nancy went to get showered and dressed and emerged from the bathroom just as Eric arrived. They all gathered in the kitchen which led onto the garage.

'We decided to buy you something you may need for university,' Eric said. 'It should come in useful.' He headed to unlock the back door. Nancy looked bewildered as she followed him, wondering how she would get a washing machine to uni. He opened the door and stood back.

Nancy's jaw fell. 'A car!' she exclaimed. Nancy had passed her test second time in January and had occasionally borrowed Maggie's VW Golf. Eric wouldn't let her anywhere near his BMW.

'Can I test drive it?' she asked excitedly.

'Of course,' replied Eric and threw her the keys. He opened the garage door and they all got in the car while Nancy reversed carefully up the drive and onto the street. It was a good little runner, and Nancy was pleased with it. They were out and about for an hour before returning home.

Nancy, Janet and Christina were going around town for their last night out together for a while. Janet was going to Leeds Uni and Chris was going to Manchester, although doing a different course than Nancy. They met up at eight o'clock in the Black Bull. Nancy was telling them about her car and offered Chris a lift tomorrow. She arranged to pick her up at 3:00 p.m. the following afternoon. They went around as many pubs as they could manage before making their way to Oblivion after last orders had gone. People were queuing up outside and they joined the queue and waited shivering. Within ten minutes they were ordering their drinks at the bar. Chris had shot off to the loo; they went and stood near the toilets, so Chris would see them when she came out.

It seemed busier than usual. Nancy spotted Shaun, a bloke who Chris had fancied for ages but didn't dare talk to. She was shy where blokes were concerned, and it was Janet who had gone to talk to him to find out what she could, then Nancy and Chris had gone over, and Janet introduced them. Janet made excuses and dragged Nancy off to the bar, leaving Chris to talk to him. She re-joined them after only ten minutes. She had got herself all tongue-tied and embarrassed and ended up standing there in silence for five of those minutes, then she ran off to the loo.

Shaun worked his way through the crowd to where they stood. 'Where's Chris disappeared to?' he asked.

'She's just in the ladies',' Janet replied, wondering where she had got to. It seemed like she'd been there for ages. She eventually emerged and went red with embarrassment when she saw Shaun.

'Hi,' he said, smiling. 'Would you like to dance?'

'Er, er, maybe later,' she stuttered back.

'OK, later then,' he said, wandering off.

Nancy and Janet looked at her. 'You idiot, you could have been in there!' they both exclaimed. 'He may not ask again.'

He didn't. The smoochy records came on. John turned up and dragged Janet off to dance, while Nancy and Christina had a wander around to try and find Shaun. There was no sign of him. Chris was kicking herself.

Nancy packed her stuff into the car and gave Eric and Maggie loads of hugs and kisses before she set off to pick up Christina. Eric had written full directions down for her, so she wouldn't get lost. She didn't really like motorways, but she would have to get used to them and it would hopefully be quiet, being Sunday.

She helped Chris pack her stuff into the car. It was a bit of a squeeze and they had to put some stuff on the back seat. Hugs all around with Chris' mum and dad and they eventually set off. Music blasting and talking and laughing all the way. Chris admitted that she was really nervous and was glad she was going with Nancy, she would probably have been sick all the way on the train. Nancy thought uni may bring Chris out of her shell a bit, meeting new people would do her good. She might even be able to talk to Shaun!

When they arrived and parked, they went to admissions where they were allocated rooms. Nancy was sharing with a girl called Susan Hodgson and Chris was sharing with Elizabeth Walsh. They were on the same floor of the building, the third of a six-floor block. The floors above them were the male sections. The rooms were average size with a single bed in each corner, a large window in between the beds with dark blue curtains tied back with cord. Two large, dark wood wardrobes with hanging space, drawers and four shelves, and matching bedside cabinets with small light blue lamps and a sink with a mirror above. The bathroom was two doors down; there was one bathroom for every six rooms, that should be fun in the mornings. Chris' room was the same. They helped each other unpack and went to the students' bar, where there were lots of people getting to know each other over drinks. Everyone seemed really friendly. It wasn't 'til they returned to their rooms later that they both met their roommates.

Chapter Twelve

Nancy recognised Susan from earlier in the students' bar, she had noticed her bleached blonde hair and classy clothes. They did the basic introductions; Susan was from just outside Priston, a little village called Darston, and her father owned a wedding dress manufacturing business. Her mother sold children's clothes. 'Are they trying to tell you something?' laughed Nancy. Susan was an only child. Nancy told her how her father Eric had inherited the fruit business which his father had started just after the war. It was split between his three brothers and her dad now had three fruit stalls in Lancashire, all in busy town centre locations. His ambition was to expand and be a local supermarket, but that ambition went out of the window when Nancy was born. Her mother, Maggie, didn't work. They had a comfortable living, probably more than Nancy realised.

Nancy told her about Christina being down the hall and Susan pulled a large bottle of vodka out of her holdall and suggested they went and introduced themselves. They knocked on the door and Elizabeth answered it with a glass already in her hand.

'Hi, I'm Chris' friend Nancy and this is my roommate Susan. We thought we'd bring a drink along and introduce ourselves.'

'Great minds think alike,' replied Elizabeth, 'and please call me Liz.' They went into the room and sat on the bed.

'Liz and I were just going to come to your room with this bottle of Martini.'

Liz started telling them that all next week, they would find their way around campus and sign up for any clubs they wanted to and generally get settled in before lectures start the following Monday, depending on the courses and timetables. 'So, we can get as pissed as we like tonight, girls,' shouted Susan. Nancy ran back to her room to get the two glasses from the sink and the bottle of lemonade she had, and they sat up for most of the night drinking Martini and vodka with a bit of lemonade.

Liz told them all about her fella who was in the army. He was twenty-three, called Steve, and she reckoned it was great as he was away for most of the time and she could do what she wanted. Chris told them about the cock-up she had with Shaun and they were all in fits of laughter. Susan said she didn't have one boyfriend, but a few she kept hanging on the line, and like deciding what clothes to wear, she always decided at the last minute which one she was going to meet that night; it always depended what mood she was in. A different bloke for every mood. And Nancy told them about Jason and Thomas, both being away and hoping they didn't show up at home together!

It was a great night with a lot of laughter. A couple of times their neighbours, whoever they were, banged on the wall and asked them to shut up. That only made them laugh more. They all got on very well and Nancy was confident that they would have a great time through their first year of uni. They agreed to meet up when they eventually got out of bed and go exploring together the next day, before Nancy and Susan staggered off in the direction of their room. They tried a few doors with the key they had before one opened, and twice Nancy had to run to the bathroom, almost wetting herself with laughing.

The next week they spent most of their time in the bar. Liz scored one night in the bar with a lad called Tim. He had long hair and wore combat clothes. He kept trying to get his mates to come over and meet the rest of the girls. When Chris got chatted up by his mate with dreadlocks who introduced himself as Ned, Nancy, Liz and Sue burst out laughing. Chris went bright red, which matched his T-shirt, he started stuttering and Chris was so embarrassed because she felt sorry for him. Needless to say, he didn't stay around long. 'You lot are cruel!' Chris shouted at them. 'You don't know what it's like to be shy, he probably doesn't have a stutter normally!' she added, bursting out in laughter, seeing the funny side herself.

They all became a little more serious when the lectures began. Nancy had two early starts in a week, Chris had four, and Sue and Liz only had one each, lucky beggars. They had more early nights and all got busy with their studies. Until the weekend arrived, Nancy, Chris and Sue all went home, but Liz came from Scotland and it was too far to go. Her mum and dad had moved up to Gretna for his work and she was rather travel sick, so she was glad to stay. They all felt awful leaving her, but she insisted she'd be OK. Tim was staying, and she would spend some time with him.

When Nancy arrived home, she had multiple questions from Maggie and Eric and certainly toned down what she told them. She'd already had three letters off Thomas which Maggie had forwarded to her at uni and there were another two at home waiting for her. She had replied to all of them, albeit not as long-windedly as she normally did.

She took the letters to her bedroom to read in peace. It was the usual, "Missing you, love you dearly" and a bit about his work, although for security reasons, he could never say where he was working or what he was actually doing. It was more like the Secret Service than the Royal Military Police, she often thought. She wrote him a long letter back, telling her who she'd met, (females only, of course) and about her lecturers, her timetable and all the boring stuff which made up three sides and then how she couldn't wait to see him at Christmas and how much she missed him too.

She wrote the address on and went to post it. When she got back, she rang Janet, but her mum said she wasn't coming home for another fortnight, but she too was having a great time. She'd told her mum the night life in Leeds was excellent and her roommate, Sally, was good fun. Nancy got her full address and room number and promised she would write to her. It was always difficult ringing; there was one payphone per floor at their uni. She presumed it would be the same at Leeds and messages rarely got passed on, so she decided she would write to Janet.

Nancy and Chris went around town that night and ended up in their usual haunt, Oblivion. They were dancing when Nancy noticed Shaun walk in. She didn't tell Chris as she would have to shout anyway, she would go to the bar near where he was and hope for the best. When the record finished, Nancy had a look around from the dance floor, which was just a step higher than the main floor, to see where Shaun had gone. He was standing at the bar talking to a bloke, who from that distance looked a bit OK. Nancy led the way to the top bar and squeezed in, a person away from him. She nudged Chris behind her and turned around and pointed Shaun out. Chris looked at him and smiled, her face reddening all the time. They got their drinks and backed away from the bar and stood at the nearest table. Shaun came over with his friend and introduced Dave to them; he had short, light-brown hair, greenish-brown eyes and was nicely dressed. Nancy started talking to him, so Shaun could talk to Chris, hopefully.

Dave had his own business making window frames. It was only a small business he'd just started three months earlier, but it was going all right. His brother was a window fitter. Dave made them and his brother fitted them, it sounded like a good partnership. Nancy kept glancing sideways to see what Chris was doing and she seemed to be chatting to Shaun easily, so when Dave asked her to dance, she left them to it.

Dave bought the next round and when the smoochies came on, Shaun took Chris' hand and disappeared to dance. About time too. Nancy turned to Dave as he, too, led her onto the dance floor. It was just a friendly dance though; Nancy didn't fancy Dave. He was a laugh and really easy to get along with, but nothing compared to Thomas or Jason. When the night ended, and they had finished their drinks, Chris started being shy when Shaun invited her back to his flat, so she gave him her number, hoping he would ring the next night. Dave just held Nancy's hand as though shaking it, with a 'See you again sometime,' and a quick peck on the cheek.

Chris was complaining about herself in the taxi home. 'Why haven't I got the guts to go with him? It's not as if I'm a virgin, I slept with Rob.'

'That was after five months of being together,' Nancy reminded her. 'Shaun could just be a one-night stand, you don't know. See if he rings you tomorrow.'

The taxi dropped Chris off and carried on to Nancy's. She staggered up to bed as quietly as possible, although Maggie was listening for her little girl to come home and heard every bang she made. Once Nancy got into bed, she was asleep as soon as her head hit the pillow.

Chris rang Nancy at tea time the next day. 'He's rung!' she shouted excitedly. 'He wants me and you to meet him and Dave tonight. Say you'll come, please,' she pleaded. Nancy thought about it and agreed, she had a laugh with Dave the night before and it would be helping Chris. They agreed to meet at 8:00 p.m.

Chris was like a nervous wreck when Nancy picked her up in the taxi just before eight. 'It took me ages to decide what to wear, I've practically emptied my wardrobe.' She had ended up with tight black leather pants on and a white gypsy top. She had her long hair twisted and clipped up at the back. She looked really pretty; Shaun wouldn't be able to resist. Nancy wasn't as dressed up, she just had her jeans on with her little black top. They walked in and spotted Shaun and Dave near the bar at the back of the pub. They squeezed through the crowd. Shaun asked what they were drinking and ordered their drinks. They stayed in the Wine Lodge for a while when it got quieter; it was well known as one of the meeting places and people had started drifting off around town. Oblivion it was, and back to Dave's for more alcohol. He lived the nearest, a suburb just outside the town centre called Livesey. It was a small terraced cottage, a quaint two up, two down. Dave opened a bottle of white wine and poured everyone a glass.

They all sat talking well into the night. When Nancy noticed Shaun looking at Chris with "come to bed" eyes, Dave nodded at Shaun as if to say OK, and Shaun led Chris up to the back bedroom while Nancy and Dave sat up watching a film. When Nancy fell asleep on the couch, Dave got her a blanket, covered her up and went up to bed himself. It was five o'clock in the morning, after all.

Nancy woke up to the smell of bacon cooking and Chris and Shaun sitting together on the armchair. 'What time is it?' she asked.

'Just after 10:30,' replied Shaun.

She sat up, still with the blanket wrapped around her, and when she focused, she could see a definite sparkle in Christina's eyes. Dave came in with a big plate of bacon butties. 'Help yourselves,' he said. Nancy couldn't face food as soon as she woke up, so she politely refused.

Later on, Dave took everyone home. Shaun promised he would ring Chris in two weeks when she was home from uni. Nancy couldn't wait to pick Chris up later on to hear all the details of what happened, although she was quite disappointed when she did. Chris insisted that nothing happened apart from a few kisses and cuddles and a nibble here and there. 'He knew I was drunk, and he didn't want to take advantage of that,' she said, which Nancy thought was very sweet of him.

Chapter Thirteen

Chris had noticed over the last two weeks they had been back at uni that Nancy was acting strangely. She wasn't dressing as nicely as usual, just seemed to be slobbing around in leggings and jumpers, so one evening before they were due to go home, Chris collared her on her own and asked what was wrong. Nancy burst into tears, so Chris put her arms around her and let her cry. When she had calmed down and wiped her eyes, Nancy told her she thought she was pregnant. 'My God,' said Chris, 'How far gone are you?'

'I don't know,' cried Nancy. 'I thought I was ages ago, but just ignored it, then I had a bad period, but it's the same feeling I had then!'

'We'll have to get you to a doctor. I'll ring for you first thing in the morning. Do you want me to come with you?' asked Chris, really concerned about her best friend.

'Yes, please, I'd really appreciate it,' replied a tearful Nancy.

Christina stayed with her for hours, her head buried on her shoulder, not moving, but the tears, Chris noticed, had dried up, apart from the ones already soaked into her jeans. She carefully laid Nancy back on the bed and tried her best to cover her up without waking her, and she crept out of the room just as Sue was approaching. Chris whispered to Sue that Nancy was upset and asleep and to try not to disturb her. Sue did ask why, but Chris just fobbed her off with she'd tell her tomorrow. Chris lay awake trying to get her head around the situation and what she could do to help her best friend. She felt helpless and ended up crying herself to sleep, hurting for herself and for Nancy.

The following morning, Chris rang the local surgery at 8:30, as soon as they opened and then argued with the receptionist that she felt it was an emergency appointment and she had to be seen that morning. The receptionist eventually gave in and booked her in for 9:25 a.m. Chris went and knocked on Nancy's room, gently at first and then with a bit more vigour when she heard Sue shout, 'Right, right, we've heard you!' She came to the door looking rather bedraggled, having just woken up. 'Nancy's in the bathroom, I heard her get up about half an hour ago.'

'Sorry,' replied Chris and went and knocked on the bathroom door. 'Nancy, are you in there?'

'Just coming,' Nancy replied and opened the door. She was just finishing off her make-up in the bathroom so as not to wake Sue. Chris noticed she had quite a lot of foundation on, but it was obviously to hide the redness of her crying the night before.

'Your appointment's at 9:25 a.m. I'm going to get dressed and ready, see you at ten past.' She looked at Nancy, smiled a "cheer up" smile, gave her a quick hug and ran back to her room.

She hurried and showered, got changed into her jeans and jumper, tied her hair up – it would have taken too long to dry had she washed it – put a bit of make-up and went back to Nancy's room. Sue had got up and gone out, and Nancy was sitting on the bed reading some letters, probably from Thomas, she thought.

'Are you ready? It'll take us ten minutes to walk there.'

Nancy got off the bed, picked her bag up and walked out. They engaged in small talk on the way to the surgery. Chris went to the reception area and checked in and they went and sat down in the waiting room. There were three doctors in the surgery; Dr Donaldson, Dr Shaw and Dr Mitchell, Nancy was seeing the latter. They waited about fifteen minutes until Nancy's name was called. Chris stood up and led her through the door. Dr Mitchell introduced himself as a locum covering for holidays for the next two months and glanced at the girls.

'What can I do for you two?' he asked.

'I think I'm pregnant,' replied Nancy with a shudder in her voice.

'And the date of your last period?' he asked.

'About four months ago, I think.'

He asked her to go into the toilet on the left and provide a urine sample. When she passed him the tube, he poured it into a funny-looking device and left it on the side. He asked her to pop onto the couch in the corner of the room and lift her jumper up. He carefully felt her stomach, his hands making his way around the small bump, pressing gently into it.

Dr Mitchell looked back at the device on the side and nodded. She was pregnant, three to four months. 'The scan will tell you more accurately, though. I'll ring it through and get you an appointment as soon as possible. They tend to prioritise the younger generation, so they have more time to think about their choices. You do know you have a choice, don't you, Nancy?' He went on to explain about terminations, adoption and coping if she decided to keep the baby.

As soon as they got outside, Chris asked her if she knew whether it was Jason's or Thomas'. She shook her head and said, 'It could be either one of them, really. Thomas left on the sixteenth of August. Jason was home for just over a month, and I met up with him the night Thomas left. He left on the twentieth of September and it's the first of December today. I'm three to four months pregnant, I'll have to try and work it out in my diary.'

When they got back to Nancy's room, they started circling the dates. The Tuesday that Thomas left, and Jason turned up would make her fifteen weeks and two days pregnant, so anything further gone was Thomas' and less would be Jason's. Chris promised to keep it secret, especially as they were going home for the weekend. Luckily, the pregnancy had not made her sick this time, that's if she ever was, and it hadn't put her off drinking either.

Chris went out with Shaun on her own on Friday night, but Janet was home, so Nancy ended up on the town with her other good friend, and as always, Janet really cheered her night up. The gossip from Leeds seemed so hilarious, she felt she was missing out. Janet told her about how the lads from the floor above kept sneaking down and setting fire extinguishers off so the girls would slip when they came out of the rooms in the morning. They reckoned they had a camera set up taking pictures of them all, but they weren't convinced until an enlarged photo of Alison running down the corridor in just her knickers was pinned up in the mess room for all to see. They were planning on how they could get them back before Christmas and were desperately trying to think of ideas. The lads at Salford were more engrossed in their hippy hairstyles than having immature good fun. All through the night Nancy laughed and relaxed after her news this morning. She didn't mention anything about the pregnancy to Janet. She wasn't the maternal type, too much good fun and Nancy knew Janet would persuade her to have a termination, so nothing was said.

The following lunch time when Nancy got up, Maggie had made a fresh pot of tea when she heard the familiar bangs of her daughter which she had missed so much since she had gone. The house always felt empty; Eric at work early mornings, Maggie being alone until Nancy got up. Even the peacefulness she had between the two events felt dull and lonely when Nancy wasn't there. This morning, however, she got the calm warm feelings back, knowing her daughter and her friend was in the house. Nancy came into the kitchen and sat at the table and sipped her freshly poured cuppa.

'Mum, do you remember ages ago, you asked me if I was pregnant? How would you have felt if I was?' Nancy asked with trepidation.

'I don't know, really, I didn't think any more about it at the time. Why?'

All Nancy could say was, 'I'm sorry, Mum,' before bursting into tears.

Maggie took her daughter into her arms, not really knowing whether to be angry, upset or disappointed. She was only eighteen and having a baby. She felt too young to be a grandmother and what on earth Eric would say, she dreaded to think. Once Nancy had calmed down, they sat and talked. Maggie felt sure Thomas would stand by Nancy, may even be pleased about it, but what did Nancy want?

'You could always have an abortion, that way we needn't tell Dad or Thomas,' Maggie suggested, 'but you really need to be sure, otherwise you could regret it for the rest of your life.'

'I have thought about it and I really don't think I could kill my unborn baby,' Nancy replied and started crying again. They talked a while longer, and Maggie urged Nancy to go for a bath and freshen up before Eric got home from work. They had agreed not to mention anything to him yet; Maggie thought it would be best if she told him once Nancy had gone back to uni and after she'd been for a scan, whenever that may be.

It was hard for Maggie not to say anything to Eric, they never kept secrets. It had always been a happy marriage. She could only remember having a few arguments with him; normally over Nancy and her mischievous behaviour when she was younger. The rest of the weekend was spent as normally as Nancy and Maggie could make it, and after Sunday tea Nancy set off back to uni. She told Chris when she picked her up about how well Maggie had taken it and that she was pretty much sure that she was going to keep the baby. She was going to talk to her year tutor at some point this coming week on what her situation would be. They may make her leave, or she may want to drop out. There was so much to think about, she was starting to have a headache, so she tried to forget about it for the time being and asked Chris about Shaun.

He had taken her for a pizza on Friday night and then to a pub near to his house, which had a live rock/pop band on called The Headleys. They were pretty good, and the pub stayed open while after midnight. They walked back to his house and had sex on the sheepskin rug in front of the fire. She nearly burnt her leg, it was bright red, but she couldn't feel any pain because of the pleasure she was having. 'He was absolutely fantastic,' she drooled. 'I must have had at least three orgasms during the night, but once I thought I was peeing myself. It was so embarrassing,' she added excitement rising in her voice.

'No, that's pretty normal. When you think you're peeing, it comes out in spurts and that is a full orgasm, not pee. Jason told me,' Nancy added, laughing. 'I was really embarrassed when it happened to me for the first time with Jason. He loved it though, most fellas do, apparently.'

They carried on the journey, nattering about all sorts, when Nancy spotted a sign for Warrington, which is about thirty miles south of Manchester. They had been talking and laughing so much that she had not realised they had missed their turn-off. That evening, Sue, Liz, Chris and Nancy caught up on all the weekend's gossip with a bottle of vodka before making their way to bed.

Later on in the week, Nancy managed to catch her tutor alone in her office and asked if she could have a chat with her. Mrs Townson invited Nancy in to sit down and asked her the usual questions on how she was finding the course work and had she settled in, which Nancy replied to. When she eventually asked why she wanted to talk to her, Nancy calmly explained that she was pregnant, yet she wasn't sure how far gone she was until she had a scan. Mrs Townson didn't even look shocked and explained that if she was going to have the baby, she would be able to stay until she was seven months and then take a year off if she wanted to return to her studies, but it was recommended that when deciding her finish date, it was at an end of a term, whether that be Christmas or Easter, depending on how pregnant she was. Nancy was to inform her when she had the results from her scan.

The next morning Nancy had two letters in her pigeon hole, one from Thomas and the other from the local hospital. She was booked in for a scan on Thursday, the fourteenth December, at 11:45 a.m. She had to drink a pint of water at least an hour before and not go to the toilet. She rang Maggie and told her the scan was next Thursday, but she would speak to her before then, and went back to her room and opened Thomas' letter. He didn't sound as happy as he normally came across in his letters, Nancy felt there was something wrong, or maybe it was just her. She hadn't told him about being pregnant, felt it wasn't right telling him in a letter; plus, the fact that it may not be his. Would he finish with her, would he accept it? Would Jason come back and be with her if it was his? The days dragged, and she couldn't concentrate on lessons at all. The only person she could talk to was Chris. She would have a chat with her tonight, maybe go for a walk if the weather held up. It looked like it could snow earlier on; the grass this morning had been white with frost and it was freezing. Nancy managed to hide her growing belly in the big thick jumpers she was wearing. Sue or Liz hadn't noticed, or if they had, hadn't said anything. After they had some tea, Nancy and Chris got wrapped up and went for a walk in the nearby woods. The scan was two days away and Nancy was getting scared. Chris tried to reassure her and pointed out she couldn't do or decide anything until she knew exactly how far gone she was, and a scan was pretty much accurate. At the moment, it was just a waiting game and every hour felt like a day.

Chapter Fourteen

The morning of the scan finally arrived, and Nancy got showered and dressed. The hospital was a half hour train ride away, so she bought a bottle of water from the university tuck shop to take with her. Nancy and Chris walked to the train station and waited for the 11.02 train which would arrive at the hospital station at 11.19, then it was a five-minute walk, so they should arrive in plenty of time, providing the train wasn't late, of course. It was only a minute late and they boarded and found a seat. It wasn't that busy but there were three more stations where more passengers would board, most carrying on into Manchester where they could change at Victoria to go on to London. The train stopped at their station and they got off and headed towards the main entrance of the hospital. The antenatal department was on the second floor and when they went through the double doors the room was packed with pregnant women, some of whom were so big they looked like they could burst. There were quite a few toddlers running around and arguing over the few toys they could find. They went to the reception desk and were sent into a different waiting room. It was quieter in here; only two other people waiting and no screaming kids.

Nancy was dying to go to the loo so when her name was called, it was a relief that it would soon be over and done with. She had to get dressed in a white gown which tied at the back of the neck and a dressing gown to cover up. She asked if Chris could come in with her and beckoned to where she was sat in the waiting room. They were led into a dimly lit room with a bed and a large screen. Nancy got up on the bed after taking her dressing gown off and lay down. The nurse explained that she would put some gel on Nancy's stomach and rub the scanner over, which didn't hurt at all. She would be able to measure the baby's head which would estimate how far pregnant she was. The gel was cold and made Nancy jump and the nurse apologised and started the procedure. After about five minutes of the nurse being glued to the screen, she turned it around so Nancy and Chris could see it and pointed out the baby's heartbeat, which was a good strong one, according to the nurse, and ran her finger across the screen so they could make out the shape of baby, head, arms, body and legs, all scrunched up inside her. The nurse told them the earlier you have a scan, the more accurate on baby's age but she thought Nancy was fifteen weeks pregnant and everything looked normal and healthy. Nancy wiped her belly and went to the loo, a big relief, then got dressed and met Chris back in the waiting room.

'I need a drink,' said Nancy quietly, so they made their way out of the hospital grounds and into the pub near the station for a stiff drink. They sat down and looked at each other before both saying at the same time, 'It's Jason's,' and started laughing even though they knew there was nothing to laugh about. When the giggles stopped Chris asked Nancy what she was going to do. Surely, she would lose Thomas if she told him the truth, but could she live a lie?

They stayed in the pub for a good few hours, talking. The trains ran quite often and there was nothing to rush back to uni for. Nancy eventually decided to pretend that she was further gone than they had said, to make everyone think it was Thomas'. Maggie didn't know anything went on with Jason, she thought they were just friends, so it would be better that way. The nurse had given the expected arrival date of the twenty-third of May, so she would tell people she was eighteen weeks pregnant and due at the beginning of May, then hope and pray it was born early. They swore each other to secrecy and got more vodkas. They were due home for Christmas next week and no one should notice before then.

The following day, Nancy went to see Mrs Townson to let her know she wouldn't be returning after Christmas but depending on what happened, she may resume her studies next summer. She also rang Maggie to inform her she was four and a half months pregnant and due at the beginning of May. Maggie asked if she had told Thomas and said she should try and get a message to him. Nancy told her she would be seeing him next Wednesday and would prefer to tell him face to face. She had to convince herself first, before she could face him.

That evening Nancy packed all her things into the car and said goodbye and Merry Christmas to Susan and Liz. She had told them earlier she was dropping out of uni but hadn't told them why and that she would keep in touch through Chris and visit now and again.

They set off for home and Nancy was dreading facing Eric. Maggie said she was telling him today when he got home from work; she didn't know what to expect at all. He would probably have calmed down a bit before she arrived, and Chris offered to go home with her for moral support, which Nancy refused. 'I'll have to face him on my own, but thanks for the support and being there for me the last few weeks. I'm dreading telling Janet even more, you know!' They laughed.

'She'll be dragging you to the abortion clinic, you know, you'll ruin her fun. We'll face her together tonight,' Chris said reassuringly.

'That's if I'm allowed out. Dad might ground me!'

Nancy was feeling a lot better about herself now, she was looking forward to seeing Thomas on Wednesday and telling him. She was sure he'd be pleased, and she could cope with Eric; he wasn't that bad at heart.

Nancy arrived home just after 6:30 p.m. and Maggie came out to help her unpack the car. Eric was reading the paper in the front room and didn't bat an eyelid apart from a nod of acknowledgement. When the car was empty, Nancy and Maggie went into the living room and sat down. Eric folded his paper up and looked at Nancy.

'I always thought you were a sensible girl and your mother tells me you've got yourself pregnant,' he said.

'It takes two, Dad,' she replied.

'What has Thomas said about it?' he asked.

'He doesn't know yet, I couldn't tell him in a letter. I wanted to see him, but I'm sure he'll be pleased.'

He seemed to have taken it better that she imagined, but when she spoke to Maggie later on, apparently, he had gone berserk at her. Nancy apologised.

'He was more upset about you dropping out of uni.'

Nancy went back into the living room and told Eric she was sorry, but she would go back to uni and she was sure everything would be fine. He stood up and put his arms around his little girl, who was carrying his grandchild. She asked if he minded if she went out for an hour to see Janet; he didn't. Nancy rang her and arranged to meet her and Chris in the Black Bull at 9:00 p.m. She quickly went and showered and put her jeans on, although she couldn't fasten them; and a warm jumper that was good enough to go out in. She booked a taxi and picked Chris up on the way. Janet was waiting and had ordered the drinks.

The first thing Janet said to Nancy was, 'Bloody hell, you've put a bit of weight on. It suits you.'

Chris looked at Nancy, and Nancy told Janet quietly that she was pregnant. Janet's face changed to a look of shock and then the barrage of questions which were asked so quickly that Nancy had to concentrate on the answers she was giving. Her life of deceit had begun with her other best friend and she felt guilty about not being truthful to her, but how she felt when she told Thomas was going to be the ultimate test.

Nancy and Chris were surprised how maternal Janet became during the night, in between hearing her stories from Leeds Uni. The blokes she had met and dumped, the one she really liked who dumped her and John whom she couldn't get rid of. Talk of the devil, he just walked in. They stayed in the Black Bull all night and then went home after last orders. Janet told John she would see him in Oblivion, knowing full well they weren't going.

The following few days were spent with Maggie and Nancy getting things ready for Christmas, shopping for presents, ordering food and replacing worn-out decorations. Maggie had invited Thomas' family around for Christmas Day, which she thought at the time was a good idea. They didn't yet know they were going to be grandparents, but Thomas was due to find out, so she had suggested to Eric they invite them around and sort out wedding plans. Eric was an old-fashioned person, and Maggie seemed to think he would prefer them to get married before the baby was born. They arrived home laden with shopping bags, and Nancy enjoyed wrapping the presents. Eric was collecting a tree at the weekend and all the presents would sit waiting under the tree, to be opened on Christmas morning.

When Wednesday came around, Nancy had really bad stomach ache. She put it down to nerves and maybe trapped wind; she was getting really scared about meeting Thomas. His train was due at 2:15 p.m. and Nancy had arranged with his parents to meet him at the station alone. She drove down, parked in the thirty-minute waiting area, locked the car and headed towards the platform. Thomas hadn't seen her car yet; he probably wouldn't like it as he preferred sporty models, but it suited her for now. She sat on a bench; 2:11 p.m., the clock said, and the train was supposedly running on time. God she was scared, and her nails were getting the brunt of it. The clock ticked slowly, and she could hear every tick. She felt like she was alone, even though the platform was busy. She heard a train rumble in the distance. Shit, she couldn't do this, she felt like running, felt like throwing herself under the train. She had accepted the baby, but what would Thomas say? Would he believe her? She had lied to her parents and Janet, could she lie to Thomas? When he looked into her eyes, would he know she was lying?

The train came to a stop at the platform and she stayed on the bench. She couldn't move, the pain in her stomach was horrendous now. She tried to stand up before the doors of the train opened. She went dizzy, held on to the bench and took deep breaths. She saw Thomas in the distance, he must have been sitting near the front of the train. Baggage in hand he raced towards her, dropped his suitcase and picked her up. She flung her arms around his neck and let him spin her around, which made her feel dizzier. When he put her down and kissed her, she pulled back whilst clinging onto his arms for support.

'I have some good news,' she said, smiling. He looked at her, rather bewildered.

'I'm, er, we–we're having a baby.'

With a shocked smile he held her tightly. She could feel his tears when they dripped onto her hair. She looked into his eyes, wiped his tears and said softly, 'I love you so much.'

'This is the best moment of my life. I love you,' he replied, and they stood on the platform, holding each other as if their lives depended on it.

Thomas looked bemused when she opened the door to the car. 'It's a bit bright, isn't it?' He put his suitcase in the boot, and they set off to his parents' house. Nancy had apologised for not telling him about the baby sooner, but she had wanted to tell him face to face rather than in a letter. They had decided to tell his parents straight away when they got there, and Nancy's growing belly was getting more and more difficult to disguise.

All Thomas' parents said when they broke the news was if he was happy, they were happy. Nancy left after a while to go home. Maggie and Eric were going out, and Thomas was coming over later to watch a video. After Nancy had some tea, she waited until Maggie and Eric had finished in the bathroom and went and had a long soak in the bath, lots of bubbles, her stereo on from her bedroom playing soft music and when she heard her mum and dad shout, 'See you later,' she wallowed in the suds and must have drifted off.

She woke with a start. Thomas was sitting over the bath with two glasses of champagne in his hands.

'You made me jump,' she said.

'Sorry,' he replied, passing her glass to her. 'Can you still drink, because I feel like celebrating,' he said with a large grin on his face.

'Is the Pope a Catholic?' she replied as she sipped the Moët & Chandon he'd bought.

He passed her a towel and when she stood out of the bath, he couldn't take his eyes off her slim body with the little bump in her stomach. He helped her dry herself, carefully over the baby, caressing the lump. He couldn't keep his hands off her. He dried her arms, her back, her boobs, her vagina and her legs and carried her to her bedroom. Nancy was by this stage feeling really horny and all he could do was stroke her stomach. When the baby kicked, he was amazed and put his head on her stomach while his fingers were entering her vagina. She was writhing and getting frustrated as she wanted him so much and it took a lot of convincing that he wouldn't or couldn't harm the life inside her through sex. He was a lot more gentle than usual though, teasing her, slowly putting his penis in and out. She wanted to scratch his back to make him make love to her with more vigour, but she had bitten all her nails off at the station. She pushed him on to his back and sat on top of him, placed his penis in and moved up and down while he sucked and nibbled each nipple in turn and moved with her rhythm. Nancy always struggled to come on top, but tonight she managed it quite easily. When she got tired and couldn't move as actively, she rubbed her clitoris constantly against his pubic bone, moving gently, slowly, her breathing deepened and she soon felt the pulsating of her orgasm which in turn made Thomas come, not at quite the same time but near enough for them both to get the pleasure of their love for one another.

They dressed, went downstairs and finished the bottle of champagne before Maggie and Eric came home. Eric started interrogating Thomas about his plans, while Maggie was trying to get him to shut up. There was no point discussing anything when you'd had a few drinks. But Thomas was answering his questions. Yes, he was still planning on marrying Nancy. He was shocked when she told him, but he told Eric, 'She's having my baby, that's a wonderful way to tell me how much she loves me.' Nancy felt a stab of guilt but smiled at him. This was going to be so hard for her, she was never a good liar, what would make it easier for her now. She had sort of convinced herself and everybody else who knew. The only person she could talk to when she felt guilty was Chris. She would ring her in the morning and arrange to go shopping with her. She still had to buy Thomas a present for Christmas, so a good excuse for some retail therapy.

It felt weird as they didn't have to sneak about any more, but they were careful not to make any noise; very difficult as Nancy was one for moaning with pleasure, but they had got their frustration out earlier so just had a quickie before lying in each other's arms, and all Thomas wanted to do was stroke the baby. Every now and again he would feel it kick, and he felt on top of the world, a life growing inside the woman he loved so much. It made him feel complete. He lay back on the pillow. Nancy's breath was getting deeper as she drifted off to sleep. Thomas lay there thinking about the future; would he leave the Military Police and set up home with Nancy, do a civilian job, or would he stay and live in married quarters in Germany? So much to think about and what would he buy her for Christmas now? Clothes, she would need clothes for when she got bigger; he couldn't wait. He would take her shopping and they could get some things for the baby. Thomas wanted a boy, to play football with and teach him as he was taught. It was a long time before he got off to sleep, holding Nancy tightly yet lovingly so not disturbing her.

Thomas was disappointed when Nancy said she wanted to go shopping with Chris, and as she didn't want to hurt his feelings, she agreed she would go with Christina another day. Nothing had been arranged anyway, she just wanted to offload some of the guilt she was feeling after yesterday. They went into Blacklodge and Nancy was hoping he would give her some indication of what he wanted from her for Christmas, but all he wanted to do was look at baby clothes and fat clothes. The maternity wear was horrible and frumpy, and Nancy wasn't impressed with the grey dress he pulled off the rack, with a white collar. She tried to convince him that her clothes were OK at the moment, it was winter, and she got away with jeans unfastened, with Eric's belts to keep them up, and a baggy jumper. To keep him happy she chose a pair of dungarees. Then the pram section. Oh, no, he was acting like a child in a sweet factory, pushing each pram around the shop floor. Nancy was a little embarrassed but ended up laughing.

'We are not buying a pram yet, it's meant to be unlucky to have one in the house before the baby comes home from hospital and we've got months to choose yet,' She said as he came to a halt in front of her after screeching around with the fourth pram he tried.

'I'm enjoying myself, I can't wait!' he replied with a sad, silly look on his face and leaned over to give her a peck on the cheek. Nancy eventually managed to drag him away, and she stopped to look at watches in a jeweller's window to see what his reaction would be.

'That one's just like mine,' he stated, lifting his sleeve to reveal a watch that Nancy didn't recognise. That idea out of the window, she thought. She would ask his parents for ideas later.

Nancy dragged him into a trendier shop and found a couple of nice jumpers to cover her growing belly. One was a plainish navy blue one with a V-neck collar; the other was black, grey and silver with bits of glitter, which she would be able to wear for nights out.

They walked past a television rental shop with a big sign in the window: "COMING SOON – ORDER YOUR PORTABLE PHONE IN TIME FOR CHRISTMAS". Portable phones, what would they think of next? But it did give her an idea for his Christmas present. She would enquire tomorrow on how much they cost when she came in town with Chris.

She had managed to keep him away from baby shops for the last half hour and she complained she was feeling tired, so they went home. They had been in town for almost four hours. It was busy everywhere, people getting prepared for Christmas; well, it was only a week away.

That evening they went out for a drink with Maggie and Eric, and they all had a good talk about what was going to happen in the near future. Thomas admitted that he hadn't really thought about it. After all, his life had only changed completely yesterday, but he wasn't very happy in the Military Police. Eric suggested to them both that whatever happened, whether he leave his job or not, they could both move into Mrs Bannister's bungalow.

Nancy was flabbergasted, it had stood empty since she died, and she often wondered why it had never been put up for sale.

'What do you mean, Dad?' Nancy asked.

'Mrs Bannister left it to you in her will, along with a bit of money when you reach thirty,' Eric answered.

'Why thirty?' Nancy asked.

Eric couldn't answer why, just presumed that because of Mrs Bannister's son, who lived an unruly life and died when he was seventeen, she wanted to ensure that Nancy was settled and happy before the money was released to her. When Nancy asked how much, Eric said he didn't know. Maggie squeezed his knee, pleased at how subtle and sensible he'd been.

'We may be able to get some money released. I'm sure the executor will if he knows you would be moving into her house.'

Nancy and Thomas looked at each other and without any words being exchanged, knew it would be perfect for them.

'But myself and your mother would rather see you married first.'

There was always a catch and there was so much more to organise and arrange. Mrs Bannister's house had three bedrooms, one being very small; a dining kitchen, bathroom and a living room. Her taste was rather extravagant and the carpets Nancy would never have chosen. This would be more exciting than a shopping spree for prams and baby clothes, shopping for carpets and furniture. Eric said he would ring the solicitor from work on Monday and see what he could sort out.

'Thanks, Dad, I love you, and you too, Mum.'

What a wonderful night! Nancy and Thomas felt like everything was going their way and nothing could have dampened the happiness they felt at this moment in time. Thomas' parents had sort of got used to him spending all his time at Nancy's and they were happy for them both, but just wait 'til they heard this news. Maybe they had better wait until they found out for definite.

When they eventually went to bed after talking with Maggie and Eric about the future, Thomas cuddled Nancy. She could tell he wasn't interested in having sex; his gentle hands when he touched her cheek to pull her towards him for a kiss meant more to her than anything. She felt his love as he held her face in his hands and caressed her hair. Little things meant a lot and the way Thomas touched her was the most precious feeling in the world. He stroked her until she fell asleep in his arms, her stomach pressed against his, so he could feel every movement their baby made throughout the night. It totally amazed him, he would spend the rest of his life with this beautiful woman who lay next to him, bodies entwined into one being; well, actually, three beings were what they would become in May next year.

Thomas lay awake thinking about Germany. He wasn't happy in his job, but he could jeopardise a lot by giving it up so soon. He could maybe put in a transfer back into the normal police force, or he could take advantage of his heavy goods vehicle licence he had acquired through the Military Police. He would stick at it for a while, until at least they got married and he would then have a whole new perspective on life. But he had now; he loved this woman lying so close to him with all his heart, he would do anything for her, even die for her. He would find out his options when he returned to base in January. He drifted off into a confused yet contented sleep.

Eric rang the solicitor and arranged to have five thousand pounds released from the estate and transferred to Nancy's bank account for furniture, carpets and redecorating. He thought that would be plenty and the solicitor said he could transfer more if need be and he could pick the keys up when he finished work about three o'clock. They also arranged a monthly allowance of two hundred and fifty pounds a month from her inheritance for Nancy and the baby, starting in May.

They all went over to the house to have a look around and decide what they wanted to do with it. It was a bit eerie; Nancy had been coming here since she was a little girl and it felt weird. She expected to see Mrs Bannister, with her green china cup and saucer in her hand, drinking the awful-looking strong tea she used to drink. Maggie said it wouldn't feel like that once it had been decorated. The money would be transferred in three working days, so it should be in Nancy's account on Thursday, but Eric pointed out that they may as well wait for the January sales, they were only a couple of weeks away.

Nancy, Thomas and Maggie went around some DIY shops, looking for ideas while Eric went home for his usual afternoon nap. There was loads of beautiful wallpaper to choose from, so they took lots of samples and would firstly agree on a colour scheme. Nancy wanted warm colours; deep reds, oranges and creams and Thomas fancied cool blues. They had all the samples with them when they went around the furniture shop looking at three-piece suites and sideboards and things. Nancy found a really comfy burgundy and cream settee which Thomas pulled his face at; he thought it was too old-fashioned. He saw a navy blue, loose covered one which you could take off and wash. Maggie liked that one as well, as it would be practical with a new baby and it was only five hundred and ninety-nine pounds at the moment and with money off in the sales, they could get a bargain there. Nancy said she'd think about it as it was two against one. They went home laden with brochures and sample wallpapers, and Maggie rang her decorator to come around and give them a quote for doing the work. He said he would come at eleven o'clock the following day. Joe had become a good friend of Eric and Maggie's. He had decorated their house every year for the past fifteen years. He was getting on a bit, probably almost sixty, although he looked younger and was always laughing and joking.

He arrived on the dot and had a look around. The smallest bedroom, they were going to leave for now, but their bedroom, which overlooked the garden, they were decorating. The nursery would be painted in pale yellow, as it had blown vinyl on the walls and Nancy would hang some posters up to liven it up a bit. The kitchen and bathroom would be decorated, and the living room. He quoted them three hundred pounds for the lot, and he would be able to do it between Christmas and New Year if they were pushing. He normally took a couple of weeks off for Christmas but as it was them, he didn't mind. They said they would let him know when they had decided on and bought the wallpaper and paint he needed. He wrote down exactly how much they would need for each room and went back to the other job he had nipped out of.

They stood in the kitchen. It was well fitted out, plenty of cupboard space. The fridge would need replacing and the washing machine was like something out of the dark ages. Nancy remembered watching Mrs Bannister standing over the washer all through the wash, lifting the lid up and transferring all the clothes into a separate section to be spun. Maggie said her mother had once had a twin tub; they were good washing machines, but nothing like you could get nowadays, which saved a lot of time.

Thomas nipped to Maggie's, got some Sellotape and got to work sticking all the samples on the wall so they could get a better idea of what they wanted, some in the living room and some in their bedroom, while Nancy and Maggie went around each room and made a list of what they needed. Living room: wallpaper, carpet, curtains, ceiling light, three-piece suite, fire, television with stand, stereo, sideboard, mirror. Kitchen: wallpaper, new lino, cooker, fridge, washing machine, some new cutlery, pots and pans, plates, dishes, cleaning cloths, tea towels, food. Bedroom: carpet, curtains, wallpaper, double bed, blankets, sheets, bedside cabinets, lamps. Nursery: paint, carpet, cot, sheets, blankets, nappies, sleepsuits, clothes. And they had probably forgotten things but at least they had made a start. For all the larger and expensive items, they would wait for the sales, but wallpaper and paint were priority, so Joe could get on with doing the job.

They all stood in the living room looking at the samples. Thomas liked a blue and cream striped one which could go around the bottom half of the room and a cream one with small flowers on the top, with a wooden dado rail between the two, 'And the navy suite would look brilliant,' he added with a grin on his face. Nancy thought it was nice but didn't admit it as she liked the one with large burgundy flowers on, but it was too flowery for all around the room, and they hadn't seen anything that would match it. In fact, it would probably look better in the bedroom as there were only two walls to do really; the fitted wardrobes were all down one wall and the window was almost as big as the wall. She finally agreed to have the cream and blue wallpaper and probably the navy suite they had seen, if it was in the sale; and he agreed to the burgundy flowers in the bedroom. They had both compromised and Maggie was pleased they had done so quickly. She knew how stubborn Nancy could be sometimes.

They had a quiet night in that evening, Nancy helped Maggie cook tea, which was minced steak pie with carrots, swede, cauliflower and roast potatoes. She would have to get used to cooking on her own soon, she always enjoyed helping Maggie when she was younger and picked up some good, although traditional recipes, as Eric preferred good old English food. She would buy some recipe books and experiment on Thomas, he'd eat anything.

Over dinner, they were telling Eric what they were going to do on the house, and he just nodded and grunted in agreement, more interested in his food than decorations and furniture. It was an exciting time: a new house to decorate and furnish, Christmas around the corner; a baby next year and a wedding to organise. Nancy wasn't sure about the wedding, knowing that she was living a lie. She didn't know whether she could go through with it and she would rather wait, but that would take a lot of convincing on Eric's part, that they should wait while after the baby was born. Maggie asked them if they had thought of any names, and they started suggesting some which had them all laughing, Guinevere, Bartholomew, Ethel, Frederick.

'What was Mrs Bannister's name?' asked Nancy.

'Victoria Alice,' replied Maggie.

'Then if we have a girl, I think we should call her after Mrs Bannister. What do you think, Thomas?'

'Well, as long as we don't call a boy Victor,' he replied.

They still had plenty of time to decide anyway, so they started talking about Christmas. Thomas said his family were looking forward to coming as they hadn't seen that much of him since he'd been home. They would arrive around two-ish, so the men could go to the local pub for an hour or so, while the women prepared the food. That was somewhat traditional when you had visitors at Christmas, which Nancy thought was a bit unfair as she would rather be at the pub as well.

They carried on chatting well into the night and went through four bottles of wine. Eric was the first to doze off in the chair, so Maggie nudged him, and they went to bed. Thomas and Nancy had a kiss and cuddle on the settee before they went upstairs. Nancy could tell Thomas was frightened of hurting the baby during sex; he was being ever so gentle and wasn't inserting his penis all the way into her vagina until she dug her short nails into his back and told him no harm could be done to the baby, it was well protected inside the womb. They eventually went to sleep in each other's arms.

Chapter Fifteen

Christmas Eve arrived, and Nancy was going out with Chris and Janet and they were meeting Thomas, John and Shaun in Oblivion later on. They had bought tickets, which were five pounds each. They arrived in town to queues to get into almost every pub. The atmosphere was brilliant but the waiting for drinks wasn't, so they decided they would get pints of lager or cider, rather than vodkas in each pub, so as not to keep queuing. It also meant they would stay in each pub longer and keep out of the cold. Christmas songs were blasting out in each pub; some people were in fancy dress and a lot of people were adorned in tinsel and singing along to the music. They were going to Oblivion at around quarter past eleven, in case they had to queue for ages, although the pubs were all open later.

Nancy had managed to disguise her growing bump. No one had noticed yet so the only people who knew were those who they had told, which was a good job when she bumped into Jason, who was home visiting his mum for Christmas. They talked for a while about where he'd been this time around and general chat. He told her that he'd missed her tremendously and asked if he could meet her later. She looked away from him and told him with a tear in her eye that she'd met someone else. He held her hand and asked if she was happy. 'I think so,' she replied, hoping in her heart that he wasn't going to be at Oblivion.

He noticed a tear drip down her cheek and gently wiped it away. 'I'll always love you and I think I know you'll always love me.' He gave her a gentle kiss on the lips and walked out of the pub.

Nancy went into the toilets and cried at the rush of love for Jason that had just shot through her body, knowing that the child she was carrying was his. She wanted to run and find him and tell him the truth, but how many people would that hurt? Chris had told Janet to leave her on her own for five minutes and then Janet came into the toilets with their drinks and asked if she was all right. She had stopped crying and she wiped her eyes and reapplied her make-up as best she could so as not to look as though she had been.

'Do I look OK?' she asked Janet.

''Course you do, you look fantastic,' she replied.

They finished their drinks in the toilets and with her head held high they went back to where Chris was standing, talking to Shaun. It was half past ten and they were going to the Black Swan, which was just around the corner from Oblivion. Shaun kissed Chris and said he would see her later.

John was in the Black Swan, it was a bit of a rough pub, but it was en route and with everyone in the Christmas spirit, there shouldn't be any trouble. They tended to stay away from the rough pubs since they were once in the Rising Sun, the pub almost next door to the Black Swan, when it got raided by police looking for drugs and they had ended up being locked in for almost an hour while police searched everyone, including them!

They were back on double vodkas in here as they sold them pretty cheap. Chris asked Nancy what Jason had said but she said she didn't want to talk about it at the moment. She knew she would fill up again and was dreading him walking into Oblivion later. She had never seen Jason and Thomas together and knew she wouldn't be able to cope if they were both in the same place. She should have asked him, but he knew her and where she went and would hopefully stay away. She kept her fingers crossed. She promised herself that she would ring him tomorrow and wish him and his mum Merry Christmas.

They finished their drinks and went and stood in the queue, which to their surprise wasn't as long as they had expected, probably because the pubs were open until one o'clock. They could hear someone arguing with the doormen, because he'd forgotten to bring his ticket with him, and they wouldn't let him in. They all checked if they had theirs; they did. If you didn't have a ticket, you didn't get in. The bloke probably hadn't bought one anyway. He was sent on his way to go and get it if he wanted to get into the club. It held about four hundred people and apparently the tickets had sold out very quickly. Maggie had gone to the club and bought Nancy four the day after they had been put on sale; she had been checking the local paper every night for the advert announcing them. New Year's Eve tickets were seven pounds, which Maggie thought was far too expensive, so she didn't get them.

The first point of call when they got inside was the toilets, a wee and touching up the make-up. Nancy's eyes still looked a bit swollen and red from crying earlier and she was careful to not put too much make-up, which could make them look worse. Janet offered her some eye drops which made your eyes sparkle. They stung at first when she put a drop in each, but the immediate redness soon went and true to Janet's word, they put a sparkle in her eyes, plus it was fairly dark, and Thomas hopefully wouldn't notice. They went out of the toilets to queue at the bar, back on pints, looking at the four deep at the bar. Nancy went to wait at the bar while Janet and Chris managed to find a table to stand at. There were no seats left, but they preferred to stand anyway. Nancy spotted Thomas further down at the bar and went to join him; he would get served quicker and buy the drinks.

'Two pints of lager and a pint of cider, please,' she said, looking at him with come to bed eyes which she knew he couldn't resist. Thankfully, the DJ was playing pretty normal music and only the occasional Christmas tune; you could get pretty fed up with them, especially as they had been playing in shops and pubs all through December. Not that Nancy had noticed much, she had so much more on her mind to worry about. The worry had sort of gone now, apart from the normal first baby stuff and the house and what would happen in the future and the wedding. She hadn't spoken to Eric about trying to delay it, but she and Thomas had agreed earlier in the week they would both tell him and his family tomorrow. They knew Eric had an ulterior motive about getting them all together for a day even though it was Christmas, they would be bombarded with wedding talk.

They took the drinks over to the table where Janet was. Shaun had already dragged Chris onto the dance floor, and it would be a case of not leaving your drinks or else they would get pinched, and certainly not leaving the table. Thomas went to tell his mates where he was standing, and they came over to join them. Dave and Terry she had met before, they used to work with Thomas before he got transferred, but she and Janet were introduced to Ian; he was a newish recruit, nearly twenty and almost finishing his three-month probation in the beat patrol, as they called it. He was tall, blond hair, blue eyes and very, very muscular. Janet's eyes were popping out of her head, and Nancy had to almost kick her to remind her to stop dribbling. He was very attractive, though. Janet made a beeline for him and put herself in flirty gear, which blokes found very sexy. After talking for a while, they went off to the dance floor. Nancy looked at Thomas and he looked a bit worried.

'He won't be at home in the morning,' Nancy said to him, laughing.

'I've noticed,' he replied, slipping his arm around her waist.

Nancy felt a tap on her shoulder and when she turned around John was standing there. 'She's just dancing with an old friend,' she told him, and he disappeared back to his friends.

'This should be interesting. Looks like John is going to get dumped tonight, poor bloke,' Nancy said to Thomas.

'You would never do that to me, would you?' he asked with all seriousness. Nancy just elbowed him in the ribs and grinned at him but inside wondered if he had noticed or even read her thoughts to make him ask such a question.

Terry's girlfriend, Clare, joined the small crowd which was now gathering around the table, and Dave was eyeing a girl up. Everyone was egging him to go and chat her up, but he was quite shy and just blushed. There seemed to be a lot of baby talk during the night. Thomas had told his mates as it was the first time he had seen them since arriving home and he was such a proud dad-to-be, it was to be expected really, although Nancy could have done without it, especially when Clare started giving her an in-depth account of her labour. Her daughter Hayley was two this year. She had left her husband after six months of violence but was not yet divorced, as you had to wait two years before you could apply in case of reconciliation. She had first met Terry when he and a colleague came around to her house and arrested her husband for beating her up and putting her in the hospital. Domestic violence was only just being recognised by the police; they ignored it normally, but some politicians were fighting for women's rights. She had always been too frightened to leave him and had let the police take her to a women's refuge, which was a secret address and well protected from violent husbands and partners. She had stayed there for four months until the council found her a house in a new area where, hopefully, her husband wouldn't start looking for her. Her parents had died within a year of each other four years ago and her sister had emigrated to Australia, so she had no one to turn to until she met Terry. He visited her in the hostel a couple of times and had been reprimanded by his boss for getting involved, so he waited until she had got her house before he asked her out. They had been seeing each other for almost a year now and she could soon apply for a divorce. Nancy understood, after talking to her for a while, although she would never say she knew how she felt. It was a pet hate of Nancy's when people said, "I know how you feel," when they had never been in that situation. Everyone is different and has different feelings. Clare was a nice girl, even though she was originally from the roughest area in town. She had been through a lot in her life, but Terry was a great bloke and they were all right together. Clare felt safe with him and she invited Nancy and her friends to her twenty-first birthday party in February and promised to send her an invite. They swapped phone numbers and said they would ring each other.

The DJ announced over the microphone that the bar would be shutting for fifteen minutes shortly, so those who had not much drink left made a beeline for the bar. Terry and Shaun came back to the table laden with drinks, followed shortly after by Dave and Thomas. The countdown soon began, it felt more like New Year's Eve than Christmas Eve and as midnight fell, everyone hugged and kissed each other and strangers came up to them and wished them Merry Christmas. The girl Dave had been eyeing up came over to him and planted a big kiss on his lips. Poor bloke went bright red, but she didn't seem to mind; Dave took her on the dance floor, and they didn't see them again for a while. Nancy had fourteen blokes kissing her, but Thomas managed seventeen women. Then they held each other. Their last Christmas on their own. Next year they would have a baby to find babysitters for if they wanted to go out. A person to care for, rather than just each other. Nancy felt relaxed and happy and had pushed the earlier moments of the night to the back of her mind. She went to the toilet, topped up her lipstick and when she walked out of the door, felt a hand going to grab her. She turned around, a bit shocked. Jason, shit.

'Merry Christmas. I know I shouldn't have come, but my friend had a spare ticket and I had to see for myself if you were happy,' he said.

'Jason, I am happy. Please believe me.'

'I don't, though.'

God, what a situation to be in. She had been dreading this happening, had her fingers crossed since she saw Jason earlier. She talked to him for a short while but was dreading Thomas coming to look for her.

'I've got to go, I promise I'll ring you,' and she went back to Thomas.

'I take it there was a long queue in the ladies?' he asked.

'No, I was talking to an old friend,' she replied, hoping he wouldn't ask any more questions.

They went to dance; she could sense Jason watching her every move and put a smile on her face as she danced with Thomas. When the record finished, Thomas took her in his arms. She saw Jason watching from the edge of the dance floor and smiled at him. He looked absolutely gorgeous from where she stood, so she pulled Thomas off the dance floor, out of eye shot of Jason, looked him in the eyes and said, 'I love you so much.' He held her tightly for a minute before replying to her with a long, lingering kiss.

The club was open until three o'clock but by half past one Nancy was shattered. They said goodbye to everyone and wished them all a good Christmas Day and walked out hand in hand. Nancy avoided Jason's stare as they walked towards the door, hoping Thomas wouldn't notice, but he did. 'Who was that bloke staring at you on the way out?' he asked.

'Which one? You know I always get looked at!' Nancy replied, trying to sound devious, and they laughed it off.

There were plenty of taxis waiting outside so they got in the first one and set off for home. Thomas was staying at Nancy's but was going to his house early in the morning and bringing his family back later. He hadn't spent much time with his family, so tomorrow would be extra special. Even though they knew they had to persuade Eric they wanted to put off getting married until after the baby was born, they were thinking of July the fourth, American Independence Day, which would hopefully be enough time for Nancy to get her figure back. If everyone agreed, they would book the church and a venue. There had been a few places suggested but nothing looked into as yet. They had talked about going abroad to get married but that wouldn't be fair on their families. They both wanted a quiet do, and they would start organising things once Eric had agreed. Nancy would like to wait until the baby was walking so it could be a bridesmaid or a page boy, but Thomas wanted to get married sooner rather than later.

When they arrived home, Maggie and Eric were still up and had not long been in themselves, so they opened a bottle of wine and talked for a while, mainly embarrassing Nancy by reminiscing about when she was little. Eric blurted out in a little-girlish, whingeing voice, 'I don't wear trousers and what would I want with this horrible jacket?' They were all in fits of laughter, when Nancy suddenly winced in pain and took in a deep breath.

'What's wrong?' they all asked in unison.

'I don't know, I've just had a really bad shooting pain through my stomach.'

Maggie took her upstairs to the bathroom while the boys sat downstairs in silence. Nancy sat on the loo, had a wee and waited to see if any more pain came. Maggie asked her to check the loo roll when she wiped herself in case of any blood. There wasn't any. Maggie helped her undress and lie down on her bed. 'It's probably the baby kicking you hard, but if you do spot any blood, wake me up, all right?' She had had a pretty rough time with Nancy, was rushed into hospital two months before Nancy was due as she had preeclampsia toxaemia which could have killed both her and her baby. She had had very high blood pressure and had to rest for six weeks before Nancy made an appearance into the world, a couple of weeks early. Maggie stroked her daughter's hair and told her everything would be all right. The pregnancies weren't similar, Nancy had had an easy time of it up to now, could do all the normal things and hadn't really suffered morning sickness at all; well, not that Maggie had known of.

They talked for a while. Maggie couldn't, didn't tell her about her problems or the miscarriage she had had after Nancy was born and not being able to have any more children. Nancy lay there with her mum sitting on the edge of her bed, when she felt the baby kick.

'It's kicking,' she told Maggie.

'It was probably telling you earlier that it wanted some sleep when we were laughing so much. Everything will be all right, I promise you,' Maggie replied, as convincing as possible.

'Will you send Thomas up, please, Mum?' asked Nancy.

''Course, love. If you need me during the night, I'm only across the hallway. I love you,' replied Maggie as she got up off the bed.

'I love you too, Mum.'

She lay totally still for a while and when Thomas came in, she said, 'I'm sorry for frightening you, but any pains I get, I don't know whether it's normal or not and it really hurt at the time.'

'As long as you're all right, that's the main thing. Although I do think we should get a couple of baby books and find out what goes on more,' he replied. Nancy agreed with him. They were both young, didn't really know what to expect, and Maggie hadn't been forthcoming with answers; not that Nancy had asked her much.

Maggie told Eric that she thought everything was all right, and they finished the bottle of wine and Maggie went up to bed. Eric always wandered around the house to make sure all doors were locked and plugs turned off before he could relax. Eric got into bed beside Maggie. He was an old-fashioned type of bloke, didn't show his feelings much yet he loved Maggie with all his heart, and she knew it without him having to tell her. The scare tonight made him remember the pain that Maggie had gone through when she lost their second child. He had tried to be strong for her, had never cried or shown his hurt in front of her. He held her close to him tonight as he knew she would be feeling the same pain he felt. He loved children and even though he was angry with Nancy at first for getting pregnant so young, he was looking forward to having a baby around. He and Maggie had showered Nancy with love and given her everything she wanted to try and disguise the pain they both felt when the doctor told them they couldn't have any more children.

Eric turned to kiss Maggie goodnight, yet a flame had been ignited in her and for the first time in months, the passion was rekindled. They kissed lovingly and the wanting of Maggie that Eric felt at that moment made him wonder why they didn't have pleasure like this more often. They both felt like youngsters as they made love, trying not to make any noise that Nancy and Thomas could hear, and they giggled every now and again as they shushed each other to be quiet. Their bodies entwined as one and just as Eric was about to ejaculate, he felt the throbbing of Maggie's orgasm around his penis, which turned him on so much he reached a full climax. They held each other all night. They had taken each other for granted, but Maggie hoped to herself that this was the start of a truly rekindled love affair. It was the first time in ages they had had beautiful sex and she was hoping it wouldn't be the last.

It was almost four o'clock and Thomas lay on the bed with his ear against Nancy's stomach while he stroked her gently, trying to listen and feeling every movement until he had reassured himself that the baby was all right. He held Nancy in his arms as they dozed off.

Nancy woke up and went to the toilet. No sign of blood, thank God. She climbed back into bed next to Thomas. The clock said quarter past six. This was about the time she would be sneaking down as a little girl to open her presents before Maggie and Eric got up. It was different this year, she had responsibilities; well, she would have soon. She made her mind up as she snuggled up to Thomas that she would stop drinking as much as she did and start trying to be the sensible adult that a baby needed. She felt horny and started stroking Thomas' penis. It soon went hard but he didn't seem to be waking up. She sat on top of him gently and kissed his lips, then moved down his neck and onto his chest, licked each nipple in turn, and her tongue slowly made its way down his torso until it reached the tip of his penis. She curled her tongue around the tip as it grew bigger, and then put her mouth over it, moving up and down. She heard a slight groan of pleasure as he started to move in rhythm with her mouth, up and down. He was still half asleep and as she opened her mouth wider his penis slid right to the back of her throat, which made her heave. She knew he was enjoying this, so she turned him, so he was on top and she was underneath with her head arched back, which felt comfortable when his penis slid down her throat. He was now awake and pushing his penis into her mouth, her jaw was aching yet the pleasure she was feeling was beyond comparison. She tried to hold her lips around his penis, being careful with her teeth, while he slipped in and out and then she felt the throb when he ejaculated into her mouth. She heaved again yet it didn't make her sick. It was nice in a way; she had enjoyed giving him so much pleasure in such a short period of time, probably five minutes, if that. He kissed her passionately then moved slowly down her body to her boobs. Nancy enjoyed sexual pain, and she writhed when he bit hard on her left nipple and chewed on it with his teeth. His tongue ventured further down till it reached her vagina. It flipped up and down on her lips until he felt her clitoris had hardened, then he gently wriggled his tongue up and down over her clitoris before he sank his teeth right into it, nibbling at first, then biting, alternating with sucking and licking. It was pleasurable pain and she orgasmed in minutes. The juices that flowed out he tried to lick up, but the bed ended up damp anyway. For the first time they have given their own to each other and had the best sexual experience without penetration of their lives so far.

Chapter Sixteen

They went downstairs just after nine o'clock. Maggie made them both a cup of tea and they went into the lounge to find Eric flicking through the channels to see if there was anything on television worth watching. He turned it off when they all appeared in the room and Nancy passed the presents around. There certainly weren't as many as there used to be when she was a child. A beautiful, thick, solid gold necklace for Maggie; a starter set of golf clubs for Eric, he'd been on about having a go for ages. Nancy had a few gorgeous tops and jumpers and elasticated trousers and Thomas his portable phone and a lovely jumper.

When Thomas left to go and pick his family up, Nancy and Maggie went into the kitchen to prepare the vegetables. The turkey had cooked overnight, and there was a joint of ham cooking in the oven. When that was ready, they could fit in the two large baking trays full of potatoes and parsnips to roast. They normally ate around half past three, as the men would be back from the pub by then. With everything prepared, Nancy went for a bath and to get dressed. She wore the black trousers with a stretchy bit for her bump and the sleeveless black and white A-line top that Thomas had bought for her and pinned her hair up, leaving bits dangling at the side. Thomas and his family arrived at half past one and, the formalities over with, more presents were handed out. Then the trip to the pub for the boys, while the girls stayed at home, nattering and drinking wine. Pat, Thomas' mum was asking about wedding plans. Nancy told her they were hoping to delay it until July, but they had to make sure Eric was happy for them to do so. They all went over the road to Mrs Bannister's house to have a look around. Nancy was going through each room and saying what they were going to do, all the wallpaper and paint had been bought and Joe was starting the day after Boxing Day. They had seen and finally agreed on the bigger items; the suite, carpets, sideboard, fridge and washing machine, but they were waiting to see how much cheaper they would be in the January sales, and hopefully, they would move in and have a few days together before Thomas went back to Germany.

Shelly noticed the little room and asked if she could move in with them. Nancy told her she couldn't move in as her mum would miss her so much, but she could come and stay sometimes when the room was decorated. That gave Nancy an idea, she would decorate the room so Shelly would like it. They may as well get everything done at the same time, so another trip to the wallpaper shop when it reopened after Christmas, and a single bed and small wardrobe to add to the rapidly expanding shopping list.

They went back across the road, and Nancy took Shelly to the stable and showed her Sammy's pictures and the rosettes they had won when she was younger. They went back in the house and started watching telly and playing with the game that Shelly had got from Nancy and Thomas: Scrabble. They didn't get very far in it and Nancy did let Shelly cheat with a couple of words and before long, they were setting the table. Shelly put a cracker on each place setting while Nancy was putting orange slices and cherries on cocktail sticks to put on the melon boats. The potatoes and parsnips had gone into the oven, the pans full of veg were simmering and only the gravy was left to make. Quarter past three, Pat had wanted to watch the Queen's annual speech and the boys would be home soon, so they tidied the game away for the time being.

They sat down to eat at twenty to four, swapped the cracker pulling and put the paper hats on. Thomas made Nancy swap her blue one for his pink one. Thomas and Nancy sat together on one side of the table with Shelly and Maggie, Pat and John opposite them, with Eric at the head. Eric was telling them whom he introduced John and Thomas to; it sounded like the pub was busy. Thomas looked at Nancy and pulled a funny face which Shelly saw and started giggling. They ate their melon, then Nancy and Maggie took the dishes into the kitchen while Eric carved the turkey and put the meat onto a large serving plate which already had sliced ham on. Warmed plates were brought out and given to everyone and the veggies were brought out in large dishes with the stuffing and gravy, so everyone could help themselves to whatever they wanted. Maggie was complimented on the food, it was absolutely delicious. Shelly did her bit and went around topping up everyone's drinks. After the Christmas pudding, or cheese and biscuits or ice cream for those who didn't like pudding, they all settled in the lounge. Thomas squeezed Nancy's hand to encourage her to ask Eric the dreaded question.

'Dad, Thomas and I have been discussing the wedding and we would both rather wait until after the baby is born, if that's all right with you?' she said, squeezing Thomas' hand back, waiting for his reaction.

'Well, seeing as everybody concerned is here, what does everyone else think?' aiming the question at everyone.

The first person to reply was Shelly, who whinged that she wanted to be a bridesmaid. Nancy told her she would be and also told everyone they had sort of decided on July the fourth, American Independence Day, to make it that little bit extra special. Everyone seemed happy enough, so Eric went along with it. They started talking about where they could have it. Northgate Manor was mentioned, along with the Foxgroves, not quite as posh as Northgate. Nancy said she would ring a few places and enquire, they should be able to get in somewhere as it fell on a Wednesday, but if they let people know well in advance, those working could book the time off if they wanted to come. Pat offered to help with the organising, and Nancy promised Shelly she could come and look at wedding and bridesmaids' dresses with her.

They had an excellent day all in all. Nancy, Maggie and Eric got to know John and Pat quite well and you could tell Pat was really excited about becoming a grandmother. They stayed until Shelly started getting restless around ten o'clock and booked a taxi home; it was double fare as it was Christmas Day, but it didn't matter. When they'd gone, they carried on talking, Eric fell asleep in the chair and Nancy and Thomas went to bed, followed shortly after by Eric and Maggie.

They talked about the house, and they were both excited about shopping for the more personal items like the big double bed and couldn't wait for Joe to get started so they could organise deliveries. They would ask him to start on their bedroom first. They cuddled up. The baby was kicking a lot. Nancy wanted Thomas to make love to her, but he wanted to wait while the baby was asleep, so she lay on top of him and pinned his arms above his head. He could have moved if he'd wanted to; after all, he was a lot stronger than her, so he let her try her best to keep him held down and pleasure herself by moving her vagina up and down his penis to turn them both on. They ended up giggling at her efforts and couldn't do anything for a while for laughing, then Thomas went on top and tormented her by positioning his penis just touching her lips. He kissed her passionately and gently pushed his penis in just a little, then pulled it back out. This made Nancy want him more and more. God, it was so sexily annoying; every now and then he would put it all the way in for a couple of seconds, making Nancy think this was it, then he'd pull out again. Nancy was really turned on and he knew by her soft groans and her nails in his back that she would orgasm very soon. He added to the torment by nibbling her nipples, stopping while he thrust his penis in, then nibbling again when he pulled out. He was getting near to orgasm himself, enjoying Nancy writhing with delight, so he hurried himself by enjoying the moments. He teased her for a little while longer, then thrust in hard, his body rubbing against her clitoris every time. She wrapped her legs around him tightly, so he couldn't pull out any more, and within minutes they relaxed as they enjoyed each other's throbbing orgasms. Nancy always held back any noise when Maggie and Eric were in the house; she normally screamed in pleasure when she orgasmed, but Thomas felt the brunt of it as she buried her head in his chest and bit him. Not too hard, but he did have a few sets of teeth marks. That was another reason they wanted to move in across the road.

On Boxing Day, they drove around to the wallpaper store; it was closed. It reopened Tuesday, shut again New Year's Eve and reopened on Monday, the second of January. In fact, all the shops were the same. The January sales were all advertised in windows, starting on December the twenty-seventh. The roads were all quiet, so they just drove, not knowing where to go or what to see. Well, there was nothing to see. They ended up in Rigchester, a small village between Blacklodge and Priston, parked in the village car park and walked slowly hand in hand along the river bank. It was very cold, and they weren't really dressed warmly enough for walking, but it was so wonderfully peaceful and serene, apart from the ducks and the odd bird chirping. They walked for miles, stopping every now and then for a warming cuddle and kiss. The time flew and by the time they realised they should be getting back, they had been walking for over three hours. They walked quicker back to the car, which took an hour and a quarter. They headed back home to yesterday's turkey made into sandwiches and a small buffet. They spent the night cuddling on the sofa when Maggie and Eric went out, the fire on full as they were both still cold from their earlier walk.

Joe was arriving at the house at ten o'clock to start work. Nancy and Thomas were already there, armed with cleaning gear for the kitchen and bathroom. He said he would start in their bedroom and they left him and went to the stores. They chose the wallpaper for the spare room which Thomas said Shelly would like; not too young girlish, but feminine, with deep pink and cream swirly patterns and some cream paint for the woodwork. Then to the furniture store. The blue suite they had seen was reduced by a hundred and fifty pounds to four hundred and forty-nine, but it would take two weeks for delivery if they paid by cheque or if they paid cash, anything they bought that was in stock at their warehouse could be delivered on January the second. They decided they would go to the bank and withdraw the cash once they added up what they bought. They carried on looking around and bought a redwood sideboard with a glass display section, which was half price at two hundred and fifty pounds; two matching large gold lamps with navy shades for the front room, half price at forty pounds the pair; a couple of gold smaller ones with burgundy shades for their bedroom at fourteen pounds the pair; a coffee table in brass with a glass top, thirty-five pounds; and a matching nest of tables, twenty-eight pounds. They were just going around the store, pointing things out, with the salesmen trying to keep up with them, jotting down code numbers. It felt exhilarating. How much did they have to spend? Five thousand pounds. Then they came to the beds, and while the salesman had a rest, they lay on each double and king size bed, seeing how comfy they each were. Thomas embarrassed Nancy when he dived on one and got some laughs off other shoppers. They decided on a king size divan at three hundred and twenty pounds and then picked a single divan for the spare room, which was only ninety-nine pounds. The salesmen gave them three bedside cabinets, two for their room and one for the spare room, which would have been fifty-five pounds. He checked everything was in stock and they drove into the town centre to the bank. Nancy withdrew three thousand pounds as they still had the carpet and electrical shops to visit. They also rang Maggie to meet them back at the store; Eric had gone to work, and she would enjoy helping them spend. She was also good at negotiating, which could probably come in handy.

They were counting out one thousand two hundred and thirty-five pounds as Maggie walked in. Thomas took her around the store, showing her what they had bought, while Nancy sorted out the money. They arranged delivery on the third of January, so Nancy could arrange to have carpets fitted on the second.

Next stop, the electrical store. There didn't seem to be as many good offers; twenty pounds off, fifty pounds off, certainly no half price items. The salesmen reckoned people had been queuing up all night and all the half price items had been sold. Still, they had a good look around and found a washing machine for two hundred and twenty pounds, a dryer for eighty pounds, a twenty-four-inch television for two hundred and sixty-nine pounds, a stereo for a hundred and forty-nine pounds, a gas cooker for a hundred and eighty pounds, a fridge with a small freezer above for a hundred and thirty-nine pounds, a three-stem gold ceiling light with cream glass shades for thirty-five pounds, a set of three spotlights for the kitchen for eighteen pounds and a plain ceiling light for their bedroom with a burgundy shade for fourteen pounds, totalling one thousand, one hundred and four pounds. Maggie managed to get the lot for a thousand pounds, including getting the washing machine and cooker fitted; they knew she would come in handy.

The washing machine and cooker would take four weeks for delivery and fitting; the rest could be delivered on the third. Would they have enough money for carpets and curtains with almost eight hundred pounds left? They had to nip home as Thomas hadn't brought the measurements with him, so Nancy left her car there and they went in Maggie's back to the carpet shop. They ordered a beige carpet for the living room which was really thick, no pattern in as such but shaded bits of swirls, and ordered the extra yardage to fit in the nursery; a long pile burgundy one for their bedroom and the only thing they had in deep pink was a thick cord one. It was very cheap though and some foam backed in sky blue for the bathroom. It all came to seven hundred and twenty pounds, including all the underlay. Luckily, it was free fitting if you spent over five hundred pounds, but the salesman said they wouldn't be able to do it until the tenth of January. Maggie had words with the salesman, and he agreed to do it on the second, although they were very pushed. They paid him the cash and headed home.

'What did you say to him to make him do it on the second?' Thomas asked, grinning.

'Never you mind,' she answered back. 'I used to be in sales myself before I married Eric, you know.'

'Thanks, Mum,' Nancy chirped up from the back seat. It was very tiring, spending money, but all they needed now were curtains and bedding and the baby's things.

They uncorked a bottle of wine when they got home and took a glass over to Joe, who had finished stripping the wallpaper in their bedroom and was glossing the woodwork. There were bin bags full of the old wallpaper and the carpet had been neatly folded up ready to go outside for the rubbish collectors. Joe appreciated the wine, although he had to finish the glossing, so he would drink it shortly. They had arranged for a second-hand store to come and buy what they wanted on Thursday. They had already had the beds collected by the council, but the suite and some other things may be appreciated by someone and it meant they had somewhere to sit when they were there. Joe worked hard over the next few days and Thomas and Nancy helped him whenever they could.

The second-hand store men came and took the suite, the sideboard and lots of bric-a-brac which they had found in the attic and gave Nancy a hundred pounds for the lot; not a great deal but someone would benefit from them. Nancy kept some of the stuff they had found in the attic to have a proper look through when she had time once they had moved in. Joe taught Thomas how to paste properly and with Thomas pasting and Joe hanging, the wallpapering was getting done quicker. When they had finished the kitchen, Nancy got to work scrubbing the tiles, bleaching the tops and wiping all the cupboards out. When Joe and Thomas ripped up the old lino, Joe said it had been levelled with bitumen and if they could get that off, he would bet any money it was the original stone floor underneath. He would ask a pal of his to have a look tomorrow if they wanted.

The house was coming along nicely. Once a room had been stripped, Joe went in and sanded then glossed the woodwork. Nancy would be picking wallpaper up, sweeping and keeping it as clean and dust free as possible and once the gloss had dried in each room, the wallpaper went up. Thomas and Joe made a good team, he even helped him paint the baby's room. The living room was last to be done and they worked until ten o'clock that night putting up the wallpaper, half above and half below the dado rail. Joe said he would come back tomorrow to have a good look around to make sure he hadn't missed anything and to touch up any paintwork that might need it. He would bring his mate with him to have a look at the kitchen floor, as it would certainly look better than lino. They said goodnight to him and wandered into each room, gazing around at the transformation. It looked fabulous. They couldn't wait to get the carpets fitted and all the larger items in. It was going to be perfect. In six days' time, they would be cuddling on their own new sofa, in front of a lovely new real flame gas fire in their very own house; well, Nancy's house, officially.

They had a well-deserved lie in on New Year's Eve. They were having a big night out around town and they had both worked hard on the house. They were meeting everyone at 11:30 p.m. in Times Bar for the midnight bells. They would no doubt bump into people earlier than that but with it being so busy, if they had lost their friends or family, as Thomas had done one year when he didn't know where his friends were going to be at midnight, the poor chap had ended up on his own. Although he did get a lot of attention off a group of older women, or so he said, so they had decided on the Times Bar to meet up.

When they did get up, near enough lunchtime, they had a brew with Maggie, then they started packing things to go across the road. She would ferry things across on the third as there would be a house full on the second: the carpet fitters; the electrician; Joe's friend Stan who was going to do the kitchen floor, using a substance to melt the bitumen and once that had been scraped off, he could polish the stones up to their original splendour.

Maggie had been doing some research on the house at the library. It looked older than all the other houses on the road, so she thought it may have some historical interest. Apparently, it had been built for a man called Herbert Everest who couldn't walk as he was paraplegic. His friend, an engineer, Harry Jennings made a folding tubular steel wheelchair for him in 1932. They together founded Everest & Jennings, a company that monopolised the wheelchair market for many years. They also bought an acre of land and had the house built on one level for accessibility, an idea taken from a Colonel Bragg who built a bungalow in Norwood, South London in the 1860s after returning from service in India. Nancy started packing a suitcase with the clothes she wouldn't be wearing over the next few days and when she pulled out her silver dress, she realised she hadn't bought anything new to wear for tonight. She tried the silver dress on, but it was pulling. It was that figure hugging, you could see how big her bump was. All her posh dresses would probably be the same. Shit, it was New Year's Eve and she had been so busy with the house she hadn't even thought of what to wear. 'Mum,' she shouted, 'What time do the shops close today in town?'

'I would imagine four o'clock,' Maggie replied. 'Why?'

Nancy was already running downstairs, trying to find her shoes. She grabbed Thomas and set off to town in the car. Thomas was dumbstruck.

'What are we doing?' he asked, confused.

'I've nothing to wear tonight,' she replied with panic in her voice.

Thomas laughed, realising what she would be thinking. She had been too excited about the house and all the furniture shopping that a new dress went completely out of her mind, how careless of her. Nancy was getting annoyed at Thomas laughing, until he told her what he had just thought what she would be thinking, if that made sense, and they both ended up laughing. They parked on the main car park and ran into the precinct. Thomas made Nancy think about where she had seen or recently bought something, so they weren't wasting time. They went to Sequins first, but Nancy had to be careful to choose something that would hide her bump. Thomas didn't mind but for reasons known only to Nancy, it had to be hidden tonight. They had an hour and a half. Nancy tried three dresses on in Sequins: one that was really nice, a black just above knee length on the left side, cut diagonally at the hem so it was longer at the other side, with a drop neck and silver shot through. It only hid her bump if she held it in but that was hard work. The other two were definite no's. A fit and flare would be ideal, but she didn't see one; they weren't the height of fashion. Then she saw it, a bright blue mini dress with a diamante pattern on the front. The skirt was tight and very short, the top had elbow length sleeves, a split neck with a one-button fastening at the back and split right down the back until it joined the skirt, and it was baggy. Perfect. She tried it on. The higher she pulled the skirt, the baggier it was around her midriff. Thomas liked it and was amazed that it had only taken half an hour. But she needed shoes to match, and some sparkly tights and diamante jewellery to jazz it up, it was New Year's Eve. It was another half hour before she was happy and had bought everything she needed: diamante dangly earrings, bracelet and choker, blue ankle boots and some tights with just a hint of silver sparkle as she didn't want to go too much over the top.

Thomas felt knackered and at this moment in time, as they arrived back at Maggie and Eric's, he didn't even feel like going out. Whilst they all ate their tea, they decided on a running order for the bathroom; Nancy first, then Maggie, Thomas and finally Eric.

'You should make another bathroom out of one of the spare rooms,' Nancy suggested.

'You're moving out next week, we won't need one then,' Eric replied with a little sarcasm in his voice.

Nancy went for a bath straight after tea, and Thomas helped Maggie clear up, get him in training early, thought Nancy and she lay back and relaxed amongst the bubbles. She was pleased with her new dress, it wasn't too fancy, and she would be able to wear it on normal nights and most importantly, it would hide her bump. She knew she would probably see Jason tonight, which was why she was glad she would be with Thomas all night; he wouldn't be able to talk to her much or tempt her. She snapped out of her thoughts and washed her hair, shaved under her arms and legs, and washed herself. She got out of the bath, wrapped one towel around her hair, turban-like, and another around her body and swilled the bath out.

Maggie came upstairs, knocked on Nancy's bedroom door and peeped her head around.

'Thomas has invited me and Eric into town with you two. We're only thinking about it, but would you mind?' she asked.

Nancy's first thoughts were to kill Thomas for suggesting it. She wouldn't be seen dead in town with her parents, but they could be trendy sometimes and she did love them dearly, and what a brilliant idea.

'That would be lovely, Mum, but do you know how packed it will be in every pub? You know how Dad likes the comfort of his local,' she said and actually meant it.

'Like I said, we're only thinking about it. I'd love to but it's up to your dad,' Maggie whispered and went for her bath.

Nancy went downstairs in her dressing gown, still with her hair in the turban towel. She sat in the lounge putting her make-up on and egging Eric to come into town. 'Come on, Dad, it'll be a laugh. Just think of all your old girlfriends you'll bump into.' She laughed as he said, 'I've only ever loved your mother.' He knew she was trying to wind him up, and Thomas rang his parents and invited them along too. They couldn't because Shelly was too young, and it was too late to find a babysitter, but they were very pleased that he had asked. Eric was warming to the idea. It would be fun, better than spending it with all the whingeing oldies in his local, but Nancy insisted it was only on the condition that Thomas picked him out something to wear; he certainly wasn't wearing one of his cardies.

Nancy went back upstairs to Maggie's bedroom and told her to dress for town, in other words not frumpy, although she had always been fairly trendy. Nancy remembered from junior school, she used to notice Maggie always looked better than some of the other mums. She was slim, always dressed nicely, when a lot of the other parents were fat and frumpy. Nancy rooted through her mum's wardrobe and found the dress Maggie had worn for her surprise eighteenth do, a bronzy-coloured shiny dress that made her brown eyes stand out. She had looked fantastic at her party and she would look great tonight. Nancy would be proud to introduce them to Thomas' and her friends.

When they were all ready, they ordered a taxi and went to the White Bull. The music was blaring out and Eric instantly pulled his face. He'd get used to it. They found the quietest corner after they had eventually been served, where they could just about hear each other. The pub was packed, it was used as one of the meeting places as later on there would only be the regulars in the White Bull. On to the Wine Lodge next, then Toffs and through the precinct to the Ribblesdale, the Jubilee and then to Times Bar, where those they hadn't already bumped into would be. The town centre had quietened off slightly as those who were going to nightclubs were leaving the pubs and they got served pretty quickly in Times Bar. They were all on pints, but Maggie had a half glass which she kept topping up; too unladylike to drink out of a pint glass. When a group of people left their seats near to the small dance floor, they went and sat down; it was only twenty past eleven, so everyone would be here shortly. Nancy could see Maggie was dying to get up and dance, so they went onto the busy dance floor. They played popular music in here, all stuff that was well known and "sing-along to" songs. Maggie was really enjoying herself.

Janet and Chris came in with Ian and Shaun; John had definitely been dumped. The boyfriends were introduced to Eric and Maggie, then Nancy and Maggie carried on dancing. Terry and Clare followed shortly afterwards and just before midnight, Dave appeared with the girl he was with on Christmas Eve. She was called Julie, lived in Feniscliffe and seemed a nice girl. The women danced most of the night and let the blokes keep them topped up with drinks. Occasionally, the blokes joined them. Maggie was trying her hardest to get Eric up dancing, while Nancy was telling her to leave him, he couldn't dance to save his life and it could be embarrassing.

The music stopped, and the DJ started the countdown which everyone joined in with. 'Ten, nine, eight, seven, six, five, four, three, two, ONE!' and the bells of Big Ben came through on the PA. Then the usual kissing, shaking of hands and hugs and near enough the whole pub joined hands for *Auld Lang Syne*. Nancy noticed Jason in the group at the opposite end of the pub and he winked at her. She glanced away quickly. When the song had finished, she went upstairs to the toilet. She was dying to go even though she knew Jason would follow her.

When she came out of the loo, he was waiting for her. 'Why haven't you rung?' he asked.

'Sorry, I've been meaning to, but I've been busy with Christmas and the house and things,' she replied. He took her in his arms and kissed her. She melted in his arms, trying to breathe in as much as she could so he wouldn't feel her bump.

'Happy New Year, you know where I am if you ever need me and you know how much I love you, don't you?' he told her, his voice soft and sincere.

All she could do was nod at him whilst a tear emerged from her eye and dripped down her cheek. He made her feel so guilty, she was carrying his child and he didn't have a clue. She made her excuses, dried her tears, went back downstairs and put a false smile on. She went over and whispered to Chris that he was here and whenever Nancy went to the loo after that Chris made sure she went with her.

Maggie was quite drunk and still dancing. Well, everyone was pretty drunk really and they were all having a great time. It was disappointing when last orders were called at one o'clock, but Eric bought everyone a drink as well as everyone buying their own. The music finished at two o'clock, so they had another hour or so before they were thrown out and they made the most of it. Maggie managed to get Eric up to dance, so Nancy went and sat down. He was being daft and had everyone in stitches trying to copy the moves everyone else was doing to the *Locomotion*, and then Abba came on, which he was singing and trying to dance to. At least he was having as good a time as everyone else.

Nancy saw Jason talking to a woman. He was leant with his shoulder against the wall, one hand in his trouser pocket and one leg across the other with a drink in his spare hand. The girl had long dark hair and a big bum from behind. Nancy caught his eye and he raised his drink to her and smiled; he looked absolutely fantastic and sexy, she could see his piercing blue eyes sparkling and his blonde-streaked hair. She looked over at Thomas. He was beautiful but in a different way; bright green eyes, dark spiky hair. Both these men were in love with Nancy and she was in love with both men. Nancy sneaked to the toilet without Chris seeing, hoping that Jason would follow. She had to walk past him to get to the toilets and she glanced at him as she walked past. The woman he was talking to was quite attractive, but she looked around thirtyish. Nancy went to the loo and topped up her lipstick. Sure enough Jason was waiting outside. Her stomach jumped when she saw him, or it could have been baby kicking.

'When do you go away again?' she asked outright.

'No plans to as yet. I've got a flat, I pick the keys up on Friday,' he replied.

She didn't know whether that was what she wanted to hear or not; confusion was an easy state of mind when you are drunk.

'I'll ring you when Thomas goes back to Germany, I promise,' she said and kissed him gently on the lips. His strong arms wrapped around her, but she quickly pushed him away, as she heard Eric and Thomas talking as they were coming up the steps to the toilets and went back into the ladies', leaving Jason standing there.

Jason went into the gents' and overheard Eric ask Thomas when they were seeing the vicar of St Paul's about the wedding in July. Jason felt sick. His heart had just been ripped out. He couldn't let her marry someone else, she wasn't happy with him, she couldn't be. He could, would, make her happy. He had to get out of there. He went downstairs, drank the rest of his drink and walked out, leaving the woman he was talking to staring after him.

He walked towards his mum's but ended up in Corporation Park. He was drunk but seemed to have a clear head until the fresh air got to him. He sat down on a bench, his head in his hands. God, he wanted that woman, but how could he win her back? He would somehow manage it when she rang him, but could he wait until then? When did she say she was going to ring? When Thomas went back to Germany, but when was that? He would just have to hope it would be soon.

They queued at the taxi rank for a while and got home just after three o'clock. Eric was shattered, thanked them for a good night and went straight to bed. Maggie offered wine around. Nancy couldn't face another drink, she'd been on vodka and cider all night and wanted to go to bed. Maggie and Thomas stayed up for a while, talking. Thomas asked Maggie if she thought Nancy was coping; he had noticed her looking a bit upset tonight, as though she was going to burst into tears. Maggie explained to him about pregnancy, how hormones affect moods and New Year's Eve is an emotional night for everyone. Maggie promised to look after Nancy when he went back to Germany in two and a half weeks. They talked for over an hour before they went to bed.

Eric woke up with a stinking hangover, so he ended up going back to bed. Nancy and Thomas stayed in bed till lunch time and Maggie was up and about at nine o'clock.

Chapter Seventeen

Nancy and Thomas were at their house early to let all the workmen in. Stan, Joe's friend, arrived first and opened all the windows and doors as the chemicals he would be using could be poisonous if not used correctly; it had to be well ventilated. He also advised Nancy to leave as they could affect the baby. He would sort the other workmen out and if he needed anything, he could nip across the road. Nancy went back to Maggie's and finished packing. They could start moving things over later on; she couldn't wait. She saw the carpet fitters arrive with rolls sticking out the back of their van and realised they didn't have a vacuum cleaner, so they went to the electrical shop and picked up a cylinder cleaner for fifty pounds. They then went to the bedding shop to have a look for bedding for the spare room. They didn't see anything that they thought would match perfectly, so they got a plain deep pink and cream reversible quilt cover and a single quilt and some plain deep pink curtains.

They would find out what else they had forgotten to buy as they went along; they still had just over two thousand pounds left.

When they got back, Nancy was dying to go and have a look to see how it was coming along. Maggie had already poured them both a cup of tea, so they would nip over after they had drunk it. They could smell the fumes as soon as they walked through the front door. The carpet fitters had white face masks on which Stan had given to them to avoid inhaling the fumes. It was a cold day and the poor fitters must have been freezing. They were fitting the beige front room carpet, they had just the main bedroom and the bathroom to do.

Stan was scraping away at the kitchen floor, he had already cleared some of the stones. He ushered them out the back door and came out. He was sweating. 'They're old quarry stones that were probably bought specially. To buy them now you'd be looking at around ten pounds each,' he told them.

'It's looking really good,' said Thomas. 'Will you manage to finish it today?'

'I hope so. I'll get all the bitumen off, and I can come back early tomorrow to finish off, probably just to polish them properly. Leave the windows open tonight as the fumes may linger,' he informed them.

'Will do,' both Nancy and Thomas said in unison.

That night, everything that was going across the road was in the hall in boxes and suitcases ready to be moved. It was a strange feeling for Maggie; she was losing her daughter who had grown up quickly over the last few months. Being pregnant she looked radiant, the glow made her even more beautiful than ever. She was thankful that she was only moving across the road, where she could help her and still look after her. Maggie had ordered a big bouquet of flowers to be delivered on Friday after they had their first night in the house, and knowing that Nancy would come and borrow a vase, she had bought her a modern blue dappled-effect one for the living room.

Nancy was really excited about all the new things that would be delivered tomorrow, and she was even excited about going to the supermarket, it would be their first time shopping together. They were going once the fridge had been delivered. Maggie had said she would wait in for any deliveries that hadn't arrived whilst they went. She laughed as she remembered her first shopping spree; they only had supermarkets in bigger cities, she had to trawl around the market on her own. Eric was always working; in fact, she didn't think they'd ever been shopping together.

Nancy got up at 7:30 and had a quick shower. She wanted to be over at the house by half past eight in case anything came early. She was so excited now, she took the vacuum cleaner over and pinched a few teabags, a bit of sugar and milk. When she opened the door, she could still smell fumes from yesterday even though all the windows had been open all night. She opened both the back and the front doors wide so as to get a good draught blowing through. It was freezing so she got to work on wiping all the woodwork down in each room and then vacuuming. The fitter had advised them to let the carpets settle for a couple of days before vacuuming but she wanted to get rid of all the bits before her new furniture arrived. Stan turned up to finish the kitchen floor.

She polished the tiles in the bathroom, cleaned the bath, sink and toilet then sat at the dining table they had kept, which was currently in the living room, and started writing a shopping list out. Food: they would decide when they got there what they would buy. Shampoo, conditioner, soap, sponge, toothbrushes, toothpaste, other toiletries as they saw them; sod it, she couldn't be bothered. She was wandering around the house, wondering what she could do now. She made a brew, sat back at the table; over an hour had passed and she was getting impatient.

Thomas came in. 'We haven't organised a telephone, do we need one?' she asked him.

'I think we should, especially nearer the time you're due. If anything happens, you would have to get in touch with me,' he replied.

'I'll probably be at Mum and Dad's most of the time when you're not here. We'll see over the next couple of weeks, then decide.'

He took her hand and pulled her up off the chair and wrapped his arms around her. 'Fancy christening the carpets?' he asked mischievously.

'Sshhh, Stan's here, wait until later, then we can christen everything,' she whispered. She started feeling horny just at the mention of sex and was thinking about later, when she heard a van pull up. She ran to the window; it was the electrical store van. She went to put the kettle on, and when they brought the first large box in, she offered the men a brew. It took them over an hour to bring everything, unbox and set things up where they wanted them. The telly was set up in the corner near the window; the picture was a bit fuzzy, they would have to get the aerial checked. Maggie came across and asked when they wanted to go shopping. They looked at each other and decided they'd go now.

They arrived at the supermarket and Thomas got a trolley. They went slowly up and down each aisle, getting all sorts of things from frozen food to a set of stainless-steel pans, an extra set of sheets for their bed and a few new records for the stereo. The trolley was piled high over an hour later and their total spend was £187.48. They worked out later that the food they had bought came to £68.32 and that was stocking up, so it should be a lot less than that on a weekly basis, especially for Nancy on her own. It would be nothing, she thought, she would eat at Maggie's.

They noticed the suite in the front room when they walked in. The beds had been delivered whilst they were out, and Maggie had made them with the crisp new sheets which she had washed for them. Nancy and Thomas went into the bedrooms; they looked fabulous. There was only the nursery that needed a cot and some pictures on the walls, and it would be finished.

Nancy and Maggie put the shopping away. The new fridge-freezer looked good full. They hadn't bought any fruit or veg as Eric said he would bring them some home on Friday when he got Maggie's. The new plate set, pans and cutlery were put next to the sink to be washed before they were used; they'd forgotten washing up liquid and dishcloths. Maggie suggested she write everything down when they realised they'd forgotten it, they could nip to the local shop for bits. The smell of the newness of everything soon overrode the smell of fumes from earlier.

When everything had been put in place, the suite was moved around a couple of times before they settled on the settee against the back wall, a chair near the window and the other chair in the corner near the stereo. The tables where they wanted them, the lamps and the fire switched on and the curtains closed, they left the windows open to get rid of the last of the fumes. As soon as Nancy settled on the settee next to Thomas, he started undoing the buttons on her blouse.

'Give over, I need a shower yet,' she remarked, pushing his hands away.

'Come on then, we'll have one together,' he replied with a rampant twinkle in his eye. He locked the front and back doors as it was only half past eight and went and turned the shower on to warm up. He led her into the bathroom and finished undoing her buttons and slipped her blouse off, then her bra. Her nipples hardened as he nibbled them gently. He undid her trousers, which just fell to the floor. He stroked her bump before taking her panties off. Nancy felt the hardness of his penis as she unzipped his jeans and teased him with her tongue when she bent down to take his jeans and underpants off. They stepped into the shower, which was a bit cold. Thomas washed Nancy while she was shampooing her hair and then quickly washed himself. He picked her up and slipped, nearly dropping her. This could be difficult, he thought to himself. Nancy wrapped her legs around him when he had got his balance and tried to position herself; her bump was in the way though and they just ended up laughing. They tried it backwards, standing up and they were both slipping, so they gave up, they were laughing too much. They each got a towel and went into the front room. Thomas laid Nancy down in front of the fire and kissed her all over before settling his tongue in her moist vagina. She made him turn around, so she could play with his penis in her mouth. The harder she sucked, the more he nibbled on her clitoris. When her muffled groaning became louder, he turned around and entered her vagina, lifting her buttocks up as he moved in and out, slowly at first then faster, and slowly again as he felt they were going to orgasm, to try and make it happen together. He was holding back until he knew Nancy was ready. He held her buttocks harder and thrust in as far as he could, and when his body rubbed on her clitoris for a while, he knew he could let go and relax to fulfil his pleasure, their pleasure, while they still could.

Thomas went into the kitchen, opened a bottle of wine and brought two glasses in. A film was starting shortly that sounded quite good, so they cuddled up on the settee and watched the film. Nancy fell asleep about half an hour after the film had started, so when the film finished, Thomas carried her to bed. She woke up as he was resting her on his knee and trying to pull the quilt back, so she kissed him passionately, which made him drop her on the bed, so he got on top and made love to her again.

The bed felt a bit weird. It was quite hard, but it would get comfier with all the activity that would get the springs bouncing. It was a restless night for both of them, sleeping in a new bed in a new house; they would soon get used to it. The privacy was great and the two of them together in their own house was a good feeling.

They were wide awake by nine o'clock the next morning. Thomas brought Nancy a cup of tea in bed. It was Friday, and Nancy was cooking tea for Maggie and Eric before they went to their local pub for a drink. Thomas and Nancy were going out with their friends and meeting up later on. They had thought about having a party but decided against it. They didn't want anything getting ruined. They could invite a couple of friends back, they would see how they felt. Nancy started preparing tea, she was cooking a meat and potato pie which would just go in the oven for a few hours in the new large casserole dish they had bought, and she would make the pastry and warm some peas up just before she dished out. She put the casserole in the oven and went into town; she wanted some disguising clothes. Thomas nipped to his mum and dad's for an hour. They were visiting tomorrow afternoon to have a look at the house. As soon as he walked through the door, Shelly was nagging him as to when she could sleep at his. He said he would ask Nancy, but probably next week sometime.

Nancy went in a few shops and bought two pairs of trousers and some longish blouses. She also found a black A-line dress, with beads all over it in a criss-cross pattern; quite expensive at sixty-five pounds but it was nice and hid her bump well. She had only been an hour in town, she drove home and walked in to the gorgeous aroma of the potato pie. She had only had a couple of slices of toast earlier and was quite hungry. She got the casserole out of the oven and tested it for seasoning and taste. The meat wasn't quite tender enough yet. She put it back in the oven and started preparing the pastry; she remembered Maggie showing her how to make pastry when she was younger, and she had ended up absolutely covered in flour. She heard Thomas coming in, and he came up behind her and put his arms around her.

'That smells gorgeous,' he said.

'It's only meat and potato pie,' she replied.

'I meant you, not the food,' he added, laughing. She flicked some flour at him which went all in his hair and made him look grey. He got some flour out of the bag and rubbed it in her hair, then the doorbell went. They looked at each other and burst out laughing; they both looked daft, what the hell. Nancy answered the door and was greeted by a big bouquet of flowers. The delivery person looked at her with a strange look and she just smiled sweetly at him and thanked him for the flowers. They were from Maggie and Eric; how nice, but they didn't have a vase. She left them in the bathroom sink for now, she would borrow a vase off Maggie later.

Nancy finished the pastry and put it in the oven, then went to have a quick shower before Maggie and Eric arrived at half past four. She got dressed and dried her hair. When they arrived, Maggie had a blue vase with her. 'I thought you might be needing this,' she said.

'Thanks for the flowers, they're lovely,' Nancy replied.

Eric had brought a bottle of wine, which they opened. The table was set, and Nancy brought out red cabbage and pickled onions for them to help themselves and a plate of meat and potato pie, peas and pastry each. It didn't seem as good as Maggie's, but she got compliments and four empty plates, so it must have been all right. They finished the wine off and when Maggie and Eric went, Thomas and Nancy got changed and went into town. Nancy wore her new black trousers with a bright pink A-line blouse she had also bought earlier. They had arranged to meet their friends in the same pub at the same time, so they could share a taxi. Thomas' friends were all there, including Ian. Janet was late as always but Chris was there, and she had already bought a round. Janet turned up five minutes later. They drank their drinks and set off to the next pub. Chris was meeting Shaun in Oblivion, Janet was meeting Ian in Times, when Nancy met Thomas before they went to Oblivion. Nancy was telling them about the house, and they said they would call around on Sunday to have a nosey around.

Town was busy, and Nancy managed to mingle in the crowds when she spotted Jason from a distance. She did miss him, wish she could be with him sometimes. Even though she and Thomas had only been in the house a couple of days, she felt like an old married woman. She could feel the spark between them fading and the feelings of being taken for granted already setting in; probably her hormones all over the place, she would feel differently once he went back to Germany. She would miss him then rather than Jason, you just always crave more what you can't have.

Chris could tell Nancy was getting maudlin and snapped her out of her thoughts. 'Forget Jason,' she nudged her friend. 'We're out to have a good time. Janet and I are back at uni next weekend, so you've got to make the most of it.'

Nancy smiled back at Chris and suddenly realised she was going to be left all alone. Janet and Chris back at uni, Thomas in Germany and Jason left to keep her company. Stop thinking these wicked thoughts, she grinned. That couldn't happen. Jason wouldn't want to know her, being pregnant with supposedly someone else's child and if she told him, it would ruin Thomas. She had already promised to ring him when Thomas went away, and she would go out for a drink with him and explain that even though she did still love him and probably always would, she was staying with Thomas for their baby and she wanted to stay friends with Jason. That would work, keeping everyone happy, surely.

They met up with Thomas and Ian in Times, finished their drinks and headed off towards Oblivion. The queue wasn't that big, so they didn't have to wait long in the cold. Straight to the bar for the boys and the loo for the girls when they got inside; it was one way to make sure the boys got the drinks in. Shaun was nowhere to be seen, and they hadn't seen him in town, so they presumed he had stayed around his locals and would be coming down later. They found a table near the top of the dance floor, and Janet and Chris went to dance while Ian, Thomas and Nancy tried to talk above the loud music. The place soon filled up. Nancy spotted Shaun and she nodded to Chris who was still on the dance floor. A big smile covered her face; she was falling for him in a big way. Nancy didn't get bad butterflies in her stomach anymore when she thought of Thomas, but when she looked him in the eyes and he looked back at her with love, a slight flutter came back as he leant to kiss her gently.

Shaun came over to the table and nodded at Chris when Nancy told him she was dancing. She didn't come off the floor for a while, trying to play it cool, or in her case maybe too shy. The next moment Nancy seemed to freeze and felt her heart pounding so loudly it could be heard over the music. Jason was heading directly for them. She turned slightly towards Thomas, put her arm around him with her thumb in his belt loop, yet not quite touching, else he might sense her fear.

Shaun got the tap on the shoulder. 'Hi, Shaun, haven't seen you for ages, mate, how are you?' Jason asked. A bit of a gush of relief came over Nancy but she was still rooted to the spot as Shaun carried on talking to Jason and when Shaun turned around and introduced her and Thomas to him, all Nancy could do was mumble and try and be polite. She noticed Thomas was looking at him with curiosity; he knew this bloke from somewhere but couldn't place him. Nancy stared at Jason without Thomas noticing, urging him to not say anything, but she knew in her heart that he wouldn't. She excused herself and went to the loo. Chris saw from the dance floor what was happening, and she and Janet followed Nancy to the toilet. They decided on a plan of action; they had to get Jason away from Thomas. Janet would be the best to do it; Ian knew she was a flirt and she could have him eating out of her hand, he wouldn't mind. Janet and Chris sneaked back on to the dance floor and came off as though they had just finished dancing. Janet spotted Jason and threw her arms around him. 'Hiya, haven't seen you for ages chic, how's it going?' Jason looked a bit stunned but he realised what they were doing and went along with it.

Janet took him to the bar and asked him to stay away while Nancy was with Thomas. Apparently, he'd gone to school with Shaun, they were good friends then but had lost touch when Jason had gone travelling. Janet promised to pass his phone number on but asked him to promise not to hurt Nancy or Thomas. He agreed, but only because he loved Nancy so much. He would collar Shaun later when he was on his own. Janet gave him a peck on the cheek for the half of lager he had just bought her and came back to the table and sidled up besides Ian in her flirty way, which always made him have a stupid grin on his face. Thomas asked Janet who Jason was. 'He's a mate of one of my ex-boyfriends,' she told him and nothing more was said, although the face still preyed on Thomas' mind.

As promised, Jason started chatting to Shaun at the bar, away from them, and refused when Shaun had asked him to come and join them. 'It's a bit awkward, Janet went out with my best mate and broke his heart, but thanks anyway,' Jason told him the story they had concocted together. Nancy knew Janet could do it, she had got herself out of some close calls before now, she was bound to come up with something good for her. Janet told Nancy and Chris later on what had been said to Jason and Thomas, so they were uniform in their stories if needed, and Nancy realised she would need them with the atmosphere in the taxi home.

They dropped Chris and Shaun off at Chris' house, her mum and dad were away for the weekend, but Thomas refused when Chris invited them both in for a drink.

'I'm really tired and just want to get home, but thanks anyway,' he replied courteously. He had been tense all night since Jason had turned up and had nearly bitten Nancy's head off for trying to persuade him to go to Chris' for a drink. The rest of the journey was in silence and when they pulled up outside the house, Nancy felt like going home, not to her home but to Maggie's. She knew she couldn't, but something really didn't feel right. They paid the taxi and Thomas got his keys out. He stormed into the kitchen and poured himself a vodka and coke.

'Will you pour me a vodka and lemonade, please?' Nancy asked in the softest of tones. He poured her a drink and went in the front room, put the telly on and sat on the settee not speaking, not touching, nothing. Nancy really didn't know what to do or say, so she did nothing for a while.

They sat in silence for what seemed like an eternity, then Nancy slowly edged her way closer to him. She was frightened, had never seen him like this before, but she had to do something. She laid her head on his shoulder; nothing. She slowly wrapped her arm over his stomach and caressed him gently. Movement; she could feel he was beginning to relax, come out of his anger, and as she looked up at his face staring at the telly, the tears slowly started. His arm made its way around her shoulder and pulled her tightly towards him, he was crying as well.

'I'm so sorry,' he said, pulling her as tightly to him as was comfortable. 'I love you so much, but I had this feeling tonight that I was going to lose you. I can't explain why, it was weird.' They held each other and cried together. Nancy knew then that every single move she made, Thomas could read and decipher. He knew that he was not going to stay in Germany for much longer, he was hurting, and he didn't know why. Nancy was hurting, and she knew that living a lie would just get harder and harder, but what could she do?

Chapter Eighteen

Things sort of returned to normal during the week before Thomas was due to go back to Germany. They had talked endlessly with each other and their respective families, and they had decided he should ask for a transfer to somewhere nearer to home as soon as he got back. He wanted to be around for the baby, and he didn't know how long the process would take; he had spoken to his old station boss, who had agreed he could go back to his old job if for whatever reason they wouldn't or couldn't agree to a transfer.

Nancy helped him pack his things the night before he was due to leave, and they went out for a snack rather than cooking, although Thomas had done most of that over the last three weeks. Nancy had been out here and there over the last week. She hadn't changed her address yet at the doctor's and a routine scan date came through on Thursday the twelfth of January. She hadn't told him, as she knew he would have wanted to go with her, and he could have easily worked things out. She had ripped the letter up and thrown it in Maggie's bin. Chris went along with her, so she wasn't on her own, and she had told Thomas she was spending the afternoon with Chris before she went back to uni the following week. They also had a girls' night out on Saturday, so Thomas went out with his friends and they all met up later in Oblivion.

The next morning, they called around at Thomas' parents for him to say goodbye to them and then Nancy drove him to the train station. It wasn't as emotional as normal as they waited for the train to pull into the station, especially not knowing how long he would be gone. It could be a matter of weeks or three months before he was officially on leave again. He promised to ring her at Maggie's the next day between 11:00 a.m. and 2:00 p.m., depending on his schedule, to let her know what they say about the transfer. Thomas stood behind her, his arms around her body with his hands on her small, for nearly five months pregnant, belly. He remembered when his mum was pregnant with Shelly, she had been really big from three months, when they broke the news to him. Nancy told him everyone was different; some women didn't even know they were pregnant until the pains started, and they went to hospital not knowing what was wrong and they ended up having a baby.

The train chugged into the station, and Thomas kissed her passionately and clung to her until the whistle blew, grabbed his bags and jumped on. They waved to each other until the train disappeared around the corner and Nancy got in her car and went home, only shedding a few tears when she arrived home, over the emptiness of the house now he'd gone. She went across to Maggie's later for her tea and while she was there, rang BT and ordered a telephone to be installed.

She stayed at Maggie's until almost ten o'clock, went home, put the fire on and lay on the settee, watching telly for a while before going to an empty bed. She slept like a log; it had felt weird at first, but she soon went to sleep and felt totally refreshed when she awoke just after ten the next morning. She showered and dressed and went to Maggie's, waiting for Thomas to call. It got to half past twelve before the phone went. She rushed to answer it and even when he said, 'Hiya,' he had a happy tone. He told her his sergeant would agree to the transfer because of the circumstances, although he would be disappointed to lose such a promising private. It would take about two weeks just for the request to go through the relevant departments, and it could end up taking at least a couple of months, maybe longer, before he found out where he would be transferred to and they would then give him a transfer date, which again could be a month later. All in all, it could take up to five months. He had requested two weeks special leave for when the baby was due if it did take that long for a transfer, and he would still have the leave, wherever he was, if he was already back in England. He sounded disappointed at the prospect of it taking that long, yet excited that his sergeant had agreed to it without much fuss. It was just a waiting game.

Nancy told him she had ordered a phone for their house and was waiting for an installation date. 'I felt so isolated and lonely last night without you, a phone will make me feel more secure and able to contact people if I want to.' He promised he would ring Maggie and get the number off her in a few days, so he could be the first person to ring her, hopefully with some news. They didn't stay on the phone long, and when Maggie nipped to the shop, Nancy rang Jason. 'I need to talk to you, meet me tonight at eight in the Alex,' she said.

''Course I will, see you later then,' he replied. He wasn't impressed with her tone of voice and knew he shouldn't be looking forward to it as much as he actually was. He could win Nancy around, always had done and hopefully would be able to again tonight. He had to persuade her not to get married, that was his main aim.

Jason was early; in fact, he got to the Alex at quarter to seven, needing a drink before she turned up. He had been going over and over in his mind what he was going to say all afternoon since she rang at ten to one. He sat at the bar, near to a couple of blokes who seemed like they were part of the fixtures and fittings. They were always there, every time Jason had been in, anyway. There was a disco later on; Thursday was quite a busy night, so if they wanted to talk, they would have to go somewhere else. A couple of pints later, Nancy walked in at five to eight. He got her a drink. The DJ had started the music, so they went in the slightly quieter back room and sat in the corner. Nancy had worn her comfiest, tightest black trousers to pull her belly in as much as possible, and the white A-line blouse, with a long black baggy cardigan. If you didn't know, you certainly wouldn't guess at her being pregnant. They both started talking at the same time, trying to get out what they had both prepared, but it made them laugh. His eyes seemed to be even more piercing and sparkling than she remembered, and it made her stomach churn just looking into them. She turned away to avoid his gaze; the laughter had gone.

Jason finally got his words out. 'Don't marry him, I could make you a lot happier, you know,' he said to her in the soft tone of voice that she loved.

'I'm sorry, Jason, I have to.' A huge lump came to her throat and she struggled to get the words out. 'I'm pregnant, I'm having–a–his baby.' She didn't dare look at him, just kept looking into her drink and when she picked it up to take a sip, she was shaking.

Jason felt like he had just been hit by lightning, he was in shock, he certainly wasn't expecting that. All that he had rehearsed over and over in his mind had gone. He couldn't think straight. After what seemed like ages, he turned around to look at her, she had her head bowed and he noticed tears gently gliding down her cheeks. He reached to touch her hand and she clasped his tightly. She wiped her eyes discreetly, hoped he hadn't noticed and carried on drinking her drink.

'How far gone are you?' he asked gently. 'F–five months,' she replied, still stuttering.

He looked puzzled 'Then, it could be mine,' he said with a little excitement in his voice.

'I was already pregnant when I met up with you. I've worked the dates out,' she replied with great difficulty and sorrow. God, she wished she wasn't here, this was harder than lying to Thomas. The pub seemed to be getting louder and was starting to get busy. They finished their drinks and started walking up the hill to a small pub just up the road. Jason held her hand as they walked in silence. As they got near to the pub, Jason pulled her around to face him and put his hand under her chin, so she was looking at him.

'I could still love the baby, whether it's mine or not. Please–please don't marry him.'

The sincerity in his voice made the tears flow and he held her for an eternity. She wiped her eyes. 'I need a vodka,' she said with a slight smile. They walked into the pub and Jason ordered the drinks, two double vodkas, his with cola and hers with lemonade, while she went and sat in a corner out of the way. She didn't want anyone to see she had been crying.

Even though they were both jangled, they managed to have a civil conversation; no laughter but not mentioning the baby while they were in the pub. Last orders were called. It had gone so quick, they ordered a double around, still on vodkas and they ended up being the last people to leave. As they were walking slowly towards the Alex where her car was parked – she hadn't intended on staying for long or drinking for that matter – Jason turned to Nancy.

'Stay with me tonight. Please, I need you and you've had too much to drink to drive. Please. It might help me accept what is happening. I promise I won't do anything you don't want me to,' he quickly added.

As he held her tightly with one arm as they walked, she thought about staying, no more harm, in her mind, could be done. Thomas was away, and she felt she owed it to him. She was worried about spilling the beans, yet she wanted to stay, to say goodbye, if, of course she could. She turned so she was in front of him and looked into his eyes. Now it was dark they weren't quite as sparkling as earlier. All she did was smile sweetly at him with her big brown eyes and as he leant to kiss her, she returned the passion that was overflowing between them.

They walked into his flat and Jason offered her a drink, he had bought some vodka specially. He poured them both one while Nancy was looking through his records. He got his guitar out and sat on the arm of the armchair and played. He was good, and he looked sexy. A couple of his friends were talking about starting a band and they had asked him to join them; his first band had split when he went travelling.

Nancy stood up, went over to where he was sat and stroked his hair; he put his guitar down. 'That was brilliant,' she told him before putting on an LP by Killing Joke. *Requiem* was his and her favourite on the album, a bit morbid but a fantastic tune. The guitar bits reminded her of Jason's playing. Jason came over to the bed where Nancy was sitting, put his arm around her and started unbuttoning her blouse. 'I won't touch you if you don't want me to.' All she could do was kiss him. He took her blouse off and laid her down on the bed. At least while she was on her back, her bump didn't show as much. She didn't feel any guilt whatsoever as they made love, and my God, did they make love. Jason was so gentle, so loving, so caring. She knew how much he loved her, and she knew her feelings for him now. It was his child she was carrying; her heart was telling her to tell him, yet her head was telling her no. Jason wasn't working, was always disappearing to foreign countries. The love she felt for him tonight was more than she had ever felt in her life before. They went on for what seemed like hours, both of them having had too much drink to orgasm fully and as Jason held her close to him, she drifted off to sleep.

'*Shit, what have I done?*' she thought as soon as she woke up in his arms.

She tried to cast her mind back to the night before, had she told him? She couldn't remember. That's good isn't it, pregnant and pissed. '*Good mother I'll make,*' she thought to herself ashamedly, yet she felt comfortable in his arms. She hadn't said anything, she didn't think, but he'd let her know when he woke up.

She sneaked out of bed and put the kettle on, made two cups of tea, got dressed and went over to wake him up. 'Good morning,' she said as she woke him by kissing him on the lips.

He slowly opened his eyes. 'God, woman, I love you,' she smiled at him.

They drank their tea and Nancy had to go, it was almost eleven o'clock. As she walked out of the door she said, 'I'll ring you,' and headed off towards the Alex car park where she had left her car.

When she pulled up on her drive and got out of the car, she noticed Maggie waving at her. She waved back, went inside and straight into the shower. She heard Maggie coming in.

'Just having a shower, Mum,' she shouted. 'Won't be a minute, put the kettle on.'

Maggie got two cups out of the cupboard, put teabags and sugar in and sat in the kitchen, waiting for Nancy.

When she came out, wrapped in a towel and into the kitchen where Maggie was sitting with a face on her like thunder she blurted out, 'I've had to lie to Thomas this morning, and I don't like it.'

'Why?' asked Nancy.

Thomas had rung after their telephone number. 'I had to tell him I hadn't seen you since last night. You were probably still in bed, being so tired. Nancy, you didn't come home last night. Where were you?' she asked.

Shit, she hadn't thought this one out properly. Quick as a flash, she replied, 'Do you remember Sharon and Geoff? Well, Sharon has thrown him out and wanted cheering up, so I went around, and we ended up drinking vodka. Sharon was upset, I couldn't leave her, Mum.' Maggie seemed convinced. She would have to ring Sharon later, see if she would back her story up. 'Anyway, Thomas knows I won't get the number for at least a couple of days,' Nancy added.

She rang Sharon later that day, asking to meet her in town on Saturday. Chris was at uni and she had to tell someone. Sharon didn't know the family, she just knew her and Thomas, but she really needed someone to talk to.

The confusion she felt that night in bed on her own, knowing that she could be with Jason, was horrendous. She met Sharon as arranged and they went to a café. Nancy asked how she and Geoff were. 'Just about still together,' Sharon replied and went on to tell her how possessive he was, and she couldn't do anything without twenty questions. Nancy was thankful in a way that neither Thomas nor Jason were over possessive with her. At the end of the day it was her life and she was a strong character and wouldn't let a bloke rule, or ruin, her life.

Sharon was a little shocked as Nancy explained about Jason. She told Sharon everything apart from the fact that it was Jason's baby rather than Thomas'. Sharon couldn't really offer advice as she was quite naïve, but it helped Nancy by talking to someone else. A problem shared is a problem halved as they say; not that Jason was a problem as such. She was in love with two men. Both different. Thomas had a good career but was away a lot of the time, which left Nancy on her own. Jason wasn't working, could be there, but then again could disappear abroad at the drop of a hat.

She felt relaxed after having a good afternoon talking and shopping with Sharon, and they had arranged to go out the following weekend. Sharon would tell Geoff they were going out on someone's birthday do around town. It turned out that she couldn't do the following week, so it was left to the week after. Nancy didn't ring Jason after the wonderful night they had spent together, she couldn't face him, and she hadn't been out to bump into him.

The weekend came around. Chris and Janet were both home, so the four of them went around town. Nancy was big, it really could not be hidden now whatever she wore. She was nearly six months pregnant, telling people she was six and a half months. She got a lot of odd looks from people, but she really didn't give a shit. She was still attractive and slim apart from the bump, and she wasn't after any blokes, just out to have a laugh. At one stage she did get a bit paranoid and ordered a lemonade without vodka! That was a first. She was surprised not to see Jason in Oblivion, but why would she be looking for him? They all had a dance and were having a good laugh. When Nancy was tired and went back to the table where their drinks were, she was standing on her own for a few minutes when she felt a tap on her shoulder. Her heart jumped.

'Jason?' She turned around to see a friend of Jason's, Brian.

'I take it by that you don't know he's gone,' he said.

'Sorry, I didn't hear that right,' she replied.

'He's gone to see his mum, she's moved to Eastbourne to be near her parents; then heading back to Salzburg, Austria,' Brian added. 'He's gutted about you getting married, you know.'

'I know, he's been trying to persuade me not to,' she told him. In her heart of hearts, Nancy had sort of expected it, not so soon though. She hadn't rung him since that perfect night; she knew he wouldn't ring her at Maggie's, and he didn't have her new telephone number.

'If you want her address, give me a ring,' Brian said, giving her his number. He sounded upset that his friend had gone.

'Please tell him I'm sorry if you speak to him,' she asked.

''Course I will. See you.'

She seemed to see a lot of Brian over the next couple of months, and it made her wonder if Jason had asked him to keep an eye on her. Saying that, she only went out when Janet and Chris were home, normally every couple of weeks and she was getting ever so big, she was officially seven and a half months pregnant, but people thought she was eight months and it was annoying when they kept saying, "Only a few more weeks to go". Thomas was due to transfer back to Allington on the sixteenth of April, so he would be coming home next Friday. She had missed him a lot more since Jason had gone but she had a lot of time to think when she was alone in the house. She had rung Brian and got Jason's mum's address and telephone number but had not written or rung. Well, Jason would be abroad now anyway, and she had to try and get him out of her mind. She had a good future with Thomas. She had also done a lot of organising for the wedding, had bought and started writing the invitations, and started looking for her dress, although she certainly couldn't try any on.

She was counting the days, the hours and the minutes as the week went so slowly by. She had been so bored over the last few weeks, she had spent the rest of the money that had been transferred from the solicitor and there was only Thomas' wages which went into his account. She had a cash card but didn't like dipping into his money and they had never got around to opening a joint account. She had loads of frumpy maternity dresses that she wore during the day and had found a couple of decent ones for if she went out. She had asked Eric if she could have some money for when the baby was born and when Eric had spoken to the solicitor, he arranged for a thousand pounds to be transferred and for the allowance to start, which they had spoken about; and it would have an annual increase for inflation; that way she would learn to live within her means. It would be set up to start the following week.

At last Friday came, Nancy had agreed to pick him up from Priston as the train wouldn't have arrived in Blacklodge until sixteen forty-five, whereas at Priston he arrived at fifteen twenty, which just missed the connection to Blacklodge at fifteen fifteen and the next connection was at sixteen fifteen. It was only a thirty-five-minute drive and she was dying to see him, but this was it now, he would be there with her every day. Her stomach was churning, had been all day and baby was kicking like mad and it kept getting her right under the ribs, which hurt. At one stage she smacked her stomach, as though smacking the baby; it kicked her back, cheeky little bugger.

She made herself a sandwich at lunchtime, then wallowed in a hot bubbly bath. Baby seemed to relax and so did she. She dried herself, put on her make-up and styled her hair, then got dressed in the only pair of trousers that were half decent, plain black ones which had a massive piece of stretchy cloth over the belly, and a blue and black blouse. She looked all right and at half past two she got in her green Escort and drove to Priston. She had been hinting at Eric that she could do with a new car as hers was on its last legs, but he hadn't taken the bait, so she kept her fingers crossed that her car would make it there, not overly bothered if they broke down on the way back. She parked up in the short stay car park and waddled on to the station; at least here it didn't remind her of Jason. She checked the timetable to see what platform his train would be arriving on, Platform four, and went and sat down. She noticed an old tramp at the end of the platform, slumped against the wall with a brown paper bag in his hand which he kept raising to his mouth. '*Probably either meth or cider,*' she thought.

She stood up when she saw the train coming in the distance, only a couple of minutes late. Her heart was beating fast and baby started kicking again. It'd been asleep since she had her bath. The train got nearer and nearer, her heart beat faster and baby kicked harder. As it pulled to a halt and all the doors opened, she glanced up and down the train a few times before she spotted him running towards her, trying not to bump into anyone. He threw his bags down and picked her up before very quickly putting her down again; she was heavy and he struggled to get his arms around her belly. Instead, he kissed her and held her tightly. He picked his bags up and they headed to the car. Nancy was cooking thick fillet steaks later and had set the dining table with candles and flowers. The champagne was cooling in the fridge. She couldn't wait to get home. They were talking non-stop all the way home, and as they pulled onto the drive and went into the house, they ended going straight into the bedroom. With the bump, it was difficult in the missionary position, so when they were both ready, Nancy got on her hands and knees for Thomas to enter her from behind. He held her thighs whilst he thrust into her, and Nancy felt the full length of his penis. When Thomas felt he was near to coming, he reached Nancy's clitoris with his fingers and rubbed it to try and induce her orgasm. Her breath was getting deeper and faster and after a couple of minutes he heard a pleasurable groan as Nancy's orgasm started. A few seconds later Thomas relaxed as he started to ejaculate, still playing with her clitoris but keeping his penis still inside her so they could feel each other throbbing with ecstasy. They lay in each other's arms for a while and when Nancy went to start cooking dinner, Thomas went for a bath.

They had a lovely meal. The steak was the nicest Nancy had ever managed. Thomas preferred his medium to well done, yet Nancy liked medium rare. She normally burnt Thomas' and undercooked hers, so she made sure she had timed them properly tonight and they were near enough perfect. They slopped on the settee after the meal when the phone rang. Maggie and Eric were nipping over shortly. They brought a bottle of wine, which Nancy put in the fridge and brought them both a glass of champagne. Constant laughter, the champagne and two bottles of wine later, Maggie and Eric went home, and Nancy and Thomas went to bed.

Life soon got into a routine. Thomas was on split shifts, it was weird cooking for him when he came home after his two-to-ten shift, eating around eleven o'clock and the nights were lonely, but it was always nice when he woke her for sex at half past six.

May was fast approaching. She had always made sure she booked doctor's appointments and antenatal clinics when Thomas was working. She was trying all the old wives' tales she had heard to try and encourage the baby to come early; lots of hot baths, eating fresh pineapple and lots of sex!

Thomas finished work for two weeks on Friday the fourth of May, so he could be there all the time just in case and after a week of him constantly pampering her, not leaving her for a second and nagging her to go to the doctor's as the baby was overdue, Nancy was fed up. She made him ring one of his friends and go out for the night, so she could have some peace. He reluctantly rang Ian to ask if they were going out and arranged to meet him at eight o'clock. As he showered and got ready, he kept asking Nancy if she would be all right. This annoyed her more and she banned him from coming home until at least one o'clock.

His taxi came and as he walked through the door, she relaxed, opened a bottle of wine and lay on the settee, watching telly. She knew she had almost two weeks to go if she went full term. Thomas would be gutted, would only be able to have time off when she was in labour. With the weight she was carrying she had really bad backache, so she moved some cushions under her back and made herself as comfortable as possible. She went to bed with the cushions at almost midnight. Thomas had listened to her, probably dying to come home but not daring to, the moods Nancy had been in recently. She eventually dozed off even though the pain was bad, and when she felt Thomas' arm gently cuddling her stomach, she turned her head to him, so he could kiss her.

'Have you been all right?' he slurred in a whisper.

''Course I have,' she whispered back. 'Go to sleep.'

He kissed her on the back of her neck, which sent shivers down her spine and made the backache worse for a second; she flinched.

Nancy woke up in a wet bed at half past three. Thomas must be drunk if he'd wet the bed. She got up and went to the toilet, she would sleep in the spare bedroom. She sat on the toilet for ages, couldn't stop weeing. She started worrying when she was still sat there ten minutes later. Her waters must have broken. Shit, if Thomas didn't get his sleep after a drinking session, he was really grumpy, and he certainly wouldn't be able to drive. The pain was in her stomach as well as her back now. She tried to shout for Thomas; he wouldn't hear her, she'd shut the door when she came out. She got a towel out of the cupboard, put it in between her legs and went back into the bedroom. She knelt down at the side of the bed and stroked his hair to try and wake him up gently. No movement. She tried whispering in his ear and in the end, she shook him violently. He jumped up, nearly knocking her backwards.

'Thomas, I think the baby's coming,' she shouted to him.

He started panicking, throwing his clothes on quickly. 'Thomas, come here and sit down,' she shouted to him. He stood still for a moment then sat next to her on the bed. 'Calm down,' she whispered to him and she stroked his back. She then started giving him instructions. 'Ring Maggie to take me to hospital, put my bag near the door, find me some clothes, an old dress will do.' She didn't bother with a bra as she would be getting undressed again soon. He went to get her shoes ready. 'Please, make a brew for us all before we go,' she asked him. He put the kettle on then went to let Maggie in. She went to Nancy to see if she was all right. The pains in her stomach were getting worse but at least she couldn't feel the backache now. Maggie started timing the pains; six minutes apart. By the time they had drunk their tea, they were every five minutes. Thomas took everything to the car and with a blanket wrapped around Nancy's shoulders, led her to the car.

They arrived at Bramley Mead Maternity Hospital just after five o'clock in the morning to be met by the duty midwife. Nancy was taken into an examination room while Thomas and Maggie waited outside. The nurse examined her cervix, she was seven centimetres dilated; probably another three hours at least. Thomas and Maggie were invited into the room, it was cosy with cool colouring in pale blue. Thomas held Nancy's hand and whenever a pain started, she gripped it hard. The nurse had given her a mask so when the pain got unbearable, she could breathe in the gas and air to ease the pain. She had been offered an injection of pethidine but refused. She wanted to feel everything. Two-and-three-quarter hours later the mask was getting well used, the pain was coming every couple of minutes, and she realised that if she started breathing the gas and air when the pain stopped, she wouldn't feel the next one as much. The midwife came in again and sent Thomas and Maggie out. Her cervix was nearly ready, so she was taken to the delivery suite in a wheelchair; a lovely light room with lots of equipment in. There was a birthing chair where you squatted on the edge of the seat and gave birth in a sitting position. Nancy tried it but wasn't comfy as you had to hold on to the chair. She wanted to hold on to Thomas, so she got on the bed, Maggie holding one hand and Thomas the other. Maggie was holding the mask for her and when Nancy squeezed her hand, she put it over her mouth.

'I want to push,' Nancy shouted but the midwife told her not to just yet. The pain was constant now, with extra pain when the contractions came. The midwife, after measuring her cervix again, told her to push as soon as her next contraction started. Nancy took a deep breath and pushed, after ten minutes when they said they were going to give her an episiotomy, cut her vagina, she refused and a couple of minutes later she heard the nurse say, 'It's a boy!'

It – sorry – he – was taken to be weighed. Five pounds nine ounces and was born at 08:36 a.m. Nancy hoped to God that Maggie or Thomas didn't say anything about it being small, seeing as it was overdue.

Thomas wiped Nancy's forehead and kissed her. 'Thank you, darling, I love you,' he told her. Nancy didn't have the energy to say anything, she just smiled at him. She struggled when the nurse told her to push again for the placenta to come out, and the nurse pressed on her stomach so hard, it felt worse than having the baby. The baby was placed in a cot, wrapped in a blanket. Nancy thought it – he – looked like a skinned rabbit, bony and thin.

Baby and mother were both fine and taken to a small ward with six beds in it. Nancy was in the bed near the big bay window. She went for a bath. It stung a bit as she had torn slightly; they said it was pointless stitching such a small tear, it would soon heal. She got dried and put on a clean nightie, then went back to her room. Thomas was sitting on the bed, holding the baby. Maggie had taken a couple of photographs of them. The nurse came in and suggested they leave Nancy to rest and come back at visiting time, three 'til five or seven 'til nine. Thomas kissed Nancy and the baby, whom they had decided to call Damon Mark, and Maggie gave Nancy a hug.

When they left the nurse showed her how to breastfeed and she had Damon on each breast for five minutes. It felt weird, but the nurse said she would get used to it. When she put him back down in his cot, she tried to get some sleep herself. She awoke to a nurse asking if she wanted any lunch and she asked for a small portion, as it was hospital food, after all. They brought her braised steak with carrots, cauliflower and boiled potatoes, one of her favourite dishes, so she was annoyed that she had asked for a small portion. Damon hadn't woken up since she put him down before she went to sleep, and he hadn't cried. The other babies in the room seemed to be non-stop screaming; she would ask Maggie to bring some earplugs in. The nurse came to see Nancy just after two to see how she and Damon were getting on. Nancy told her he hadn't woken up since she put him down around half ten, so they woke him up, he fed for twenty minutes and went back to sleep again. Nancy put a bit of make-up on and brushed her hair before visitors arrived.

She stayed in hospital for five days and when Thomas came to pick her up to take her home, the house was spotless. The heating had been on in Damon's room. Maggie was there to help if she needed it, but she soon settled into a routine. Damon was a good baby, hardly ever cried, only when he was hungry, which soon started being every two hours, which proved difficult when they were out, so as the wedding drew nearer, she started to wean him off the breast with formula milk, and she also fed him bits of baby rice and rusks as that would be easier for Maggie. They were going to take him on their honeymoon, but Maggie had offered to have him for the ten days they were going; where to only Thomas knew. Nancy's figure had sprung back into shape almost as soon as Damon was born, so she only waited a few weeks before trying wedding dresses on.

Janet and Chris had organised Nancy's hen night for two weeks before the wedding. Thomas was having his stag night the week before, so they weren't struggling for babysitters as Maggie was going with them to Blackpool. They were staying overnight, and they set off on Saturday just after lunch, it was only a forty-five-minute drive and four cars, sixteen people in total. They were lucky to find a hotel for the one night; most only did two-night stays and they had booked four family rooms at the White Feather Guest House in the North Shore area. They went for a few drinks in the afternoon and had a meal, then back to the hotel to get changed to go out for the night. Nancy was made to wear a net curtain on her head with a big L-plate pinned to it and she wore a black and white, rather psychedelic mini-dress with black tights and ankle boots. They went around a few pubs in North Shore. A couple of them were gay pubs and the blokes were really friendly; each pub had a disco on and before long it was last orders and they were heading to a nightclub. Surprisingly, nobody had been lost. Liz and Sue were there from uni with a couple of their friends from home, some friends of Janet's from Leeds Uni. Sharon, who had managed to get away from Geoff, Barbara and Maggie. It was a fantastic night, full of decent-looking blokes from all over the country. Nancy met one from Kirkcaldy in Scotland who was down for the weekend and he was asking her not to get married and go and live in Scotland with him. He was gorgeous and seemed a very nice person, but Nancy was struggling to understand his broad accent. He gave her his phone number anyway and, eventually, he took her for a takeaway then walked her back to her hotel. Well, you're allowed to be a little bit naughty on your hen night. She politely kissed him goodnight and went into the hotel. The owners were still up and offered her a drink from the bar; in fact, they reopened the bar as they knew the rest of the party would be back soon. Maggie was already in bed and she had told the landlady the rest of them had gone for a snack. They soon wandered in laughing, they had got totally lost and couldn't find the hotel. They had eventually stopped a Black Maria, Janet had put on her sexy smile and asked if they could take them home and they had all been sitting in the back chatting the policemen up. Janet had even pinched a pair of handcuffs but didn't get the keys so a bit of a pointless exercise, although she asked Nancy if Thomas could get some for her. She had her perverse head on, and they were laughing at what she was saying she was going to do to Ian with the handcuffs.

They had to be down for breakfast before ten o'clock if they wanted any, so there were fifteen rather hungover people in the dining room. Maggie was the only one who wasn't looking too bad, it was a good job she was driving home. They had their breakfast and then all went for a walk along the sea front to clear their heads before setting off for home. It had hit home as they were walking along that was really Nancy's last night of true freedom, yet she could still pull the blokes. Did she really want to get married or did she want to be a single mum? Thomas adored her and Damon. Luckily, he looked more like Nancy now; she was dreading him ever looking like Jason. She convinced herself she did want to marry Thomas and spend the rest of her life with him.

Thomas went on his stag night the following week to Manchester with about thirty of his friends and colleagues. He just said it had been an expensive, excellent night. They had ended up in a casino and lost a lot of money between them.

The Friday before the wedding, Nancy was in town with Damon in the pram, doing some last-minute shopping for the honeymoon when someone suddenly appeared in front of her, making her jump. 'Jason!' she almost screamed. 'Are you OK?'

'Are you still going through with it?' he asked. She bowed her head as she nodded.

'Come out with me Tuesday night for a drink. I take it you'll be staying apart the night before the wedding?' he asked.

'Well, yes, but I have Maggie coming around and Chris and Janet staying at my house, so I can't really,' she replied.

'Meet me for an hour then early on, 5:00 p.m. at the Alex,' he asked with pleading eyes. She just said she would try. The Alex was open all day because of a funeral or something. What excuse could she make to Maggie? She would get Janet and Chris to think of something and they would cover for her.

She went home and finished packing for the honeymoon. All she knew was it was abroad somewhere, and they were flying from Manchester on Friday at 11:35 a.m. and were being picked up at half past eight in the morning. At least they had a full day to recover from the wedding.

Maggie wasn't due around until seven-ish. Janet and Chris arrived with loads of stuff just after four o'clock. They unpacked three bottles of vodka, a bottle of champagne and their clothes which they hung up, ready for the big day. Nancy told them about Jason. Janet thought she should go but Chris disagreed and said she shouldn't, but she would cover for her and say she'd nipped around to Thomas' mum's to make sure Shelly's bridesmaid dress fitted her properly. They would make sure they answered the phone in case Thomas rang as he was at his mum's, but she had to be back for eight.

Jason was sitting at the bar when she walked in. He ordered her a drink and they went to sit down.

'I really didn't think you'd come, but I am so pleased you have,' he said sweetly.

'I wasn't going to,' she replied.

They talked, Jason trying to persuade her not to get married to Thomas, saying he could treat her better and love her son as much as he loved her; Nancy telling him she was sorry, but she was going through with it as he would never settle down, always having itchy feet, liking being abroad so much. It was a sad time for both of them and when Nancy had to go, he produced a record by The Jam. 'Play it and listen to the words, I'll be there tomorrow.' Nancy was a bit frightened by those words until he added, 'Just in case you change your mind.' He was very upset.

When she got home, she put the record on. It was *The Bitterest Pill* and tears came to her eyes as she listened to the words. Nancy tried to control her tears in front of everyone and wondered if Jason knew that Damon was really his. She hadn't lied to him about anything else, ever. She would never know. They went through two and a half bottles of vodka before they went to bed at around one-ish. Maggie had left just after eleven. The wedding wasn't until three o'clock, so they would have time to sober up. The beautician was coming around at eleven o'clock to do hair and make-up for everyone. Pat was bringing Shelly around at half past one and the cars were due at quarter to three to take them to church.

Chapter Nineteen

Nancy was in the house, alone with Eric; everyone else had gone. He stood looking at his daughter with pride. Her dress was backless, in ivory with half sleeves and pastel multi-coloured sequins and diamante all over the bodice. The skirt was full, layered with diamante and pearls scattered over the lace and a long train; her hair had been pinned up with ringlets falling sexily over her ears and a long headdress attached to a tiara with pearls and diamante on. She looked wonderful and Eric actually felt quite sad; he was losing his baby daughter to a man and she was no longer his baby. The car arrived for them and they locked up and got in the car. It was five past three when they arrived at church. The photographer was standing outside the car, taking photographs as they got out. The guests who had been waiting in the churchyard made their way into the church when they saw the car pull up and the bride arriving. There were a lot of people, both adults and children, milling about outside the church. Nancy tried to look around for Jason, but she couldn't see him anywhere.

They walked through the gates and approached the bridesmaids who were waiting. Shelly looked beautiful and was so excited, they had to tell her to shush. They stood outside the church, waiting for the nod from the usher when Nancy just had a last glance behind her. Jason was standing at the hedge just bordering the graveyard. Their eyes met, and she could see the glistening of a tear. She loved him, but she also loved Thomas. She gave him a sorry look, then pulled her veil over her face as they made their way into church to the wedding march and slowly up the aisle. All eyes were turned to her, with gasps at the beauty of her dress. With her veil, no one could see the tears she was trying to fight back. As she reached Thomas, her bridesmaids lifted her veil. Her eyes were sparkling through the tears and she smiled at him. Thomas thought her more beautiful than he had ever seen her before. The vicar started the service and when it came to Nancy saying her vows, she was struggling to get her words out and through nerves, started laughing. When she controlled herself, the vicar carried on and they eventually emerged, husband and wife. As they came out of church, Nancy glanced over to the hedge and watched as Jason walked away with his head hung low. They had photographs taken and went on the Foxgroves for the meal. They greeted everyone as they made their way through to the restaurant and the food was served; melon or soup for starters and chicken in garlic or beef in a red wine gravy with seasonal vegetables for the main course, then a sorbet, sweet and coffee. Then the bar.

Whilst they mulled around in the bar, the tables were cleared so more people could fit in for the night do. They started arriving at half past seven. Thomas was quite tipsy by then. Nancy had been trying to take it easy. When the disco started, they played the record that Thomas had asked for to start the dancing off, *Something's Gotta Hold of My Heart*, the Gene Pitney record they had danced to after he had proposed to her in the Lakes. They had their smooch and then the disco started. They were both mingling with everyone and didn't really talk to each other much during the night. Nancy was shocked when Jason turned up with Shaun. After she had spoken to him and said sorry that she had gone through with it and married Thomas, he gave her a peck on the cheek and didn't stay long after that. Nancy relaxed and enjoyed the night. She was getting hot in her dress and went to her room to get changed into a lovely dress she had bought, a purple, figure-hugging satin with embossed spots on, split down the back with sashes falling from the shoulders. She came back down to the ballroom to be grabbed by Thomas, who was staggering slightly, and was dragged on the dance floor. He promised he wouldn't have much more to drink when Nancy told him what she was going to do to him that night. In fact, he tried to take her to bed then but she refused, it was only ten o'clock and the night was still young.

Everyone seemed to have a good time and after eleven, people slowly started drifting off home. Nancy was still fairly sober but in the heat of the place, she decided to go outside for some fresh air. She walked around the wooded grounds, taking in the fresh but damp country air. No one else was about. It was so peaceful until she heard taxis pulling into the car park and drunk people talking loudly. The odd light flickered in the farmhouses in the distance on the hill behind and the stars shone brightly. She suddenly felt a shiver and started walking back to the hotel when she felt an arm grabbing her from behind. She tried to scream but a hand went over her mouth. Her body stiffened with fear until she heard the gentle voice of Jason. 'It's me.'

She broke free and turned around quickly. 'You frightened me to death then, you bastard!' she shouted at him with tears dripping down her face.

'I'm really sorry. I've been walking around, wondering what I can do, and then I saw you come out for a walk, I had to see you,' he said.

'But you left hours ago. Look, Jason, I made a big decision today. Right or wrong, I've married Thomas. I'm sorry, but I can't see you anymore,' she told him, near to tears from the terror she had felt for a moment and the guilt that she always felt when she was near Jason.

'Damon's mine, isn't he?' he almost shouted at her.

Her tears were coming now, in fact she was sobbing as she said over and over, 'No, No, no.'

He held her and tried to dry her tears. He wasn't stupid, she had married the wrong person, but he'd be strong and leave her to it. When she had calmed down, he went to phone a taxi and left her with the words, 'I will always love you, and I know I should have stayed around. Things would have been different.' He went.

Nancy went back into the bar and ordered a double vodka and lemonade, then another, then another, then another. People were talking to her, but she couldn't hear them, she just kept hearing Jason's words in her head over and over again. Thomas came to the bar and ordered them both a drink. In the last hour Nancy had drunk seven double vodkas and was slightly, to say the least, pissed, while Thomas had seemed to sober up slightly, although he hadn't, it was just that Nancy was more drunk than he was.

When most people had left, they staggered up to their room. Maggie and Eric were staying overnight, as were Thomas' parents and Shelly. Maggie had Damon in her room. When they got into the room, a bottle of champagne was waiting for them. Thomas opened it and poured two glasses. Nancy was tired and drunk and pulled away as he tried to kiss her. 'Just sleep for a couple of hours, please,' she asked, but as they undressed each other and got into the four-poster bed, horniness got the better of them and they made love until they fell asleep, entwined together forever, husband and wife, 'til death us do part: Mr and Mrs Bradshaw.

They got dressed and went down for breakfast. A few of the guests who had stayed over were already eating and Nancy and Thomas sat with Maggie, Eric and Damon. A bottle of champagne was opened by the waiter and they all had a little bit in their orange juice. They planned to stay at the hotel until after dinner, then go home and relax before their flight tomorrow. Maggie and Eric were leaving shortly after breakfast. Thomas had paid for the room for an extra night, so they could, if they wanted, decide to stay. When Maggie and Eric left, Nancy and Thomas went for a walk. It was a cold morning for July, as the sun was struggling to get through the clouds. They walked through the woods at the back of the hotel, saw a few squirrels scurrying about, birds were chirping happily. When they reached the edge of the woods, they noticed a path which they presumed went up to the top of the hill. Neither was dressed for hiking up a hill, which looked a couple of miles or so, houses and farms scattered about. They looked at each other and both shook their heads. They sat on the nearby fence and took in the view, hand in hand, then Thomas pulled Nancy towards him, locked his arms around her and kissed her. 'Mrs Nancy Bradshaw,' he said, grinning at her, 'Fancy going back to our room?' She smiled at him and he jumped off the fence and was almost running. She pulled him back and they walked slowly back through the woods. When they reached the edge, the hotel was nowhere in sight, they must have taken a wrong path, so back in the woods,

Nancy took the lead and they eventually got on to the hotel car park, through reception and up the stairs to their room.

When Nancy said she was going for a shower, Thomas decided to join her. He gently rubbed the shampoo through her hair and massaged her body with soap as she rinsed her hair. Her nipples were erect as his tongue and mouth played with each of them in turn and as his fingers slipped into her vagina, she reached for his penis. He stood up and kissed her as they carried on playing with each other. Thomas put his hands under Nancy's bottom and lifted her up, so she could ease his penis into her waiting wetness. She wrapped her arms around his shoulders for extra balance and lifted herself up and down in harmony with his movements, the water still belting out of the shower. They got off-balance a couple of times, which made them giggle. Thomas climbed out of the shower with Nancy still clinging on to him, both of them dripping. Thomas sat on the bed, Nancy put her legs behind him and as they moved together Thomas was nibbling, sucking and biting her nipples as Nancy was groaning with pleasure. Thomas recognised her groans and knew she would soon orgasm, so he held her buttocks up slightly and helped her by pulling them towards him, so she could get the full length of his penis. Her groans were shorter and quicker until she threw her head back with one loud groan, and as she felt the first throb of Thomas' orgasm, she held herself closely to him, so they could feel each other throbbing with passion. Thomas stood up and gently placed Nancy on the bed while he stayed on top and moved very slowly in and out of her vagina. After a few minutes, Nancy was orgasming again and really felt that she wasn't going to stop; her first multiple orgasm. She had never felt so relaxed in her life. 'That was absolutely wonderful, Mr Bradshaw, thank you,' she whispered to him.

'It was a pleasure, Mrs Bradshaw,' he replied cockily. She picked the pillow up from behind her head and whacked him with it, which made him grab her arms and pin her down as he kissed her between laughter. Nancy just glimpsed the time on Thomas' watch, it was half past six. They laughed as they wondered where the day had gone; it was almost noon when they'd got back to their room, six and a half hours of perfect sex.

They got ready to go to the restaurant for dinner. Nancy wore a strapless black velvet knee-length dress with a white satin band around the top of the bodice and pinned her hair up. Thomas wore his suit pants with a blue shirt. They both missed Damon and rang Maggie, who assured them he was fine, so they decided to stay the night, so they could both have a drink. Breakfast was served from seven o'clock so if they managed to be in the restaurant at seven, they could still get home in time for the taxi to the airport at half past eight and hopefully spend a while with Damon before they left for the airport.

Soft music was playing in the background. The waiter came over to their table in the bar with a bottle of champagne, 'With the manager's compliments,' said the waiter as he popped the cork and poured them each a glass, then went and brought the menus over. They glanced through and both decided on garlic mushrooms for starters; well, if one had garlic the other had to; and steak to follow. When their table was ready the waiter took them into the dining room. It all looked different from the day before; individual tables with flowers and lit candles on each, all flickering in time to the music and dim lights around the walls, very romantic and cosy. There were three other couples already eating as they were led to the table. By the time their main course came, the restaurant was almost full. They had another bottle of champagne and had a lovely quiet evening. They booked an alarm call at reception for six o'clock, then went up to their room just after ten and collapsed on the bed, made love and went to sleep in each other's arms.

They managed fifteen minutes with Damon before their taxi arrived to take them to the airport. They loaded the suitcases into the boot, and Maggie and Damon waved them off. Nancy was excited, she still didn't have a clue where they were going. They checked into the domestic departures. Nancy was confused, they were going to Gatwick Airport, so were they staying in London? She sulked and pulled her face all during the hour flight so when they arrived and changed terminals at Gatwick rather than get in a taxi, she cheered up a bit. Another check-in desk, this time to Antigua. She hugged Thomas so hard; he had enjoyed winding her up. She wanted to ring Maggie to tell her where they were going, but Thomas told her she already knew, it was Maggie who helped him choose the destination.

They boarded the plane for the eight-and-a-half-hour flight and sat there waiting for take-off for just over two hours, as it was delayed for some technical reason. They eventually reached the runway and the plane sped down and took off into the cloudy skies of England, the houses getting smaller and smaller as they headed higher into the skies. Soon the stewardesses came around with lunch, then drinks, more drinks and then dinner and more drinks. The flight seemed quick and they were soon landing at Antigua airport. They were taken to their apartment, where they dumped the suitcases and changed into some fresh clothes. It was 7:00 p.m. and two hours after landing, collecting suitcases and transfers that they went off to explore.

There was a restaurant and bar in the main building and the beach was practically on their doorstep. As they walked down the beach, the sun still shining although it was getting low in the sky, there were plenty of other bars and restaurants to choose from. They stopped in a bar and had a drink. They weren't hungry, but they had a look at the menu; lots of meat in strange-sounding sauces, all kinds of fish dishes and Caribbean snacks. They wandered down the beach and went in a few more bars, then got a snack. It was strange walking on sand and going in bars, but they had a good laugh. They wanted a quiet night; the long journey was getting to them now, and they just had a couple more drinks before heading back to their apartment.

During the holiday, they sunbathed, swam in the clear blue sea with a multitude of brightly coloured fish swimming around them. They had a go at waterskiing, paragliding and scuba diving, and they hired a car to explore the island in the evenings and found an array of little village bars which were a lot cheaper than the main beach bars. There were three hundred and sixty-five beaches on the island, one for every day of the year. Some were busy, some were quiet coves. One day they found a small cove and found themselves alone. They made love on the sand and both ended up covered almost head to toe with the fine grains of sand, it got everywhere. They went in the sea to wash it off and made love in the clear blue sea. A small shoal of yellow and white fish was swimming around them, and a couple kept butting their legs, which made them collapse in giggles. They spotted a jellyfish heading towards them and made a sharp exit from the water and lay on the towels in the blazing heat after they had smothered each other in sun tan lotion.

It went so quickly. Nancy rang to see how Damon was a few times during the ten days but before they knew it, they were packing to go back home and back to reality from this paradise island in the West Indies.

After their meal on the plane, they made themselves as comfortable as possible, and with Nancy's head resting on Thomas' shoulder, they both managed to sleep. The plane landed at Gatwick at 6:10 a.m. and their flight to Manchester was at 7:30. They rushed from the terminal building to the domestic departures and just managed to check in at 7:10 a.m., with the lady behind the desk pulling her face and saying check in closed ten minutes ago so she was doing them a big favour by letting them through. They giggled as they walked towards the departure lounge and were called to board the plane just as they sat down.

They arrived in Manchester, collected their baggage for the second time that day, loaded it onto a trolley and walked out of the arrivals lounge to hopefully a waiting taxi, which they had booked for 9:30 a.m. It turned up at 9:45 a.m., so they weren't waiting long.

They were both dying to see Damon's face light up when they got home, but he was still asleep when they arrived. He'd had a restless night, Maggie was saying, so she wanted to leave him as long as possible. Maggie thought he was ready for weaning onto solids; he was drinking all his milk and was wolfing down the rusks and baby rice. As soon as Nancy heard him stir an hour or so later, she shot upstairs to get him out of this cot and gave him the biggest cuddle as she brought him downstairs. He seemed a little confused as he kept rubbing his eyes; they let him come around and he was soon laughing and gurgling. Maggie had kept their house warm and they collected their things and disappeared over the road to relax for a while. They were going back to Maggie's later for tea, a good home-cooked British meal, delicious, just thinking about it was making them hungry. Thomas went to the fridge to see if there was anything in it to eat. Maggie had stocked it for them, so he made a chicken sandwich each. When Nancy put Damon down for his afternoon nap, they both went and lay on their bed and drifted off to sleep.

Chapter Twenty

Thomas had the whole weekend before he was due back at work on the Monday, and once he went back, life soon settled into a routine; cooking, cleaning, shopping, washing, feeding and yet more shopping.

It wasn't long before Nancy noticed Thomas becoming distant towards her. He wasn't cuddling her on the sofa or in bed as much. Sex was once a week if she was lucky, and she couldn't remember the last time he kissed her passionately. She didn't say anything at first; maybe he was just tired. She knew he worked hard, and he had been putting quite a bit of overtime in but after a couple of months, she'd had enough and spoke to Maggie about it. Maggie stuck up for Thomas until Nancy suggested she thought he might be having an affair. 'But you've only been married, what, four months? Impossible,' replied Maggie.

'Almost five months, and it would explain how he's been behaving and all the overtime he's put in. I don't know what to do, Mum,' cried Nancy.

Maggie put her arms around her daughter and comforted her while she went over in her mind what she should do. Maggie had been in that situation but had never told anyone and she didn't want to now, either.

'I think you should just ask him. Try and sit him down and explain your fears like you have done to me,' said Maggie eventually. They talked and talked well into the afternoon before Nancy went home, with everything she planned to say going over and over in her mind as she prepared the tea. She fed Damon while their tea was cooking, then got him into his sleep suit so he could spend half an hour with Thomas before she put him to bed. He was due home around half past six, after doing another twelve-hour shift.

He walked in and shouted he was going for a shower. Nancy's stomach was churning, and her heart was pounding. Why did she feel so scared and nervous? A tear trickled down her face. She was trying to control herself from crying more, she wasn't even going to mention anything before they had eaten. She wiped her tears away, checked her face in the mirror and tried to smile to hide the way she was feeling; it was hard. Thomas came in to the kitchen and said, 'Hi, what's cooking?'

'Mincemeat pie, roasties and veg,' Nancy replied. He walked out and went to play with Damon. Nancy could hear gurgling laughter, which actually made her smile. Thomas doted on Damon, he was a good dad. When Nancy shouted through that tea was nearly ready, he said he would take Damon to bed. She lit a candle on the table, turned the lights down low and dished tea out. Thomas came in, sat down and said, 'Have I forgotten something? Is today the day we met?'

'No,' replied Nancy, 'I just thought it would be nice.'

Thomas gave her a strange boyish look and then kissed her on the cheek. They ate almost in silence, glancing at each other every now and again. Nancy cleared the table while Thomas went into the living room and switched the television on. Nancy came through and sat next to him on the settee. She put her feet up and leant on his shoulder. His arm stayed resting on the back of the sofa. She nuzzled up to him and put her arm around his chest. His arm went around her shoulder and she snuggled up to him more. It made her feel more at ease as he started caressing her shoulder. He lifted her chin up with his other hand and kissed her gently on the lips. 'I love you,' he said.

Nancy's stomach knotted tightly and as her tears started trickling slowly down her face, Thomas kissed her passionately, with love. Nancy shuddered with all the familiar feelings that she hadn't felt for a while and the doubts she had earlier just simply disappeared. He carried her to the bedroom where he slowly undressed her, kissing and licking her body as he did, while Nancy was unbuttoning his shirt and then his trousers. They fell onto the bed and Thomas reached her stomach with his tongue, slowly, teasingly, while Nancy writhed with pleasure and when his tongue reached her clitoris, she orgasmed very quickly, he carried on licking and nibbling her lips and clit, then made his way back up to her nipples, Nancy pulled his face to hers and kissed him passionately, then rolled him over, straddled her legs over his body and rubbed her vagina teasingly over his penis. Starting at his mouth she kissed him, all over his chest, down each side, which she knew tickled him in places. As she neared his belly button, she could feel his penis, hard against her chin. She put the tip of her tongue on the end and licked around the helmet as he groaned with pleasure. Her mouth slipped down his shaft, up and down as she managed to go further and further with each thrust. His hands were holding her hair tightly as his penis slid right down her throat; his groans got louder and heavier. Another loud groan and Nancy felt the throbbing of his orgasm. She heaved as the warm thick liquid collected in the back of her throat and then she swallowed it; well, the protein is meant to be good for you. She enjoyed pleasing him that much.

They kissed and cuddled for a while, then Thomas eased her legs open and lay between them. Nancy was still very wet, and Thomas' penis was erect again. He gently pushed it in, very slowly at first and gently, lovingly. She kissed him, holding his head tightly and passionately as he thrust faster and harder, his hands digging into her buttocks, pulling her nearer and nearer to the final thrust. She bit his neck, not too hard; he liked it. She could feel they were both nearing climax; her nails scratched his back as she raised her legs, grabbed each buttock with her hands and using her stomach muscles, raised her bum so his body was thrusting in the perfect place against her clitoris. His thrusting went slower, frustratingly he kept his body against her clit and just as she was on the plateau, he moved it out so as not to push her to full orgasm. After a few minutes Thomas gave in to her frustration and kept his pubic bone rubbing hard against her clit and as he felt the throbbing of her orgasm, he relaxed just at the second he started to ejaculate. His body writhed with the most immense pleasure he thought he had ever experienced. The pulsating sensation he had when he came was the most intense feeling, then his whole body had an ecstatic sensation which started in his head and went all the way through his body to his toes. His body felt numb, like he couldn't move, yet warm and calm.

What had happened? Had he had his first ever full orgasm? He'd heard his mates talking about them. He thought he'd had one before, but never like that. *'Wow. This woman, my wife, who I adore with all my heart – what have I done? Sleeping with the new office junior from work. I don't care for her. Shit. I won't see her again. I want to tell Nancy. I've never lied to her before. No, it'd destroy her. Tell her you love her, idiot!'* He held her tightly. Tears came to his eyes, but he held them back. 'Nancy?'

'Hmm?' she replied.

'I love you so much,' he said. Nancy knew he meant it.

'Love you too,' she said as she kissed him gently, then snuggled into his chest.

Thomas lay awake, things running through his mind. Charlotte, the office junior, had made a beeline for him as soon as she met him and went out of her way to try and get him on his own, making suggestions and being very forward in letting him know she wanted him. He had finally given in to her; well, sex handed to him on a plate. Nancy had been tired a lot, what was any man going to do? Nancy's breathing soothed him as she fell into a deeper sleep, and he held her as tightly as he could without disturbing her, as though he would never let her go. He would tell Charlotte tomorrow that is was over and he didn't want to see her again. Easier said than done, but he had to do it.

She told Maggie the next day that everything was all right and she hadn't even had to ask him; all the doubts she had yesterday soon disappeared. She felt awful for even suspecting something could have been wrong. He loved her and was probably overtired with all the overtime he'd put in lately. He'd mentioned before he went to work this morning that because of some new people they had taken on, he wouldn't have to do as much, if any, once the intake of administration staff was fully trained, as it would take a lot of tedious paperwork from him. He also promised her that he would book a few days off work, so they could go away for a long weekend in a few weeks. Pleading eyes looked at Maggie, hoping she would have Damon. Maggie smirked at her and said, 'Of course, I will.' She knew that look on Nancy's face and she had to admit, she looked a lot better than she had done lately, she was glowing.

It was lunchtime before Thomas bumped into Charlotte in the canteen. She came and sat at his table. 'I need to talk to you,' he said as seriously as he could manage while he watched her smile; it gave her the most gorgeous twinkle in her blue eyes.

'Meet you in the usual place in half an hour then,' she replied as she winked at him sexily and tantalisingly put a forkful of pasta into her mouth. Could Thomas resist her young charms? Blonde hair, natural by the look of it, and her bright blue eyes. He had always loved Nancy's dark brown eyes and dark hair, they made her mysterious and sexy. He couldn't ever remember even dating a blonde before he met bubbly Charlotte. He was drawn to her character, she was a real extrovert and a flirt! Charlotte finished her lunch, winked at him and left the canteen. Another five minutes and he would be alone with her in the last office along the corridor on the second floor. No one ever seemed to use it and Charlotte found it by accident, or so she said. His stomach started to churn. This was going to be one of the hardest things he ever had to do. He knew he was falling in love with Charlotte, but he was committed to Nancy and he was deeply in love with his wife. He'd do anything for her, even die for her.

Charlotte was sat on the edge of the large board room table, her legs crossed with one foot on the chair, the split of her skirt showing a glimpse of her thigh. Her slim legs looked very sexy in black stockings! Resist, stupid. 'Charlotte, I can't see you any more, sorry,' he managed to splutter out.

She looked shocked. 'You don't mean that, you can't be serious!' she shouted. 'Tom, I love you,' she cried. He went to put his arms around her, and she pushed him away as she sobbed uncontrollably.

'I'm sorry, really I am.' He held his hand out to her, and she slapped it away.

'Go away,' she spat. 'Go on, fuck off, bastard!'

Shit, what had he done? OK, she's a bit upset, she'll get over it, he thought as he walked out of the room. He felt bad, yet it felt like a huge weight had been lifted off his shoulders. He was totally at ease all afternoon and even rang Nancy and said he would be home early, about four or five-ish. If she wanted, they could go out for tea with Damon. Maggie and Eric as well, he said; he would leave it up to her. He thankfully didn't see Charlotte for the rest of day, he would have felt really guilty.

He arrived home and Nancy looked stunning in some bronzy-coloured tight jean type trousers and a low-cut cream T-shirt. Her hair was clipped up at the back with sexy bits dangling around her beautiful face. He could have taken her to bed right then. 'Go and get showered and changed then, and put your tongue back in!' she laughed at him as he edged over, put his arms around her slender neck and kissed her. He could feel his penis getting hard and he held her hand and rubbed it against his trousers. She laughed and pushed him away. 'You can wait for that! I'm starving!' She pushed him towards the bathroom. 'Go on, get ready!'

He danced towards the bathroom, trying to be sexy. Nancy just laughed, pulled her tongue out and wiggled her hips at him.

When Nancy asked Maggie earlier if she and Eric wanted to come for a meal, Maggie said she would babysit for Damon, so they could be on their own. She knew they needed to talk and taking a baby for a meal can be difficult. Nancy had booked a table at a pizzeria in Langhall called Nico's. They had been before, but it was a long time ago. The table was booked for 7:30 p.m., so they stopped at the Wiltshire Arms for an hour as it was only six o'clock once Thomas had showered and changed and Nancy had finished her make-up. The pub was fairly busy with workmen, obviously having a pint before they went home to their families. They arrived at Nico's and sat at the bar. There were only four other people in, but it was a weekday and normally quiet. They were handed menus. Nancy ordered melon for starter and beef stroganoff; Thomas opted for garlic mushrooms and spaghetti Bolognese, and they shared garlic bread.

'Thanks for last night,' Nancy smiled at him.

He put on his beautiful boyish grin and winked at her. 'Sorry I've been distant lately. Work was getting on top of me, and I only realised last night what I'd put you through. Sorry,' he told her in his softest voice.

She held her hand on his. 'I was worried,' she replied. 'I thought you were having an affair!' She laughed. He smiled back but remained silent, just held her hand tighter. Feeling guilty, looking at this beautiful woman sat opposite him, her eyes glittering in the dim lights, he felt a frog in his throat and felt like he could have cried, but excused himself, kissing her on the cheek as he passed, still holding her hand, and went to the toilet.

The night passed quickly, and they had promised Maggie they would be home before eleven as Damon was hard work at the moment, wouldn't settle for any long period as he was teething. They asked the waiter to order them a taxi and Thomas paid the bill, it was a reasonably priced place, only £11.60. Maggie had just managed to get Damon to sleep and shushed them when they walked in. She'd had a pretty hard evening with him, and she did look tired. Thomas walked her home while Nancy made them a nightcap. She poured Thomas a whisky and water and she had a vodka with lemonade. They sat on the sofa for a while, Nancy lying on his chest. It wasn't long before she heard him gently snoring. She nudged him, he jumped and groaned. Nancy sent him to bed. She peeped in on Damon and gently stroked his cheek before she went into their bedroom, undressed, then got into bed next to Thomas and gently snuggled up to him. His arm went around her shoulder and pulled her towards him; true warmth went through her body, Thomas felt her shudder and held her tighter. They both fell asleep, huddled together.

Chapter Twenty-One

Nancy was pacing the floor, waiting for Thomas to come home from work. She'd been on tenterhooks for the last week, although not showing it to Thomas. He'd been called back to do overtime again and with Damon being extra hard work, she hadn't really seen much of Thomas to have a proper conversation. Her period hadn't come and today had been the first chance to do one of those new pregnancy kits that had been brought out recently. Although Nancy hadn't realised you had to wait seven days after your period was due before it could be ninety per cent accurate. She'd bought it the other day from the chemist and was gutted when she read the packet. She would have to wait three days. She was never late; even after having Damon, her periods went back to normal after the post-birth bleeding.

She kept looking at her watch. Half past four, then five o'clock, quarter past five. Damon was screaming. She went to him and suddenly realised she hadn't fed him since his lunch. SHIT, she felt a huge pang of guilt. She picked him up from his playpen, sat him in his high chair and gave him a rusk to nibble on while she made him something to eat. She put cauliflower florets in a pan to boil and whisked up cheese sauce. Damon couldn't get enough of it and it would do as a side dish for their tea, when he eventually turned up! She felt so angry inside, where was he when she needed him! Half past five, where the bloody hell was he! He'll be working until six, knowing him. Anything to please his bosses. He was never this late on a Friday! Damon was banging his rusk happily on his plastic tray, she turned around and smiled at him. He'd eaten over half of it, greedy little bugger, she thought. It was so difficult to be nice and kind to her child while she felt so badly inside; she was bubbling with anger. Have you ever tried smiling when you've felt that way? Your face feels so false and the imaginary string pulling the corners of your mouth into the shape they call a smile. She fed Damon his cauliflower cheese with a false sense of motherhood, then put him back in his playpen with the rest of his rusk. He needed changing but, in all honesty, she couldn't be bothered. She may as well wait until bedtime now, it was only just over an hour away.

Where the fucking hell was he? It was almost ten to seven! She poured herself a glass of vodka with just a drop of lemonade and downed it in one. She poured another, then another. *'Sort Damon out!'* she suddenly thought to herself.

She went into his bedroom, got a clean nappy, and his pyjamas, went to pick him up from his playpen and laid him down on the rug in front of the fire. '*He doesn't know he's going to bed early; what sense of time do babies have? I know they're smarter than we actually think most of the time. He would miss seeing Thomas, though. Let's see.*' She topped and tailed him, put a clean nappy on and his Babygro, trying to be as normal as possible, cuddled him for a while as she walked him to his cot. She put his dummy in and stroked his cheeks. It seemed really dark, so he soon went to sleep. He hadn't had his afternoon nap today, he'd kept himself busy.

Half past eight, over half a bottle of vodka later, she heard a car pull up. She waited in the kitchen. She hadn't made any tea for him, there was only the cauliflower cheese she had made earlier. She felt so angry, she picked the knife up used to cut the cauliflower and held it tightly in her fist. It was a small knife, but her favourite one to prepare veg, and she preferred this knife to peel potatoes rather than the peeler. She heard Thomas say, 'Hello,' when he walked in. She stayed in exactly the same position she had been a few minutes ago, leant against the sink with the knife clasped firmly in her hand.

He walked into the kitchen and went to put his arms around her from behind.

'Where the fucking hell have you been!' she shouted. The knife dropped into the sink and she turned around and started punching him in his chest; she would never have had the guts to use it.

'Nancy, calm down,' he pleaded with her as he felt every blow. He grabbed her wrists to stop her punching him. She was sobbing. 'What's wrong, love?' he tried saying to soothe her.

That made her worse. 'Where've you been?' she shouted, still trying to hit him with her fists.

'Whoa, darling, what's happened?' he was starting to get worried. 'Where's Damon?' he asked her, quite abruptly.

She managed to free her wrists and ran out of the kitchen into the bedroom and threw herself on the bed, sobbing into the pillow. Thomas went to Damon's room and sighed with relief when he saw him asleep. He crept in and stood over his cot for a while, listening to Nancy crying and wondering what the hell was the matter with her. Had she found out about his affair? He dreaded going to her. The sobbing eased eventually, and he plucked up the guts to go to her.

He sat on the edge of the bed and slowly, gently put his hand on her back and rubbed carefully. She took a big gasp in between her tired sobs. 'Nancy?' he whispered. No response, her body shuddered with every breath. 'Please, talk to me?'

'Leave me alone,' she told him.

He got off the bed, went to the kitchen and poured himself a whisky. She was pretty drunk, but what on earth could have happened that was so bad? She must have found out about Charlie, she was still on the scene. Not as often as before he'd told her it was over, but nevertheless, he was still seeing her. She wouldn't take no for an answer. He tried so hard, but he'd made sure he hadn't left Nancy out. How could she have found out? Could Charlie have spoken to her? No one else knew, they'd managed to keep it under wraps at the station. He poured himself another whisky and downed that in one as well. He'd just put another glass to his lips.

'I'm pregnant!'

Without thinking, he spat the mouthful of whisky out in shock. How long had she been there? Could she tell what he had been thinking? What did she say! Pregnant?

He turned around and faced her. Her eyes were all puffy, her mascara was smudged underneath her eyes. She still looked beautiful. He smiled at her and looked straight into her eyes for some kind of response from her. The light caught her eye which gave it an intense sparkle.

He held his arms out to her. 'Come here, darling,' he said in his beautiful dulcet tone. Nancy burst into tears again and fell into his arms. He held her for what seemed like hours, his shirt was wet through, but he held her tightly. Eventually, when his back was aching, he said 'That's wonderful, darling, I love you.'

He led her into the living room, and they sat together on the sofa and talked. Nancy was scared because she hadn't been coping with Damon lately, and he was only seven months old. Maggie had been helping her a lot, she needed it, but she felt so tired all the time. Thomas reassured her that it would be all right. She only felt tired because she was pregnant, and Damon would be sixteen months when the baby was born; it'd be company for Damon, and it could maybe make life easier for her. She had stopped crying now and had just been lying on him for the past hour, in silence, listening to his words, too tired to even open her mouth. Thomas poured them a drink and brought it into the living room; it was the first time he had felt he could even leave her for a minute.

She took the drink from his hand and sat up slightly. 'I'm sorry,' she said after she had taken a big gulp of her vodka, then put it on the table and leant back against him. The thought was going around and around in her head: she could not have this baby.

When they went to bed, Thomas tried to cuddle her, but she didn't respond. He just held her until she fell asleep, her breathing went heavier, and he felt her body more relaxed than it had been. He lay awake thinking about Damon and thought about whether Nancy would be able to cope with another baby. He knew Maggie helped a lot, but she was a good mum. Drank a bit too much, but so did he. Charlie sprang into his mind and he found he couldn't push her out. He smiled to himself, closed his eyes, held Nancy tighter and drifted off to sleep.

Nancy woke up before Damon, my God, he'd slept all night. She looked at the clock; quarter past seven. Maybe keeping him busy in the afternoon helped him sleep. She went to the bathroom and looked in the mirror. Her eyes were all puffy from her tears the night before, she splashed water on her face to wake up and try and remove the puffiness and started running a bath, with any luck she could have a peaceful bath before Damon woke.

While the bath was running, she went and made herself a cup of tea, then peeped in on Damon, who was still fast asleep, before getting in the bath. She was just rinsing her hair when she heard Damon stirring. He wasn't crying, so she left him to play in his cot. She hadn't made any bottles up the night before, she'd had too much on her mind, so hopefully, he would be happy in bed with Thomas while she made a bottle from the recently boiled kettle and cooled it down. Once she dried herself and wrapped a towel around her slim, yet pregnant body, she went in and picked Damon up. He was gurgling and smiling and when she put him on her bed next to Thomas, he pulled his hair. Thomas opened his eyes and smiled at him.

'I just need to go and make a bottle for him, are you all right for a couple of minutes?' she asked Thomas.

''Course, darling,' he replied and started tickling Damon. He screeched with laughter. Nancy went to the kitchen and scooped the milk formula into a sterilised bottle and added the boiled water, shook it and ran it under the cold tap until it was cool enough for Damon. She took it into the bedroom, and Thomas fed it to him while Nancy got dressed. Thomas suggested they went out somewhere for the day. Blackpool or St Anne's? Nancy thought about it for a while and went and checked the weather forecast. It wasn't going to rain, but did she feel like walking along the prom or the sand dunes in the cold, crisp December air and there wouldn't be much open on the front? It would clear her head with a walk, let her try.

They needed to talk. She wouldn't let him make her keep it, he could listen to her, he would listen to her.

It was quarter past ten by the time they set off for the hour's journey. They had decided to go to Blackpool and walk from the South Pier (it was always easier to park here, and it was just beyond the last of the sand dunes) right up to the North Pier, visiting some of the few open places along the Golden Mile. Damon loved all the lights on the slot machines, it kept him fascinated for ages.

All day she couldn't face talking to Thomas about the baby, bringing up the fact she didn't want to keep it. She knew Thomas wanted it so much, so she decided to keep quiet and she would talk to Maggie on Monday when Thomas was at work. They hadn't told anyone yet, anyway; at least, Thomas had promised not to mention it to anyone, not even at work. There would be a time and a place for telling people once Nancy had made up her mind and decided what SHE wanted. She had been brought up with everything she had ever wanted and that was affecting her now. She was spoilt, always had been, she thought to herself, she could be a proper bitch when she wanted. If she had an abortion, it would break Thomas' heart and she was sure they would split up. Could she risk that? Or could she live a life with two screaming kids, Thomas always at work. Why hadn't she gone back on the Pill? She was annoyed with herself, she could easily have hidden them from him.

They had a good day, walking along the prom, nipping in the handful of open amusement arcades, watching Damon's face as he was mesmerised by the lights and spending the coppers they always threw in a jar in their bedroom. It seemed exciting, winning ten two pence pieces on the "ski slide", the one where you put the penny or tuppence in the slot at the top, it falls down through metal bars and hopefully, landing on the top slide and being pushed onto the bottom one without slipping on top of the other coins there. Once they'd finished spending their winnings, they, of course, walked further back along the prom and found a family bar! Thomas only had a couple of halves of lager as he had to drive home later, but Nancy was on vodka. They left the pub, Damon still gurgling in his pram. They had sat near the slot machines which had kept him amused, even though he had been staring at them most of the day! He hadn't slept again all day, but it would ruin the night as he would probably fall asleep in the car on the way home. To try and keep him awake, they drove the scenic way, through Bamber Bridge and stopped off for something to eat at a pub there on the edge of the River Ribble. They only ordered snacks as they had eaten earlier, and it would be going dark soon. Nancy wanted to head home shortly to get Damon to bed and chill out, all the fresh air had made her tired.

Thomas undressed Damon, gave him his bottle, winded him and put him to bed while Nancy got her nightie on, then put her feet up with another glass of vodka. He'd borrowed a video from a friend at work – *Indiana Jones and the Temple of Doom* – which had just been released. Thomas topped their glasses up before he pressed "play" on the machine, and they settled down on the settee with their feet up. It was almost an hour into the film when Nancy drifted off to sleep and after midnight by the time Thomas picked her up and carried her to their bed. She stirred as he put her under the covers, and they kissed. Nancy got back up and went to the toilet and to get another drink while Thomas got undressed and climbed into bed. They cuddled for a while before Nancy drifted back to sleep.

Chapter Twenty-Two

Nancy had decided not to mention anything to Maggie. Instead, she rang Sharon and arranged to meet her in a coffee bar at dinner time that day. Luckily, she was off work; however, Nancy did wake her up from a late shift last night. She felt so relieved when she confided in her, Sharon would know what to do. She disagreed with her having an abortion. She knew how happy they were together and if he ever found out, she thought it would ruin the relationship, and it would occupy Damon more as he grew up with a brother or sister, but if she was so insistent, she would go with her. They rang directory enquiries from a phone box, and she booked an appointment for later in the week at a private clinic in Cheshire, one o'clock on Thursday for a first consultation.

They plotted a story. As far as Thomas would be concerned, Sharon rang her today asking her to go to Chester shopping for old times' sake, she was off work and would love to meet up again. Nancy would ask Maggie to have Damon for the day, and they would set off about half past nine. It was about an hour and a half drive away, so they would have a good couple of hours to have a look around before the appointment as Thomas would expect Nancy to spend a lot of money. It would be good therapy too, maybe try and get Nancy's mind buzzing and her thoughts clear before her consultation.

Thomas was pleased that Sharon had been in touch; it would be nice for Nancy to get out for the day. When she told him over dinner that night, well a takeaway actually; Nancy couldn't be bothered cooking, so they had decided on pizza. They had decided to go to Chester for the day, Sharon had been before and said it had some great shops. Damon wolfed the garlic bread down, so they always got plenty, it was just a pity about the nappies the next day! Nancy felt a pang of guilt. It brought up the other lie which hurt her every single day. She swallowed back the tears that could have started and managed a smile at Thomas as he bit a piece of garlic bread and then passed it over to her for a bite, then went and teased Damon with it by passing it near his mouth. He had opened his mouth to take a bite and Thomas whisked it away. He promptly started crying! They laughed, and Thomas gave him the piece they had both had a bite out of, which made him smile.

'Did you tell Sharon you are pregnant?' Thomas asked. Nancy pretended to be chewing more than she was and pointed her hand to her mouth. Shit, she thought, why did he do this to her? What should she tell him?

'No, I didn't,' she replied when she decided to continue lying to him. 'I might tell her Thursday, it depends. She rang me out of the blue, she might have more gossip than I have,' she laughed. That shut him up about it. She felt awful, one about lying yet again, and secondly calling her pregnancy "it".

Thursday soon came around. Nancy picked Sharon up as arranged, and they set off down the M6 to Chester. 'Are you nervous at all?' Sharon asked Nancy.

'Not at the moment, but nothing's going to happen today,' she replied. 'They do a pregnancy test. If it's positive, they examine me to find out how far gone I am, then talk to me about the risks of abortion, physically and emotionally, then we leave, and I have to decide whether or not to book another appointment within the time limit, so, no, I'm not nervous. Can we change the subject?'

They chatted about trivial things and what plans they had for Christmas for the rest of the journey, and Nancy was getting annoyed, trying to find parking near enough to the town centre, got lost a couple of times with the one-way system and eventually parked just over the bridge, about ten minutes' walk from the shops. They found a tourist information shop and bought a map of Chester, so they could find exactly where the clinic was, whether it was walking or driving distance. They found the street on the map and decided by the time they had visited all the shops on the way there, it would be shopping distance!

The shops were expensive, but what the hell, she certainly couldn't go home empty handed. She bought a dress which was seventy-five pounds and a few tops. She didn't buy any trousers or jeans as she wouldn't, of course, get into them soon. Sharon bought some jeans and a top.

When they arrived at the clinic, they were pleasantly surprised at how nice it was. It certainly didn't look like an abortion clinic, it was a converted mansion, seemed to be newly decorated and the staff were well dressed and very pleasant. The receptionist guided them to a waiting room, more like a very posh lounge with leather chesterfields, a roaring coal fire with a Christmas garland over the mantel, a large tree with blue and silver baubles and expensive-looking pictures on the walls.

A nurse came to see them and carefully explained the procedure to them and asked for Nancy's urine sample she was told to bring. She left her with some forms to fill in about herself and any health problems she may have had. She filled in the questionnaire truthfully, not that she had ever had any real health problems, only the usual childhood diseases. It went into depth about any previous pregnancies. Well, she had sailed through having Damon.

The receptionist came back in and leaving Sharon in the waiting room, took Nancy through to see a consultant, Mr Palmer-Harvey. He was very well spoken and told Nancy about himself. He did his medical training at Kings College in London and started his career in the Freeman Hospital in Newcastle as a junior doctor. This was a specialist heart hospital which was famous for training some of the best heart surgeons in the world. He then decided to continue his training in gynaecology and ended up doing private clinics here. He had looked after quite a few famous ladies; he couldn't mention any names, of course. He smiled a warm smile at Nancy and asked her to tell him about herself. She explained that she already had one son who she adored, he was only seven and a half months old and she was recently married to a wonderful man with a good career. He did start looking confused until he noticed a tear rolling down her cheek and she went on to explain how she didn't think she could cope with another baby at this moment. He listened and took everything in. They talked for what seemed like ages. He explained the dangers, he also asked if she had been to her own doctor, not about the pregnancy, but he seemed to think she may be suffering from post-natal depression, which could be treated and that may be clouding her judgement. He told her he'd had three children all within a year of each other and they were so close now they were older. Once the consultation was over, he asked if she wanted her friend with her when she had the scan. She nodded, and he buzzed through to reception. He took her along the corridor where Sharon and the receptionist were waiting outside a room. They went inside for a scan, which would measure the foetus' head to get an almost exact date of conception. From that he would give her a time limit to go away and think about what she wanted to do.

Mr Palmer-Harvey was staring at the screen. There wasn't much to see so she was, as she said, in the first trimester (up to twelve weeks). He could make out the faint flicker of the heartbeat on the screen. He looked again at her forms to find the date of her last period and the dates she had sex, so he could be as accurate as possible at this very early stage. The longest she could be if her dates were correct was six weeks, which tied in with what he saw during the scan. The embryo wasn't large enough to obtain measurements, that was normally done between twelve and fourteen weeks. She had plenty of time to make up her mind; he advised her to talk to her GP about the possibility of her having post-natal depression before she made her final decision on whether or not to keep the baby. If she decided to go through with the termination, he would like her to be in touch just after Christmas as it could take up to a week to book an appointment.

He gave her a card which just had his name and telephone number on for privacy. She paid the receptionist the fifty pounds consultation fee and left in silence. Sharon tried to interrupt her thoughts as they walked along the quiet street. She told her some of the things he had said, the post-natal depression which she had already decided to go to her own doctor about and his children, who were grown up.

They headed back to the car as it was almost three thirty and she wanted to get home to Damon. She hadn't expected it to go on that long, but she was glad. She had an awful lot to think about and talk over with Thomas and, of course, Sharon on the drive back home. They were talking so much, Nancy almost took the wrong turning onto the M6, nearly heading to Birmingham.

Nancy dropped Sharon off at home and headed to Maggie's. She pulled up to her drive and nipped across to pick Damon up. Maggie was just giving him some shepherd's pie, so Nancy put the kettle on to make a pot of tea. Maggie was asking how Sharon was and how their day had been. Nancy felt a bit guilty lying to her mum, but she would have to get used to it as it could go on for a while. Thomas came in shortly afterwards, he'd finished work at six and gathered Nancy would be over here. She made him a brew and Maggie asked if they wanted anything to eat, she'd made plenty of shepherd's pie. Thomas fed Damon the rest of his, while Maggie dished the food on to plates. Eric came into the dining room and they all sat down to eat, Damon gurgling in his high chair by the side of the table. Eric poured them all a glass of wine and they talked and ate.

It was after eight o'clock before Thomas and Nancy gathered Damon's things together and set off home. Thomas undressed Damon and put him to bed while Nancy poured them both a drink and settled down on the settee. 'I'm going to book an appointment with the doctor tomorrow,' Nancy said as he walked into the living room and sat down next to her.

'For the baby?' he replied.

She told him that Sharon thought she could be suffering from post-natal depression; she had come across it recently and from their conversations today, it seemed a possibility and it would be worth checking. It would certainly explain the way she had been feeling recently. At first, he thought it was because of him, but when Nancy explained what Sharon had told her, he realised it was common after the birth of a baby.

They talked for a while. There was a film on at ten that Thomas wanted to watch; he liked his films. Nancy normally fell asleep shortly into it, but she always enjoyed the after-effects when Thomas carried her to bed, undressed her and made love to her, although she wasn't in the mood tonight. She cuddled up to him, while the day with Mr Palmer-Harvey went around and around in her head and one of the biggest decisions in her life needed to be made, or did it? Was that not the day she married Thomas, when she still loved Jason, or lying to Jason on her wedding day about his baby? What if this baby looked totally different from Damon, would that plant a seed of doubt in Thomas' mind? Was that the real reason she didn't want it? She had three weeks to decide.

She had arranged to meet Sharon again in a couple of weeks. Sharon had promised her she would stand by her and be her alibi whatever she decided to do. They had even concocted her staying at Sharon's overnight when, and if, she decided to go ahead with the termination. Then a couple of days later she would ring Thomas at work, tell him she had started bleeding, call the doctor out, who would tell her to rest, and she would have a miscarriage. Prior to eight weeks and if her own family doctor hadn't a record of her being pregnant, they wouldn't take her into hospital for a D & C. It was good having a great friend like Sharon, especially with her nursing background. A couple of vodkas later, Nancy soon fell asleep and woke as Thomas was tucking her in. She still wasn't in the mood, so when he got into bed, she put her arm over his chest, cuddled him and fell back to sleep. Thomas felt disappointed, but he knew she was tired, so he didn't persist, especially as he had been with Charlie earlier. He soon fell asleep.

When he got to work the following day, there was a message for him to go and see the super. Shit, he thought to himself, has someone sussed him and Charlie out? He knocked on the door and walked into the office.

'Thomas, thank you for coming,' DC Patterson said. 'I'll get straight to the point – we have selected you to attend a course at headquarters in Hutton on customer and management liaison. It's for three days on the eighth of January. Obviously, you would be put up in a hotel near to the site, unless you wanted to travel every day,' he added. 'It would certainly help your career progress, as long as you're not after my job,' he laughed.

Thomas was a bit gobsmacked; he certainly wasn't expecting this, he'd thought he was in the shit. 'I'll talk to my wife tonight, if that's all right, and let you know tomorrow?' he questioned, thinking he may want a decision on the spot.

'That's fine. I'm booking a few of you lot on it, so I've more people to see to get the final numbers,' the super replied.

'Thank you, sir.' Thomas saluted him and walked out of the office. Nancy won't like that, he thought to himself, but if he went on the course, he could get promoted, more money, more status. He could persuade her it would be a good idea. '*I hope she got in at the doctor's today.*'

He had a great day, thinking about his possible promotion, about how pleased Nancy would be. It would cheer her up, he was sure. Woah, stop, until he told her it was a three-day course and he would be away for two nights. He sailed through his morning's work and during lunch in the canteen, Charlie flirted with her sexy eyes from another table. She was a sensible girl, knowing if the super found out it could lose him his job. But after lunch, she dragged him into "their office", gave him a blow job before he bonked her over the boardroom table.

Nancy wasn't in a particularly good mood when he arrived home, even though he was earlier than usual. She never had tea ready nowadays, but she never really knew when he would turn up home; sometimes he went to Charlie's after work if he didn't see her during the day. He thought it would be better not to mention the course yet. If she cheered up, he would tell her later.

'Do you want to nip out for something to eat if Maggie will have Damon for an hour?' he suggested.

'I fancy a takeaway curry,' she replied.

Thomas went for a shower and Nancy poured them both a drink. He came into the living room with a towel wrapped around his midriff. Nancy was sitting watching telly, Damon was in his night clothes, sitting on the floor playing with some toys. Thomas knelt next to him and Damon grabbed his hair, laughed and fell backwards, hitting his head on the floor. His laughter suddenly stopped and the tears started. Thomas picked him up and soothed him, bouncing him on his knee when he sat next to Nancy on the settee. They were trying not to laugh; whenever he fell, his facial expression changed so suddenly, it was amusing.

They ordered a curry once Damon had gone to bed. Nancy had seemed to have cheered up, so while they were waiting for the curry, once he'd asked how her day had been and whether she had been to the doctor's, he told her about the course at the beginning of January. He couldn't remember the dates, he would confirm them tomorrow. Nancy seemed concerned that he would be away, but inside she thought to herself, perfect timing, less lies to tell. She hoped when he got the dates, the clinic would be able to fit her in.

When Nancy met Sharon a week and a half later (she'd arranged it earlier to make sure she got an appointment when Thomas was away), she had done nothing but think about the consequences. The guilt she would have to live with, even though she was used to that, and even the prospect of him leaving her if he ever found out! Yet she had still decided to go ahead with the termination. They rang and booked an appointment. Nancy gave them the dates she could have it done, the dates of Thomas' course; that way she would only need an alibi for Maggie. Luckily, they could fit her in on the eighth of January. She had almost three weeks to make a final decision, but they told her they wouldn't mind if she changed her mind seconds before the operation, and to really think hard and carefully about it.

Sharon also tried to persuade her to keep the baby, but in her heart, she had made up her mind. The doctor had put her on antidepressants for her post-natal depression and did tell her it would be at least three weeks before she noticed any difference in herself, so she could change her mind once they had kicked in, if she wanted to. Thomas had been more attentive over the last few days, probably feeling guilty about going away. She played on it though, she could make him feel bad sometimes even though she felt like a bitch. She'd lied to him for months and cheated on him. She knew how much he loved her, yet she would twist him around her little finger when she felt like it.

It only dawned on her when she was wandering around town that she had nothing prepared for Christmas! Or Maggie's birthday, for that matter. It was their first Christmas together, so she tried to put the pregnancy out of her mind, drew some money out of the cash machine and bought some blue and silver baubles to go on a five-foot white tree; a string of multi-coloured lights and some blue and silver ceiling decorations. She bought Maggie an Estée Lauder gift set; at thirty pounds it would be both birthday and Christmas present. It had a fifty millilitre bottle of *Beautiful*, foundation, a double eyeshadow – gold and brown, and a coffee lipstick.

Laden with large bags, she was glad Maggie had Damon and her spirits lifted; in fact, she felt happy and warm from within. She unloaded the car and put the bags into the cupboard, then went across to Maggie's. It was two days before her birthday and as in tradition, she always put her decorations up on her birthday, so she had been going through what they had from last year to see if any needed replacing. Eric was bringing a tree home on his way from work. They always had a real tree; in fact, Eric had bought a small one last year with roots and planted it in the front garden just outside the front door, but it was too small yet for it to be decorated. Nancy told her what she had bought.

On the morning of the sixteenth, Nancy put her tree and decorations up in the front room. Damon sat on the rug watching her, cushions placed around him, so he wouldn't hurt himself if he fell over. He wasn't that steady and had a few bangs to his head; it was funny, the sudden change of his expression, but it wasn't nice when he cried. After lunch she took Maggie's present over and spent the afternoon helping put her decorations up.

She was finally in the mood for Christmas and they arranged to go shopping for presents the following day, mostly for Damon, although he wasn't old enough to realise what they were buying. They got him some cute Care Bears and a Cabbage Patch Doll, a couple of wooden jigsaws and some other bits.

Christmas Day quickly passed. Damon showed more interest in the boxes his toys came in until Shelley turned up with Pat and John around two. It was a good day although Nancy was glad to get home, put him to bed and go for a long soak in a candlelit bath.

New Year's Eve was spent at Nancy's with a few bottles of wine and Big Ben at midnight on the telly, and then it was soon back to the normal routine, if you could call anything normal! Just over a week to decide what she was going to do about her baby.

Thomas was feeling super guilty as he had told the super he was taking his wife with him, and they had booked into a different hotel further away, so he would drive there, but nearer to Manchester, so Nancy could relax and enjoy some shopping and being pampered in a luxury hotel. He could claim some of the money back on expenses, but he wasn't really bothered. Charlie had booked the week off work; she had got a last-minute cheap deal to Majorca. Well, that's what she told personnel. They had sunbeds in the hotel, she'd checked.

Chapter Twenty-Three

Thomas packed a holdall on Monday night, then set off at half past six on Tuesday morning to arrive at Hutton for eight-ish, depending on traffic. The course started at nine, but you were meant to be there for 8:30. Charlie would check in the hotel sometime after ten; she was taking the train and getting a taxi from the station. Thomas had given her twenty pounds, which would cover the fares; he would see her at five-ish, when the day's course had finished. He paid for the hotel on a new credit card he had applied for, through another bank account which was still registered at his mum's address, so Nancy wouldn't find out about it. He had told Charlie to pamper herself in the hotel and put it on their bill.

Nancy took Damon to Maggie's and set off to pick Sharon up. Sharon wanted the company, so she was stopping overnight, then she could have a drink without driving home and would be back around three the next day. The clinic had recommended a nice bed and breakfast place within walking distance, where Sharon would stay for the night. They parked in the clinic car park and went into reception. They were again shown into the waiting room until the consultant was ready for them. Mr Palmer-Harvey soon came through to take them to his consulting room. He explained to her the dangers again and that she could change her mind at any time prior to the actual operation. She explained to him even with the antidepressants her doctor had put her on since her last appointment, she still wanted to go ahead with it. She signed a document which he had explained to her, but she wasn't really listening.

He showed her to a changing room, where she changed into a gown. She then lay on his couch, where he gave her a pre-med injection. He took her to a small nicely decorated room where she lay in the bed until she was ready for the anaesthetic. Sharon could stay with her until she was taken to the operating theatre. Sharon asked her if she was a hundred per cent sure she wanted to go through with it. She nodded, although Sharon could see she was getting upset. She was thinking about Thomas and how upset he would be. Half an hour passed before she had the anaesthetic; this was the last point at which she could change her mind. She had around ten minutes before she would be asleep. Sharon

138

squeezed her hand and when she was wheeled off, Sharon cried for her. Nancy was such a strong person.

Charlie arrived at the hotel just after eleven, booked in as Mrs Bradshaw and took her bag to their room. It was perfect; the wardrobes and dressing room were there in the entrance, the king size bed was in the corner of the next room. There was a huge settee, a dining table and a compact kitchen for those mad bastards who would come here and cook! She unpacked the few things she had brought and went for a nosey around the hotel. She had taken a towel and her bikini and swam, sauna'ed and sunbedded to her heart's content; well, she was meant to be abroad. When she got back to their room, she ordered a sandwich from room service for a late lunch and a bottle of champagne on ice for when Thomas arrived.

She had never met anyone like Thomas. He was gorgeous; sparkling green eyes and a cheeky look permanently on his face. When she went out with her friends around town, almost every weekend, she had immature young lads trying to chat her up or older perverts gawking at her. She knew her boobs were big for her age and she had a fantastic figure. She thrived on it, but she had never met anyone who matched up to Tom. It pissed her off he was married. She'd never met Nancy but had heard about her from some of Thomas' colleagues and had seen a picture of her. She was beautiful, she couldn't deny that, but Charlie was younger, blonde, blue eyes, had no stretch marks and was hornier than Nancy was, from what Thomas told her. She had stayed on the sunbed a bit too long, was burning slightly and her chest was rather red. She ran herself a bath and poured herself a Bacardi and Coke from the minibar, got in the bath and relaxed. Thomas wouldn't be long now, she thought, and she was so excited. Spending two nights with her beautiful bloke. It was just a pity she wouldn't be with him during the day, but she would make it up with the nights!

Sharon stayed at Nancy's bedside, holding her hand when she came back from theatre. She looked so peaceful, maybe it was the right thing to do. Even though she herself disagreed with abortion, she was there for her. That was what good friends were for. It was a few hours before Nancy woke up. She was hurting, a horrible pain in her stomach. Sharon called the nurse and they gave Nancy some painkillers. It was a funny kind of pain though, she didn't have any regrets at the moment, but it was a heart-rending pain. She knew she had to lie through her teeth to get around this, and she and Sharon had concocted this story to get around it. It was a damned sight easier as Thomas was away on his course, but she hated lying to him. She loved him, but obviously not enough to keep his child and not let him think that Damon was his! They were keeping Nancy in overnight just in case of any complications, so Sharon left and went to the bed and breakfast

Nancy had paid for; she would be back early in the morning. There was a bar at the B & B and Sharon took full advantage of it. Nancy was driving home tomorrow. She got chatting to a bloke called Mark who was working in the area from a company pretty local to her. It turned out he lived only a mile or so away from her. He knew her local pub and promised he would look her up when he was back home. She thought he was gorgeous and ended up having a great night, they talked for the majority of it in the bar. Well, residents could drink all night if they wanted to! They swapped phone numbers and Sharon went to her room. This promptly started spinning when her head hit the pillow; she didn't realise she was that drunk!

She had a bit of a headache when she got up for breakfast. Mark was already seated at a table and he invited her to sit with him. She was due at the clinic around 10:00 a.m., once the doctor had been around and officially discharged Nancy. Mark was heading to work at half eight, so she had time to have a bath before she walked around to see Nancy. Mark wouldn't be home for almost a month; she couldn't wait!

When she got to the clinic, Nancy was still in pain, but according to the consultant, it was normal. He discharged her, and they drove home. Sharon tried to cheer her up, telling her about Mark, but she could sense something deeper was on her mind and she wasn't really listening. She dropped Sharon off at home, thanked her for being there and said she would ring her later, then headed to Maggie's. Maggie put the kettle on and made Nancy a chicken sandwich. They talked but Nancy seemed distant. Maggie presumed she was missing Thomas.

'He'll be home tomorrow, cheer up,' said Maggie.

'I'm OK, just a bit of period pain,' Nancy replied. She then suggested going shopping the next day, to try and get her mind off what had happened, or more to the point, what she had done.

She opened a bottle of wine when she went across the road, put Damon in his playpen and chilled, watching telly. The dull ache in her stomach felt weird; they had given her some pain killers from the clinic and for obvious reasons, she was bleeding pretty heavily. They had advised her to use towels rather than Tampax, which she preferred, as she had to watch out for any big clots of blood. If she spotted any, she had to ring her doctor straight away. She put Damon to bed just after eight and when she had finished the bottle of wine, she poured herself a vodka. Damon was fast asleep when she checked on him before she went to bed. The dull ache hadn't gone but it wasn't much worse than a bad period pain. She took a couple more painkillers before she eventually fell asleep.

She went over to Maggie's pretty early the next day. They had decided to go to Priston; it was ages since they'd been shopping there, it would certainly take Nancy's mind off the pain. She had taken four painkillers already this morning, and she could have some more at two o'clock. They parked in the multi-storey car park above the main shopping centre, put Damon in his pram and got the lift to the ground floor, to start at the bottom and work their way back up to the car. It was on three levels, with loads of different shops. Nancy was particularly looking for a small present for Thomas and she was looking for ideas; she wanted it to be something special. Three hours later, they went into a café as they were all hungry, they hadn't bought much, and Nancy still hadn't spotted anything for Thomas. They were racking their brains as they sat waiting for the food to come. Maggie was trying to think of things she had bought Eric, but didn't come up with anything super special, it was the usual socks and handkerchiefs for birthdays, and more expensive things for Christmas; a watch, shirts, suits etc.

'What about a surprise holiday or even a weekend away?' Maggie blurted out excitedly. 'It would be nice for Damon, too.'

Nancy thought about it. She would have to go behind Thomas' back and clear it with work before she could book anything, but she could invite his boss and his wife over for dinner one evening; it was ages since she had entertained anyone. She would have to get Thomas to invite his boss, otherwise it would look suspicious, and when he agreed on the holiday dates, he would invite him around the Friday before they left, and she would get his boss to leave saying, "See you in a fortnight, then". That would be a surprise.

'What a good idea!' Nancy replied with a sly grin on her face. Once they had finished their food, they set off to shop again. Nancy saw a cute cuddly teddy bear with "Missed you" in a heart around its neck. She paid extra to have it boxed and wrapped but it was worth it; it would probably end up in her collection anyway but never mind, it was the thought that counted.

Nancy was driving home the ten miles or so, when she suddenly got a very sharp pain in her stomach. It made her scream and she pulled the car over. Maggie had jumped, and Damon started crying.

'What's up?' Maggie asked. Nancy was taking deep breaths; her face was screwed up and her hands were holding her stomach.

'Please get my pain killers out of my bag, Mum?' she asked. 'I'll be OK in a minute.' She took the tablets and Maggie offered to drive the rest of the way home.

When Nancy got up off the driver's seat, that and her trousers were covered in blood. They were on a busy main road between Priston and home. Maggie went into the boot, emptied two carrier bags into others to put on both seats for the rest of the journey. They were about ten minutes from home. Nancy was praying for the tablets to work; her stomach felt like someone had stuck a knife in and was twisting it around.

'How are you feeling?' Maggie asked. Nancy was still struggling to talk. They arrived back home. Maggie took Damon in and set the bath running for Nancy, then went out to help her into the house; she was doubled up walking the short distance. Maggie was concerned, she normally never had heavy periods or pain. While Nancy was in a hot bath, Maggie nipped across to her house to get some clean clothes, then some hot water and cleaning fluid in a bucket to wash the car seat before it dried.

Maggie knocked on the bathroom door. 'Can I come in?' she shouted through; no answer. She tried the door; it was open. Nancy was lying in the bath, her eyes closed, but the bath water was very red.

'Nancy,' Maggie said, hopefully loud enough to wake her up. She opened her eyes, tears welling up.

'Mum, I was pregnant. I think I've miscarried,' she told her. Maggie could see the pain in her daughter's eyes.

'You should go to hospital, then,' Maggie replied.

'I was only in the early stages, it doesn't matter,' said Nancy.

'Did Thomas know?' Maggie asked.

'Yes, but he's on his course, there's no way of getting in touch with him at the moment. It'll be all right, he'll be home soon.' She was pretty worried herself, this was not meant to happen. She was hoping the bleeding and the pain would soon subside; the painkillers weren't working, but the bath was relaxing her. She needed to ring the clinic to see what it could be, but she couldn't do that while Maggie was there, or Damon for that matter; she needed to get home.

'Mum, can you have Damon tonight, just in case?'

Maggie nodded. Nancy emptied the bath water and refilled it while Maggie went to look after Damon, playing happily in the front room with some toys and a biscuit. Nancy sat on the loo while the bath was running, the blood was just flowing out, the pain excruciating. She had a quick wash in the bath and put three sanitary towels on when she got dressed. Maggie had brought her some old trousers and some "period knickers" around just in case of any further accidents. Maggie wouldn't let her go home until Thomas arrived; she needed someone looking after her. Six o'clock came, then seven o'clock; no sign of Thomas.

'Mum, I need to go and lie down. Thomas won't be long, I'll be fine,' she insisted. Maggie left Damon with Eric and went across the road with her, put her to bed and took her a cup of warm milk, a glass of water and more painkillers. She sat by her side until she heard a car pull onto the drive. Thomas came through the door and Maggie pulled him into the living room.

'I'm so sorry, but Nancy's miscarried today,' she told him gently. 'Do you know how far gone she was, as she may need to go to hospital? She's been insistent she doesn't need to.'

Thomas didn't answer her and rushed into the bedroom. He saw how pale Nancy looked and sat by her side. She started crying. 'I'm sorry,' she spluttered.

He stroked her face. 'Hey, come on, love, it's not your fault. Come here.' She winced in pain as she tried to sit up, so he could cuddle her. 'I should take you to hospital, love,' he said gently.

'I'll be all right, honestly. I really don't want to go,' she cried.

'Try and get some sleep then.' He kissed her forehead and told her to shout for him if she needed anything. Maggie and Thomas left the room, Thomas told Maggie she would be about ten or eleven weeks pregnant. They decided if she was still in as much pain tomorrow, they would ring the doctor to come out.

Maggie went home, asking Thomas to keep her informed no matter what time. Thomas rang the station and explained briefly to the desk sergeant what had happened and that he wouldn't be in work tomorrow, then poured himself a whisky and automatically poured Nancy a vodka. He went into the bedroom and sat on the edge of the bed. She looked very pale and her eyes were heavy, opening and closing as though she was just on the brink of falling asleep. He didn't think she was aware of him sitting there. He sat for a while just looking at her, then went into the front room to watch a bit of telly. He kept the volume as low as possible, in case he heard her calling for him, and he checked on her every half hour.

It started sinking in what had happened. They had lost a baby, a brother or sister for Damon, they would never know. He was upset but more concerned about Nancy. How would she feel when she recovered? She hadn't wanted the baby at first, so she may be glad it's happened, yet she had been getting used to the idea, so she may be upset. He would just have to wait. She seemed to be sleeping peacefully when he checked on her, so he had a few more whiskies before he climbed into bed beside her and gently put his arm around her, kissed her gently on the lips and whispered, 'I love you.' She didn't stir, her breathing seemed heavier than usual. He held her close to him without disturbing her and went to sleep himself.

He woke up and looked at the clock; ten to five. Nancy wasn't in bed, she must have gone to the loo. Five minutes passed; no noise, no toilet flushing. He got out of bed and put his dressing gown on. The bathroom door was locked so he knocked on the door. 'Nancy are you all right?' he asked, no reply. 'Nancy!' he shouted and knocked on the door. He banged the door repeatedly with his thigh until the lock snapped off.

Nancy was lying on the bathroom floor in a pool of blood. He rushed to the phone and automatically rang Maggie, who groggily came straight over. Thomas was panicking; all his first aid training went right out of his mind, he hadn't even checked if she was breathing. Maggie told him to ring an ambulance, as neither of them were fit to drive, while she tried to wake her up.

Nancy opened her eyes, Maggie saw the pain in them. She managed to sit her up onto the toilet and got her cleaned up as much as she could. She was so weak, since she had lost a lot of blood. Thomas carried her to the bedroom while Maggie cleaned the carpet in the bathroom. The ambulance was there within ten minutes. Maggie showed them where Nancy was and left them to it. Thomas had been pacing the floor in the kitchen with a glass of whisky. He offered Maggie one and she nodded.

The paramedics strapped Nancy onto a stretcher and carried her off to the ambulance. Thomas downed his whisky and went in the back of the ambulance with her. Maggie said she would lock up and go back to her house to look after Damon, as Eric would be up soon to go to work. They put an oxygen mask over her face to help her breath and took her to casualty. When they arrived after the ten-minute journey, which seemed like hours, they rushed Nancy into a room and Thomas was at reception being asked loads of questions, half of which he couldn't answer. He wasn't thinking straight, he wanted to be with his wife, but they wouldn't let him. The receptionist assured him the doctor would come and talk to him as soon as he knew anything.

What seemed like hours and a lot of shoe leather later, the doctor finally took him into the family room.

'Your wife has lost a lot of blood; she is unconscious at the moment. The next twenty-four hours are crucial,' he told Thomas. 'We're confident she will make a full recovery, but we need to do a few more tests, and you may need to prepare for the worst. The abortion could have made her sterile. She may not have any more children,' he said as gently as he could.

'Abortion?' Thomas asked. He was gobsmacked.

The doctor timidly excused himself with, 'We'll let you know as soon as you can see her,' and left Thomas in the room.

He couldn't believe it. Abortion! She wouldn't have killed his child. He sat there, oblivious to anything, and cried. He was gutted, heartbroken, how could she have done this to him? His mind was spinning. How, when, where? He'd been away on his course; she must have planned this. What should he do? At this moment in time, he hated her, but she must have had her reasons. He sobbed uncontrollably and only stopped a bit when he felt an arm around his shoulder. He couldn't even look who it was, but they were there to comfort him when he needed it. When he eventually controlled himself and wiped his eyes, the nurse told him he could go and see Nancy now. She was still unconscious, but it may help if he was by her side. He looked the nurse in the eye and shook his head. He thought for a minute, '*Can I face her, can I ever forgive her?*'

He swallowed his pride and went and sat by her bedside. Doctors and nurses were frequently there, checking on whatever they had to check on. She had numerous drips attached to her and a face mask on, feeding her oxygen. His mind wasn't with it. He was sat there looking at this woman, his wife, who looked so peaceful and content. He felt like killing her, but he couldn't, he loved her too much. Why hadn't she talked to him? So many questions needed to be answered, but how? When? And by whom? Was he in the wrong? He was thinking back. She had tried to talk to him, she had told him she didn't want this baby. Fucking hell! He was so confused, he loved this woman with all his heart, yet he was shagging an eighteen-year-old. Could she have found out about him and Charlie, is that why she had done it? SHIT, SHIT, SHIT! He leant his head on the bed, held her hand and drifted off to sleep.

He woke with a start, looked around him and wondered where he was. He had been lying against an empty bed. He panicked and ran to the nurses' station at the end of the ward, 'Where's Nancy?' he shouted.

The nurse gave him an apologetic smile. 'Sorry,' she explained. 'You were sleeping so peacefully, I didn't have the heart to wake you. Nancy's gone for a scan, she won't be long, sorry,' she replied with a sheepish grin.

'Has she woken up?' he asked.

'Not yet,' the nurse replied.

Thomas went to the phone to ring Maggie to let her know what was happening, not that he had a lot to tell her, or did he? It was half past eight in the morning. He decided to ring work instead as he didn't know what to tell Maggie. He told work Nancy was in hospital as she had miscarried, and he would let them know when he found out from the doctor, when they could expect him back in work. He had to ring Maggie, it was only fair. He told her what he knew, apart from the abortion bit. She said she would be up later when Eric got home from work.

It was a long morning. The nurses kept asking if he was all right when they came over to monitor Nancy. 'Have you talked to her? It helps, some people say they hear voices when they are unconscious, and it makes them wake up. It's never been proven, but it's worth a try. Talk about a good holiday you've had or something special that's happened to you both. I won't listen in, I promise.' She smiled sweetly, she was obviously trying to cheer him up a bit, but he didn't think anything could at this moment. What would he say to her when she did wake up? How could he talk to her about anything good that had happened when he felt this way? He didn't even know how he would feel when he saw Maggie. Could he, should he tell her the truth? He had never had feelings like this before in his life, all his emotions were causing havoc inside him. He thought about what he could talk about; the wedding, the honeymoon, Damon's birth, but everything he thought about brought tears to his eyes. Could he stay with her after she had done this? He didn't trust her. When the nurse came over again, he asked if Nancy would be all right if he went for a walk, he needed some fresh air. She nodded.

He walked through the grim corridors of the hospital and squinted in the sun when he got outside. The morning sun was bright for January. He wandered through the gardens of the hospital and sat on a bench. It was quite chilly, but he didn't care. What he would do to have Nancy here now, just to hold him, reassure him and tell him why. He put his head in his hands and cried.

Maggie arrived shortly after four o'clock; she could tell Thomas had been crying, his eyes were red and swollen. She felt sorry for him and put her arms around him. He cried on her shoulder, even though the doctor had told him Nancy was stable. He must love her so much. If only she knew.

Chapter Twenty-Four

Thomas nipped home to freshen up while Maggie was at the hospital with Nancy. She had come in Nancy's car, so Thomas wouldn't have to mess around with taxis as one of them would be there constantly while she was still officially on the critical list, even though the doctor had said she was stable.

Maggie talked to Nancy, told her what Damon had been doing: playing with the activity centre they bought him for Christmas; his laughter; how he had learnt to climb on his feet against the settee. How upset Thomas had seemed and that he would be back soon. For some reason she thought of Sammy and started recalling Nancy's younger years, most happy but some sad memories.

She had been talking for well over an hour when she noticed Nancy's eyes flicker. She held her hand tighter. 'Nancy, wake up, darling,' she said, she felt a slight squeeze of her hand. 'Nancy, open your eyes love.'

Thomas had just arrived back and put his hand on Maggie's shoulder.

'I think she's coming around. You'd better get the nurse,' Maggie smiled up at him.

The nurse came over and did her checks, while Nancy's eyes opened. 'Where am I?' she appeared confused.

'You're in hospital, love, but everything's going to be all right,' said Maggie.

When the doctor came around the following day, Nancy was a lot brighter, he asked a lot of questions. Luckily, Thomas wasn't there, he had gone home last night to Damon. He would come at visiting time as she had been moved from intensive care to a ward which had two visiting sessions – 2–4:00 p.m. and 6–8:00 p.m. From the tests and scan they had done, they had found her uterus to be punctured; all he could think about how it had happened was the surgeon slipping with the curette. They had glued it together, and she would need another scan tomorrow to make sure it was healing all right. If it was, she would be able to go home tomorrow afternoon.

When Thomas came, she told him what the doctor had said, and he could probably pick her up after work. For the two hours he was there, he hardly spoke a word, just answered her when it was needed. She had no idea he knew about the abortion, so she wondered what was wrong with him.

'Are you OK? You look tired.' He just nodded. When four o'clock came he stood up, kissed her on the cheek and went. Maggie and Eric were coming at night, so she wouldn't see Thomas again until he picked her up after two o'clock when he finished his shift, or even later if he was doing overtime.

In the morning, she went for her scan and apparently was healing nicely so she would be discharged later on.

Thomas arrived at quarter past three, Nancy packed the few things she had, and they drove home. The ten-minute journey passed in silence, as did the rest of the evening. Thomas cooked some tea, spaghetti Bolognese, which was very tasty after the bland hospital food; then he put Damon to bed. Nancy wasn't allowed to lift anything heavy for four weeks, when she had to go for another scan to make sure the cut had healed properly. Sex was out of the question, although the mood Thomas was in, she wouldn't have got any anyway. She had never known him this quiet. She tried to talk, but just got grunts and nods out of him. She went to bed just after ten.

When Thomas eventually came to bed, Nancy tried to cuddle him, and he just turned over. She left her arm around him but felt very uncomfortable. The next few days were unbearable when he was around. Luckily, he was doing plenty of overtime. She made an effort by cooking him nice meals, with Maggie's help, but she hardly got a word out of him.

Nancy had asked Maggie if Damon could stay at hers tonight, so she could talk to Thomas. She didn't go into truthful detail and Maggie didn't pry, just agreed as a brilliant grandmother does. She set the table with candles, prepared the tea as she didn't know exactly what time he would be home. The fillet steak was marinating with pepper and mustard, the veg and potatoes were all in the pan ready to be switched on when she heard his car pull up, but the minutes ticked by, then the hours. It was after ten o'clock when he eventually came home. Nancy had been crying, worried about him. When he walked through the door, it was obvious he had been to the pub; he was pretty drunk.

'You could have let me know you were going for a drink. I was worried,' she said sorrowfully.

'You could have let me know you were having an abortion!' he spat back at her.

Now she knew why he had been acting as he had been. She was a bit gobsmacked, didn't know what to say and all that came out of her mouth was, 'I'm so sorry, please forgive me,' and she went into the kitchen and poured herself a drink. The antibiotics she was on to prevent infection said she should avoid alcohol, but she needed it. She stood against the sink, looking out on the back garden and drank. Tears came to her eyes again. He was going to leave, she could sense it. How could she live without him? She loved him so much, but she knew she had broken his heart with irreparable damage. She stood there for ages, crying, sobbing silent tears, hoping he would come in and put his arms around her, tell her everything was going to be OK, but she was living in a dream world.

She got a pen and pad out, poured herself another drink, put the food in the fridge as it would have to keep 'til tomorrow and went to their bedroom. She sat in bed and pondered, pen in hand, tears dampening the paper. He wouldn't understand, whichever way she put it, but she had to try.

Darling Thomas,

For the last few years I have loved you with all my heart. I love Damon so much as well, but I really could not have had another child yet. I'm depressed, sometimes, when you are late home from work, I get so worried I cry and feel suicidal. So many times, I have stupid thoughts you are having an affair, but you always reassure me when I have any doubts. I have never understood your moods and probably never will, but please believe me when I say I love you so much.

Having another baby with Damon only sixteen-months-old, I really wouldn't have been able to cope. You're at work every day; you don't see how I struggle with him. Mum helps a lot and I know she would with two kids, but I really didn't feel ready. I tried to talk to you about it when we went to Blackpool, but you didn't take anything in, so I gave up. I know how much I've hurt and disappointed you, but it really was for the best. Maybe six months on, I'll be ready to have another baby, but I really couldn't now. I am so, so sorry, but I love you with my life.

Always, Nancy. X X X X X

Nancy went into the front room and left the piece of paper on the table in front of him. He looked, then carried on watching telly. Nancy went back to bed and waited for any kind of reaction. Nothing. He didn't even come to bed. She woke in the morning alone. Thomas had already gone to work. She went into the kitchen and put the kettle on, made herself a cup of tea and sat down in the front room and turned the telly on. It was relaxing not having Damon to look after, feeding, changing nappies and dressing, then keeping him amused. She would go to her mum's later. She rang Sharon – answerphone. She left a message for her to ring her as soon as possible. She flicked through the channels, why was telly crap in the mornings? Sharon rang back an hour or so later; they arranged to meet in town for lunch. Nancy went to get showered and when she opened the wardrobe, it looked different. She got dressed then looked again.

Thomas had cleared his clothes out. Frantically, she ran around the house, searching. The big suitcase had gone, his clothes and all his belongings. She found his wedding ring near the front door! SHIT, SHIT, SHIT!

She was hysterical. She rang Sharon, crying on the phone. Sharon came straight around. Nancy was sobbing as she tried her best to tell her what had happened. Sharon went and poured them both a drink of vodka; it might calm Nancy down a bit. She couldn't really suggest what she should do. Maybe she should ring him at work when she had calmed down and just ask to talk about it, maybe even leave it till tomorrow in case he has a change of heart. Where would he have gone? She could ring him at his mother's later, rather than at work.

When she calmed down, she rang Maggie to see if she would keep hold of Damon. She told her they had an argument last night and she wanted to try and sort it out tonight. Maggie didn't pry and agreed. Sharon said she would stay the night, unless of course he came around. They talked and reminisced about their lives, a lot of tears were shed, especially later that evening when the soppy music went on and plenty of vodka had been drunk. Nancy always made sure she had plenty of alcohol in. Her heart jumped when the phone rang; it was Maggie asking if she would say night-night to Damon. Crikey, was that the time? She spoke to him and he gurgled over the phone. He cheered her up a bit and when she came off the phone, she asked Sharon if she was hungry; they certainly hadn't eaten and there was the uncooked food left from the night before. They went into the kitchen. Sharon was staggering and nearly tripped up. Nancy laughed at her and they both started giggling. It felt good to laugh, all she had done was cry all day.

They just about managed to conjure up something that looked edible and armed with more vodka, sat in front of the telly to eat. 'Do you think I should ring him, then?' she asked between mouthfuls.

'It's up to you. I think I would.'

She thought about it while she finished her tea. She dialled his portable number, but it was switched off, so she tried his mum's number with her heart pounding. His mum answered.

'Hi, Pat, is Thomas there?'

'No,' she replied. 'Is he meant to be?'

'He said he may call around after work,' Nancy quickly lied. 'If he calls in, will you ask him to ring me before he comes home? I'd like him to pick something up for me.'

'How are you feeling?'

'Traumatised, but getting there slowly,' she replied politely. 'I'll call around one day next week and bring Damon to see you,' said Nancy, desperate to get off the phone.

'Brilliant, see you then. 'Bye,' Pat replied.

She went back in to the front room and told Sharon he must be at one of his mates. She would have to wait to see if he got in touch. What on earth would she tell Maggie? Her marriage was over before it had really started. Six months, could it be the shortest marriage in history! Eric had traditional family values, he would be devastated, and if she told them the real reason why, he would hit the roof. Maggie would probably understand; she had seen the state Nancy had been in sometimes. They tried to concoct a story which sounded plausible and came out with some right crap like Thomas realised he was gay and ran off with another bloke from work. But at least it got Nancy laughing.

Chapter Twenty-Five

A couple of months passed, and Nancy settled in to being a single parent. She went on holiday to France with Maggie and Eric. Because of his love of boats, they went on a cruiser on the canals of Normandy. They drove down to Dover and boarded the ferry across to Calais. Nancy left Damon with Maggie and went for a wander around the ferry. She stood on the top deck, as high as she could get and just gazed at the sea, hoping and praying that by a miracle, she would bump into Jason. He travelled a lot and would always go by ferry as it was the cheaper option. Where was he now? France, Austria, Germany, Holland? She cried, what she would give for him to be there with her now! He promised her the world. When she saw land, she went back to find the others after a good wander around the ferry just in case Jason was on it. Then she had a thought! She wondered if she could ask someone if he was on the passenger list. She almost ran around the ferry until she found a steward.

'Could you please tell me if there is a Jason Hampshire on board? He's a good friend of mine and I'm sure I've just seen him,' she said without even taking a breath. He could see by the pleading look in her beautiful eyes that she was dying to see him, so he took her to Robert, who was the purser on the ferry. She looked at him with her sexy look and explained. He checked the passenger list for his name, and he wasn't there. Oh, well, it was certainly worth asking. She made up her mind to write to his mother when she got home from holiday.

The holiday was beautiful and relaxing, sailing along the French canals. There were plenty of pubs and hotels along the route when they moored up each night. Damon loved helping out, holding the ropes whenever they came across a lock. But all Nancy dreamed about in a foreign country was seeing Jason, but she knew she wouldn't. She would ask on the ferry back though.

Beautifully tanned when she arrived back in England, she arranged a girlie night out with Sharon, Janet and Christina and whoever else they wanted to bring along, any friends from uni or whoever. Ten girls met in the Brewers Arms in town and went on the rampage, pretty much literally! What a scream! Twelve pubs and then Oblivion. They were all rather pissed but what a good night at the end of such a relaxing holiday! Nancy got chatted up by so many blokes; she looked stunning when she was tanned, in a miniskirt and a top that didn't leave much to the imagination. She let them buy her a drink and then walked off. What a bitch she felt, but she loved it. She wasn't after sex, as they were, but it helped boost her confidence. Her self-esteem had dropped drastically since Thomas had left. He hadn't been in touch, and she had tried her best to get him out of her mind all the time, mainly by thinking of Jason while she was away.

When the night was drawing to an end and the sloppy music came on, one of the blokes who had bought her a drink earlier came over and asked her to dance. They went on the dance floor and smooched. He wasn't bad looking, but she wasn't interested; she needed to sort her head out properly. The record finished, and she made her way back to the bar. They had all ordered double drinks as last orders had been called. She nipped to the loo and spotted a familiar face. He stood there, looking cool as fuck.

'Enjoy your dance?' he asked.

'I really need a wee, back in a minute,' she replied and shot off. Her heart was pounding, and her stomach had done a double back flip. She felt a bit sick, yet excited. When she came out of the toilet, he was sexily leant on a pillar; his sparkling blue eyes shone, more piercing than she remembered. She gazed into his eyes.

'Would you like to dance?' he asked. *Only You* by Yazoo had just started playing.

'Love to,' she replied.

He held her so close, it felt like they would never be apart again.

The song meant so much. Nancy held him tight and noticed the bloke she had been dancing with earlier standing on his own at the edge of the dance floor. She didn't care. She had found what she was looking for. He stroked her cheek and pulled her face up to his. Their lips met, the tears came. God, she had missed him so much and wanted him so badly, she could have sexually abused him there and then. He showed her so much love in return; actions always spoke louder than words.

When the record finished, she made her way back to her friends with Jason, holding hands and both of them grinning like Cheshire cats. They finished their drinks and stood outside, waiting for a taxi.

'Yours or mine?' Nancy asked with a cheeky look on her face.

'Whatever,' he replied.

'Come back to mine if you want.' The look in his eyes when she said that made him think either her husband was away, or they had split up. 'I'm glad you said that 'coz I'm staying with friends on the settee. I'm only here visiting, I go away again next week.'

Nancy looked at him with a disappointed look, and she didn't know how she would cope sleeping with a bloke in "their" bed, even though Jason was special, so special. She poured them both a drink. Jason wanted vodka, thank God he didn't want whisky! That would have been too reminiscent. She felt uneasy at first, was very nervous. Jason put some soft music on, and when she walked back in the room, he was sat, well, more half-lay on the settee. His black shirt made his blonde streaks look sexier than ever. Nancy put the wall lights on and turned the big light off, it made it more cosy.

He reached his hand out to her and she put her hand in his. He gently pulled her towards him; she knelt down on the floor in front of him and their lips met, gently at first, but soon the passion they had when they were on the dance floor came back. Nancy felt at ease now and pulled him off the settee onto the floor. They laughed. He got astride her and pinned her hands behind her head, kneeling above her. The love shining out of his eyes as he gazed at her was unbelievable. Her long hair was spread over the carpet, showing off her tanned face; eyelashes so long, brown eyes glistening with the faintest sign of tears, her high cheekbones and then she smiled at him. He leant down to kiss her, first on the lips, then her neck and pulled her skimpy top off to reveal beautiful brown boobs, she had obviously gone topless on holiday! He licked and nibbled her nipples, one after the other, again and again. With her knee and leg, she rubbed against his penis; she could feel it was already hard. God, she wanted him so much. Her hands were free, so she unbuttoned his shirt; he was pretty tanned too. She'd thought Austria was all snow; obviously not. He took it off. He made his way down her stomach, unzipped her skirt; she lifted her bum off the floor, and he pulled both her skirt and her knickers down. 'That's cheating,' she giggled, then suddenly groaned as he pushed her legs apart and buried his face in her. She couldn't reach him. 'Turn around, darling,' she groaned. She wanted his penis in her mouth, she had never given him deep throat, and she so much wanted to please him; didn't know whether she would be able to, but she wanted to try. He turned around and she unbuttoned and unzipped his trousers. His penis stood to attention and as she licked around the end, his tongue went into overdrive. He was trying to have sex with her mouth, thrusting his penis too far. It was making her heave and it wasn't pleasurable. She asked him to turn over, so she was on top, it was easier for her to control. She slowly put more and more of his penis into her mouth, slowly, tantalisingly, as he nibbled her clitoris. She eventually managed to get most of his penis into her mouth, her head was tilted back for ease of it gliding down her throat, and she played with his balls with her hands. He asked her if she was near to coming. She momentarily took his penis out of her mouth and said, 'Not so far off, love,' and put his penis back in her mouth. She soon felt a sensation through her body as he fingered her vagina and nibbled her clit. His penis was as far down her throat as she could manage and as she felt herself orgasm, she felt a throbbing down her throat. She nearly felt sick, but she knew it pleased him. He relaxed and pulled his penis out of her mouth. The semen, she swallowed it; it was manky but what the hell! He pulled her around to face him.

'I love you, I always have done,' he said.

'I know,' she replied, and they hugged, tightly. She couldn't say it back; she didn't know how she felt. She got hurt so badly by Thomas, and she knew Jason was going away again next week. She had to be cool, she couldn't give her heart to him. They went to bed, leaving all their clothes strewn over the front room floor. They made love a few times during the night, before they fell asleep in each other's arms.

Nancy woke when the telephone rang; she answered it.

'Hiya, love, it's Mum. What time are you coming over for Damon? It's just me and your dad were planning on going out this afternoon.'

'What time is it?' Nancy asked.

'Half past twelve,' Maggie replied.

'*Shit*,' she thought. 'OK, give me half an hour, please, Mum.' She looked over at Jason and felt her heartstrings tug. She kissed his cheek. He smiled, a groggy smile, turned over and kissed her tenderly on the lips. She grabbed his bum and pulled him as close to her as she could. Well, that was it, his penis grew instantly, and they were making love, neither of them needed any turning on, they were both ready. It didn't take long before they were in ecstatic heaven. God, why was it so much better when you were sober? Quicker maybe, just by an hour or so! But so beautiful.

So, thirty seconds later Nancy threw her jeans on and a T-shirt, went across the road to collect Damon. He laughed and gurgled when he saw his mum. She cuddled him and kissed his cheek. Nancy walked across the road with Damon in her arms. Shit, she thought, Jason's still here, what would Damon do? How would he react to a strange man? She put Damon into his playpen and went into the bedroom. Jason was lying there, his arms laid back above his head, a grin on his face, torso above the sheets. Nancy pulled the sheets down to his knees and sat astride him, teasing him. She felt so naughty, it turned her on. He practically ripped her jeans off. God, why was she such a turn-on? He only had to look at her to realise the answer.

With Nancy on top and pushing down on him as hard as she could, her clitoris rubbing hard against his pubic bone, she soon orgasmed. He took a little bit longer, but it felt like she was having a permanent orgasm. The bed was wet through. Fantastic.

She got up, put her jeans back on and went to make a brew. Damon was happily playing in his playpen; Maggie had given him his lunch. She took the brews into the bedroom and sat on the edge of the bed. He winked at her with a cheeky grin on his face and put his hand on her leg, moving it from her knee closer to her thigh, edging his way towards her inner thigh. She shook her head, laughing. 'Have you not had enough last night and this morning?'

'I always want more with you, love,' he replied. She smiled at him and he couldn't resist. He pulled her towards him and kissed her gently on the lips, stroking her hair lovingly. She pulled away as she was getting more and more turned on.

'Behave, Damon's only in the other room,' she laughed. 'Anyway, it's time I took you home.' He gave her a look with his beautiful eyes that said he wanted to stay. She didn't know what to do or say. He could, she supposed, but her mum would be a regular visitor and it wasn't that long since Thomas left, and of course Damon; how would he be?

Nancy went into the front room to where Damon was playing and picked him up out of his playpen. Jason got dressed and came into the room. 'Hiya, little buddy,' he said to Damon, smiling. He got a gurgle back.

Jason looked at Damon, then looked at Nancy. He thought he looked a bit like he did as a baby, the same cheeky smile and colour of hair, but Nancy had always denied it and told him he was Thomas'. Nancy smiled and went to put the kettle on again. The phone rang. Her heart jumped as it always did, just in case it could be Thomas. It was Sharon, just ringing to see if she was all right; well, being nosey, really. 'Yes, he's still here, if that's what you want to know.' The next few questions were yes and no answers; Sharon was trying to be discreet. When she came off the phone, she told Jason who it was and some of the questions she had asked, as well as how she was a good friend and had been there for her when she needed her. They spent the day relaxing and talking and decided they would go somewhere the next day. Nancy had noticed Jason was fine with Damon, but they couldn't decide where to go. What choices did they have locally? Blackpool, St Anne's or nearer to home, walking in the woods down at Salewheel? Difficult with a pram. Last time she went to Blackpool she was with Thomas, so she tried to put him off that idea.

Nancy cooked some tea for Damon; they were getting a curry later. There wasn't anything decent to watch on telly, so Nancy nipped out and got a video and some drinks. Maggie just happened to spot her going out in the car on her own, so as soon as she walked back into the house, the phone rang.

'Is Thomas back?' Maggie asked in anticipation.

Talk about being put on the spot, Nancy didn't know what to say. 'Er, no, it's an old friend who's called around to see me,' she spluttered out. 'We're just having a drink and watching a film and whatnot,' she replied.

'What film is it? I might come over, Eric is tired and is going to bed soon,' Maggie suggested.

'Mum, it's an old friend!' Nancy said again.

'All right, I get the message, I'll ring you tomorrow, love.'

Nancy gave Damon his supper and let him stay up for a while. Jason was playing with him while she went for a bath. She came out dressed just in a towel and got a look from him which meant so much to her. She picked Damon up and took him to bed. He was tired and starting to get a bit grumpy. With his mobile spinning above his head in his cot, mesmerised, he didn't even cry when she walked out of the room.

'Is it all right if I have a shower?' Jason asked.

''Course, you need one!' she laughed and rang for a curry from the Khyber Café while he was in the shower.

Damon was quiet, the curry wasn't coming for three quarters of an hour. She sat on the settee, then decided she would join him. He hadn't locked the bathroom door, luckily.

'Do you mind if I join you?' she asked.

'Hell, no,' he replied.

She let the towel drop on the bathroom floor, opened the shower door to a barrage of water spilling out on the floor. She quickly got in and his arms went around her. They kissed, water pouring on them from above. He nibbled her nipples and holding her buttocks, lifted them to be in line with his penis; typical bloke, already hard and wanting. She had no room to talk, she was wet and willing. Beautiful sex, horny, rampant and exciting. It didn't stop there; the film, what film? Once they'd eaten their curry, they ended up going to bed and making love for most of the night.

Jason stayed at Nancy's and whenever Maggie came around, he stayed in the bedroom to avoid her. Nancy had explained to him why they had split up. Jason thought Thomas was a bastard for leaving her to cope with a miscarriage on her own, yet he wondered how he would be able to deal with the pain. Nancy tended to take Damon to see Maggie to avoid her coming over to hers. The couple spent blissful days, evenings and wonderful nights together. Nancy tried to keep her feelings hidden to try and avoid it hurting too much when he left.

The phone rang at just after eight on Thursday morning. Groggily, she answered it; she hadn't had a lot of sleep, yet she knew Damon would be awake shortly. It was Thomas. 'Any chance we can talk?' he asked with a sorrowful tone. Jason was lying at the side of her but still asleep.

'Can I ring you later at work? Damon's literally just woken up,' she asked, her heart pounding with the unexpected shock. When Jason was in the shower, she rang Thomas. They arranged to meet up that night. Nancy told Jason she was meeting Sharon, and he arranged to go out with his mates and then meet up with her later.

Nancy sat at the bar in the Bull's Head where she had arranged to meet Thomas. The minutes ticked by, she waited over an hour. He didn't even turn up! She was annoyed but it was probably for the best. She rang Sharon from the pay phone to see if she could persuade her to come for a few drinks. She didn't need much and said she would be half an hour. At least she wasn't lying to Jason, and they could both go to the Alex. They got a taxi up to the Dog Inn, and between there and the Alex were two other pubs they went in. It was certainly busy for Thursday. When they arrived in the Alex, there was a disco on, it was really busy. They went and ordered drinks at the bar and Nancy spotted Jason, sitting in the corner with a couple of mates she didn't know. He introduced them as Titch and Woodsy; they were both punks with spiky hair and looked a bit frightening at first, but they were such a good laugh!

The time went quickly, and they were soon being thrown out, the landlord whingeing they were always the last to leave and they should have beds here! Jason asked Nancy if she would like to walk home or get a taxi; it was a clear night and they could walk past Sharon's and then cut through the park. That cheeky glint was in his eyes, and she smacked him on the back playfully. It would be almost three miles, they reckoned. Nancy and Sharon looked at each other and in unison said, 'Taxi!' They rang one from the phone box and sat on a nearby bench, waiting. They dropped Sharon off en route and went home. There was a note behind the door. Nancy picked it up and put it in her pocket, then she went to the kitchen and poured them both a drink. There wasn't a lot of vodka left, they had gone through three large bottles in the last four days! She quickly read the note while she was in the kitchen:

Darling Nancy

I am ever so sorry for not being there tonight; a robbery that I was called to got a bit nasty and they made me go to hospital to be checked over. Please will you give me another chance? I can't get you out of my mind. I still love you, always will do, and I will try so hard to forgive you. Please ring me tomorrow.

Love always,
Thomas XXX.

She put the note back in her pocket; she hadn't taken it in as she was a bit pissed. She would read it properly in the morning. She took the drinks into the front room. Jason, as usual, was slouched on the settee. She sat down and put his legs over her knees and leant on his shoulder. She had six more days before he left again. She was determined to make the most of it. She knew in her heart he would never settle down, even though when she was marrying Thomas, he asked her to marry him instead. He would have got itchy feet, wanting to travel all the time. He would never be happy living a family life. Maybe in a few years' time it would be a different story, but this was now. Maybe, once he had gone, she could get back with Thomas. She didn't think it would work; he would never trust her again, and love was based on trust, wasn't it? So many thoughts were going through her mind.

She didn't ring Thomas the following day, she thought she would let him stew for a bit. If she seemed too keen, it would make it easy for him. The following six days passed quickly; it was time for him to leave. Her heart wrenched with pain when he boarded the train, but she somehow managed to keep her tears back until he'd gone. He promised he would phone her and write regularly, keep her informed where he was, and she could visit him with Damon if she wanted to.

The next week passed in a blur. She felt so depressed that she went to the doctor who put her back on antidepressants, blaming the after-effects of the abortion as well as her post-natal depression. She couldn't face ringing Thomas even though she wanted to. She hit the bottle. Once Damon had gone to bed, she drank until she crawled into bed. She was letting herself go, hardly eating, wearing casual, if not old clothes, getting Maggie to do her shopping for her, which was only odd bits and vodka. Maggie soon noticed how tired she was looking and took it upon herself to ring Thomas, telling him how depressed she was and how she thought she was drinking too much. Nancy didn't know.

Just after nine o'clock one night, there was a knock on the door. She'd only had a few drinks at this stage yet with the amount of vodka she was putting in them and just a drop of lemonade, she was well on her way to being pissed. She went to answer the door in leggings and an old T-shirt. It was Thomas. She looked at him and burst into tears.

'Hey, hey love, come here.' He held her on the doorstep, and she cried on his shoulder. They edged their way into the house. Whatever he said, and he said some really nice things to her, told her how much he loved her, how he'd missed her, how beautiful she was, he just couldn't stop her tears. She eventually fell asleep in his arms on the settee. He wasn't working the next day, so he lay awake most of the night so as not to disturb her, holding her tightly.

Nancy woke up about two in the morning. She still had a drink on the table, so she finished that off. Thomas asked if they could talk. 'Tomorrow,' she replied. 'I'm going to bed. You can stop on the settee or come to bed, I'm not bothered either way.'

'I don't suppose you have any whisky?' he asked.

'Where it normally is,' she replied and staggered off to bed.

She needed him, he decided. He could stop her drinking; she was pushing herself to an early grave. He had to sort their problems out. He would have a good chat with her the next day. He went and poured himself a large glass of whisky and took it to bed, he went and looked in on Damon, fast asleep, totally oblivious to the world around him. Such a beautiful child; he didn't really look like any of them, just his own person, his own individual.

When he went back into "their" bedroom, Nancy was already snuggled up and half asleep; how he wanted to take her in his arms and make love to her, but it didn't seem right. He put his arm around her and let her fall asleep.

He left her in bed the following morning and gave Damon his breakfast. He had missed him so much, it had been nearly four months since he had seen him, heard his gurgles and his laughter. He wanted to come home. Charlie had been seeing someone else as well as him; he'd only found out the other day, so he was keeping her at a wide berth.

When Nancy got up, she went straight to the kitchen and put the kettle on. Thomas went in, put his arms around her from behind and whispered, 'I will always love you, whatever happens.' Well, that was it, the tears started again. She turned around to face him, her eyes puffy from the tears the night before.

'Do you know how much it hurt, you disappearing like you did?' she shouted. 'Never mind what you wrote, "I will try and forgive you". What about me!'

He didn't know what to say to that; it was true. Damon started crying, probably because of the shouting, Thomas went to see to him, leaving Nancy in the kitchen. He rang Maggie to see if he could take Damon over there while they talked. She agreed straight away, glad he was there. When he came back to Nancy's house, she had a glass of vodka in her hand. He took it off her and poured it down the sink, it was just after ten o'clock in the morning.

The arguing continued for about an hour. Nancy went for a bath, lay in the suds thinking. If they got back together, would it be arguments all the time, would he throw the abortion in her face every time they had a disagreement? Would it be worth it? They never used to argue, but she could sense they would and what was the point, life was too short. She'd already thought about suicide, she didn't have the guts or the courage to do it, thinking of Damon.

When she got out of the bath and got dressed, she went into the front room where Thomas was sat on the settee. She looked at him, could they really get back to what they were, NO. She would see how the day went on, not push for any arguing and see what happened. She'd lost him and Jason recently, and she didn't want to be hurt any more. Her heart was broken, she had no sense of life, didn't want to live, but the faint bit of hope she had kept her going. She didn't know what she wanted; maybe she needed to be on her own for a while. All she'd had over the last few years was Thomas and Jason, both fighting for her attention. She'd given everything she could give to both of them in her own way. She wanted to be free and live her own life. God, why was life so complicated? A song came on the radio, *torn between two lovers, feeling like a fool…* a tear slid from her eye; of course, she still loved Thomas, she married him, but he hurt her so much when he disappeared. Jason, she knew he was going, and she coped with it, supposedly. Why was she drinking so much? Why was she so heartbroken? Who had done it? Jason or Thomas? She needed a fresh start.

Through tear-sparkling eyes, she blurted out, 'I want a divorce.'

He looked at her with pleading eyes. 'We love each other, always have done, why?'

'No,' she replied. 'I don't love you anymore. I've realised over the last few months, we could never work now.'

They talked all day, cried a few times, both of them, held each other. She wanted to tell him about Jason, but she didn't, he'd been yet another secret from him, especially that he was Damon's father. There was too much deceit from both of them to carry on, even though neither of them knew. They finally decided they would give it another month apart and see how they felt after then. He would visit Damon every weekend but take him out, rather than be in the house with her.

Maggie rang as it was almost eight o'clock. Christ, the day had gone quick. 'Do you want me to have Damon overnight? Is Thomas still there?' she asked.

'Please, Mum, and yes he is,' she replied.

'Good, I hope you two are sorting things out.'

'We're trying; I'll see you tomorrow. Thanks, Mum.'

When she came off the phone, she asked Thomas if he was hungry. They had been so engrossed in the conversations of the day, they hadn't even thought about food. She went and looked in the fridge and freezer to see if she could put something together and went back into the front room with a few takeaway menus. They decided on pizza and ordered it. Nancy asked if she could have a drink now. He laughed and went and poured them both one. He felt at home, they had both shared their grievances; well, those they could, anyway, and they were getting on all right. They were comfortable together and a bit of laughter was shared throughout the rest of the evening, so when Nancy asked him to leave, he glanced at her with eyes to die for. She didn't give in until she got to the door with him.

'Thanks for being so honest with me. I will love you forever.' He leant over to kiss her and gave her the gentlest yet loving kiss she had ever had, with so much meaning.

She succumbed to him. 'You can stay if you really want to,' she whispered when they came up for air.

'You sure?' he sexily whispered back. She practically dragged him back in the house, feeling so horny she locked the door.

They walked, hand in hand and practically tongue in tongue to the bedroom. They took their own clothes off and he lay on top of her, kissing her so gently, so lovingly and meaningfully, he didn't want to do anything she didn't want him to do. They were both lying naked on the bed, he was on top of her, kissing her every second. He wanted her, he knew she wanted him, but something was stopping him. It made her more excited, the teasing, the waiting; her legs were spread, waiting for him. He heard the words he needed to hear. 'I love you so much,' she whispered to him between kisses. He put his penis into her waiting vagina and made love to her so gently, so lovingly, she was writhing with pleasure.

Chapter Twenty-Six

They settled back into normal life. Thomas moved his things back in; they were a couple again. They started planning Damon's birthday, which was a week on Monday. They couldn't have a party as such, as they didn't know any other babies his age; it would just be family and all attention on Damon, much like a normal day really. Sunday the twelfth of May, everyone turned up at Nancy's; John, Pat and Shelly, Maggie and Eric and Sharon. Damon didn't really know what was going on, but he was enjoying it! When the cake came to the table with one candle on, he was fascinated and tried to grab it. Nancy tried to show him to blow it and rather a lot of spit and bubbles came out of his mouth. He tried again, and Thomas blew the candle out. Damon burst into laughter when everyone clapped and kept saying, "Clever boy". All too soon, Damon fell asleep with all the excitement and everyone drifted away. It had been a tiring day for everyone, and they were glad when they had tidied up and slopped on the settee with large drinks.

Four months passed, Nancy's birthday soon came, and they were out for a meal, celebrating and talking about holidays, where they would like to go, in their dreams! Thomas looked into her eyes. 'Let's go to the travel agents tomorrow,' he said excitedly. She laughed at his impulsiveness. He would ring work and book two weeks off. They normally had to give a week's notice for holidays, but they schemed. He would explain his wife had booked a surprise holiday for her birthday and she had forgotten to ring work; they might be lenient, then they could book it and go straight away. On Monday morning there was normally only one member of the personnel department in first thing, as it was a busy day and they staggered the shifts, so they should be able to pull it off. They laughed and thought about who should ring, Nancy in a panic or Thomas. Nancy! They could probably pick up a bargain if they were ready to go there and then. He was like a child with a new toy, the excitement sparkling in his eyes.

She had to admit, they needed a good break; it had been hard over the last four months. To everyone on the outside, they were the perfect loving couple, but behind closed doors it was a different story. Thomas was drinking more than he used to. Admittedly, they were both big drinkers. Certainly not every night; mainly weekends and occasionally during the week. They would normally start arguing. Thomas had started hitting out, with the pain of the past in his face. Always so sorry and loving afterwards, she let it happen. She often thought she must be weird, wanting, needing the pain of him hitting her for what she had done and then to have the beautiful sex when he was so remorseful and loving. She had got pretty good at hiding the black eyes from everyone with make-up. On the worst occasions, she would have the 'flu or some other contagious illness to put off anyone coming around. It was two weeks ago since the last episode, the bruising had faded.

Nancy tried to get as excited as him about the holiday. Inside she was dreading it; holidays and drink went together. Hopefully, though, she could regain her confidence and it could be a make-or-break holiday. She played along with him. They had a good night, he was being nice, and she knew he wouldn't turn nasty tonight. Maybe he had realised what he had being doing. She looked beautiful tonight; he wouldn't be able to resist her later.

She suggested they left about an hour later; he was getting a bit drunk. They booked a taxi and went home. He was being so lovable, the excitement of the supposed holiday. Nancy got more relaxed, she was getting to know his moods. It was her fault though, she couldn't blame him for being how he was. They were in bed having sex in the spoon position, lying on the side of their legs, Nancy in front and Thomas behind, when he asked her if he could "do it" up her bum. She agreed as long as he used plenty of Vaseline. She had never done this before, and it hurt when he first put it in. He was very gentle though, and it was a weird but nice feeling. He played with her clit with his fingers while he was penetrating her. That was the nicest; she loved it, and when his fingers hit the spot, she was in ecstasy.

The following morning, she felt closer to him than she had in a long time. It had been so very intimate the night before. She was making a fried breakfast. He came into the kitchen, she turned around and kissed him with so much passion and love inside her. They ate their breakfast and Nancy rang Thomas' work.

The waterworks had to come. Tracey was one of the personnel team who was a cow. She had to really play up on the situation. She did well not to laugh, as Thomas was sitting near her, pissing himself, laughing quietly! She couldn't believe it when Tracey agreed to it; she had been very convincing though. She had learnt over the years to be a brilliant liar, she had to be! Thomas hugged her when she came off the phone, she was still crying, but laughing with it. Tracey had authorised two weeks. She went and got dressed then rang Maggie to tell her. She was a bit shocked, to say the least; she thought Nancy was expecting her to have Damon and was relieved when Nancy said they would take him, but could she have him for an hour or so while they went to the travel agent's? Armed with Thomas' credit card, they parked up and went into Thomas Cook. The lady asked a few questions, where they would like to go, for how long, how many adults, children under twelve, and when they answered each, she gave them a strange look when they said, 'Now!'

She did a search on her computer. It was a slow process but eventually she had a list of destinations. There weren't that many leaving today, and they all seemed to be Spain. They were certainly cheap enough though, most were less than half the brochure price. She looked at some more exclusive tour operators, and they came across a ten-day holiday in the Seychelles, on a beautiful island off the coast of Africa; it was going for two hundred and ninety-nine pounds per person and Damon was free! A quarter of the brochure price, they snapped her hand off. The only problem was they had to at the airport for the three o'clock flight. It was half past ten now, it would take a good twenty minutes, half an hour to sort tickets and everything out. They really needed to be at the airport for two at the absolute latest and it was forty-five minutes away if there was no traffic on the roads, which there would be. Nancy left Thomas at the travel agent to go and pack, while he sorted the tickets out. He could get a taxi back home. The lady made a few phone calls to secure the booking and the price had been reduced even further! Two hundred and eighty pounds per person, but with insurance and airport taxes and transfers when they got there, it was a total of six hundred and sixty-three, still an absolute bargain.

Luckily, Nancy was pretty straight with the washing and they could buy Damon some more clothes when they got there. She rang Maggie and she offered to come and help her pack as well as take them to the airport; she could do some bits of shopping she needed at the local Spar shop on her way back. She wondered why Nancy wasn't as excited as she was for her. Thomas came back with the tickets almost an hour later, grinning from ear to ear. Nancy was throwing anything into the suitcase; they could sort it out when they got there.

They managed to set off at just after half past twelve and got halfway up the road.

'Passports!' They went back to the house, it was a good job they had only just set off. Nancy ran in and was going through everything in her mind: passports, got them; the tickets, Thomas had them; Damon's buggy; cash? She got back in the car, waving the passports and asked Thomas if he got some currency at the travel agent. He'd got travellers' cheques, five hundred pounds' worth and they had the credit card. They were on their way! They were lucky, no roadworks and no major hold-ups, and they got to the airport at twenty to two. They checked in and went into the departure lounge. Damon was excited seeing the "big birds" arriving and departing. He was starting to talk incessantly. Sometimes they couldn't shut him up! The other passengers were amused by him, he wasn't being over-loud or annoying, but people were more patient as they waited to board their planes for their holidays.

As they walked to the plane, Nancy made Damon hold their hands, and he wanted them to swing him as he walked. He was laughing, Nancy felt a lot more relaxed, she was hoping the holiday would be great. They climbed the steep steps to board the plane and found their seats. They sat Damon next to the window, he would have to kneel up to see out though, and buckled him in. He didn't like it, so Thomas explained he could leave the belt off until the plane started moving. He looked out of the window and watched all the other people getting on. Thomas reached out for Nancy's hand and held it tightly. He was always nervous about flying and he hadn't had a drink as they were rushing. He'd never told Nancy, as she was used to all the foreign holidays she'd had as a child with her parents. It was good to get Damon used to it at such an early age.

As the plane started its engines, Thomas made Damon sit down and strapped him in again, telling him that when the light went out above his head, he could take it off. For his age he was a pretty obedient child. Nancy saw other children, similar age to him, screaming and misbehaving in the supermarket and it made her thankful. Nancy had her hand luggage packed with a couple of colouring books and crayons for him to scribble on, to keep him amused during the ten-hour-forty-minute flight. Once the plane had taken off, Thomas loosened his grip on her hand. It had made her feel a bit nervous, as she didn't know what he quite meant by it, whether it was love or excitement or nervousness! She turned her head to him. 'I never knew you were frightened of flying!' He grinned back sheepishly.

'I haven't had a drink to calm my nerves; it's the taking off and landing that scares me the most. Why do you think I always took you to the lakes?' he laughed, 'When we went on our honeymoon, I was hungover to start with and had a drink at the airport, if you remember, so it wasn't too bad.' Nancy giggled, which made Damon giggle, even though he didn't understand what they were saying. They all laughed, which made other passengers laugh. What an ice breaker! They were more than likely all going to the same resort, different hotels or apartments, maybe.

They were chatting to the couple on the seats opposite and they were staying in the same resort. They seemed quite a bit older than Nancy and Thomas. They were from Essex and it was their tenth wedding anniversary, so they were treating themselves. They introduced themselves as Ray and Judith; two children, left with grandparents. With much persuasion, they laughed. When Nancy finally got a word in edgeways, she told them who they were. That's all. Ray talked above her, so she didn't bother. '*THIS HOLIDAY WAS GOING TO BE FUN!*' she thought firmly to herself. Why had she sat on the aisle seat? Thomas leant over towards Damon and pretended to go to sleep. '*NIGHTMARE FLIGHT!*'

They broke off their conversation half an hour later when the stewardesses came around with the food. My God, they only shut their mouths when eating!

The drinks followed. Nancy ordered two double vodkas; they needed it! They were whispering ideas on how they could avoid them at the hotel. They eventually, after what felt like days, they landed in the Seychelles.

When they got off the plane, they could feel the heat; beautiful. They went into the terminal building, through the smallest passport control she had ever seen and were then escorted to a rather tatty coach. It was half an hour's drive to Fisherman's Cove where they were staying, and the rep was telling the coach party about the activities they could do. Thomas gave Nancy a cheeky look. 'She is talking about water sports!' She nudged him playfully. Damon was fast asleep on his knee; he had scribbled and slept on the plane for a while as well, but even being so young, he was probably over excited and tired himself out, little love.

They arrived at their apartments, checked in at reception and were given the keys to number sixty-four. The hotel was set in lush tropical gardens on the southern tip of Beau Vallon Beach, in a small secluded cove. The usher took their cases and showed them to their apartment. It was made of wood; the framework outside was similar to an old western movie ranch. They were in the downstairs apartment with a terrace, and as they walked in, they encountered luxury. There was a king size bed and a cot had been put next to the large bed. The bathroom was large and open plan, with a bath and a shower. They left their cases and went to explore. The sea was a gorgeous turquoise blue with scattered palm trees and plenty of sunbeds. The pool which overlooked the sea was inviting, and the restaurant was open and had amazing views over the cove.

It was an immensely relaxing holiday. They went to Victoria, the capital, which was good for bits of shopping and was only four miles away. Taxis were very cheap and, amazingly, Damon was very easy to keep entertained with his bucket and spade. The food was buffet style and very varied so there was always something they could make a meal of, and there was entertainment on most nights, which they enjoyed. Damon loved the colourful outfits the dancers wore and the music.

The days went quickly, and they had managed to avoid Ray and Judith; they seemed to have hooked up with a couple more their age, thankfully. They packed the suitcases and were taken back to the airport for the long flight home. They were all a lovely colour of golden brown, although Nancy had kept Damon covered most of the time. He got really excited when he saw the planes, especially when they started boarding, and he loved looking out the window. He fell asleep in Thomas' arms and they were soon landing back in Britain.

Chapter Twenty-Seven

The holiday had done them all a world of good. Damon struggled to get back into his night time routine as they had kept him up late in his buggy; it took almost a week before he went to sleep without crying! Thomas settled back into work, and Nancy settled into being a housewife and mum again, going shopping with Maggie, cleaning, washing, ironing. Surely, there was more to life than this? She could get herself a part time job perhaps, in a pub or nightclub, so Thomas could have Damon in the evenings. She would talk to him when he got home from work.

It was their first argument in nearly five weeks! And it ended violently. He was NOT having her working behind a bar! She took her bottle of vodka, lemonade and some frozen peas for her eye to bed until he calmed down; then he would be all sorry, with promises he would never do it again and how much he loved her. He would make love to her so gently, telling her all through how much he loved her and how he couldn't live without her. It was the first time it had happened in a while, so she would give him another chance again! The violence only came after she had the abortion, she felt the guilt and blamed herself anyway. They had talked on holiday about having another baby, but Nancy had gone back on the Pill when he had left, "just in case". He didn't know, and she'd keep on it, blaming the abortion for not being able to get pregnant. She made herself remember to take it every night as it was hidden in Damon's room, so every night when she checked on him, he was a reminder for her to lift the mattress and take her Pill. It also meant she had to have a period every month; she had been taking it constantly to avoid having them, but now they were back together she had to put up with bleeding for three or four days every month, else he may get suspicious.

He came into the bedroom about an hour later. Nancy was reading a magazine with one eye, her hands holding the peas on her other, and she ignored him until he got into bed. He stroked her cheek and started with his usual spiel; when Nancy shed the tears, so did he. He held her, and they cried together. She was shaking, it actually sometimes made him feel good – dominant and totally in control. He ended up making love to her gently and they eventually fell asleep in each other's arms.

She didn't leave the house until the swelling had gone down. She could cover the bruises, and she arranged to meet Sharon in town one day. They had a good chat about life in general, and Nancy confided in Sharon about the violence. Sharon told her about some victims she had come across in hospital and some horrendous injuries. Nancy didn't realise how common it was and at least she only got a black eye every now and again. Sharon told her she should see a counsellor, but talking to Sharon helped a lot, no one else knew. Sharon convinced her it wasn't her fault and that made her feel strong. She decided there and then that when it happened again, she would stand up to him before it got any worse. She didn't have to live her life in fear, and she had put up with it for seven or eight months.

It was a couple of weeks later when she received a phone call from a woman. 'Ask Thomas about Charlie,' was all she said and hung up.

Charlie, male or female? She rang Sharon. She was on shift but would be finished at 2:00 p.m., so she would call around after work. They decided Charlie was a woman after they rang the police station and asked to speak to Charlie and no one of that name worked there. Nancy was a bit scared though. She knew if it turned out to be a woman and that he had been having an affair, the argument would more than likely turn violent. Should she say anything? What? How? They talked about it, and Sharon suggested she casually mention it once they had gone to bed. He wouldn't hit her there, and if he was having an affair, he wouldn't hit her anyway, as it wasn't her in the wrong.

Sharon left just after five. Nancy never knew what time Thomas was going to be home; tea was always prepared and ready to switch on when he got home. If he was having an affair, it would certainly explain all the overtime he had been putting in, but she didn't know whether she wanted him to leave or not. OK, she tried to weigh up the pros first: she loved him; he was good in bed; he took her out every now and again. She couldn't think of any more at the time. The cons: he hit her; she was on tenterhooks most of the time because of his moods; he was hardly ever there; he didn't help with Damon as much as he used to; he didn't give her much housekeeping, she basically supported herself and Damon with her allowance; she didn't go out on girlie nights anymore because he always ended up hitting her. There were more: the cons outweighed the pros, but did she have the guts to tell him to leave?

The thoughts and the things Sharon had told her swam around in her mind all night, even when he arrived home. She acted as normally as possible, poured him a drink, switched tea on, took him his drink while he sat in front of the telly, 'Tea will be ready in about three quarters of an hour, if you want a bath now?' she said nicely.

'I'll have one later,' he replied. Nancy pottered between the kitchen, watching tea and the front room, where she watched a bit of telly. She dished tea out and brought it in to him on a tray and sat next to him on the settee while they ate.

Nancy ended up pretty drunk and confused. She went to bed first, checked on Damon, took her pill. Thomas went for a shower. He came into the bedroom with a towel wrapped around his waist. Nancy watched and studied him; she didn't know at this moment in time how exactly she felt for him. If she threw him out if he was having an affair, would she be bothered? Did she love him deeply like she thought she always had done? Her feelings for Jason were different; that was real love. Thomas was dependable love. When he got into bed and put his arm around her, she snuggled into his shoulder and put her arm around him. It was now or never, she thought to herself.

'Who's Charlie?' she asked him in a soft voice.

He flinched a little and said, 'Who?'

'Charlie,' Nancy said again.

He paused as though he was thinking. 'Oh, it's a new bloke at work. We've been taking the mickey out of him because he's ginger-haired. Why do you ask?' He was panicking a bit now. Nancy didn't really know what to say to that, so a minute or so went by.

'It doesn't matter,' she replied. She would ring work back up tomorrow and ask about a new bloke.

Thomas was lying awake for hours; had he convinced her with his quick thinking or not? He didn't know.

When Nancy got up, Thomas had already gone to work. She made a brew and rang his work. 'Could I speak to Charlie, please?' The operator again replied, 'I'm sorry, there's no one here of that name.' Nancy explained it was a new chap with ginger hair.

The operator put her on hold while she checked out the new staff. She came back on. 'The only person we have similar to that name is Charlotte, one of the junior office staff.' Nancy apologised and put the phone down. Junior office staff, she thought to herself. She rang Sharon and explained. They decided he was definitely having an affair, and she should pack his stuff. Nancy asked Sharon to come around later; then she didn't have to face him on her own. She could wait in the bedroom while he was there.

Nancy spent all day sorting his stuff out when there was a knock on the door. Presuming it was Sharon, she shouted, 'Come in, I'm in the bedroom.' Maggie walked in and asked what was going on. Nancy burst into tears. She had been crying on and off all day, dreading the moment when she threw him out and ended her marriage. Maggie held her while Nancy explained about his affair. She got her on her side for a change; normally, Maggie was always in favour of Thomas. She even helped her pack some stuff.

'Eric had an affair, you know!' Maggie said. Nancy was shocked as Maggie went into details. Once they had got married, and Maggie was pregnant with Nancy, Eric had had a very brief fling with a woman who worked on his stall. She soon found out and he ended it and to her, it made them stronger together. 'Could you not try that?' Maggie asked.

'No, Mum, I'm not as strong as you,' she replied.

Maggie took Damon to hers before Thomas arrived home, as no doubt there would be shouting. Sharon came around and they hit the drink. When they heard a car pull onto the drive, Sharon went into the spare bedroom and Nancy, as calm as she could be, sat on the settee watching telly. Sharon had the door ajar, so she could hear every word which was said. Thomas walked in the house and saw the suitcase and a couple of bin bags near the door.

'Planning a surprise holiday, love?' he shouted before he got into the front room.

'No, darling,' she replied as cool as a cucumber. 'It's all your belongings from my house. You're moving out.'

He walked into the front room and looked at her. 'You mean it as well, don't you?' he asked. 'What have I done? You know I love you and only you?'

Well, that said it all. She stood up off the settee and the arguing started. Sharon was listening for any signs the violence could start. 'For one, Charlie's a fucking woman, in fact a junior office member! How long have you been seeing her?' Thomas was silent. 'Come on,' Nancy shouted. 'How long?'

Nancy couldn't stop her tears and he didn't even try and approach her, all he could say was, 'Sorry.'

'Get out of my life, once and for all. I don't need you, just get out!' she screamed and sat back on the settee, sobbing as he took his stuff and put it in the car. Sharon stayed in the bedroom. Once all his stuff was packed, he came back in the front room.

'Do you not want to talk about this? We could make it work. I love you,' he said.

'No, I just want you to go, please.' He left, tail between his legs, with so much regret it hurt. How had she found out about him and Charlie? It was a best kept secret! He realised when he drove away what he had put her through over the last six months. He'd hit a woman, not any woman, but the one he loved with all his heart. What the fucking hell had he done? He drove until he was out of sight of the house they shared, her house, parked up and sobbed his heart out. He didn't know where to go. He couldn't go to Charlie's; it was because of her his life had just been ruined! He slept in the car.

Sharon came out to her as soon as he had left and hugged her. She needed the reassurance. She was sobbing but, in her heart, she felt a little bit relieved; or did she? After a few more vodkas, Sharon decided she had better stay the night as she wasn't fit to drive home. They were both pretty drunk and it was only ten o'clock! They were both hungry and decided to order a takeaway; they ordered a pizza and garlic bread to share. It would be an hour, so they had yet another drink. Nancy had been crying on and off most of the night, she wasn't sure whether she regretted what she had done or not. Every now and again, they laughed, usually at something stupid and daft, or something on telly that amused them, and some of the stories Sharon was telling Nancy about the antics of some of the junior and trainee doctors.

Their pizza arrived, and they tucked in. That soaked some of the alcohol up, so another drink. Sharon wasn't working the next day, so it didn't matter what time she went to bed. It was almost midnight when they hit the sack. It felt weird being on her own in a big bed; she would have to get used to it, she supposed. Sharon was in the spare room. Nancy cried herself to sleep quietly so as not to disturb Sharon; she had done enough tonight by being there, it was good to have such a good friend, how glad she was they had met in the Lakes. The night Thomas proposed. She cried more, remembering the early days, before she fell asleep.

Sharon woke her with a brew around ten o'clock and could immediately tell she'd been crying, with the puffiness of her eyes. 'Did you have a good sleep?' she asked.

'On and off. I dreamt about him and that woke me up in tears,' replied Nancy.

Sharon hugged her. 'Everything will work out all right, you know. I'll always be there when you need me,' she answered her as any true friend would. When Nancy got up and dressed, she suggested they go into town and do a bit of shopping. That would certainly cheer her up. She put some make-up on while she was having another brew, mainly to hide the puffiness around her eyes. She always felt a lot better once she had her face on, as most women probably did, rather like getting dressed up to go out. At the beginning of the night, she always felt fantastic and as the night wore on, most women didn't give a shit what they looked like when they were bladdered. She got her purse. Sharon was just brushing her hair, she had got ready earlier, and armed with cash and credit cards they hit the centre of Blacklodge.

As well as clothes, Nancy bought some stuff for the house; new things for a new start. She got loads of ornamental candle holders and brightly coloured candles to go in them to cheer up the front room, some large floor cushions for her bedroom and a new bed for Damon, he was getting too big for his cot even though they had taken the sides off, so it was a small version of a "big" bed. He had only fallen out twice! That would be delivered on Thursday. It would give her chance to move the cot tomorrow and clean his room properly. They loaded their shopping in the boot of the car after struggling up the car park stairs; the blooming lift was out of order again. She was sure it saw her coming, laden with shopping, and decided to pack up. Every time she had been into town over the last couple of months, the flaming lift was broken and typically they were on the fifth floor; ten flights of stairs to climb!

They laughed at each other once the boot was full. Both out of breath. 'We should start going to the gym,' Sharon laughed.

'Yeah, but sex is the best exercise. Are you working on Saturday?' Nancy asked.

'What day are we on, my brain's knackered after that climb!' Sharon answered.

'Tuesday, pension collection day, that's why there's always the zimmer frames to tackle!' They giggled.

After all that, Sharon wasn't on rota for an early on Saturday, she was on a late. Sharon suggested having a girlie night out, somewhere different. They each suggested local-ish towns; Priston, Arlington, Blackpool, Manchester! They looked at each other and smiled. 'Good idea,' they said in unison. Sharon invited some of her friends, as did Nancy. Christina and Janet would meet them in Manchester, and others would meet them near the train station in Blacklodge; well, the pub on the train station, where Nancy often visited, waiting for Thomas' arrival. They were good memories, so she didn't get upset.

As soon as they got off the train in Manchester, they found the nearest pub. Shirley, one of Janet's friends, was offering cigarettes around the group, and Nancy took one. She had smoked during her teens with Barbara, her school friend, but had given up when Eric found out. During the night they went into what must have been the smallest pub ever. It was not even six feet wide, built between two larger buildings. It really looked like it had been crushed. It was one human width that could fit behind the bar and you'd be lucky to fit two bar stools around it. You could not come in here if you were over fifteen stone! Then they hit Deansgate and went in every bar along there, working their way to the centre and the decent clubs. The Hacienda was suggested; that was an indie music club, New Order had something to do with it. The queue wasn't that big, so they waited. When they got near the front, Janet starting flirting with the doormen, and they ended up letting all nine in free. Well, if you've got it, flaunt it! What a fantastic night! The music was excellent and they danced most of the night with some really hunky blokes. Janet got chatted up first, what a surprise. Sharon was being extra flirty; they had a brilliant night. They had to ask four people for directions to the hotel they had booked into, since they seemed to be going around in circles. They came across China Town, all lit up. People sat outside the restaurants down the narrow street; how fabulous! Nancy had only ever seen it during the day, not the hustle and bustle of it at night. They wandered around the square garden with beautiful plants and trees. Other cultures certainly made you wonder about British people.

After what seemed like ages and walking for miles through various different culture areas, they found the Britannia Hotel. The night porter looked at his watch in disgust when they waltzed through the doors. They got their room keys after signing in, a lot more pissed than sober. Who gave a shit! A fantastic night, followed by hopefully a long comfy sleep.

'Breakfast is served between 7:30 and 9:30 IN THE MORNING,' he grunted at them. They said goodnight so pleasantly, yet slurring, he actually smiled as they headed to the lift. It was working; well, at twenty-four pounds each, it bloody well should be. The family rooms each had four beds in. Christina had got a taxi back to her uni room, so that meant four in each room. They were very spacious though, and who really gave a shit what they looked like as long as they had comfy beds!

Six of them managed to drag themselves downstairs before half nine for breakfast. A greasy fry-up, for some an excellent hangover cure! For some, a sick bag, running back to their room to puke their guts out at the smell of cooking oil. Nancy just had a few slices of toast with butter. She never got hangovers or headaches but could never face a cooked breakfast.

They collected their things from the room after breakfast and went around the shops, calling in at a few pubs along the way from the hotel to the train station. Well, they may as well make a day of it; well, an afternoon. Sharon was the only one not drinking, she was at work at four until one in the morning, so even though she'd be knackered later, at least she wouldn't go in smelling of booze. They got on the ten-past-two train, after downing five pints apiece and were all giddy and feeling sorry for Sharon as she had to go to work. They could tell she was thinking of ringing in sick by the look on her face!

They arrived at Blacklodge Station and went into the pub. Sharon went to the phone box near the shops about fifty yards away to ring work. She blamed her absence on being up all night with sickness and diarrhoea, the classic excuse. She got a double vodka. Well, she had to catch up with the rest of them, didn't she? They all ended up pissed as farts in a curry house, stuffing their faces with poppadoms, mango chutney and onions, onion bhajis with lots of lettuce, and then the curries. They had ordered a selection; chicken korma, madras, dopiaza and vindaloo! They shared them all. Nancy tried the vindaloo and liked it. Very hot, but very tasty! They ordered two taxis when they had finished their meal and laughed as they tried to organise who was in which taxi. They managed to sort out the easiest way around the different areas of the town they lived for the cheapest fares.

Two days on the piss. Maggie wasn't over impressed when Nancy turned up after dinner the following day for Damon. As normal, he had been as good as gold for her, so she soon softened when Nancy explained she had needed the time away from him to get herself back to as normal as possible, both for her own and Damon's sake. She stopped for a while and had a late lunch there. Well, it was almost three o'clock by the time she felt remotely hungry. Eric came into the kitchen, said his usual hello and invited Nancy out for tea with them later on. 'Thanks, Dad, are you sure you don't mind?'

'I wouldn't have asked if I had, would I, lady!' he replied. They were only nipping up to the Spread Eagle at Miller; it was fairly decent food and reasonably priced. They allowed children in till 9:30 as long as you were eating, so they booked a table for eight. Nancy left to go home just after four and bathed Damon, shoved him in a Babygro for now and went and had a shower herself.

She put some cream trousers on with a newish khaki top. Not too tight or revealing; classic style if anything. Certainly suitable for going to the Spread Eagle. She got Damon into some decent clothes and went back over to Maggie's. They set off at 7:30 for the ten-minute drive up the country lanes to Miller, a small village on top of the hill. They had to go straight into the restaurant as they had a child with them and rather than a high chair, they brought him a big cushion to sit on. They ordered drinks and then food. Eric hadn't really spoken to Nancy properly since she and Thomas had split up. He knew what had happened. Maggie kept him informed regarding what she knew, so Nancy got a barrage of questions off him. What are you going to do now? How will you manage? What about Damon without a father? She was honest with him and told him she didn't really know what to do next, she had been thinking of getting a part time job, but never got around to looking for nurseries or childminders for Damon.

They got through the rest of their meal with the odd few questions and suggestions, including divorce on the grounds of adultery or even getting back together! She told them both she would leave any decisions for a few months. Sharon had told her she would have to wait two years before she could even apply for a divorce; she was still waiting to get one from Geoff. She would tell them exactly what she was going to do when she decided.

They went home, and Nancy put Damon straight into his pyjamas and to bed. Maggie stayed with her for a couple of drinks, apologised for Eric but said he was only being a concerned parent. She went home just after eleven, knowing Eric would be already in bed. It was early morning market day on Monday, and he would be up at four. She had another couple of whiskies before she went to bed, trying not to disturb him. He stirred and put his arm around her. He wouldn't be wanting sex, would he? She wondered to herself, and she cuddled him gently to see what response she got; a snore in her ear. Oh well, there's always another night. What wonderful years she could have thrown away if she had the guts to throw him out when she found out about his affair with Nora all those years ago. Smiling to herself at the many happy years they had spent together, the ups and the downs, she drifted off to sleep in his arms.

Nancy had noticed the answerphone flashing shortly after Maggie had left and couldn't decide whether to listen to it. It could have been one of her friends from the weekend, Thomas or even Jason. She waited till she had quite a few more vodkas, then sat and listened. There were three messages, one was Sharon on Friday night. Basically saying she was sitting in the pub on her own and hurry up; the second, no message was left; and the third, Thomas, slurring his words somewhat, must have been Friday or Saturday night, begging to come and see her to talk about things. He'd finished it with Charlie even before she found out, and he still loved her and felt he couldn't live without her. What a shame, he didn't leave a contact phone number. She poured another drink, lit a cigarette and went to bed. She couldn't sleep so she read for a while.

She was feeling really horny; what she would do for a bloke to be here now. Jason or Thomas would do. She put her book down and rubbed her fingers over her nipple – how quickly it went hard – then the other. Her other hand played with her clitoris. She was amazed how soon she was very wet. Her fingers went into her vagina and bringing the juices out, rubbed hard on her clit. It really was like a mini penis, the more turned on she got, the harder it became. She squeezed it between finger and thumb; what a sensation! But it was better being rubbed with three fingers together across the area. Thomas had once bought her a dildo. Where could it be? They had only used it a couple of times; they both agreed the real thing was better. She had a quick search for it. Well-hidden at the back of her undie drawer. No batteries. She had just replaced those in the telly remote control. She felt like a naughty school child, sneaking around the house, knowing what she was going to do.

Once back in the comfort of her bed, she started again. Nipples squeezed between finger and thumb 'til they were hard, her other hand rubbing against her clit. She teased herself with the dildo, on soft vibrate at first just near the entrance, then turned it up full blast. One hand slowly in and out, the other rubbing hard on her clit, her hands moved perfectly together. Her legs were wide apart, bent at the knee; her stomach muscles pulling her hips up to enjoy the dildo, all seven inches of it; her left hand pushing it in and out while her right hand still rubbed against her clit. She could feel herself reaching orgasm. She relaxed her body as she felt herself throbbing in ecstasy but kept on rubbing her clit and pushing the vibrator in and out. Within seconds, the juices flushed out of her in big, throbbing, pulsating sensations; the full orgasm that the majority of the time women are embarrassed to do with a fella and stop themselves, so they don't think she's weed in the bed. Well, fuck that, she was on her own and she wanted to enjoy the moment. She even enjoyed lying in her wet patch! She finished her drink, lit another cigarette and wallowed in her pleasure. Who needed a man? She didn't, well not for now anyway.

She smiled as she drifted off to sleep. Her dream was vivid and sexual, featuring Thomas, Jason and a stranger. The stranger was rugged-looking, bigger built than both Thomas and Jason, stronger, forceful, powerful. When she woke in the morning, she tried her hardest to remember the stranger's face, but she couldn't. Maybe one day, if she ever bumped into him, she would know. Maybe her dream was telling her this was her perfect partner. She would probably never know.

The following few months passed pretty normally. Her friends had finished uni for the summer, and they had their regular weekends out, although they tried different places; Priston, Blackpool, Belton and Manchester, to name a few. Sometimes they would stop over in a B & B; other times they would catch the last train back to Blacklodge and carry on their night there. Nancy had got to love the Hacienda in Manchester and dressed "poser punk"; not the tartan pants with loads of zips on, but long black dresses bought from a second-hand shop, spiky hair and black eyeliner. Christina and Janet stayed normal. There was always a bunch of punks at the Hacienda from Blacklodge. Nancy got to know them; Tom, Paul, Ken, Mick, Moff, and Moggy were the regulars. They were all about the same age but seemed a lot younger than the girls.

Christina started going out with Mick. He was tall, dark spiky hair with a big white lovely, cheeky smile. She hadn't seen Shaun since she got home from uni and hadn't been in touch with him either. They started meeting up in Blacklodge. Cheaper night out for all of them. Janet drifted off; she wasn't into the music and didn't like any of the blokes. Nancy stayed because of Christina. She got on well with Paul but didn't fancy him in the slightest. He seemed too puny compared to what she was used to. She did, however, have a very brief fling with Tom, more of a one-night stand.

Then one night, Mick came on to her. Christina wasn't out that particular night, and being pissed, Nancy ended up back at Mick's house. He put the B side of a Sex Pistols record on; *I love you*. He looked at Nancy, sitting on his bed, and he went over and kissed her. His tongue went straight down her throat, which she wasn't used to but enjoyed. She felt awful because she didn't feel guilty about sleeping with her friend's boyfriend. Mick invited Nancy around the following evening. His parents were going out, so they would have the house to themselves 'til about eleven o'clock. They were just getting down to business when there was a knock on the door. Mick asked Nancy to answer it, which she complained about, but she had more clothes on than him. She grabbed a towel to hide the rest of her body, opened the door to find Christina stood there. Her face dropped.

Nancy didn't know what to do either. They stood there looking at each other, not saying anything, for what seemed like hours. Nancy was the first to break the silence when she heard Mick shout, 'Who is it?'

'Sorry,' she said to Chris. 'It just happened, last night. I didn't mean it to.'

Chris looked at her with disappointment written all over her face. 'It's OK,' she said and walked off the estate. Chris knew Nancy would have slept with him and was more pissed off that she hadn't; maybe she was being too naïve in this day and age, making the blokes wait for sex until they proved they loved her. Saying that, Nancy had hardened since her split with Thomas and had one-night stands with a couple of blokes; she felt she had been used, so she was all out to use the blokes, give them a taste of their own medicine.

The latter statement proved very much to be true over the next few months. Nancy was called a slag by the females of the species and a dick tease by the blokes. Janet never did, even though she probably had more blokes in bed than Nancy had hot dinners! Saying that, she was very attractive but wasn't a patch on Nancy. Christina knew that practically every bloke found Nancy a challenge and they did their best to try and get her. Not many succeeded, but the few who did were proud of their conquest.

Chapter Twenty-Eight

Nancy found a part time job in an MOT Centre, the boss's friend called in most days. He was a lot older than Nancy and kept asking her out, but she timidly refused each time. It wasn't long before she started to receive flowers at work from Mark. He was thirty-eight, seventeen years older than Nancy and married with three children. She didn't encourage him at all; well, not that she was aware of. He took her for lunch at least once a week. Even when she went with her colleague from work to the Pump House, he would follow her. The flowers kept arriving. She would not, could not split a marriage up. In a way, Charlie had split hers up. The first time she went out with him at night, he took her to a posh restaurant in Darwin, about five miles from Blacklodge. The menu was weird; carrot and fish soup, which Nancy tried. It wasn't that bad, but she didn't eat it all. The fillet steak with pepper sauce was very nice, though.

Mark had his own business and was by all accounts pretty loaded. He showed it most of the time, showering gifts on her. He told her he and his wife had eloped when they were both seventeen and got married without their parents' agreement. They were the best of friends and he had told Deborah about her. To Deborah, Nancy was Mark's Achilles' heel, his weak spot, he adored her. For obvious reasons it pissed Deborah off, but she had to live with it; she knew it was Mark and not Nancy, so she didn't have an argument with her. Yet it was the first time she knew that her husband had started even thinking about straying. It was six months before Mark actually left Deborah and moved into a flat above a bank in Darwin but even then, she knew Nancy had not been with her husband. Nancy was his fantasy.

Mark asked Nancy to go to Scotland with him for the weekend a week in advance, she and Damon. She said she'd let him know. He asked Deborah if he could take his youngest daughter, Marian, with them, but Deborah was reluctant. Her oldest daughter was only five years younger than Nancy. Even though he had left on good terms, it was hard for her to believe he'd gone after twenty-one years together. He had always been a dependable husband; how the fucking hell would he cope with a young, beautiful woman? A woman who could have anybody she wanted (according to him).

Deborah had only ever seen Nancy once when she first started working for Max, their friend in Blacklodge, and she hadn't taken much notice of her then.

She didn't often visit. They lived just outside Belton, nearly ten miles away, but Mark had property dealings with Max, and she was secretary for any new transactions they managed to concoct together. She wanted to see Nancy again, so when Mark and Max bought their next piece of land in Wigan and applied for planning permission to build a new shopping centre, Deborah had to go and see Max for something or other. She needed a cheque signed for solicitors' fees and couldn't get hold of Mark. She walked into the reception of the MOT Centre. The young girl with long dark hair opened the glass which separated them. 'Hello, can I help you?' Nancy asked with a smile. Deborah was stuck for words. What was she doing with an old bloke like her husband, with thinning hair and a stomach any beer drinker would be proud of? He wasn't even funny most of the time, and she really couldn't imagine Mark making love to her, maybe they hadn't done yet.

'Is Max in?' Deborah asked, returning her smile.

'Who shall I say wants to see him?' she asked pleasantly.

'Deborah Williams.' The look on Nancy's face didn't show any recognition of her. She buzzed Max, who said he would be through in two minutes. Nancy asked Deborah to take a seat as Max wouldn't be long. Deborah was dying to make conversation and try and get to know Nancy, but what would she say? Point out the weather? It just came out. 'Are you looking forward to going to Scotland next weekend?'

Nancy looked at her, quite shocked, suddenly realising who the woman was. 'I haven't decided whether to go yet,' she replied. 'I take it you are Mark's wife?'

Deborah smiled. 'It's nice to finally meet you.'

'Likewise.' The atmosphere had gone a bit tense, so Nancy was relieved when Max came and took Deborah into his office.

Nancy carried on with her job, taking messages for Max and typing customer invoices. When they emerged, Nancy gave Max his messages, smiled at Deborah and went for her lunch. She had been dreading Mark turning up. She wandered down to the sandwich shop, thinking of Deborah. She seemed a nice woman, attractive for her age, short dark red hair going slightly grey at the sides, slim, with a bit of a stomach and very well dressed.

She asked Max if she could have the following Friday and Monday off work and rang Mark to tell him she would go to Scotland. He was thrilled, and the following week seemed to drag. In fact, every moment dragged until he was with Nancy, then time seemed to fly by. Friday morning, they set off to Kirkcudbright in Mark's Mercedes, Damon strapped in the back with a colouring book and some crayons to keep him amused. She didn't know how long the journey would take as she had never been to Scotland. She felt a bit funny when they drove past the junction for the Lakes; all the times she had been with Thomas. They arrived at a little holiday camp and checked into reception. Mike had booked a huge wooden cabin, "For their comfort". It was basic but tastefully furnished. Three bedrooms, was he presuming they would sleep separately? She doubted it. They walked around the campsite for an exploration. There was a swimming pool and sauna under construction; a mini-market which sold everything, so they stocked up on alcohol for later on. They didn't buy any food as they would eat out. They went back to the chalet after walking for what seemed like miles, and Nancy unpacked the few clothes she had brought for herself and Damon. On their travels they had spotted a few country pubs, and each had a varied menu. They had three nights, so they could try them all. The restaurant at the campsite could be used for lunch, as the evening menu was pretty basic.

They showered, got ready and drove to the Hope and Anchor, a quaint pub with a welcoming real fire in the lounge bar. Everyone seemed friendly, although hard to understand with their broad accents. The food was delicious, tasted so fresh. They had coffee and liquors sitting by the fire; it had turned into quite a chilly night. Damon fell asleep with his head resting on Nancy's knee, probably from the warmth of the fire. When they left, Nancy laid Damon carefully on the back seat to try not to disturb him and they drove back to the campsite. Damon briefly woke up as Nancy was putting his pyjamas on but soon nodded back off. Mark had poured them both a drink and was sat on the settee. Nancy downed her drinks, and Mark kept them coming. She had to admit she was a bit nervous, not through lack of experience, but wondering what it would be like with an older man! She couldn't remember even kissing Mark before, and here she was, in a strange room, a different country, with a man who adored her, yet she didn't have the same feelings for him as he had for her and she would have to sleep with him.

Mark took Nancy's hand, picked up his drink and led her up the stairs to the largest bedroom. He closed the window and the curtains. Nancy sat on the bed. Should she get undressed or would he want to undress her? She didn't know. He came and sat beside her and asked if she was all right. She looked at him and nodded. He leant to kiss her gently and his arm went around her shoulder, caressing her neck and back. His kisses grew more passionate, and his hand slipped into her dress and he rubbed her breast. She started to get turned on and returned the passion in his kiss. He unzipped her dress and when they stood it slipped to the floor. He undid her bra at the back and his lips hooked onto her nipple. She moaned gently as he sucked on one, then the other. He prised her legs slightly apart and knelt in front of her. She had nothing to hold on to, and she so much wanted to open her legs as wide as she could, to feel the full pleasure of his tongue in her vagina and thrashing against her clit. He could tell she wanted more; his hands went under her buttocks and he steadied her as he spread her legs wider. He lifted her onto the bed and buried his face in her vagina, sucking hard on her clit, then thrusting his tongue into her vagina, whilst his fingers took over on her clit. Her nails dug into his head as both his fingers and his tongue stimulated her. Her moaning became louder and before she came to full orgasm, he thrust his penis inside her. He was turned on by giving her pleasure and wasn't too far off ejaculating himself. He thrust gently, then harder, and once he'd felt the throbbing of her vagina when she came, he came himself. He kissed her, said, 'Thank you,' and held her tightly. He had wanted to make love to her from the minute he had seen her behind the reception desk, that was almost nine months ago.

Nancy lit a cigarette and finished her drink. He started playing with her nipples again when she sat up; they were just at mouth level. Nancy let him carry on, she had been nicely surprised. He was a lot better than what she had expected; in fact, she absolutely loved it. Once she put her cigarette out, Mark made love to her again then they both fell asleep.

The weekend passed quickly, and they returned fully refreshed and relaxed. Max was winding Nancy up when she went into work on Tuesday because, he said, she had a very bright twinkle in her eye.

Nancy was starting work half an hour late on Friday as Eric had asked her to follow him to the garage to take his car in for servicing. She hadn't even told Maggie about Mark, thought they might disapprove because of his age. The first five minutes of the return journey were in silence; Nancy was plucking up the courage to tell Eric about Mark. 'Dad, what would you do if I said I was seeing an older man?' she asked timidly.

He unexpectedly replied, 'You're better off being an old man's sweetheart than a young man's slave!'

She started telling him about Mark and what he did. Eric seemed extremely pleased, saying he was sure he would keep her in the lifestyle she had become accustomed to.

The next evening when Mark came to pick her up, Nancy took him to Maggie's to introduce them. Mark and Eric got on extremely well and Maggie seemed to like him as well. Over dinner, Mark told Nancy he had a surprise for her. 'Let me guess?' she smiled. 'A trip to Paris?'

'How did you know?' he asked disappointedly. She could read him like a book. A couple he knew well had mentioned they were going when he had a drink with them the other night. They had suggested Mark and Nancy went along with them as they were dying to meet her. Nancy suggested they went out for a meal with them beforehand. It would soften the blow of just meeting them at the airport. Nancy could tell Mark had something else up his sleeve, but she wouldn't push to get it out of him. She was sure it would be lovely, whatever it was.

They booked a meal at the Lime Tree, just outside Manchester. At weekends, you had to book well in advance as they were always full, but as it was a Wednesday, they managed to get a table. Mark picked Sylvia and Frank up on the way and when they pulled up outside, there were BMWs, Jaguars and Mercedes parked outside a scruffy-looking café. Once they had ordered the food, she could tell why the posh cars were outside; the food was exquisite. Nancy had the best tasting fillet steak ever. Mark had smoked salmon, Sylvia also had a steak, and Frank had opted for the beef stroganoff. Frank and Sylvia were a nice, down-to-earth couple. He was head teacher at the boys' grammar school and Sylvia was a maths teacher. They had met at teaching college when they were eighteen and got married when they were twenty-one. They both got on with Nancy and they were talking about Paris, when Sylvia slipped up and mentioned they would be travelling back on their own. Mark gave her a dodgy look and nudged her leg under the table.

'I knew he had something else planned,' Nancy laughed. 'It's a good job I did find out, then I know how many clothes to take!'

They had a good laugh, Mark paid the bill and they set off. They nipped into Frank and Sylvia's for a nightcap, and Nancy had arranged with Maggie to stop at Mark's flat. It would be the first time since Scotland, and she was looking forward to it. She wasn't disappointed either, it seemed more sensual, her feelings for him were growing. She cared for him; certainly didn't and probably never would love him in the way she loved Thomas or Jason, but caring was the nearest thing.

The next day, Nancy and Maggie went shopping in Belton for some new clothes for her holiday. She spotted a beautiful red dress. It was a Frank Usher, bright-red lace dress in a sort of Charleston style, and there was a matching hat which rested on the back of her head. She put a deposit on it, saying she would pick it up later once she had been to the building society as it was three hundred and sixty pounds sixty pounds! She and Maggie went to Mark's office and Nancy told him about the dress. They had a brew with him and then went to the building society, where Nancy drew out five hundred pounds and went to collect the dress. They arrived at the shop where another woman was trying on the dress. Nancy was a bit shocked, but it turned out she was trying it on only for size, she wanted to order it in a different colour, red didn't suit her anyway. They packed the dress and put the hat in a hat box and off they went.

Nancy spent some quality time with Damon later. It was a shame, he probably got confused as to who his mum was, he spent more time with Maggie at the moment. She didn't mind, Nancy had gone through a lot recently and she was happy for her with Mark. Maggie knew it was going to be a short-lived thing, but what he was doing for her was good.

It was a four-day trip to Paris and their hotel was pretty basic, although it had a minibar which Nancy ransacked as soon as they arrived. They freshened up and met Frank and Sylvia in the bar.

Nancy had never been on a city holiday before; she was more of a sun worshipper, preferring to lie on the beach all day in the blazing sun. They wandered around the cobbled streets of the older part of town, where street artists were drawing and painting. Some were drawing caricatures of people; others, portraits and scenery. Mark asked if he could have Nancy on canvas. She fobbed him off with, 'Later on,' once they had eaten. They found a café on the edge of the River Seine with plenty of chairs outside and ordered their food while they watched the sun go down, sparkling reflections on the river. It was nice, and she knew why they called it the city of romance.

The next day, Nancy woke with toothache which got progressively worse. Sylvia and Mark went wandering and found an English-speaking dentist; however, Nancy refused to go, saying it would be all right. She didn't mention it again and put up with the pain. On the morning of the last day, Mark and Nancy got a taxi to Charles de Gaulle airport and boarded a flight to Vienna. He had booked first class, the seats were wide and comfortable, they were brought champagne and food – caviar, a thick slice of roast beef with salad and potatoes and a slice of chocolate cake. They arrived in Vienna and were taken to the Grand Hotel by taxi. The room was massive; she had stayed in similar rooms before but not as plush. As they walked in, there were mirrored wardrobes on each side of the entrance room, a huge king size bed and a raised area with a dining table laden with fresh flowers and a bottle of champagne on ice awaiting them. The view from the small balcony was of the central park.

When they went out for a walk and had their meal later on, Mark noticed Nancy playing with her food and only putting tiny pieces in her mouth at a time. She still had toothache and it had got to the stage she could hardly open her mouth. The following day, he asked at reception for the nearest dentist and took her. He paid a hundred and twenty pounds, but it was worth it. He didn't like seeing her in pain. All the dentist did was put some cleaning gauze under her gum where her wisdom tooth was pushing its way through. He tried to explain she had developed an infection as some food must have got trapped between the tooth and the gum. It took a day, but the pain started fading and she could eat properly again. He told her that evening that they were going back to London the next day, but it would take them three days to get there. 'The Orient Express!' she squealed and leant over to kiss him. She was glad she had brought all her posh frocks.

Once back in their room, Nancy showed him her appreciation. He was more of an old-fashioned lover, always missionary position, so tonight, she climbed on top of him and kissed his body from his neck down to his penis. As she slowly and teasingly slipped it in her mouth, his groans of pleasure turned her on. He didn't let her do it for long before he pulled her up to sit on his face. She loved it this way; she felt in charge and she could pleasure the bloke into biting, licking

184

or whatever the mood took her. She wanted him to bite. She pulled her lips apart, so he could get easy access to her hardening clit, and he nibbled gently at first and as she pushed herself harder on him, he bit sensually. She moved down and sat above his penis. He guided it in to her waiting vagina and sat upright. She moved herself up and down on his cock, rubbing her clit against his pubic bone whenever she was close to him. She was about to orgasm and sensing this, Mark turned her over, back to the missionary position, where he knew he could give her full pleasure and he did.

Nancy went to the hotel hairdresser in the morning and had her hair plaited from the bottom going to the top; that way it looked better with her hat on and she could pin the hat to the back of her head. She wore what she called her Dallas dress – a purple, figure-hugging satin dress with embossed spots, split down the back and sashes hanging from the shoulders. She was a bit shocked when she got to the train station. Tramps sat outside, begging, the place was scruffy, and she felt very out of place, even more so when they got to the platform. There were a lot of Chinese or Japanese people getting on the Orient Express, dressed in jeans and T-shirts! She was quite disappointed until an American couple started talking to them in their Texan drawl. All she kept saying was what a beautiful couple they made, very flattering. Mark felt so proud of Nancy. He hadn't overdressed, just had trousers and a jacket on, but he certainly wasn't underdressed! They were shown to their room, very small but exquisitely furnished. There was the settee, which doubled as a bed, and the other bed was to be pulled down from the wall. There was a tiny wardrobe and a small toilet with the tiniest sink you could imagine; a small table against the window, with a lamp. Suitcases were stored under the chair. Nancy just unpacked the clothes she would wear on the train. Even when she dressed for dinner, she didn't know what to expect. Would the Chinese/Japanese people still be in jeans, children running around everywhere? The trip for her and Mark cost around two thousand pounds, although he wouldn't give her the exact price. The Orientals must be loaded, why couldn't they have got a normal train? It was the only thing that was disappointing about the trip.

The food was excellent, they had soup or melon to start, then monkfish with salad and sautéed potatoes, followed by a selection of sweets. They went to sit in the lounge after the meal, where the grand piano sat at one end of the carriage. Waiters were coming around offering drinks. Wine and liquors were free after the meal, any other drinks had to be paid for. They were talking to the American couple they had met at the station; he was an oil baron in Texas, and they were touring Europe for their twenty-fifth wedding anniversary, for two months.

When they went back to their cabin, the movement of the train was perfect to make love to, very cramped but wonderful and exciting. The scenery they sped past was wonderful. They had to change driver carriages at every border, and they stopped in Salzburg, Austria. Nancy made her excuses and went for a wander, just in case she saw Jason. This was the last place she knew he was. She had an hour or so, and she just wandered the streets, hoping, praying for a glimpse of him. She didn't know how big Salzburg was, and started panicking a bit when she realised an hour had passed. She had to ask directions back to the station, and Mark was standing on the platform, worried sick. She apologised, saying she had lost track of time looking around the shops. He was angry, the train was going to leave her behind, and he had had to persuade the guard to wait, they weren't impressed. They boarded the train and Nancy was silent; Mark could tell she had something on her mind, and when he questioned her about it, she told him she had come on her period. She didn't have any Tampax and had to go and ask the young concierge who looked after their cabin; what an embarrassment! It was true, she had forgotten to bring another packet of pills, not knowing how long they would be away.

'I presume you cleared it with Max that I would be away for so long?' she suddenly asked Mark.

'Of course, love,' he replied. His voice had softened now. There was something really bothering her; it wasn't her period, there was something he just couldn't put his finger on.

They travelled through Germany and Nancy gazed out of the window for the majority of the journey. How much he wanted to hold her and reassure her, but not knowing what was wrong, how could he? How he loved this woman. He knew she didn't love him, but she gave him everything she had the heart to give. He couldn't ask for any more; well, he could and how often had he thought about asking her to marry him? She wasn't divorced, neither was he. He didn't think Deborah would ever divorce him. He would see how she was later.

She was quiet over the meal and he decided to ask her. 'I know there is something bothering you, would you like to confide in a friend?' was the best way he thought to ask her. He noticed her eyes welling up with tears. She tried her best to hold them back and managed to, just about, a couple of tears rolled down her cheeks. Mark could see the hurt she was feeling and wanted to hold her tightly. What would life be like if she could love him? What a perfect partnership they would have! He held her tightly that night, cramped on the one bed. During the night he woke a few times to her sobs, his chest hair wet from her tears. How he wished he could take all the pain she was feeling away. If only things were that simple. He knew it was nothing he'd done, so he was just there for her.

They arrived back in Paris and had a couple of hours there. All the oriental people got off the train and other passengers got on. Their next stop was London, so most of the passengers were British. She wore her red dress and hat and looked like a film star, and she didn't feel at all overdressed. The Brits with their stiff upper lips, politely nodding to other passengers. She was probably the youngest person on board the train now and according to Mark, the most beautiful! She seemed to have relaxed and wasn't as tense as she was the previous night. They made the most of the time they had left on the train, one more night before they landed in England. This was more like it, the piano was being played in the corner of the cabin, people were singing along to the music, all old school. Nancy hadn't heard of any of the tunes. People were talking to each other and to them. A perfect end to a near-perfect journey.

The following morning, they disembarked from the train at Calais, boarded a ferry to cross the channel, then they got on the English Orient Express at Folkestone. They were stopped by customs at Folkestone and Mark wasn't very amused. Nancy kept calm; to them, a younger woman with an older man could well be suspicious. Mark was shouting at one stage. The second time on the trip the train had been held up for them! It was a different train, still as plush but not as authentic, more British. They travelled through Essex up to London. Mark had one last surprise for her. They got a taxi from Victoria Station to the Ritz. It seemed to be full of Arab-type people, very rich looking, most with turbans on. They were taken to their room. Nancy wasn't over impressed, the foreigners certainly did it better than the British and at half the price. There was a biro mark on the sheet, the corners of the blanket were turned back. This was meant to be the Ritz!

They ate in the restaurant, which admittedly was very nice, then went in a black cab to the Apollo Theatre to see *Starlight Express*. The whole production was fascinating as they were all on roller skates! They had a couple of drinks in a quaint little pub near the theatre before heading back to the hotel, where they had a nightcap in the bar.

When they eventually went to their room, there was a bottle of champagne on ice and a bowl of strawberries and cream. This wasn't tennis season! The strawberries made the champagne extra tasty and extra potent! As well as both of them very horny. They hadn't had sex, sorry, made love for three days as Nancy had come on her period. It was only very light now, so she didn't mind when he went down on her. She had taken her Tampax out when she went to the loo earlier, there was hardly anything on it. She had another wash and freshened up while he was dishing the strawberries out and pouring the champagne. They sat on the bed and Mark dipped strawberries into the champagne and seductively teased Nancy's taste buds with them. She lay back on the bed, her head felt light and soon he was nibbling her clit while his fingers were inside her vagina, probing and looking for her G spot, she asked him to turn around then they could do a "69", but he didn't. She had only ever given him one blow job and she knew she was good at it. Thomas and Jason and some of the other few blokes she had given them to all said she was good. So why didn't he let her? She supposed some blokes weren't that keen. She had never met one before who wasn't, but Mark was old-fashioned, maybe that was it. He always made sure she came before he did. Honourable, she supposed was the proper word to use. She stopped thinking, so she could enjoy what was happening to her; she relaxed and enjoyed the present. Before she came, he thrust his penis inside her, slowly, teasingly at first until she bucked and took him full length for the duration of them thrusting in rhythm until she had a full orgasm. He kept it tightly inside her as she came, rubbing his pubic bone on her clit to give her the most pleasure. Once he knew she had been totally satisfied, he thrust into her wetness until he came. At the point of his ejaculation, he totally relaxed so he felt the force of a bloke's full orgasm as a woman felt it, from head to toe. Apparently, the Japanese have that to an art; not a lot of blokes thought they can have full orgasms, but if they could manage to relax just at the point of ejaculation, the ecstatic feeling rushed through their bodies as it did with a woman.

They went shopping the following day, looked around Harrods on Knightsbridge. They didn't buy anything though, surprisingly. They looked around a few other shops before finding a pub for lunch; they hadn't got up in time for breakfast! Well, they had been screwing most of the night! Nancy looked at Mark over lunch, thinking about the last few days and how brilliant they had been, but just looking at his face, a permanent grin, she could never love him. She could be happy with him, but could that be enough for him? She didn't think so.

The following day, they boarded yet another plane, Gatwick to Manchester, and that ended their holiday, two weeks long altogether. Mark went back to his house, Nancy to hers and straight over to Maggie's. Damon screamed when he saw her. It pleased her he hadn't forgotten her! She left Mark a message on his answerphone, saying how grateful she was for the fantastic time they'd had. She also said she wanted to spend some time with Damon, and that she would ring him in a couple of days. Mark had booked her the full week off work, so she wasn't due back until Monday; she had two full days, plus the weekend to enjoy with just herself and Damon. She took him to St Anne's and the sand dunes, Blackpool, the Pleasure Beach and the smaller rides. Nancy couldn't go on them, but she stood at the side, waving at him each time he sailed past. They got to know each other again. He had grown up so much over the last two weeks; he was jabbering away in a foreign tongue, expecting her to understand him.

When she put him to bed that night, she sat alone with her vodka and cried. She felt guilty, used. Although she had used him. She cared, God damn it she cared, but why? He was nothing to look at, had a gut, was balding; was she really taken in by his fortune? Why, she had her own money, she didn't need his. It must have been the attention he gave her, devoting everything to her; gave her everything she asked for, gave her money when she didn't want or need it. It was security! That was what she had missed out on all these years, however happy she had been with Thomas, Jason, none of them made her feel secure. Was this her answer to life itself? Should she ignore the good-looking blokes who had only ever brought her heartache? Fuck that! She needed a challenge. She rang Janet, Chris and Sharon and arranged a night out that weekend. Between themselves they arranged Saturday. They would decide later where they would go. She jumped when the phone rang; she picked it up, and recognised the voice straight away.

'What do you want?' she asked.

'I've been trying to get in touch for weeks. I just want to talk to you, pllleeeeasseee?' he asked beggingly.

'We're getting a divorce, what on earth do you want to talk about?' she asked coolly. She agreed to meet him the following evening at the Spread Eagle at Miller, it was enough out of the way for her not to be seen by anyone she knew. She drove up for eight o'clock, planning not to have a drink.

Thomas was smiling as she approached the bar. God, he looked so sexy, she could take him to bed there and then. They had a laugh together. When Nancy got up to leave a few hours later, Thomas grabbed her hand.

'I still love you so much.' His eyes were pleading with her, sparkling with passion and wanting, what should she do? Damon was at Maggie's. What a surprise, he practically lived there now! She had just come back off holiday with Mark, a good holiday. He was giving her space to spend time with her son, he understood family values. She couldn't hurt Damon by letting him see Mummy and Daddy together. She wanted him, he obviously wanted her. She gave in.

Thomas had got a taxi there. Nancy drove home, to HER home. Thomas went straight to the drinks; his whisky was there, still intact. Nancy had brought people back, but no one liked whisky! He poured them both a drink and sat on the settee, pouring his heart out to her. He still loved her. Always would as long as he lived. She tried to tell him she had her own life now, was seeing someone else, but he knew by her reaction she didn't love the new bloke. Her eyes said it all. Whenever she looked at him, he could see the love she had for him would never die. He took her hand and sat on the floor in front of the fire that wasn't on. The telly was on the music channel. A song came on, Dina Carroll; she wasn't too sure of the title, but the words seemed meaningful. They made gentle, loving love to the music. No passion, just true love between two people, perfect, totally breathtaking, the most fantastic night of her life.

The tears came slowly from Nancy's eyes; she had never, ever made love so meaningfully. Thomas noticed her tears, didn't ask why, he had no need to and gently wiped them from her cheeks, then kissed them away. She held on to him, not too tightly, that would ruin the moment. She felt so confused. She had only loved two blokes in her life, Thomas and Jason, each a different love, but so deep. She didn't know what to do. How could she hurt Mark? Two days after they got back from a wonderful holiday, she ended up back with her husband, would he understand? She sort of decided, if Thomas wanted to, to take it slowly, not move back in straight away like he did last time, but to start seeing each other again. That could be sort of a tester for both of them. She didn't mention anything that night; she would talk to him in the morning. They went to bed and lay in each other's arms. Even though they both wanted to, neither could match the perfect moment they had shared earlier.

Chapter Twenty-Nine

Janet, Chris and Sharon were all waiting when Nancy turned up in the Bull's Head. She ordered herself a drink and told them about her holiday. They caught up with each other's gossip, then ordered a taxi into Blacklodge. The first pub they went into, some of Jason's friends were in. Nancy made a point of, well, not ignoring them but not going over to chat. Instead, Brian came over to her. He was skinny with brown shoulder-length hair. He looked out of place really, old-fashioned like a Beatles fan.

'Jason's in hospital,' he said. She took him to one side, out of earshot and asked him to explain. He told her he had gone to Amsterdam when Jason was there, and he had seemed weird, talking to himself a lot and blocking other things and people out. Half the time he didn't realise who Brian was. Jason, being Jason, wouldn't see a doctor abroad, couldn't afford to for one thing, so when he came back to England, his mum took him. After seeing a psychiatrist, they sectioned him with a mental disorder to do more tests. They put him on tablets for schizophrenia, and he was made to stay in hospital under their watchful eye. Nancy said she would ring his mum and she would arrange to go and see him in the next month or so.

She pushed the worry to the back of her mind, and they carried on and had a great night, ending up in Oblivion as usual, then the normal curry place before they all went home, pissed as farts. Nancy had bumped into Thomas and given him a key for her house as she didn't know what time she would be home. He was already in bed when she arrived. Staggering into the bedroom, she slumped on the bed, fully clothed and waffling about something or other he couldn't make out. When she started snoring softly, he took off her clothes and put her under the covers. He put his arm around her and went to sleep.

When she rang Mark on Tuesday, he immediately asked her out to dinner. She agreed but told him she needed to talk to him. He picked her up at eight and they drove into the country, a quaint little pub outside Mitton, the Three Fishes. Nancy had been there before as a child; she remembered the aviary outside. They just had a bar snack; Nancy, chicken and chips which was served in a basket, and Mark, the scampi. She found it extremely hard to even get onto the subject she wanted to discuss. It waited until they were on their way home. She started with an apology and told him the full sequence of events; Thomas ringing her, begging to talk, and the decision they would try again but take it slowly. She could tell he was upset, but he didn't show it. When he dropped her off at her house, she didn't invite him in, just kissed him gently on the lips, whispered her apologies again and promised she would keep in touch. She could have sworn she saw the glisten of a tear in his eye in the bright moonlight and she felt totally shit!

She poured herself a drink and lit a cigarette. Sat up for ages with soft music on, smoking and drinking. She thought about the men in her life: Jason, mentally ill in hospital in Eastbourne; Thomas giving her the breathing space she needed, but would he go back to hitting her if she let him move back in? And Mark, the gentlest man she had ever met, who would do absolutely anything for her! She was so confused, she got pissed and went to bed.

Thomas was coming around later to see her and Damon, and they were getting a takeaway. He only came around to hers by invitation. Sometimes he rang and asked but if she said no, he wouldn't pester her or give her grief. But after three months of pussyfooting around, she sat Thomas down and told him she loved him and always would, but she didn't feel it was working out. They spent their last night together.

She started going out with the girls more, having a laugh and a good time, fobbing blokes off whenever they tried to chat her up. She would let them buy her drinks first though! She wanted to be on her own with Damon, no one else to answer to, apart from Maggie, for going out too much, but she could handle her. As soon as Nancy told her she was happy, she let her get on with it. She bumped into Thomas a few times in town, spoke to him, melted inside but was strong. She was determined not to let him back into her life. Easier said than done, especially one night at Oblivion, when he introduced her to his new girlfriend, Suzanne! Nancy was gobsmacked to say the least. She was a big girl, not fat, but tall and broad, with long dark hair and a permanent grin on her face. She couldn't have been much over eighteen! Shit, was she jealous? No, just in shock. She had filed divorce proceedings and didn't stop them, even though they had got back together before, so it shouldn't be long before they would be free of each other to get on with their own lives.

The following Thursday, she and Sharon were in the Bull's Head. The disco was on, they were in the back bar having a laugh when Brian came over. Last orders had just been called and they had ordered double rounds.

'Have you heard?' Brian asked.

'Are you about to tell me a joke?' Nancy laughed, but his face remained serious.

'Jason's dead.'

The room started spinning. She held on to the bar, felt like she had been stabbed right through her heart. She felt weak, her body screamed. Brian held her arm to steady her. He could see the hurt in her eyes and thought she was going to pass out. The tears rolled down her cheeks; she was in public, but she didn't care, she was sobbing uncontrollably now. Brian had never felt so shit in his life as he told her Jason had jumped off Beachy Head in Eastbourne. The song in the background, *I Miss You Like Crazy* by Natalie Cole, was all Nancy could hear – every word meant more pain.

For the last six months, she had been meaning to go and see him, ring his mum to find out how he was and had never got around to it. She knew she could have helped him, stopped him, shit, shit, shit. She wanted to die herself, the pain was excruciating. He had never truly known that Damon was his baby. Shit, shit, shit. May the thirtieth 1989, she found out on the thirty-first.

The following few days passed in a blur. She didn't have the guts or the heart to ring his mum; she found out the details of the funeral from Brian. She bought a card for her and posted it to the address Brian had given her years before, when she had written to Jason and his mum had replied to her. The letter stayed safely in her keeping; she thought his mum had read between the lines and realised she had a grandson with the letter she received back.

Chapter Thirty

Nancy and Sharon set off to Eastbourne the day before the funeral. Once they reached the M25, they needed fuel. They came off at the next exit, filled the tank, and when they got back on the M25, they noticed they were following a lorry from Blacklodge! They had got back on the wrong way! They laughed, something Sharon hadn't seen Nancy do over the last few days; all she had seen her do when she was with her was cry. She didn't realise heartbreak could affect anyone so much. Nancy had died on the thirty-first of May 1989; well, her soul had. She could see that. Her friend, her close friend who she had got to know so well, was a mess. On the drive down, she seemed to be lightening up; she probably had to summon the strength from somewhere.

'I went into Blondie yesterday, you know that clothes shop on Darwin Street?' Sharon nodded. 'I tried a black chiffon and silk skirt and blouse on; the label on the blouse said thirty pounds. Perfect funeral outfit, sexy and classy. I took the suit to the till and when the clerk said, "A hundred and ten pounds, please," my mouth dropped!' she laughed. 'I didn't realise they were sold separately!'

They turned the music up in the car and took the next turn-off, which would take them back onto the right direction, forty miles out of their way. They found their way onto the M23 towards Brighton, turned east towards Eastbourne, found somewhere to park and found a B & B with vacancies a few streets away but very close to the town centre. It was just after half past six. They dumped their baggage and found a pub. God, did they need a drink! It was a strange pub, on the edge of the market, with curved glass windows and a kidney-shaped bar. Nancy rang Brian and told him where she was, he met them for a drink, and it turned out they were in B & Bs just on the next road from each other. They all got pissed as farts. The funeral was at 11:00 a.m. at St Joachim's Church. It made Nancy wonder how the hell Jason's mum could have wangled a Catholic funeral for someone who had committed suicide!

Nancy had in all intentions planned to take the flowers she had brought with her to the funeral parlour and see Jason in his coffin before the funeral. Absolute bollocks! She woke up at quarter to ten, too late for breakfast. She woke Sharon and rushed her on to get ready. She had Sellotaped the under-silk lining to the waist band of her skirt, so in effect she had a black miniskirt on that flowed with chiffon down to almost the floor. The matching top was cap sleeved and covered everything.

After what seemed like hours, they eventually found the car. It was parked four streets away, but they had wandered a while before they found somewhere to stay. There was half an hour before the service, and they didn't know where it was. Brian had given them directions the night before, but she had been that pissed, she could hardly read her own scrawl. They got to St Joachim's and parked up just as a van pulled up beside them. The doors opened, and four or five beer cans fell out. Nancy and Sharon got the giggles. Woodsy, Titch, Brian and loads of his friends from Blacklodge. The two-car cortège turned up. Nancy stifled her laughter and watched the coffin being carried into church. The woman who got out of the second car looked haggard and worn, bent over as though an old woman. A chap helped her out of the car. Nancy soon realised she was bent over with pain. She had black hair, tied back in something that could resemble a pony tail. Her clothes hung off her body as if she had lost that much weight, she couldn't afford a new wardrobe. And the dark glasses, to hide either the swelling of her eyes, or the fact she was pissed or not. Her gaze stopped on Nancy for a moment as she followed the coffin into the church. Everyone followed, seating themselves as they walked up the aisle. Jason's coffin remained at the front of the church throughout the service. The vicar then led the way to the waiting cars outside for the drive to the cemetery.

The road was very busy as they followed the cortège, slowing them down immensely, and Nancy's car started to overheat. She switched on her hot air fans as high as they would go amidst the June heat, and followed the funeral cars for the next ten minutes. Nancy parked her car at the top of the cemetery and walked to where the funeral cars had stopped. All in all, there were about thirty people standing around the grave. The vicar gave the usual sermon; ashes to ashes, dust to dust, and the coffin was lowered into the grave. Nancy couldn't stop the tears, she sobbed, the quietest she had ever done. She felt someone staring at her and when she glanced up and wiped her tears, Jason's mum, Kay, had her gaze fixed right on her. It made her feel a bit nervy, but Kay was intrigued by this beautiful woman. She felt she was looking at herself twenty-odd years ago. She had to know about this woman, find out all there was to know. She would find her later. In the meantime, she could hardly take her eyes from her; she certainly distracted her from the pain she was feeling.

Nancy had already noticed that Heather wasn't there, one of Jason's short-lived girlfriends; in fact, the only other girl she knew he'd been with apart from herself! She never did pry though, just in case they asked her! Woodsy dropped a big cross-shaped arrangement of flowers on top of his coffin and nearly fell in, which got a smile from most of the people stood around the grave.

The Seven Sisters pub was the next venue. The first drinks were free, Kay had paid for them. Nancy and Sharon were standing next to a pillar, talking, when Kay suddenly spoke from behind. It startled Nancy, she jumped.

'Who are you?' She was glaring straight at Nancy. Her sunglasses had been removed and her eyes were brown. The bags covered with as much make-up as she could have managed.

'This is Sharon, and I'm Nancy,' she replied courteously.

'I knew it was you from the moment I saw you outside the church. Jason always spoke so highly of you. I instinctively knew it.' Nancy flushed as she spoke. 'Can we talk later?' Kay asked politely. Nancy just nodded, and Kay went back to join her little party of relatives.

Heather turned up and immediately started giving Nancy dirty looks. It had always been a competition between the pair of them, who could wear the shortest miniskirts, look the sexiest; Nancy normally came out on top. If Heather wanted to start any trouble, she could. She would only make a fool of herself, as she already had, missing the church service and the burial! Nancy just ignored her, left Sharon talking to Woodsy and went and sat with Kay, who introduced her sisters, their partners and her mum and dad, who were both in their spritely nineties. Both Nancy and Kay were a bit pissed.

Nancy asked for directions for Beachy Head; she wanted, needed to go there. It was only about eight o'clock. She stupidly got in her car, after nicking a load of roses from the outside of the pub; there was a trellis full of them outside. She started the car and drove. She parked up near a pub called the Beachy Head and walked. It was twilight and she could see pretty clearly, although with blurred vision. She found the point that Kay had briefly described to her, sat not too near the edge and talked to Jason, annoyed with him until the tears came thick and fast. 'Why the fucking hell?' she shouted which echoed amongst the cliffs. 'You bastard!' she shouted. Not another soul was in sight, and if they were, she didn't care. She went nearer to the edge and threw the roses over the cliff face, all the time shouting, 'Why, you bastard? I loved you!' She sobbed uncontrollably; she had kept her nerve for most of the day, and now it was all coming out. She eventually composed herself and made the trek back to the Seven Sisters. Sharon immediately collared her. 'Where the fuck have you been?' Nancy just mumbled an apology and went to the loo to sort her face out. The swelling of her eyes was excusable, they were at a funeral, but she added more lipstick and a bit more blusher; she couldn't, wouldn't let Heather take the scene.

Sharon and Nancy eventually said their goodbyes to those who needed it. Kay invited them back to her flat before they headed off for home the next day; they agreed, and she gave them the address. Sharon drove as she was the soberest, they got back to their B & B and the bar was still open. Well, it was

196

only just after eleven. They had a few more drinks before going to their room. Sharon bollocked Nancy for driving earlier; she could have killed herself.

'In all honesty, I think that was the intention!' she replied. 'At the time,' she quickly added.

They turned up at Kay's flat just after one o'clock the following afternoon. She had so many cards and flowers, they practically filled the room. She told them that the vultures had been around, asking for his record collection. She didn't let them take anything.

'Bad time to ask then,' Nancy blurted out.

'What do you want?' Kay asked abruptly.

'The purple shirt he always wore, that's all. We used to laugh at him, saying he had no other clothes, but he loved that shirt and I would absolutely treasure it, if you don't mind?' she asked with sincerity.

Kay thought about it for a while as they talked. She was impressed with this woman and it wasn't long before she disappeared and came back with the infamous purple shirt. Nancy held it to her and smelt the aroma; she closed her eyes and he was there. Kay watched her every move and knew she had genuinely loved her son. Once they had gone, she had time to dwell on meeting Nancy for the first time; she had spoken to her on the telephone once before when she was with Jason. She had replied to a letter Nancy had sent Jason a few years ago when he was away on his travels. She decided she would root it out and have a read through Jason's diaries.

Nancy went back to Jason's grave before she left Eastbourne. She had bought a single red rose, and it propped up between the grass and the infill. Sharon had stayed in the car, watching her friend closely. From the short distance she could see her tears as she sat at the graveside talking to Jason. She was still dressed in black, tight trousers and a black T-shirt which hugged her trim figure. When Nancy came back to the car, Sharon offered to drive for a while so Nancy could compose herself for the long journey ahead.

When Nancy and Sharon arrived back in Blacklodge, Nancy picked her post up from behind the door, went to the kitchen and poured them both a vodka after the six-hour drive. There was a note from Mark amongst the other letters, simply saying, "Please get in touch – pretty urgent!"

Once Sharon had left, she collected Damon and rang Mark. 'Sorry to be the bearer of bad news, but Max has sacked you. He was worried when you rang in sick and called around at the house. Someone told him you'd gone away!' Mark told her. 'However, I have some bad news of my own which is good for you. I've lost my driving licence, so was wondering if you'd like to be my chauffeur for six weeks? I pay well!' he added hastily.

Nancy agreed and arranged to be at his house the following Monday morning for eight o'clock. They would have to use her car for the first couple of days as his was being serviced, if it was all right with her. She should bring a book or magazines for some of his longer meetings, and he would give her money to go shopping. The only drawback was she would sometimes have to chauffeur him at nights when he had meals out with clients.

She spent a quiet weekend with Damon, walks to the park, drives out and McDonald's! They also spent time at Maggie's. Sharon called around to see her on Sunday, to see how she was. She poured them both a drink, Damon was happily playing in the bath before getting ready to go to bed. Sharon stayed, and they ordered a curry later on. They talked a lot about Jason, of the happy times they had together, and Nancy smiled as she remembered the more intimate moments they had shared.

Nancy arrived at Mark's nice and early on Monday; he was still shaving. She made them both a cup of tea. Once she'd relaxed in his company, Nancy asked Mark to explain to Max about what had really happened and to apologise for her. She told him about Jason and the funeral as he listened intently. He had lost his parents, whom he obviously loved, but it was a different kind of love. He showed her a lot of compassion, and he now understood why she could never love him, could tell her heart was broken.

After the first week, he decided to treat Nancy and Damon to a holiday. He went to the travel agent's and booked for himself, Nancy, his youngest daughter Marian and Damon. Marian was nearly ten, Damon had just turned five. He remembered her once telling him about a place she had been in Majorca with her family and even though it was a lot dearer than a standard holiday, he booked it. They would set off on the twentieth of July for two weeks, once the kids had broken up from school.

The argument he had with Deborah about taking Marian drained him that night. She didn't like it, but he told her she could lump it. When Marian came home from her friend's, the excitement shone in her face. Deborah had already hit the bottle as she was angry. Mark gave Marian a hundred pounds to get some new clothes with, it was just over four weeks away. She couldn't wait.

Chapter Thirty-One

Kay put pencil to paper a few days after the funeral and wrote to Nancy (this is a true letter written on the twelfth of June 1989, from Kay Hampshire to Nancy):

Hello Nancy,

I know you arrived home safely, I just know it.

I had a sad but incredibly glorious day.

A day with mixed emotions.

All of us wanting to possess Hammy, who always kept a distance that was of course important and vital to him.

He chose his friends carefully and warily, because he was a perfectionist. He desired and sorted out only the best.

I was drawn to you on June the ninth. I spotted your car at the entrance to the cemetery, and also before I went into church.

I thought, "Who is that lovely girl over there?" I knew it wasn't Heather. Who is she? I thought over and over again. A metallic green Fiesta. I saw it at the church and then again as I sat in the limousine. We passed it, or maybe I looked back and saw your car there. I was distracted from what was going on. Even in the church, I felt an unusual presence. I said to myself, concentrate, your only son is here at Mass. But I have to admit, I had an impelling desire to turn around.

Who is that girl I saw outside the church? Who is she? I saw her before I went into the church, just standing there, looking at me. Keeping what I supposed what a respectable distance.

But alone, in front of everyone behind me, I felt your eyes burning into me. Curiosity wanted me to turn around and walk back to ask, "Who are you? What are you doing here?" I remember thinking, "She looks like I used to do in the sixties."

All the time throughout the mass I had this impossible desire to turn around and seek you out.

I saw you at the pathway of the cemetery; you were standing back. There were a lot of people there, some with us, some tending graves. I was trying to be as Hammy would expect but all the time I wanted to turn around.

And then at last I saw you in the pub.

I was sitting down and then I spotted you, looking very beautiful between the pillars. I was just sitting with my family, just chatting. I stopped talking and thought, "There she is, there she is, that lovely girl," and then and only then could I stand up.

I said, 'Excuse me,' to my family, 'There is a lady over there I am impelled to meet.'

I tried to walk tall, with my head held high as always in my life, with dignity as I approached you.

I asked you, 'Who are you?' Who is this girl who reminds me so much of "ME"?

And then I heard this wonderful, Lancashire, beautiful voice, saying to me simply, 'This is Sharon and I'm Nancy.' And much later we really talked, and what did I think?

You in your way have eased my pain; I cherish the thought he enjoyed a beautiful girl as you are. It gives me such peace of mind, that my son could have held your precious heart for so long. He will always be with the both of us, for as long as we both still live.

You were special to him; as I said, Hammy never wasted a moment, not even a second of his time with anyone who was of no account.

We all in our own way have to deal with grief. But remember, Hammy was precious to all of us in different ways.

Let's not be morbid or depressed.

I had a wonderful day, seeing all of you I never knew before.

Hammy was not in any way an accidental pregnancy, he was vital to me from the moment he was conceived. Loved and cherished from a tiny baby into a mischievous toddler and then a bloody aggravating teenager.

There were times he almost drove me over the edge. He was exacting Everything had to be "PERFECT". No way would he accept second best. I know you loved and wanted him but inevitably as life turned out, you would have lost him anyway.

You will be happy to know, I am feeling incredibly well. Meeting all of you from Blacklodge was good fun.

Be happy, work hard and enjoy life to the full.

Goodbye for now, my love to you and precious Damon,

Sincerely, Kay.

Nancy cried at the words, as she read the letter, the first of many to come, as well as phone calls. At first, she told her the answers to her questions, what Jason (Hammy) was like with her, how he had treated her and more intimate questions sometimes. She wanted to know every detail of his life away from her. Kay was normally drunk and sometimes Nancy left the answerphone on and pretend she wasn't in; she couldn't cope!

She explained to Kay one Saturday that she was still grieving and asked her not to phone late at night as it disturbed Damon. Kay understood and the late-night drunken calls stopped for a while. She started buying Damon things, clothes and toys and sent them to him. He was always thrilled, but always wondered why the postman would buy him things. Nancy sat him down one day and explained that an old friend of hers had died and because his mum couldn't buy him things anymore, she was buying them for Damon instead. 'Is she my nana then?' he asked, not really understanding.

'You could call her Nana Kay, if you want to,' his mum replied, thinking it could do no harm, him having three grandmas.

Chapter Thirty-Two

Mark took them all shopping the day before they were due to fly on Thursday. Marian was a beautiful girl; natural blonde hair; girly chubby cheeks, although not chubby in her body in the slightest; and one tooth missing when she smiled, which made her cuter than she looked. She got on with Damon well; they laughed together in the back of the car, giggled when Mark suggested some clothing that would have looked totally silly on either of them. They had a great day together and went to McDonald's for tea, although Nancy and Mark were eating out later. They were all getting excited about the holiday. Mark had only told Nancy the week before because she could tell he had something planned but all she knew was it was two weeks in Majorca.

The holiday was fantastic, it was at Pontinental, and Nancy felt like she had travelled back in time. It had expanded somewhat, but the original buildings where she had stayed when she was five were still intact. They all went exploring. Their apartment had two bedrooms, a living room with kitchenette, a large balcony overlooking the swimming pool. The complex was right on the beach as well. The older apartment blocks still had the same rustic charm they had nearly twenty years earlier. Seemingly the trees were the same size, but obviously she had grown, as they had. The restaurant was new, well, a different one and the waiters had changed. Nancy had fancied a Spanish waiter called Paolo, if she remembered correctly. The entertainment hall seemed exactly the same, maybe had a lick of paint over the years.

Nancy relaxed over the holiday. Mark gave her the breathing space she needed; at night he never pushed her or demanded anything from her. The first couple of nights she had cried herself to sleep whilst Mark held her, and it was the third night, after they had each been thrown in the swimming pool outside before going to bed, that Nancy made a pass at him. They had a drink on the balcony and waited for the kids to go to sleep before they went into their bedroom. It had two single beds, but Nancy had pushed them together as soon as they arrived. It was quite hot at nights, so they just had a sheet covering them. Nancy snuggled up to him with her head on his shoulder, kissed him lightly, and as he caressed her shoulder, she straddled his body, bent down to kiss him again and whispered, 'Thank you.' It didn't take him long to get excited; a few rubs against him. He sucked her nipples as she dangled them at mouth's reach, and when she felt ready, she guided his penis into her. She was thrusting up and down, all the while rubbing her clit on his pubic bone. By this stage they were both upright, Mark was sucking hard on each tit in turn. Nancy moving rhythmically up and down, until the moment she was about to orgasm. She kept her clit in place and rubbed hard on his pubic bone. The gasps came faster and as soon as Mark felt the throbbing inside her vagina, he rolled her over and thrust inside her, slowly, gently, but all in, and holding her buttocks up towards him it wasn't long before she had a multiple orgasm, they came thick and fast and Mark let himself go as she was coming. They stayed in the missionary position for quite a while to get their breath back. Nancy felt all the tension of the last couple of months drain away from her body and was so relaxed and calm.

They went horse riding, on a boat trip; did practically everything there was to do. They needed a holiday to get over this one by the time they got home. It had done Nancy the world of good and helped in the healing process. It was over too soon for everyone. They landed back at Manchester in what seemed like two days, let alone two weeks!

Mark had a week before he got his licence back, so Nancy started looking for another job. She hadn't taken a regular wage off Mark, he had given her a few hundred pounds to go shopping, and taken her to Majorca for two weeks, so she didn't ask for anything else. He only needed her on Friday the week they arrived home, he had not made any other appointments and hopefully would have his licence back on Monday or Tuesday the following week. She'd enjoyed working for him but wanted to get back to having no ties. They went out for meals or a drink every now and again, but nothing was ever set in concrete. They were good friends, no more. Mark understood now exactly how she felt, in herself as well as towards him.

Chapter Thirty-Three

Nancy had started going to the Bull's Head on Saturday afternoons, there was always a big crowd there; Mick, Paul, John (whom she quite fancied), loads of them. She always sat with Paul and John and they classed her as one of the boys. It took a few weeks before she actually got with John. He was younger than her by three years, sunbed tan, cheeky grin, bleached blonde spiky hair, but as she soon realised, he loved himself too much, so after a couple of weeks, she ended it. He kept trying to crawl back, but she didn't give in to him. She had, however, got very friendly with Paul and after three months, she invited him back to hers and they ended up in bed together. As they were both drunk, it was nothing fantastic, but she certainly recognised the potential he had! They became a couple.

After a couple of months, he moved in with her. They had debated whether to move to a different part of town, but they stayed. Eric wasn't too keen on Paul, but who could come up to his expectations after Mark? Paul was six months older than Nancy, bleached blonde hair, spiky as it was the in thing at the time, and he had a steady job as assistant printer in a wallpaper factory. He worked a three-shift pattern, one week six 'til two, then two 'til ten and nights. A lot of the other time he slept. At times Nancy felt like his mum rather than his girlfriend, but it was secure, and he didn't complain if she wanted to go out. He wasn't jealous or possessive, so she still had her girly nights out, most weekends in fact.

One Friday night out with the girls, she bumped into Will, whom she had fancied years ago; a punk, dark spiky hair, nothing too special but he invited her back to his flat. Stupidly, she went, pissed as a fart (where does that saying actually come from?). They had a great laugh. He nicked a car, which Nancy found exciting; it was a pure adrenalin rush being with him. They dumped the car and walked the rest of the way to his flat at Shadbolt, the other side of Blacklodge where Nancy lived. They had sex on the living room floor and when Nancy started sobering up, she felt guilty. She had a good bloke at home, dependable, always there for her, but not loving or affectionate, which was what she needed and the reason she strayed. She booked a taxi home.

It was nearly four o'clock when she crawled into bed. Paul grunted and stayed asleep, questioned her the next day. 'Where were you till after three? Nightclubs shut at two,' he shouted.

'We went for a curry,' she replied coolly. He left it at that. He still had his regular Saturday afternoons in the pub. If he wanted to stay out, he would ring her to see if she could get a babysitter for Damon and meet up with him. Sometimes she did, but when she didn't, and he rolled in late, drunk as hell, his tea ruined, she would pretend she was angry, and he would ask her to marry him. She just laughed at him.

Her next period didn't come. Six pounds for a pregnancy test at the chemist, but they could supposedly tell forty-eight hours after her period was due. Positive, shit. Was it Paul's or could it be Will's? She didn't dare tell Paul.

Janet and Chris came around one night for a chat and a drink. Paul was working until ten. When he got home, they all had a laugh, but then Janet and Chris started dropping hints about Nancy being pregnant. She shit herself; when she saw her friends off at the door, she bollocked them for dropping her in the shit! She really didn't know how he would react to the news. She was dreading going back into the house once she had seen her friends off, but when she walked into the living room, Paul said, 'Are you pregnant?' Nancy burst into tears. He was shocked, but he cuddled her. It hadn't been planned, but she felt secure. Four weeks later, he was on nights again. He had come to terms with the pregnancy, actually felt happy about it.

Before he went to work on Friday night, they made love on the chair in the living room. Nancy straddled him, having a laugh and it just carried on, as she thrust up and down on top of him. He sucked and bit her nipples; he knew he would be late for work, but he didn't really care – sex was always fantastic between them. As they orgasmed together – they had learnt to do that through good timing – they had a quick cuddle and he got in the car and drove to work.

When Nancy went to the loo an hour or so later, she noticed she was bleeding, not a great deal, but it was worrying when she was pregnant. She dialled the number for Paul's work; it wasn't always answered at night if reception forgot to transfer it to the warehouse. She noticed her hand was shaking and she felt a bit weird. Eventually, an older-sounding chap answered, and she asked for Paul in the print room. What seemed like hours later, she heard his voice and with a tear dripping down her cheek, told him she had started bleeding. Calmly he said, 'Lie down on the settee with the phone near and if you feel any pain, or the bleeding gets worse, ring the emergency doctor. You know the number, don't you?' She nodded. He asked her to ring him if anything happened; he would try his best to answer the phone when he heard it and if she wanted him to come home, he would. 'Nancy, I love you.' The tears came, it was the first time he had ever told her, even though he had asked her to marry him twice!

She lay on the settee and watched telly. She didn't know what she was watching, just lay there waiting for anything that could happen. The next time she went to the loo, the blood seemed thicker. She rang the doctor and then Paul.

He offered to come home but she promised she would ring him once the doctor had been. Within half an hour, there was a knock on the door. She invited him in, and he had a quick feel of her stomach while she told him what happened, omitting the sex part! He couldn't feel anything but as she was only about six to eight weeks gone (what Nancy had worked out), he wouldn't be able to hear a heartbeat without specialist equipment. He told her to lie down as much as she could with her feet as high as was comfortable, and if any sharp pains or the bleeding got heavy, to go straight to hospital. He wrote something on a piece of paper, put it in an envelope and handed it to her.

Paul got home at just after six. Nancy was dozing on the settee. He made them both a cup of tea and sat on the edge of the settee, stroking her hair. 'How do you feel now?' he asked as she opened her eyes and gave him a small smile.

'Still bleeding,' she replied.

'Do you want to go to hospital?'

She shook her head. 'Not yet, you need some sleep. I'll see later.' They both went to bed and Paul carefully held her close to him. His breathing deepened as he dozed off, it was a comfort to Nancy him just being there and she managed to get some sleep.

Paul woke up with a start. Nancy wasn't there. He pulled some trousers on and went to look for her. She was making a brew in the kitchen. 'I think I need to go to hospital; would you take me, please?'

'What's happened?' he asked.

'I woke up with a dull pain and there was quite a lot of blood.'

They had their cup of tea, Paul went to get a top on, and they set off to Blacklodge Royal Infirmary. As they explained to the lady behind the desk, she was taken straight through to lie on a trolley and told once a doctor had seen her in casualty, they would decide which gynaecology ward she could go on to. The doctor was quite a while and when he did put his head around the curtain and she explained to him what had happened, she was taken to Ward E5 to wait for a scan, but it would be Monday morning now, as the radiologists finished at lunchtime on Saturdays. She was dreading staying in hospital for two nights, but they wouldn't let her go home now. She hadn't brought any night clothes with her; she thought it would just be an examination, a yes or no to whether she was still pregnant or not and straight home.

Once she was settled on the ward, Paul went home to get a bit more sleep and to bring the things she needed. She had written a list; nightie, dressing gown, slippers, clean underwear, toothbrush, toothpaste, towel, soap, shampoo, conditioner, some magazines or a couple of books and a couple of packets of cigarettes. He came back just after five o'clock and as she unpacked the holdall he'd brought, she pulled out the pink satin negligee Mark had bought her. 'I thought you'd want to look nice,' he said coyly. He was only thinking of her,

206

little love! They went into the smoking lounge and had a cigarette and chat. Maggie and Eric were coming later; Paul had told Maggie what had happened when she rang and woke him up!

Nancy went and got changed into her rather revealing negligée and got back into bed with the sheet right up to her neck, seeing as there were a lot of male visitors around the ward. Paul went shortly after Maggie and Eric turned up; they stayed for half an hour as visiting time was coming to an end.

The nurses brought tea and toast around that evening and sleeping tablets for those who wanted them. Nancy would rather have had vodka, but never mind. She read for a while and when they turned the main ward lights off just after ten o'clock, she lay there in the dark while her eyes focused around the ward. Most of the women there were heavily pregnant, probably brought in to rest prior to being induced or waiting for a C-section. She had spoken to a couple of them in the smoke room. She felt a bit silly with her slim figure when they had asked her what she was in for. Her mind was in turmoil. Was she or wasn't she pregnant? She didn't know, her boobs still felt quite heavy; then she thought to herself maybe if she lost the baby, it could be better, that way she wouldn't be going through life living yet another lie and not knowing truly who the father really was. She eventually drifted off.

The noise of the nurses clattering woke her up. She looked at her watch, ten past seven. They were bringing breakfast around; she had ordered toast and a cup of tea. As she sat up, she had a sharp pain right in the pit of her stomach, which made her gasp. The nurse who had just put a tray in front of her, helped her to the bathroom. There was a lot of blood. All the nurse could say was, 'Sorry, it's happened.' She stayed with her while Nancy was on the loo and ran the bath for her. When the bath was ready, Nancy soaked in the warm water. The nurse left her to it with the promise of fresh toast and a cup of tea when she was ready. She put her negligée back on, luckily no blood had got onto it. Put two large sanitary pads on and wandered back to bed. The nurse brought her breakfast again. 'Will I be able to go home today?' Nancy asked her. The nurse smiled at her. 'You'll have to wait and see the doctor in the morning. You'll still need a scan to make sure everything that should have come out has done. If it hasn't, you'll need a small operation to scrape out your uterus.'

Nancy drank her tea and went for a cigarette before she rang Maggie; it was too early to ring Paul, she would ring him later. 'Mum, I've lost the baby.' Maggie asked if she was all right, but she didn't know how she felt, it hadn't really sunk in. They talked for a while, then Nancy went back to bed. She couldn't settle, so she spent most of the morning talking to whoever came into the smoke room. The nurses often came in and gave disapproving looks at the pregnant women smoking, but Nancy wasn't pregnant anymore, so they couldn't say anything. She rang Paul and told him towards lunch time, before he turned up for visiting.

He didn't say much on the phone, told her he loved her and that he'd see her in a bit.

Maggie and Paul turned up together. Nancy could tell Paul had been crying and was trying to put a brave face on. She hadn't cried yet, didn't really feel any emotion, couldn't explain how she felt. She didn't feel pregnant, obviously. Maggie nipped out to have a chat with the nurses and while she was gone, told Paul she would go on the Pill to stop her getting pregnant again. 'No, you won't,' he said quite abruptly but with a bit of a smile.

The next morning, she was taken down for a scan just after nine o'clock. There was a radiologist and a doctor looking at the screen. They conferred and decided there was no need to do the D & C. She could be discharged. She rang Maggie, as Paul was on a six-to-two shift, to pick her up. She had been told to rest for a couple of days and if she wanted to see a counsellor, she should go to her doctor.

Paul was feeling super horny by the weekend. Nancy didn't bother going out Friday night. Paul cooked a fillet steak for them, Nancy's favourite, with cauliflower, broccoli and boiled potatoes and there were two bottles of wine in the fridge, chilling. Nancy had a bath and when she noticed there was no fresh blood, she got dressed in a black basque with lace-topped stockings, and a short black dress. They ate their meal on trays on their knees, and when Paul took Nancy's tray away and noticed the lace of her stockings, he could feel his penis going hard.

He went back into the living room and asked her what time Damon was due home. She told him he was stopping at Maggie's. He took her hand and pulled her up from the settee, looked into her big brown eyes with his beautiful piercing blue eyes, put his hand gently behind her head and pulled her face towards his. He kissed her as he had never done before, so gentle yet so passionate, his tongue searching her mouth sensually. Her body quivered, and tears slowly rolled down her cheeks. He wiped them away as he told her he had never loved anyone as he loved her. He kissed her again. God, she wanted him, wasn't sure whether she loved him as much as she'd loved Thomas or Jason, but the feeling in her stomach of butterflies and the way he was making her quiver could be the start of her love for him. He unzipped her dress and it fell to the floor. He held her shoulders as he couldn't take his eyes off her dressed in her basque. 'You look beautiful,' he said as he kissed her gently again. 'Are you sure you're ready?' She nodded and undid his jeans, she hadn't seen his penis so big before and she was already wet with his affection. He slowly pulled her knickers down over the silky stockings, rubbing his hands on her legs as he did it. His tongue went into her vagina, he was still stroking her stockings, she would dress up more often for him! He pulled her down on the rug in front of the fire, and slowly entered her with his extra-large penis. He was so loving and gentle, she orgasmed within

208

minutes, as did he, but he carried on thrusting gently, his penis still hard, all the while kissing her affectionately, her mouth, ears, neck and nipples. They both orgasmed a few times throughout the night, and Paul had never made love to Nancy like he did that night. She told him she loved him for the first time as he cuddled her. A few tears rolled down her cheeks when she realised she meant it. He stroked her hair as she drifted off to sleep.

Chapter Thirty-Four

Paul became a lot more loving than he ever had been, and they enjoyed spending time together, along with plenty of love-making. Nancy hated it when he was on nights, could never sleep well until he was in bed next to her, so once she had taken Damon to school, she would always get back into bed with him, trying not to wake him. If sometimes he stirred, she would rub her hand on his penis. If it hardened easily and he groaned, she knew they would enjoy the pleasure of each other.

It was over seven weeks since she had left hospital and was checking her birthday book for upcoming events when she realised she hadn't had a period since she miscarried. She rang her doctor's and asked the duty nurse about it. The nurse told her it was normal; the hormones could affect her periods and she would be back to normal after a few months. She didn't worry.

Granddad asked her one visit if she was pregnant. She didn't get over to see them often as they lived almost thirty miles away. She had put a bit of weight on and she still hadn't had a period. It got her thinking, how long ago, we are in October now. I miscarried in July. Could she be? She hadn't even thought about it. She felt normal, she put the weight down to Paul spoiling her with his rich cooking. She would get a test on Monday.

'Don't think so, Granddad.' She kissed his cheek. The smell of Nana's cooking drifting through from the kitchen, mincemeat and chips, hopefully in a nana dish. She hadn't eaten that since she was a child and loved the special taste only Nana's cooking made. They normally got fish and chips on their visits as they went out for the day, but Granddad wasn't feeling well enough and it was very cold outside.

That evening when Paul came home from the pub, he was fairly sober for a change, so Nancy mentioned it to him, although she wished she hadn't as he turned down her advances when they went to bed. 'Just in case,' was his reason when she turned over and pretended to sulk.

Nancy stopped at the chemist on the way back from taking Damon to school. She'd done a sample first thing in an old jug, so when she got home, she went straight to the bathroom and read the instructions on the leaflet. They kept bringing new ones out, it was different than the last one she had. You were meant to hold it under the stream of urine, and it would turn blue after five minutes if you were pregnant. If it stayed white, you weren't. She held it carefully over the toilet and poured the jug over the white rod, left it on the sink in the plastic carton it came in and went to wake Paul up. 'In five minutes, we'll know. If it turns blue I am. If it's white, I'm not,' she whispered in his ear as she snuggled next to him. His arm went around her shoulder and they cuddled for a few minutes. Paul went to the bathroom, had a pee and took the carton back into the bedroom with a huge smile on his face.

'Better ring the doctor's, it's definitely blue.' She went downstairs and put the kettle on while she phoned the surgery. She managed to get an appointment for the following day at 9:30.

The doctor examined and prodded her stomach, as he asked questions. He was frowning. 'It feels like you could be around four months, must be a big baby!' he smiled jokingly. 'I'll request an urgent scan, try and get one for next week if I can.' He disappeared out of the examination room while Nancy dressed and when she entered his surgery, he was on the phone explaining to someone about the risk of his patient miscarrying again and wanted a priority appointment. Four thirty p.m. on Friday that week was booked in. Paul would be at work and wouldn't be able to go with her. She was disappointed, but the doctor said they were lucky to get in that quickly.

Once Nancy told Paul what the doctor said, she went across to tell Maggie and Eric; she hadn't seen them the day before. Eric grumbled but Maggie was pleased for her. They were going on holiday the following day; she would have to take Damon with her for the scan. Maggie looked closely at Nancy's stomach. 'I bet it's twins,' she laughed.

'I'd kill myself if it was!' Nancy replied. Maggie was all packed and looking forward to Cyprus for a fortnight, she promised she'd ring Nancy often while she was away. She had a couple of carrier bags of food to give to Nancy and reminded her she wanted milk and bread for when they returned.

Friday came around quickly. Janet had offered to have Damon for her, so she picked him up from school and took him out. Paul wished her good luck before he went to work. She drove to the hospital and was given a pint of water to drink, they could see more if her bladder was full. She was dying to go for a wee but couldn't. She was called in and lay on the bed while the radiologist smothered her stomach with the sticky gel they needed and then placed the scanner on the gel. After a few minutes she was smiling. She turned the screen around so Nancy could see it. 'You're having twins, congratulations!' said the nurse. She pointed to a heartbeat, and Nancy followed her finger around the weird-looking shape inside her. She then pointed to the second heartbeat and shape. Nancy was shocked, remembering how she'd struggled with Damon when he was younger, how would she cope with two!

She walked out of the hospital in shock. She wanted to talk to someone, who? Paul was at work, Maggie was away, Sharon was at work, as was Chris, and Janet had taken Damon out. She got in the car and burst out crying. After one abortion, a miscarriage and now twins! What had she done to deserve the crap she'd had over the last few years?

When she got home, she looked through the address book to see if she could find anyone to talk to. She rang Paul's mum, Maureen, who just laughed and gave her congratulations. She cried again when she came off the phone and was so pleased to see Janet when she turned up with Damon. Janet saw Nancy and sent Damon to play in his room. She put her arms around her, thinking the worst. Had she miscarried again or was there something wrong with the baby? When Nancy stopped sobbing, and managed to talk, she told Janet about having twins.

'Two bundles of fun, there are a few advantages, you know,' trying to sound reassuring.

Paul didn't turn up at home at ten past ten. At half past Nancy started worrying; he normally got a lift when he was on day shift, he took Nancy's car when he was on nights. If he had walked, he would have been home by half past. By eleven o'clock, she was getting frantic; he knew she was going for her scan today, why the fuck wasn't he home! Janet had stayed, and they had had a few drinks. Janet had to go and meet her boyfriend at half eleven, but was a bit bothered about leaving her. She did, however, invite her around to her flat if she needed to. She would be home at midnight.

Paul turned up at ten past midnight; he'd gone to the pub, celebrating the pregnancy, his mates had dragged him. Nancy shouted, was annoyed, he should have been there for her. She stormed out, got in the car and went to Janet's. She had probably had too much to drink to drive but she didn't care.

The only beer Janet had was bitter, which her Ian had brought. She had just polished the last glass of wine off. Nancy, knowing Janet, knew she was in the way. Ian went to bed and Janet stayed up comforting Nancy. She stayed for an hour, threw up from the bitter, then drove home. Paul must have gone to bed. She poured herself a vodka and got herself comfy on the settee and fell asleep.

Her back was aching when she woke. She made herself a brew, switched the telly on, waiting for Damon to wake up. She would have liked to crawl into bed with Paul, she was dying to tell him, but she was still a bit angry with him.

Damon walked straight through to the kitchen and helped himself to a bowl of cereal. Nancy put the kettle on again for a fresh brew and she heard Paul stirring. He walked into the kitchen, put his arms around her, kissed her on the neck and whispered, 'So, so sorry.' She ignored him while he carried on kissing the back of her neck as she stirred the teabags in the cups. He pulled her around to face him and kissed her, so gently. 'You know I love you?'

She shed a few tears as he kissed her affectionately. 'I was really upset after the scan, I needed you!' she half shouted at him. He cuddled her. He thought he heard wrong when she whispered, 'We're having twins.'

Looking into her eyes, he asked, 'What did you say?'

'We're having twins,' she told him again. She had to smile at the stupid grin plastered on his face.

Whenever she told people it was twins, people were telling her how wonderful that would be, so Nancy pretty quickly got used to the idea of "double trouble". She sailed through the pregnancy, hardly any morning sickness, growing quickly larger around the midriff, and when one kicked, they woke the other up and it felt like a street fight in her stomach! They had worked out as near dates as possible and they were due on the first of April 1991. However, with twins, they normally came up to six weeks early, no one normally went full term with twins. The doctors kept a regular check on her progress, especially through the later months. Thirty-six weeks passed, then thirty-seven, then thirty-eight and absolutely no sign of them putting in an appearance into the world. Nancy was so big, she was struggling to walk, when the doctors decided to try and induce them.

She went into Queens Road Hospital on Thursday the twenty-first of March, and the Asian doctor, who looked a bit like Mr Bean, inserted tablets into her vagina, containing prostaglandins to try and "ripen" the cervix. He had fat fingers and it hurt her. Nothing happened on Thursday, or Friday, or Saturday or Sunday! They must have been a lot comfier in there than Nancy was! It was Monday morning when they took her up to the delivery suite to induce her with a drip. After three hours, even that didn't work well enough. They had built up her contractions slowly and steadily, but she wasn't dilating very quickly, and her waters hadn't broken, even though the nurse kept turning the drug up to release more into her bloodstream. Just after one o'clock, they asked for a doctor to come and break her waters to try and speed it up. Nancy asked the nurse to ring for Paul to come up to be with her. They also asked an anaesthetist to come and give her an epidural to ease the pain later in her delivery. Nancy felt really embarrassed when the doctor came to break her waters, he was gorgeous! Paul turned up within the hour and not a lot had happened. The anaesthetist was just sticking a large needle into her spine. Paul held her hand. Well, she squeezed his to try and relieve the pain of the needle. He was grimacing!

At least things should start happening now. Paul was pacing the floor next to her. At five o'clock it was shift change for the nurses and midwives. Nancy was due for another internal shortly, so she would know how many centimetres she had dilated, and they could estimate from that how long would be left. The nurse asked if she had her bladder emptied. Nancy hadn't thought about going to the loo as she couldn't feel her lower body because of the epidural. The nurse inserted a tube into her bladder and immediately a stream of urine squirted out into a bowl. It made Nancy laugh and it started spurting out in bits as she laughed. The epidural was starting to wear off and she now had slight feeling in her stomach. The nurse gave her an internal and she was ready, it was probably her full bladder that had prevented them coming earlier.

At 5:16 p.m. a baby girl was delivered normally. They immediately asked what she would be called but they couldn't name her until the other baby came out. They had agreed on a name for one girl and one boy, but they hadn't agreed on names for a second child, whatever sex they turned out to be. The second baby didn't seem to want to follow their sister. Nancy was tired from pushing the first baby out and was struggling to push hard enough. His heartbeat was slowing down, and they decided to pull him out. Nancy's legs were put up in stirrups and she was asked if she didn't mind students coming in to view. She had lost all dignity by this stage and nodded her agreement. She was very shortly surrounded by white coats, Paul by her side, rubbing her forehead with a cool damp cloth the nurse had given him and whispering encouragement to her. He went a bit white and had to sit down at the sight of all the blood she had lost and didn't like the look of her legs in stirrups, but the doctors knew what they were doing. Nancy refused when they asked to give her an episiotomy, so they eased the forceps into her vagina until they were clamped around the baby's head. She had to push as hard as she could as they pulled. She felt her contractions quite well now but, luckily, her lower region was still fairly numb. Five thirty-six p.m. and a little boy was dragged out, battered and bruised from the forceps. They named them Danielle Faye and James Ryan, five pounds four ounces and five pounds five ounces respectively. They were both cleaned up and handed to the proud parents. Nancy was absolutely shattered and felt like she could sleep for days.

Paul and the babies were taken to the nursery while Nancy went for a long soak in the bath. The nurse was showing Paul how to give baby a bottle. Nancy was not going to breastfeed as she didn't think she could cope with two on her breasts! Nancy went back to the ward to lots of congratulations from the other patients and headed through to the nursery, where Paul sat feeding Danielle. James had just been fed and fallen straight back to sleep. When he put Danielle down in her cot, they went to the smoke room and had a cigarette. Nancy was gasping, she hadn't had one since first thing.

It was half past nine before Paul left for home. Nancy left the twins in the nursery for the night staff to feed and went to bed. Tea and toast came around at quarter to ten and she ate her toast. She had a slight pain in her chest, which seemed to be getting worse; she didn't mention it to anyone. As she took a drink of her tea from the cup and saucer, she tried to put it back on the table right in front of her. She couldn't; her arm moved in jerks to the right as she tried to put the cup on the table. As her arm got as far to the right as possible, she got confused and brought it back in front of her to put on the table. Again, her arm in up-and-down movements jerked to the side. She brought it back to the table and tried to put it down. The same thing happened. She was starting to panic. Another patient had watched her and called the nurse, who observed for a few seconds and ran to the office to call an emergency team. The cup was taken out of Nancy's hands, the curtains were drawn around her and about eight bodies in white coats surrounded her. That was her last memory.

She was rushed to the Intensive Care Unit at Blacklodge Royal Infirmary while Paul was rung. He rang Maggie, asked her to run him up to the hospital. Eric would have to have Damon; he didn't feel fit to drive. She was at his house within ten minutes, car keys in hand. They were both worried; he had only been told Nancy had had a fit and was in intensive care.

Chapter Thirty-Five

They were both allowed in to see her and a doctor came and explained what all the machines were and what had happened, to his knowledge. She was on a life support machine; she'd had a fit and lapsed straight into unconsciousness. She had stopped breathing at one stage, and they had to revive her, so the machine was keeping her alive. It would be touch and go for the next twenty-four hours, and they should determine what caused the fit when they got the blood test results back in the morning. All they could do was sit by her side, talking to her.

Paul stayed all night. Maggie went home. She had looked awful, attached to God knows how many machines supposedly keeping her alive. She was lying there naked, apart from a thin white sheet covering her body. Eric snuggled up to Maggie when she got into bed. They were all really worried, but what must Paul be going through? Two new babies and his girlfriend hanging onto life by a thread.

The blood test results the following morning revealed she had developed eclampsia toxemia, and there was a slight chance she would pull through. The doctor had been honest with them. It was very rare compared to pre-eclampsia, which was common amongst pregnant women. The signs were always there; swelling of the ankles, protein in the urine, and was easily treated through rest prior to delivery. Eclampsia Toxemia came on suddenly; chest pains, fits and it was basically a rare form of blood poisoning. The doctors and nurses were on twenty-four-hour alert, checking the monitors every fifteen minutes without fail, checking her pulse as it easily led to heart failure. Everyone was worried. Flowers and cards came by the sackful but weren't allowed in ICU. Everything was so clinical.

Maggie brought Paul some sandwiches; he had been crying and looked tired. She tried to persuade him to go home to get some sleep. He wouldn't leave Nancy's side. Paul couldn't face telling them, so he asked a nurse to explain to them what was wrong with their daughter. Maggie and Eric stayed with Nancy and Paul for a while, then went off to visit James and Danielle. The nurses had been pampering them, along with some of the other new mums; there certainly wasn't a shortage of people offering to feed and cuddle them. Everyone on the ward were concerned and asked Maggie how Nancy was. She just told them she was still unconscious and critical. Janet and Christina were regular visitors to the babies. They weren't allowed to visit Nancy; at the moment it was immediate family only while she was still on the critical list.

They brought the babies down to visit one day, to see if they could bring her around, but no use. Paul's mum became very supportive, as Maggie had been, as much as she could, to Paul; making him go home to eat and sleep and taking him to visit his babies. He cried as he held them, knowing their beautiful mother could die.

Paul spent every minute he could with Nancy. He got used to the "bleep, bleeping" of the machines and recognised if something was out of beat and would call a nurse. When he was alone with her, he talked about the ups and the downs they had been through, told her things she had told him about her childhood, even tried bringing music in she liked to play to her; anything to try and bring her around.

She developed a chest infection and another drip was inserted into her wrist with an antibiotic potion. She was still on the critical list after six days and the doctors' hopes were fading pretty fast. They took Maggie, Eric and Paul into the office and explained. The chest infection wasn't clearing and was having a devastating effect on her other organs; they were expecting them to fail and so they, the family, should prepare themselves for the worst; maybe consider taking her off the life support machine, to see if she could breathe on her own. However, that would be very unlikely. They couldn't let her die, so they refused that and asked that if anything at all could be done, it should be done.

Their only hope, which could be very risky, was draining her lungs manually. It would put a big strain on her heart but would have a thirty per cent chance of working. The doctors left them to talk and said they should let them know their decision the following day.

They dragged Paul home and sat up a lot of the night, talking about what to do. Paul obviously wanted his girlfriend to have the best chance of survival, as did Maggie and Eric. They decided to see what happened over the next twenty-four hours. There was no improvement, so they gave the go-ahead for the chest drain. They had borrowed a drain from a specialist chest hospital, so they didn't have to slice her open at all to drain her lungs. It looked to them like the tube on a vacuum cleaner, but the doctor explained how it worked. There was still only a thirty-to-fifty-percent chance of success.

Nancy was taken to theatre. Her head was strapped back so her throat was as straight as they could get it and her tongue was secured to her lip while the large tube was gently pushed into her lungs. Another tube was placed into it and the machine switched on.

Nancy was in a dark tunnel, heading towards a small light. The brightness hurt her eyes. Snow covered the ground, and Jason was sat on the snow-covered roof of a house! A snowdrift was covering the downstairs of the house, and she kept slipping as she tried to climb up. Jason was holding his hand out to her. She eventually managed to grab hold of his hand, and they struggled to get to the top of the roof. He was cold, and they sat with their arms around each other. His lips touched hers, and she suddenly felt a warm glow go all through her body.

'Damon's your baby, she said.

'I know. I always knew, love.'

They held each other for a while, then Jason told her she had to go back. She didn't want to; she wanted to stay with him.

The machine was switched off when she had a cardiac arrest. Doctors quickly revived her again. Paul, Maggie and Eric were pacing the floor near to the theatre. No one had been out to see them, and after more than three hours, they were getting very anxious. She was eventually wheeled out, looking absolutely awful. She was being taken back to intensive care. The doctors explained their disappointment at it not working effectively enough but would keep a very close watch on her. They had drained a percentage of the fluid out of her lungs; she may have a chance. They were advised to go home and rest, and if there was any news at all they would be contacted immediately.

Paul got up early, ignored the flashing light on the answer machine. He wanted to go and see Nancy. When he arrived at ICU, the wrenching pain in his stomach made him feel sick as he walked towards her bed and saw it empty, neatly made, ready for the next critically ill person. The machines were gone, and there was an eerie silence surrounding him. No one was around.

He turned around in total shock, could feel his body crumbling. He managed to walk out of the hospital, went home, collapsed on the bed and cried as his heart broke into the smallest pieces of intense, harsh pain you could ever imagine.

CPSIA information can be obtained
at www.ICGtesting.com
Printed in the USA
BVHW051033040319
541704BV00026B/2193/P